Azorean Dreams

Azorean Dreams

By Sue Fagalde Lick

Blue Hydrangea Productions South
Beach, Oregon

Azorean Dreams

ISBN: 978-0-9833894-84

Published by
Blue Hydrangea Productions
P.O. Box 755
South Beach, OR 97366
(541) 867-4692

http://www.suelick.com
sufalick@gmail.com

Acknowledgments

I owe many thanks for this book to my late husband Fred Lick, my unpaid editors Sonia Pérez Villanueva, Joe Raposo, Donna Gomes Austin, and Margarida da Silva, and the members of the Los Gatos writers group who helped me fumble along until I found Chelsea's story.

Prologue

Great Aunt Julia was the last of the Silveiras. Chelsea perched on the wooden kneeler, staring at the waxen face in the brass casket. Her grandmother and all the aunts shared that bump on the bridge of the nose and dark eyes with a perpetually worried expression. When she looked in the mirror, she saw the same features on her own face. These women, part California and part Azores Islands, all ended up here in the Santa Clara Funeral Home, with painted-on faces like olive-skinned dolls, their gnarled hands clutching rosary beads.

Chelsea felt the years passing too quickly. She was already 28, not one of the kids anymore. A whole generation had passed on. Her own children, if she ever had any, would never know these women.

She thought of her last visit with Aunt Julia, just before Easter. Her aunt, wrapped in a granny square afghan, had apologized for not making rocky road candies. "I know you kids love 'em, but I just couldn't do it this year. My legs ached so bad."

"Don't worry about it, Aunt Julia. I'm on a diet anyway."

"What for? You're too skinny already."

Chelsea smiled. If she weighed 300 pounds, she would still be too thin for Aunt Julia.

Her mind lingered on that evening as she felt a heavy weight beside her on the kneeler and her mother leaned toward her.

"She was quite a woman in her day. The stories she could tell."

What stories, Chelsea wondered. When they visited, Aunt Julia was always so busy feeding and entertaining everyone she didn't have time to talk. When she did sit down, she turned the conversation to her guests. Her own life was too boring, she said. Tell me about you.

There was no time to ask what her mother meant. Two birdlike old ladies, friends of Aunt Julia, were waiting to pay their respects. Chelsea and her mom moved on.

As she sat beside her parents in the third row of the family pews, listening to the somber organ music and gazing around the stuffy, dimly-lit chapel, Chelsea thought about her mother's Portuguese-American family. Mom had married a German-English fellow with a love of British names, hence her own name, Chelsea Anne Faust. The relatives on Dad's side were like him, tall, fair-haired, slender and studious. But Mom's family was different. She looked around at the stout dark-eyed men wedged into the leather chairs and the plump women gossiping even as their rosary beads dangled ready for the priest's arrival.

They were good, loving people, but Chelsea always felt like an outsider. She was the family star, college educated and a published writer and photographer. Just last year, she had spent six months in Washington, D.C., and had even met the president. Her aunts and cousins had all admired her newspaper work and the splashy magazine features she had published, but she knew they whispered about how she was still single and might never get married if she didn't hurry. Her three years living with her boyfriend Jeffrey McNeil, first in Sacramento and then in Washington, were a scandal. Now that she was home, she should forget about her career and settle down with a nice Portuguese man.

The organ music ceased as Father Drury walked in with the slow practiced stride of a man who comforted bereaved parishioners every day. He came down the front row, whispering his condolences to Aunt Julia's sons Jack and Harry and their wives, nodding at other family members he recognized from St. Claire's Church. Chelsea felt her mother straining for attention, but the priest didn't see her. Just as well. Mom hadn't been to St. Claire's in years, not since they moved to San Jose.

Dad wasn't Catholic. Although he had gone to Mass when Chelsea was young, they had fallen out of the habit. "It's your father's fault I never get to church," Mom had told Chelsea when she called this morning to remind her to bring her rosary beads. Dad told a different story. She couldn't stand the new pastor and his modern ideas.

"In the name of the Father and of the Son and of the Holy Spirit," the priest began. As the family eased onto the hard kneelers provided by the funeral parlor, Chelsea knelt with empty hands. She hadn't seen her rosary beads in years and couldn't find them this morning. Mom frowned in her direction as she stumbled through the "Hail Mary," struggling to remember the words.

Her abandonment of her faith was one of many things she and her mother disagreed on. But tonight she would go along, for Aunt Julia's sake.

The next day, after the funeral was over and most of the family had left the gathering at her parents' home, Chelsea was surprised when her mother called her into the bedroom.

"Come here a minute. I want to show you something."

Chelsea had been playing rummy with her cousin Tommy, a gawky 13-year-old who was still shaken by seeing his grandmother in the coffin. He wouldn't admit it bothered him, but he had been unusually quiet all day, and Chelsea had seen his face go green when he first looked at the body. She remembered the nightmares she had had for weeks after Grandpa Silveira's funeral, her own first experience with death. She was only 11.

Now, as her mother summoned her, she looked at Tommy and shrugged. "Mothers." His lips turned up slightly, almost a smile.

Chelsea's heels echoed on the hardwood floor as she entered the bedroom. "What's up?"

Mom picked up an old photo album. "Aunt Julia wanted you to have this. 'Because you're a writer,' she said."

Chelsea joined her on the white chenille bedspread, inhaling the scents of cedar and mothballs as her mother turned the black pages of the old album. Faded photos held by gold stick-on corners showed Aunt Julia in her younger days, dressed like a queen marching in a parade. In other pictures, she was on stage, singing. In another, she was making a speech.

"When did she give you this?"

"A long time ago, when she first got sick. Before you came back from Washington. She made a section in it for each of the six sisters, to pass on to future generations. They were all old ladies when you knew them, but they were really something when they were young. There's some pictures here of my grandmother, too. Aunt Julia thought you ought to write a book about the family."

"Hmm." Chelsea turned the pages slowly, reading the names written underneath in gold ink in Aunt Julia's florid script. "I feel like I don't really know much about these people."

"Well, I told you about your great grandma and how she came over here from the Azores at 15, pregnant with your Uncle Henry. She

9

had eight kids and then her husband died. She was only 35, no education, no money, no nothing. She worked in the cannery all day, then worked at the church at night, scrubbing the floors on her hands and knees. Sometimes she had to take handouts from the neighbors to feed all her kids.

"Her life was always a struggle, but here's her children, all American citizens, all with their own homes and good jobs. Look, here's Aunt Julia giving a speech--she was the president of her lodge. She was the Holy Ghost queen three times. God, how Grandma worked on those white dresses."

"1923," Chelsea read. "It's 1993 now, so that was seventy years ago. Who took these?"

"I don't know. Uncle Ted, I guess. He was a camera buff, like you and your dad. Always taking pictures."

"What are they doing in this one?" she pointed to a photo of Aunt Julia kneeling at an altar full of flowers.

Mom closed the album and stood, fighting tears. "Some silly old-country custom. The smart ones left all that behind." She opened the drawer on her nightstand and pulled out a handkerchief with hand-crocheted edging. "They're all gone. Nothing left but pictures," she said, wiping the wrinkled skin under her eyes.

"Lou," Dad said, hurrying in. "Gladys is leaving. She wants to know if you want to keep the rest of the coffeecake she brought." Chelsea watched her father rub his wife's shoulders. In the last few years, her parents had attended funerals for far too many loved ones, including both of her father's parents and his younger brother. Lately the light seemed to be gone from his eyes, and he walked like an old man.

"Oh," Mom said, handing the album to Chelsea. "I don't care. "Gladys can take the cake home for her kids. We don't need the extra calories. But I do want to say good-bye."

Chelsea rose. "Where do you want this, Mom?"

"Take it with you. Aunt Julia wanted you to have it."

"Have what?" asked Dad as Mom brushed past him.

"Aunt Julia left this photo album for me. She wanted me to write a book about the family."

"Oh yes, your mother showed me. Well, let's go say goodbye so I

10

can get this necktie off."

"And these shoes," Chelsea said, frowning at the black pumps that had been pinching her toes all day.

Chapter One

Chelsea would never forget that hot June in San Jose. It was the month Aunt Julia died, the month she met Simão Freitas and the month she got the anonymous tip about San Jose City Councilman James Slater's shenanigans. It was also the month she became Portuguese.

"They're having this big Portuguese parade downtown on Sunday afternoon. I need you to cover it," said Mel, her editor at the South Bay Weekly Times.

It was already Friday afternoon, and she had been looking forward to a weekend with no commitments.

"Why me? Because I once told you I was half Portuguese? I don't see you covering the Jewish events just because your great grandfather was a Polish Jew."

"Hey, you know that's not the reason. I heard the parade is a big deal and you're the best photographer we have. I'll give you comp time next week."

"Sure you will."

So she found herself at Five Wounds Church, surrounded by girls in white dresses, crowns and long velvet capes, and parents dressed in their Sunday best. They were dark and heavyset like her mother's family, but she had no idea what it was all about.

She had to park a half mile from the church. Frowning, she slung her camera over one shoulder, shoved a notebook into the back pocket of her jeans, and hurried toward the band music.

The parade stretched way into the distance. Behind the first band came two boys carrying a banner, a man with a flag, then a teen princess. Two little girls, also in white, marched beside her, their capes dragging on the ground. The girls stared straight ahead, weary already from their stiff dress shoes and the warm spring weather. Mothers, fathers, aunts and uncles plodded behind them. Then came another banner, more princesses, and more adults.

The onlookers called to the marchers in Portuguese and waved green and red flags. Pressing to the front, Chelsea ran quickly through her first roll of film. This looked a lot like the pictures in Aunt Julia's album, she thought. Aunt Julia was all in white like these girls, a crown

13

on her dark, curly hair. Mom had pointed out Great Grandma Silveira in the background and her own mother, then a tiny girl marching next to Aunt Julia. How come nobody ever talked about these parades, she wondered. Was this one of those old country customs her mother couldn't wait to leave behind?

She hated to admit Mel was right, but this was going to be a great feature. She squatted in the path of the parade and finished the roll with more shots of the princesses. She was hastily changing film when a man's face caught her eye.

He was younger than many of the men in the parade, too young to be a princess's father, yet he led the San Jose delegation with an air of authority. He was tall and well-built, wearing a charcoal pin-striped suit and shiny black leather shoes. His thick hair was short and wavy, his brown face intersected with a thatch of mustache. Something about his erect posture and shining eyes drew her to him.

She snapped his picture just before he broke off from the parade and hurried up the steps into the I.E. S. Hall next to the church. Chelsea stood, rubbing her stiff knees, and was gazing in his direction when she heard a sharp command no more than two feet away.

"Please move out of the way," an old man in a navy blue band uniform said in English. "You will get run over." He pounded his bass drum for emphasis.

She backed out of the path of the band and onto the feet of a woman standing behind her. "*O que estás fazendo?*" the woman scolded in Portuguese.

"I'm so sorry," said Chelsea, seeking an empty space. She raised her camera again. A long line of women marched down the street with baskets of bread on their heads. Behind them rattled an oxen-drawn cart with a five-foot tall statue of the Virgin Mary. Chelsea dashed into the street and took pictures of it all, finding it hard to believe this was happening in San Jose.

When the parade was over, the flag carriers lined the lodge steps, American flags on the right, Portuguese flags on the left. The man Chelsea had photographed earlier stepped to the center and began to speak in Portuguese. She edged closer, aiming her lens at him.

She had no idea what he was saying, but the sound was melodious, with lots of shushing and zhhzing. Growing up, she hadn't

14

heard much Portuguese, only a few curses and whispered gossip between her grandmother and her great aunts. Now she listened intently, frustrated at not understanding.

The speaker was smiling, perfect white teeth glowing beneath his mustache. He waved his arms and signaled the bands to begin. She didn't know the first song, but the second was "The Star Spangled Banner." The people around her sang along with both songs, switching from Portuguese to English.

What a great closing shot, Chelsea thought. She raised her camera to photograph the double rows of flags and the men singing with their hands over their hearts. The shutter clicked in the silence after the National Anthem. Suddenly, from behind the flags, a pair of doves rose into the sky and fluttered awkwardly to the eaves of the old church. The crowd applauded, the speaker shouted, and everyone surged toward the door. Chelsea was swept up the steps with them, barely able to hold onto her camera.

The doors swung open, and the people poured inside. Huge tables were set for hundreds of diners, and the smell of roasting beef and fresh bread was so thick she could barely breathe.

Clearly the story wasn't over yet. She eased back against a side wall, listening to the clamor of Portuguese and English, the stamping of hard-soled shoes on the wooden floor and the scraping of folding chairs as people settled in.

The tables filled quickly, yet hundreds of people still waited outside. A burly white-haired man stretched out his arms in front of the door and yelled, "*Espere*. Wait. We are full."

Outside, the people moaned.

"*Paciência*. Patience. You will be next," he said.

Meanwhile, inside, men with aprons tied over their white shirts and dark slacks brought immense bowls of steaming meat and bread to the tables. The bowls were passed from hand to hand. Green salad followed. Sons and fathers lined up at the back of the hall to purchase beer and canned soft drinks as mothers helped their children fill their plates. Chelsea watched in awe, her camera still in her hands. Someone touched her elbow.

"Can I help you?" The handsome master of ceremonies she had

15

admired through her lens stood beside her.

"Oh!" she said, startled. Up close, he seemed taller. He had taken off his tie and unbuttoned the top of his shirt. She cleared her throat. "Yes, I'm a reporter for the South Bay Weekly Times. I've been taking some pictures, and I wondered if you could give me a little background on what's going on."

His dark eyes fixed on hers, puzzled. "Are you not Portuguese yourself?"

"Half," she admitted. "My mother's side of the family. But. . ."

He glanced back at the crowded tables. "You have never been to a *festa*? Amazing. You know, I would really like to get something in the newspaper, but right now, I am quite busy." He pulled a business card from his jacket pocket. "Call me tomorrow, and I will tell you anything you want to know."

"Thank you." Simão Freitas, Entrepreneur, she read.

A sweating, aproned man came up and said something in Portuguese.

"*Sim, agora,*" Simão said, already walking away.

"Thanks, I'll phone you tomorrow," Chelsea called.

He turned. "If you are hungry, I can find you a seat. . ."

"Oh, no thanks." She felt him watching her as she slipped out a side door away from the crowd.

"Simão," she heard the anxious man urging.

"*Sim, sim,*" Simão replied.

As she walked through the dust and gravel to her truck, only the soft whizzing of cars on nearby Highway 101 broke the silence. The air was warm and heavy, promising an early taste of summer. She set her camera on the passenger seat and got in, rubbing her aching neck and shoulders and cranking the windows open..

She drove slowly back to Santa Clara Street. Now that the parade was over, traffic was light. Only a few dropped carnations on the pavement remained of those who had marched through.

On the way to the freeway entrance, Chelsea noticed Portuguese names on most of the stores--Furtado's Jewelry, Silva's Restaurant, Carvalho Insurance--and wondered where Simão's office was. As she read the signs and thought of the girls and women marching down the street, she felt a twinge of nostalgia for a life she had never known, the

16

life of her great-grandmother, Aunt Julia and other Azorean women. She felt cheated. Why hadn't anyone ever told her about her Portuguese roots?

When she got home, she would take another look at that photo album. Maybe there was a story to tell after all.

Chelsea held her breath as she pulled the wet negatives from the developing tank and held them up to the light. "These are great," she whispered. Captured in sharp black and white were girls with crowns and capes, women balancing loaves of bread on their heads, flags lining the steps, Simão Freitas gesturing with his right hand.

In the negative, Freitas' eyes, hair and mustache were white, and he looked like an old man. She stared at his face, ignoring the water that dripped down her arms and onto her father's old shirt. Was this the sort of man, she wondered, who had swept her great grandmother from the Azores all the way to California with his dreams of streets paved with gold?

She wished her father were here tonight to see these photos. When she was a girl, they developed film together in the darkroom he had made in the corner of the garage. He would examine her negatives and explain why some of the frames were too dark or too light or out of focus and praise her childlike pictures of her friends or Butch, their old Springer spaniel.

It was no wonder she'd grown up to be a photographer. Dad loved taking pictures. But he had never tried to make a living with his camera as Chelsea had. Last year, when she urged him to try sending some of his travel photos out to magazines, he said, "No, you're the photographer. I'm too old to start now, and my eyes aren't as sharp as they used to be."

Shortly after his brother died in a head-on collision on Hecker Pass Road, Dad dismantled the darkroom and stored his camera in a box in the hall closet, with the towels and sheets. She had been shocked to find it there when she came back from Washington. Her mother reported that Dad said there was nothing worth photographing anymore, that all the good memories were already stored in the family album. Chelsea tried to get him to join her on a photo trip to Yosemite

17

that winter, but he just shook his head and said he was too busy.

However, he was still proud of her work. It was her father who convinced her landlord to let her rent the defunct laundry room behind the old Victorian where she lived and convert it into a darkroom. She smiled, remembering the weekends they had spent together cleaning, painting and building shelves for her enlarger, trays and chemicals. Dad had bought her the big timer/clock for her birthday in January.

She spoke to the portrait of her father, one of the many photos hung with thumb tacks on the yellow walls. "We got some good ones, Dad."

Even as she heard her father's approving words, she knew her mother would have a different reaction: Why waste your time with that old-country stuff? Come out of the darkroom and find yourself a husband.

There's plenty of time, Mom, she would respond.

She hung the film to dry and opened the door to air out the ammonia-tinged developer and fixer fumes. In the distance, a lawnmower roared. Just beyond the back fence, children squealed in a backyard swimming pool.

Her downstairs neighbor, John Grijalva, a San Jose policeman, parked his Ford pickup in the driveway next to her truck and slid out, looking tired, still in uniform. He nodded at Chelsea standing in the darkroom doorway with her plastic apron over her jeans. "Working again, huh?"

"Always," she grinned. "What else is there?"

It was after 10 when she quit that night. Her back and neck ached from bending over the trays. Her eyes felt bruised from staring at the enlarger image, and her lungs were full of developer and fixer. She had used a whole package of photo paper and had far more prints than she could ever fit in the South Bay Weekly Times, but it was more than a one-page photo feature.

She gazed at the damp prints spread over her kitchen table and sighed. The pictures were good, but she had no words to go with them. Who are these people? Why were they wearing crowns and carrying bread on their heads?

Tired as she was, her mind wouldn't rest. Opening Aunt Julia's photo album, she studied the women inside, so much younger and prettier than when she had known them. Had Aunt Gloria ever been so slim? Look at Grandma with such a short dress and no glasses. Although the old photos were faded and out of focus, the shots were amazingly similar to the ones she had just taken. She looked from one to the other and heard her mother's voice again: "Aunt Julia said you're the writer; you'd recognize a good story."

Well, maybe she would try it. Since Mom didn't want to talk about the old customs, she would have to ask Simão Freitas what this parade was all about. Perhaps she could show him she wasn't as stupid as she had sounded.

"*Bom dia,*" said the woman who answered the phone. "*Quem fala?*"

Oh no, Chelsea thought. "Do you speak English?"

"Yes. A little," said the woman slowly.

"Great. I need to speak to Simão Freitas."

"Oh. Simão." She pronounced it like Sim-OW. "He is not in."

Nuts. Chelsea studied her watch. Mel needed this story by 4:00. It was already 10. "Okay, can you have him call me?" She left her name and number, then turned on her computer and studied her notes from the water board meeting for the drought update she was writing.

"So," Mel said, returning from his Monday morning conference with the publisher. "How was the parade?"

"Good," Chelsea said, nudging her photos toward him.

He leafed through them quickly. "You know we can't use all of these."

"I know. Pick what you like."

"What's with the ladies with the bread?"

"I'm not sure. I'm waiting for a phone call for some background."

"Didn't you interview anybody there?" He pointed to the photo closest to him. "This one's cute with the little girls."

"Thanks. And no. They all spoke Portuguese."

"Really? Just off the boat, huh?"

Chelsea felt herself bristle and wasn't sure why. "No, it's their language. Why not use it when they get together?"

19

"I guess. Anyway, I need the story today. You got the water district thing?"

"Nothing to that. Just the usual rationing reminders."

"Write it, and don't be stingy. The Matthews column isn't coming. We've got mega space to fill. And can you rewrite this stuff?" He handed her a folder of press releases. "Mandy was supposed to do it, but she's got the flu or something, and I'm backed up with sports copy."

Intern work. She would rather be writing major stories, but she was lucky to have a job. When she came back from Washington, hurting from her breakup with Jeffrey and expecting to return to her post at the Sacramento Record, she discovered the paper had new owners and her job was gone.

Chelsea was grateful to Mel for getting her this job. As soon as he heard she was coming back to San Jose, he'd called her. She had accepted immediately. How bad could it be working with her college pal again? Besides, it was only temporary, until she found another job on a big daily. It would have to be a job where she could both write and take pictures. Most editors had trouble believing she could do both-- until she proved it to them.

She had been here since just before Christmas, six and a half months. Most of the time, she had to admit, she liked it. She could be both reporter and photographer here, and she got to do a variety of assignments. In a single week, she might cover a society ladies' lunch, a city council meeting, a feature on a local artist, and a three-car crash on the freeway.

You didn't get that kind of range on dailies like the Sacramento Record. She had had to stick to her beat, transportation. It got pretty boring, but there was always the possibility of moving up. At papers like the Weekly Times, a reporter could get stuck doing the same thing for life, like Sarge Olsen, who had outlasted several police chiefs while covering the crime beat.

For now, it was pleasant enough. It was fun making a name in her home town. Big fish in a small pond, she thought, looking around the little storefront office she and Mel shared with Mandy and Sarge. The Record newsroom was four times as big, and the darkroom made the one here look like a closet.

She shrugged and opened the rewrite folder.

By noon, she was hungry and needed a break, but Simão Freitas still had not called. She dialed his number again.

"*Bom dia*," the voice began, and Chelsea started to speak, then realized it was the same woman's voice on a tape recording.

She grabbed her purse and camera case. "I'm going to lunch," she said.

Mel looked up from his snack machine lunch of diet Coke and tortilla chips. "How's the work coming?"

"Water board and rewrites are done. You can call up the files and edit them now. But I still don't have the parade thing. He's not in."

"4:00, Chelsea. If you can't get this guy, interview somebody else or write what you have. The pictures can't fly without some words to explain what's going on."

"I know, I know." She paused, staring at the pile of photos on her desk, then grabbed Simão's business card and stuffed it in the pocket of her tweed blazer.

Two old men in the doorway of Tamar Restaurant watched Chelsea as she parked her truck at the curb, grabbed her purse, and got out. When she returned their gaze, they didn't smile or look away. Despite the warm weather, a chill ran up her back. There was something predatory in the dark eyes fixed on her from under their felt hats. In her uneasiness, she dropped her keys. "Damn," she hissed, stopping to pick them up, grazing her fingertips on the hot asphalt.

Up and down the street, she saw only men standing in front of the Portuguese shops, waiting at the bus stop, walking toward the church.

She looked again at Simão's business card and turned east, away from the men. Behind her, she heard a guttural chuckle, and one of the men said something in Portuguese. She pulled herself up taller and clutched the keys tight in her hand.

It was eerily quiet here, despite the freeway. She passed Casa Nova Imports and Furtado's record and jewelry shops. Gazing in, she saw rows of colorful ceramics, Jesus statues, and books. Black iron grills barred the front windows. Handmade signs on the doors proclaimed upcoming events in Portuguese. There seemed to be no

21

customers.

At 534 East Alum Rock, she stopped and looked up at what appeared to be an apartment building. Slowly she climbed the stairs to Unit D. The white paint was peeling, and a strange sewage odor drifted up from the basement. She checked the address again. It had to be here.

At the top of the stairs, a business card was scotch-taped to the bright red door. It matched the one Chelsea held in her hand. Taking a deep breath, she knocked. Instantly the door opened and she stood looking up at Simão Freitas.

Again he wore a three-piece suit. This one was gray. His wavy black hair was impeccably styled, the sideburns precisely cut. His patent shoes were freshly shined. But the office didn't equal his personal grandeur. Behind him, Chelsea saw a sagging flowered sofa. Above the sofa in a wooden frame hung a yellowing photograph of a broad harbor, white-washed houses and green fields. On a scratched tan steel desk to the right of the door, a half-eaten sandwich sat next to a Styrofoam coffee cup in a sea of papers.

Simão wiped his lips with a paper napkin. "You are the woman from the newspaper, yes?"

"Yes." She extended her hand. "Chelsea Faust from the South Bay Weekly Times. I called this morning and left a message, but it's getting close to my deadline and. . ." She looked around, wondering where his receptionist was.

He frowned. "Oh. I am sorry. I did not check my messages yet. I was trying to--well, I was very busy. I still am. But, you are here. Come in. Tell me what you want to know."

He closed the door behind her. Chelsea swallowed. This was nothing like the busy office complex she had pictured. It was a shabby apartment living room, complete with green shag carpeting. No one knew where she was.

"Please sit down," Simão said.

The only choices were the sofa or a plastic kitchen chair next to the desk. She perched on the edge of the chair and opened her notebook. "Now, could you tell me--?"

"I'm sorry," he interrupted. "I hope you do not mind if I finish my lunch."

"No, go ahead." She ignored her own growling stomach. He had a roast beef sandwich--white bread, lettuce, tomato, mayonnaise oozing out the top, the kind Chelsea's mother used to put in her school lunchbox. She could almost smell the apples and potato chips that used to go with it.

"So."

"First, could you explain what yesterday's festivities were all about? The parade and the free food and all. What's the occasion?"

"You really know nothing about it?" he said, talking with his mouth full.

She shook her head. "My mother's family was Portuguese, but they came here over a hundred years ago. I'm afraid the customs didn't get passed down. I was looking in an old photo album and saw pictures of my aunts in a parade that looked like yesterday's, but I don't know why they were marching." She added, "My father's of German and English descent, and we're totally Americanized."

"Well, you should know about this. It is the Holy Ghost festival, *festa* (feshta) we call it. Every spring, after Easter, we have this celebration. We prepare for it all year."

Chelsea wrote rapidly as he told the story of the young Portuguese Queen Isabella who defied her tyrannical husband Dom Diniz and prayed to the Holy Spirit for food for the starving people. When the food miraculously appeared, she gave her crown to a peasant girl, as she had promised in her prayers. The Portuguese people had celebrated her good deeds ever since. In the Azores, every parish continued the custom, and the immigrants brought it to America. These days, members of the Portuguese lodges in California and on the East Coast traveled from city to city in the spring and summer to march in Holy Ghost parades, crowning a local girl as queen and sharing a banquet of meat, bread and wine.

Simão's accent was charming. The English words were perfectly formed but softened around the edges with the same shhhs and jhhhs she heard when he spoke Portuguese. He was younger than she had thought, not much older than she was. She fought the urge to stare at him instead of getting the story down in her notebook. Her mother should have shared this with her long ago instead of making her hear it from a stranger.

23

Long after Simão's sandwich was gone, he patiently answered her queries.

"You should know these things," he kept saying. "Besides, it will be good to have something in the newspaper. You must mention our Portuguese Chamber of Commerce, which did a lot of the work this year."

"Portuguese Chamber of Commerce? I didn't know there was one. Can you tell me a little about that?"

By the time she was out of questions, it was 1:30. She hadn't had lunch, and the four o'clock deadline loomed. Yet she hesitated.

"What else?" said Simão, leaning back now with a smile, his thumbs hooked in his vest pockets.

"I know I'm taking up a lot of your time."

He shrugged. "I will work later."

"Well," she said, sliding her pen and notebook back into her bag. "I'm curious. What kind of business are you in? I know your card says 'entrepreneur.' What does that mean for you? I know what it means in general, but. . ."

"Oh," he said, smiling. "Isn't that a fancy word? I thought it was American, but somebody told me it is really French. It just means businessman. I am an investor, I guess you would call it. I have been here in the United States only three years, but I am planning to invest in a business. I will build that one to make enough money to buy another business until I have a whole chain of businesses. When I can afford it, I will buy a big house in the hills and raise my family like the rich people."

Chelsea stared at him. He was serious.

"I have a dream," he went on. "The American dream, they say it is. In the Azores islands, we do not have very much land, and the business is limited. Here, as I have heard all my life, the land goes on forever, and there is no limit to what a man can do. Rags to riches, that is me."

She stood and so did Simão. "Not everybody gets rich," she ventured.

"I will. Then you can write a big story in your newspaper about me. Okay?"

She nodded. "Sure."

24

"Thank you for coming." He held out his hand. His strong fingers were warm. She was surprised to feel calluses. Why would an "entrepreneur" have calluses?

"Thank you," she said.

Then she was outside, the door closed behind her, smelling the sewage fumes again, blended with exhaust from the freeway nearby. She was hungry, and she was late.

Across the street, an old woman waited at the bus stop, her hands folded across the lap of her dark blue coat. As Chelsea came down the stairs, she saw the woman's eyes narrow.

What's her problem, she thought, looking around for a quick source of food before heading back. No fast food here. She saw a bakery down the street.

Popular Bakery. *Padaria Popular.* What an odd name. A bell jingled as she pushed the door open and went in. This was not like any bakery she knew. Where were the donuts? Or the muffins? A tired-looking chocolate cake revolved in a tiny display case to the right of the counter. Along the back wall, a refrigerator case held imported olives and spices. Big round loaves of bread filled most of the remaining shelves.

Sweet bread, she thought, vaguely recalling the yellow loaves with hard-boiled eggs baked inside. Aunt Julia always had them for Easter. The kids loved finding the eggs.

A tiny black-haired woman with a striped apron over her flowered dress bustled out of the back, staring up at Chelsea. "Can I help you?" she asked, her accent thick.

"Um," said Chelsea, the blood rushing to her face. There was really nothing here she wanted, although she had a sudden craving for sweet bread. "I don't know. I guess I'll just have a couple of these things." She pointed to a tray of brown and white pastry rings.

The woman named them so quickly Chelsea understood only "Fifty cents."

Stuffing the small white bag into her purse, Chelsea hurried out, feeling like a fool.

Mel didn't look up from his computer screen when she came in.

"Cutting it pretty close, Faust."

"I know. But I got the interview."

"The water board enacted a new drought plan today. You'll have to catch that, too."

Chelsea closed her eyes as she felt the familiar deadline stomachache coming on. "Right," she said, dialing the water district office. As she waited for the receptionist to answer, she pulled out a pastry and took a bite. "Ugh!"

"Santa Clara Valley Water District," said the voice on the phone.

She swallowed hard. "Public relations, please." Great. An authentic Portuguese pastry, and she couldn't even eat it.

In a minute, she had a promise that a copy of the new plan would be faxed to her right away. She opened a file on the computer and started typing.

There was no time to get something else to eat. This was deadline. Crank the words out, perform a miracle just as she did every issue.

Normal mortals could never write this much in such a short period of time. Chelsea was always aware of the police reporter who had had a heart attack one morning while on deadline at the Palo Alto paper where she interned. He dictated the rest of his story before he let the paramedics take him to the hospital. He was crazy, she thought, but she would probably do the same thing. Mel was waiting, the pressroom was waiting, the paper would be printed tonight and the story had to be done.

The water thing was standard, but this parade story was special. She wanted to give the feeling behind it, so different from ordinary American experience--the splendor of the little girls dressed like queens, the free food doled out in huge quantities in the hall, the flags of two countries standing together.

The clock over her desk buzzed, as it always did at the half hour.

"A little bit of Portugal came to the streets of San Jose Sunday afternoon when girls dressed as queens paraded down East Santa Clara Street.   ."

Chapter Two

"What are you doing here?" Chelsea's mother asked as she opened the door Wednesday morning. "Don't you have to work?"

Chelsea bent to hug her mother. "I worked Sunday so Mel gave me the morning off. Did you see my parade pictures?"

"What parade?"

"Holy Ghost parade. Or *festa*, as I hear it's called." She pulled a folded newspaper from her canvas bag. "Here, I brought you a copy. Page 3."

"Oh. I can't see this without my reading glasses."

Chelsea followed her mother into the kitchen and watched her put on the half-glasses she'd just started wearing a few months ago. She was struck by how much her mother looked like her grandmother.

Mom glanced at Chelsea's story and pictures, then set the paper on the table, folding her glasses carefully. "I remember when we used to sit on my grandma's porch and watch the parade go by. Then we kids would all run down to the Portuguese lodge for *sopas* and candy. We'd play games all day. Aunt Julia used to dance till way past midnight and Grandma would have a fit."

"Did you ever march in the parade?"

"Me? Nah. My mother thought it was silly. I did, too. None of my generation got into that stuff. Besides, the lodge president's daughter always got chosen for queen, even if she was the ugliest girl in town. I remember Tillie Gomes was the queen for three or four years in a row." Mom shook her head, smiling at the memory. "Well, come have some coffee and sweet rolls. I just got them fresh from Wilson's."

Chelsea watched her mother pour coffee from the old chrome percolator and fill a flowered plate with pastries from the never-empty cakebox. She recalled her mother's first words at the airport when she came back from Washington: "My God, you're too skinny."

They had fought about food for years. Chelsea was determined not to look like the rest of her hefty relatives. Mom was just as determined to keep feeding her fattening foods. That's why she had started running back in high school and kept it up ever since.

Sitting in her usual place at the table, the seat closest to the stove, Chelsea savored the hot coffee. Caffeine was the only vice she and her mother had in common. She bit into the cinnamon-coated pastry and promised herself she'd run an extra mile tonight. It was easier than arguing about it. "How come we never went to a Holy Ghost festival?"

Mom stirred milk into her coffee. "Oh, I wasn't interested. And your father's not Portuguese. He did go with me once when we were dating. But he was miserable."

"Well, I wish you'd taken me when I was a kid. Then I would have known what was going on. I felt totally different from those people at the parade."

"You are different. You're a California kid. Those people are foreigners. It's only the ones who were born in Portugal who still do that stuff. More coffee?"

"I'll get it."

Chelsea refilled her mug and brought the pot over to fill her mother's. "I was thinking I might try to write something else about the Portuguese."

"There's nothing to write about. All the people are dead."

Chelsea stared at the embroidered hummingbird pictures that hung over the table. "I'd go beyond our family. I would talk to the immigrants who are still alive. I got some great shots Sunday, not just the ones Mel put in the paper. I could take lots more. Besides, there are plenty of old photos, like Aunt Julia's, that would give it an historical flavor."

Mom scowled. "Ancient history. Nobody cares."

Chelsea watched her mother bite into a second roll, her expression distant and somehow threatened. She changed the subject. "How's Dad?"

Mom shook her head. "Not good. He doesn't want to do anything. I keep telling him to go to the doctor to see if something physical is wrong, but he just shakes his head and says he's fine."

"Well, at least he's got his job. He always seemed happy there."

She sighed. "Not any more. They've got new owners, young guys, and your father is convinced they're going to lay him off because he's getting too old."

"That's ridiculous. He knows more than anybody there. Besides, it's illegal to discriminate because of age."

"I know. That's what I told him, but he won't listen."

Her father had worked at San Jose Linoleum and Tile for 30 years. He had wanted to become a photographer, but his family couldn't afford the equipment or the training, and his parents thought it was a waste of time. So he kept photography as a hobby and made an art out of tile and linoleum, figuring it was better than the construction work his two older brothers did.

A manager now, he enjoyed helping customers pick out colors and patterns. He knew which brands were good and which were not. He would walk into someone's kitchen, look at the floor and nod. "Yep, Mannington Gold. That'll last 'em forever." Or, "Construction grade. Looks good now, but they'll have to replace it in a couple years."

He loved tile, the colors, the textures, the different shapes. He had re-tiled their own kitchen in sea green and their bathroom in soft peach and white. In the entryway, he had laid big rust-colored Mexican pavers and forbidden his wife to cover them with one of her frilly throw rugs.

"They won't lay him off, Mom. He's the best, and they need him."

"I don't know," Mom said, sipping her coffee. "Eat some more. They're good."

"No, thanks."

"You know what your Aunt Ruth told me last week? She said, 'Lou, you're just going to have to get a job.' I said, 'Yeah, doing what? Scrubbing floors like my grandmother did?' I'm too old and too fat. All I've ever done is take care of you and your father and this house. Besides, if I got a job, who would watch after your father?"

"He's not a child, Mom. And you're not that old."

"My friend Elsie, she said, 'Your kids should take care of you when you get old.' 'Hah!' I said to her. 'I've only got one daughter, and my girl can barely take care of herself.' "

Chelsea opened her mouth to protest, but her mother held up her hand.

"I know you don't make a lot of money at that newspaper. You need a husband to support you properly. You live in that old apartment and drive that pickup truck--"

"That truck cost more than your Buick," Chelsea exploded, banging her cup down on the table. "I have a good job. And I love my apartment. She pushed back her chair. "I've got to go to work. Do you want to keep the paper?"

"I guess I'll show your father."

"Okay. Thanks for the coffee."

"Next time I'll give you decaf. Be good."

Chelsea continued out the front door.

She jerked the gearshift in her blue Ford Ranger into reverse and backed out of the driveway, barely missing the neighbor's cat.

On the way downtown to the office, she stewed. Her mother hadn't approved of anything she'd done since junior high. She couldn't see why Chelsea had to go all the way to the University of California at Berkeley when San Jose State was closer and cheaper, why she had to work nights and weekends, or why she wanted to buy a truck instead of a regular car. Her mother certainly hadn't accepted her decision to move in with Jeffrey McNeil shortly after she got the job at the Sacramento Record.

Even though her mother denied her Portuguese heritage, maybe it was her ethnic upbringing that made her believe women should marry and devote their lives to their husbands and children, as she had. Or maybe it was just the way of her generation.

But now, with Dad in danger of losing his job, maybe Mom *should* think about getting one. There were a lot of things she could do if she tried. Instead, she assumed she was helpless. Chelsea would never be that dependent on a man.

She felt a pang of guilt remembering what her mother had said about children taking care of their parents. It was a burden she had never considered taking on. But without any brothers and sisters, who else would do it? It was true that she could not support herself and pay her parents' bills, but who could? She had taken quite a pay cut going to work at the Weekly Times. When she had come back from Washington and found out her job at the Record was gone, she had to take the first job she could get. Besides, it was only temporary.

Merging onto Route 880 North by the Valley Fair Mall, she considered her mother's life. What would it be like to need a man so much, to depend completely on him, even though some day he might die and leave you alone? Chelsea had certainly known love. A series of college romances was followed by her three-year affair with red-haired, bearded political activist Jeffrey McNeil. They had been passionate in bed and best friends outside of it. It had felt like a love that would last forever, but when it came to a choice between their careers and their relationship, the careers won.

She still burned remembering the night at the Sacramento Hilton that she realized their relationship was hopeless. Jeffrey had taken her to a fundraising party for Senate candidate Bob Cates. Lots of politicians, business leaders and society folk had been there. Jeffrey escorted her into the glittering crowd, telling her she looked gorgeous. But as he began to introduce her around, he said only that she was his girlfriend. No mention of her work as a reporter for the Record or the national magazine articles she had published. Whenever she started to speak, he interrupted, as if she had nothing important to say. She glared at him and tried to get his attention, but he was unusually animated, laughing too much, pretending to be pals with half the men in the room.

When she managed to drag him over to the refreshment table, she protested. "Hey, how come you don't tell them who I am? Or let me talk? You squelched me like some kind of bimbo."

Jeffrey rolled his eyes. "Tonight could you just be my beautiful girlfriend, not a reporter who's going to put whatever people say in the paper?"

"What?"

"Look, these guys don't want to deal with the press tonight. If they realize I'm dating a reporter, I'm screwed."

"Jeffrey, I'm not a gossip columnist! Besides, I know some of these people. I've interviewed them. I'll talk to them if I want to. They can see I'm not taking notes tonight."

"They're not going to believe it. I need for them to trust me."

"So, what are you saying? I should quit and devote my life to charity teas and fashion shows to help you cozy up to Congress?"

"No, just use a little discretion."

She knew her face was red and her voice was too shrill, but she didn't care. "Okay. I will discreetly find my way out. If I decide to speak to anyone on the way, I will tell them exactly who I am and what I think because I am a whole person, not just your trophy."

When she got home that night, she found the letter notifying her she had received the fellowship in Washington. She would spend six months in the nation's capital, following the activities of the senators and representatives from California and write a series of articles that the Associated Press would publish across the country. It was quite a coup, and it would get her away from Jeffrey for a while. Sooner or later, she knew he would end up in Washington, too. But when she left Sacramento two weeks later, they agreed that their relationship was over. Jeffrey had apologized "for being a jerk" that night, and he shared her apartment in Washington for a while, but they both knew their careers would always win over romance.

After Jeffrey, Chelsea's love life had slowed down. Tall, good-looking and smart, she attracted plenty of attention from the opposite sex, but the men who asked her out all seemed dull compared to Jeffrey McNeil.

When a survey published in the daily newspaper reported that women's chances of getting married after age 30 diminished dramatically, Chelsea's mother sent her a copy. Once, after she came home to San Jose, her mom even jokingly offered to send to the Azores for a good Portuguese man.

"Chelsea would have him for dinner," Dad said.

"Hey!"

He bent and kissed her hair. "I meant it as a compliment. When it's time, you'll find somebody worthy of you. No hurry."

"I want grandchildren," Mom had protested.

"I'll get a cat," Chelsea responded, quickly changing the subject.

How did I get off on this, she thought, pulling into the parking lot behind the newspaper building. She slipped her blue blazer over her white blouse and got out, gazing at the South Bay Weekly Times sign etched in redwood over the door. Inside was normal life. Her desk. Her computer. Her phone. Mel. No more arguments or guilt trips from her mother.

"Chels," said Berta, the spiky-haired receptionist with the pale skin and black lipstick. "You got messages up the yin yang."

"Good," she said, pulling the stack of pink slips out of her cubbyhole and starting toward the newsroom.

But the top message stopped her. "Simão Freitas," she read. "Hmm."

Mel was waiting for her in the newsroom. As he filled her in on the week's schedule, she studied the message from Simão, wondering what he wanted.

"Faust, are you paying attention?" Mel's eyes twinkled as he watched her fiddling with her messages.

She grinned. She and Mel had known each other for a long time, ever since their college days at Berkeley, when she was the editor and he was the reporter. They were both older now, and there were gray hairs in his beard, but they remained buddies. "Sure. I've just got lots of calls to return, and I guess I'm a little tired."

"After a morning off? Well, you'll be glad to know the Portugees liked your feature."

"They did?" She smiled. "Good. I wrote it so fast it's a wonder it made any sense. That Freitas guy said they didn't get much press."

"Apparently they don't. I was talking it over with our beloved publisher." He rolled his eyes. "When he found out how many potential advertisers have businesses in that part of town, he decided we should produce a more in-depth feature on the Portuguese section of San Jose. Of course, he wants you to do it."

Chelsea set the messages on her desk. "It always boils down to advertising for him, doesn't it? Does it matter at all whether it's a good story or not?"

"Couldn't it be good for both sides?"

"I don't know." She shoved her long hair back over her shoulders and smoothed it behind her ears. "He doesn't want it this week, does he?"

"Nope. He needs a couple weeks to sell ads. You don't sound too excited about this."

The sweet roll lay like a rock in her stomach. "It was weird out there, Mel. I felt as if I had stepped into another country, a country where I didn't belong."

"Really? That might be the element that makes the story. Think about it, Chels. It might grow into a book or something."

"I doubt it."

33

"No, really. Why not?" Mel looked out the window at a homeless man pushing his shopping cart across the street. Chelsea knew he wished he could move beyond the Weekly Times. They had both had grand plans at Berkeley, but their lives had taken different paths. The few waking hours Mel didn't spend at the newspaper were devoted to his wife Kathy and their two little girls.

"I don't know." She spread the phone messages out on her desk, trying to prioritize them. "You got anything non-Portuguese on your list?"

"Kindergarten talent show, 2:00 today. Want it?" Mel's phone buzzed. He slid the assignment sheet over to her. "Take it. It's not Pulitzer Prize stuff, but it'll be fun."

"*Bom dia*," Simão Freitas answered when Chelsea returned his call late that afternoon.

"Hello," she said, surprised to get him instead of his answering machine. "This is Chelsea Faust." She picked up a red and yellow tissue paper flower one of the children had given her at the talent show. The teacher had introduced her as "Mrs. Faust, the reporter from the newspaper." It made her feel ancient. But now she was blushing like a 14-year-old.

"Ah," Simão said, "the Portuguese lady with the English and German name."

"Right." She twirled the flower, watching the red and yellow blend into orange.

She heard in the background what sounded like a radio; the announcer was speaking Portuguese.

"What was your mother's last name?"

"What?" Why was her face so hot? "Silveira."

"Ah. Silveira." He said it like Sil-VAY-da. "Chelsea Faust de Silveira," he said, as if thinking out loud. "I like that."

"Yes. Well." Mel was watching her. She cleared her throat. "What can I do for you, Mr. Freitas?"

"Americans, always in a hurry." He chuckled. "First, I want to thank you for your photographs and story in this week's newspaper. You did a very nice job with something that was foreign to you. You write very well."

34

"Thank you." Find something to do, Mel, she thought, glaring at him. He winked before turning back to his computer screen. She tossed her flower at him. It swished against his monitor and fell on the floor. This would never happen at the Record. Here, the newsroom was so small they were like kids jammed into a playpen together.

"Second," Simão continued, "I wondered if you would be interested in coming to a meeting of our Portuguese Cultural Society Monday night. I thought it might be useful to you to learn more about our people. You seemed to be interested."

Chelsea smiled. She was interested in at least one Portuguese person. Her calendar showed nothing for Monday evening. If the publisher was serious about this Portuguese feature, this was a good way to start. "Monday night? Okay. What does this cultural society do?"

"Many things. We give scholarships to Portuguese students, hold special programs on our culture and arts, sponsor symposiums and other events. If you come, I can introduce you to some important people in the community."

"Sounds good." She wrote "P. meeting" on her calendar. "Actually, this is great. My publisher wants me to do another article on the Portuguese section of San Jose and the people who live and work there. I have a lot of research to do in a hurry, so this will be a big help."

"Excellent. My group will be pleased."

"I'm afraid you can expect the advertising staff to hit you up for ads."

"Good. I have been telling people in the community that we should advertise in the English-language papers, too. Well, I will enjoy seeing you again."

"Thank you. Same here. Where is it and what time?"

Chelsea wrote down the details and hung up, blowing on her burning face. Across the aisle, Mel flashed a thumbs up sign.

"Hush, Mel. I'll be working overtime on Monday, okay?"

"Sure. Your people want you."

"They're not *my* people." She got up and retrieved her flower. "I'm going to hide in the darkroom for a couple of hours. If anybody calls, I'm not here."

Mel shrugged. "Fine."

From the hallway, she leaned back through the door. "Except for my parents, of course."

"And Mr. Freitas?"

"Get real, Mel. He's just a source."

Thursday passed with no word about the Portuguese, a welcome relief. On Friday morning, Chelsea shot pictures of an art exhibit, coming back with three rolls of film to process. It was almost noon when she emerged from the darkroom, squinting against the bright fluorescent lights of the newsroom. Her prints were washing in the sink, and she had straightened out the mess the sports guys had left, throwing out their ruined photos and wet paper towels and dumping the used chemicals left in the trays. All the other editorial staffers were gone for lunch or assignments.

She leaned against the doorframe and looked out the window onto the quiet street that divided the South Bay Weekly Times building from the adjacent shopping center. Sparrows nudged each other in the eaves. On the sidewalk, a sheet of newsprint skittered along in a light breeze. The sky was dotted with clouds, and the light dimmed and brightened as the sun darted in and out.

Inside the office, a police radio chattered atop the unmatched gray and tan file cabinets. Like all the staff, Chelsea was attuned to the codes. If she heard about an accident, fire or hostage situation, she would grab her camera and go, but now most of the messages were about lunch or routine reports on old burglaries or vandalism. They faded into the background, along with the frequent warbling of the telephone at the front desk.

The editorial office was in front next to the reception area. They could see people passing by or coming in the front door. Passersby could also watch them working. But right now the street was deserted.

Chelsea checked her watch. Five more minutes and she could hang her pictures to dry. Sarge should be back any minute. She supposed she'd take lunch then, walking home to read her mail and eat some of last night's leftover taco salad.

Beep! Wearily she picked up her phone. The baby downstairs had cried all night, making it hard to sleep.

"Miss Faust?" said a hoarse male voice.

"Yes?"

"Have you seen Councilman Slater lately?"

"What? I don't know. Who is this, please?"

"Think of me as an informed source. So, have you seen the councilman? Was he at the last city council meeting?"

She eased into her chair, trying to identify the voice. "No, come to think of it, he wasn't."

"Don't you think somebody ought to look into where he was?"

"It was just one meeting. I didn't think much about it."

"Well, I suggest you investigate what our esteemed councilman is up to. If you call his office, you'll find Slater isn't there either."

Before she could respond, he hung up.

"Hello? Hello?

"Huh." Chelsea paged through her Rolodex and found Slater's work phone number. She dialed, wondering what she would say if he came on the line. But no one answered the phone.

The darkroom timer dinged. She dashed into the dank room lit by a single red bulb, turned off the water and fished out her prints, squeegeeing them one by one against a large sheet of glass, then clipped them to the wire that hung the length of the room.

When she came back out, wiping her hands on a paper towel, Mel was back in the newsroom, standing by the police scanner. "Better load the camera, Faust."

"What's up?"

"Big crash in front of City Hall. Three cars. Jaws of life on the way."

She grabbed four rolls of film from the supply cabinet. "Lucky me." Her bag weighed heavy on her shoulder, and she felt the familiar adrenalin rush as she shoved her notebook into her purse.

"Be careful," Mel said.

"Always." As she rushed past the receptionist, she called "accident" and shoved out the front door without slowing to sign out.

Both lunch and Slater would have to wait. He was probably just on vacation anyway.

It was one of those spring afternoons when Chelsea couldn't stand being inside, especially after what she had seen that afternoon. The accident was a nightmare. A drunk in a U-Haul rental truck had plowed into a Honda with a mother and child inside. Then the Honda ricocheted off a VW bug carrying two teenage boys. The truck driver was not hurt. He was already in the back of a police car on his way to jail when Chelsea arrived. One boy was just badly bruised, but the other had a crushed leg. He was screaming in pain. "What am I gonna do about the game this weekend? I've got to play," he kept saying. He wouldn't be playing ball for a long time, if ever.

Chelsea was sickened by what she saw in the crushed Honda. The mother was pinned against the dash, blood streaming from her head and face. The toddler in the back seat seemed unhurt but wailed nonstop in fear, and the mother couldn't move to comfort her. . .

"Ugh," she said, pushing out a deep breath, trying to expel the tension as she drove up the hill to Alum Rock Park. She had already souped her film and would print it in the morning, but now it was time to shake it off for a while.

She had stopped at her apartment after work just long enough to change into shorts and a tee shirt, stuffing her long hair into a San Jose Sharks cap. She drove through the Portuguese section of town, passing Simão's office, the bakery, the church. Portuguese names melded into Mexican and Vietnamese names. The businesses gave way to lush hillside homes as she climbed the winding road. She passed the ranger station and parked under a row of gnarled oaks.

Soon the summer heat and smog would turn everything brown, but today the foothills were still green, dotted with purple lupine and orange poppies. Between the clouds, the sky was a deep blue, and the air smelled fresh. She breathed deeply, grateful to be alive and healthy. What a horrible night it would be for the people in the accident.

Dust-colored squirrels scattered as Chelsea opened the door. Her work was all verbal and mental. She needed to do something physical. Sometimes she pictured a little girl inside her yearning to go outside and play, like a restless puppy whining to romp and run.

She stretched and set off at a trot, enjoying the chuff of her shoes against the dirt.

She could hear her mother telling her not to come up here by herself, it wasn't safe. But the only danger she had ever seen was a rattlesnake sleeping on the trail. As she approached, it shook its rattles at her and slithered into the bushes.

She liked to be alone. When she lived with Jeffrey, they sometimes jogged together, but it was hard to get away from the traffic and the crowds. She wondered how Simão Freitas would feel about it. Somehow she couldn't picture him jogging.

The park was already high above Santa Clara Valley, but the trail wound even higher. When Chelsea was out of breath, her calf muscles aching, she stopped and looked around, picking out the landmarks. Straight down, the tallest building was the Fairmont Hotel. She found Fifth Street, but couldn't locate her house. To the south sprawled the county fairgrounds and Oak Hill Cemetery. Looking northwest, she could see Alviso Bay and the hangars at Moffett Field Naval Air Station. Closer by loomed the towers of Five Wounds Church. Along the rim of the hills, she could see Highway 101, packed with rush-hour traffic. Seen from above, San Jose was a mosaic of green, gray and brown.

Something moved close by, and Chelsea held her breath. A blacktail deer was watching her, its donkey-like ears sticking up above the weeds. Behind the doe, Chelsea thought she saw the heads of two fawns. If she had her camera, perhaps she could capture the scene on film, but the deer would probably bolt at the first click of the shutter.

She stood a long time, watching the deer watching her, until finally a dog dashed down the path, followed by a young man on a bicycle. Chelsea barely got out of the way in time. "Watch it!" she grumbled as the deer bounded away. She turned and started back down the hill toward civilization.

The windows of the San Jose main library were black with night as a voice on a loudspeaker announced that it was closing time. Chelsea yawned as she put the newspaper clippings back into the folder labeled "Portuguese."

Most of the articles were about Five Wounds Church and the struggle to build it that began just before World War I and ended with its completion shortly after the war. There was a big feature, done about 15 years ago, on some of the merchants in what the article called Little Portugal. Other yellowed clips described past Holy Ghost festivals.

She felt the gray-haired librarian watching her. "I know. It's closing time."

"I hope you found what you needed."

"Well, I thought there'd be more."

"I'm sorry." The librarian's attention was on reshelving the books piled on her desk.

Chelsea rode the escalator to the first floor and went out, surprised at the warm wind that massaged her face as she walked down the wide steps toward San Carlos Street.

Friday night. To the right, the new convention center marquee welcomed software engineers. Across the street, the civic auditorium was hosting a concert by Little Joe y La Familia. To the left, the marquee at the Center for Performing Arts advertised "Evita," curtain at 8 p.m. All around, brightly lit restaurants and shops testified to the rebirth of downtown San Jose, which only 10 years before had been deserted and decaying.

Couples walked hand in hand, dressed for dinner and the theater, the women in high-heeled shoes and spangled dresses, the men in sports jackets and dark tailored pants. Chelsea wore her usual jeans and denim blazer, her bag slung over her shoulder. She felt more in common with the homeless man sitting on the library steps than with the glittery nightlife crowd.

Occasionally Chelsea wondered if she'd ever grow up. Looking at herself in the mirror each morning, she saw the same image she had carried through Cal Berkeley. Even Mel had cut his hair, trimmed his beard, and started wearing ties and suits. But why not be comfortable? She dressed up when she had to and wore slacks, blazers and loafers when she couldn't get away with jeans.

If she were going to eat at Scott's and see "Evita" afterward, she could dig up a dress, but right now there was no one to do those things with. Simão's face flickered through her mind, but she pushed him away. That was just business. She would get her article, and he would get some publicity, period.

Sometimes she hated being alone. When she lived with Jeffrey, even if they were apart, at least there was someone else in her life. And now, there wasn't. All of her old female friends were busy with husbands and children, and most of the men she met were already committed to someone else.

No point in feeling sorry for herself. She walked quickly toward home. Maybe she would stop at Lee's on the way. What she needed was a good TV show and some Chinese food for dinner.

Chapter Three

Monday morning, Chelsea had planned to sleep in, since she was working that night, but it was barely light when the telephone woke her up.

"Your father's going crazy," her mother proclaimed without a hello.

"Huh?" said Chelsea, half asleep. "Mom?"

"I thought you'd be up by now. Don't you have to go to work?"

"I'm going in later. What's wrong?"

"Well, your father is supposed to go to the doctor this morning, and he refuses to go. He says he has to work."

"Well, maybe he does. Is he sick?"

"Who knows, the way he's been acting. He can take a couple hours off for a checkup. He's been working there for 30 years."

"I know. But, Mom, he's a grown man. It's his decision."

"You haven't had to live with him lately. I really think there's something wrong."

"He's probably just depressed."

"He thinks nobody cares about him. Shall I tell him he's right?"

"Nuts," Chelsea whispered, glancing at the digital clock next to the bed. 7:28. "Okay, you win. I'm awake anyway. Give me a few minutes to dress and a half hour to fight the commute traffic."

"He says he's leaving for work at quarter to 9."

"I'll be there as soon as I can. Bye."

Is this how it's going to be as they get older, she wondered, tossing off her nightgown on the way to the shower.

Her father was sitting in the kitchen drinking coffee and staring at the newspaper when she arrived.

"Hey, you skipping work?"

She bent to kiss his freshly shaven cheek, noticing he'd missed a tuft of white hair near his left ear. "No, I've got a couple hours off."

He pointed to a column in the local section. "Jim Spielbauer died. He was only 59. Heart attack."

Her mother leaned against the kitchen counter, shaking her head.

Chelsea settled into her chair. "You're lucky your heart is in good shape. You don't have to worry."

"My Uncle Phil was in great shape, too. Then he had a heart attack and boom. He was gone."

"I remember." Her mother set a cup of hot coffee in front of her. "Thanks, Mom. So Dad, I hear you have a doctor's appointment this morning."

"No, your mother made a mistake. I have to work."

"Dad, if the appointment's set, why not go? I'll drive you."

"I can drive myself."

"I know. But I want to spend some time with you. Besides, I thought maybe you'd like to ride in a vehicle with some class."

He pushed back his chair, nearly knocking it over. "Don't talk to me like I'm a child!" He glared at Chelsea's mother. "Forget breakfast. I've lost my appetite." He stumbled down the hall to the bedroom, slamming the door behind him.

"Damn," said Mom, slapping a potholder against the side of the stove. "His stubbornness is going to kill him." She banged a cast iron frying pan onto the right front burner. "You probably didn't eat anything. Can I make you some eggs and bacon?"

"What?" Chelsea was still stunned by her father's sudden temper. "Sure, I guess so. Do you need any help?"

"No thanks." Mom cracked an egg against the side of the pan.

As her breakfast cooked, Chelsea went out to the back yard, wandering through her father's garden. Overripe artichokes peeked through the leaves on the husky plants near the fence. Rotting blackberries covered the vines between the lemon tree and the apricot tree. Weeds had come up around the plants, and snails crawled in the carefully mounded basins her father had built around them.

When Chelsea was a girl, she had spent hours back here with her father, inhaling the rich smells of earth, leaves and fruit. Together they had photographed the ripening apricots and artichokes and even the bugs, playing with colored filters and macro lenses. Now her dad had let it all go.

"Chelsea," her mother called from the back door. "It's ready."

"Okay."

43

Nothing stayed the same, she thought. Maybe her mother was right. At 28, she needed more than a good job. Most people her age were already married and raising children. She remembered her 10-year high school reunion in March. She was the only one at her table who wasn't married and a mother. She had thought her work in Sacramento and her fellowship in Washington would impress people, but all they talked about was their kids, their husbands and their houses.

She slowly walked up the steps and into the kitchen of the house where she'd grown up.

"Eat," said her mother, pointing Chelsea to her regular seat by the stove.

A Buick, a Mercedes, and a Cadillac filled the tiny paved area in front of the Portuguese Community Center that night. Chelsea parked in the nearly empty lot at the county building next door and walked over, her feet already hurting in her beige pumps.

Having been the only woman in slacks the last two times she visited Little Portugal, she had decided to make an effort to blend in. She needed to make a good impression if these people were going to help her with her article. She wore her brown suit with a lacy white blouse and pushed her hair back from her face with tortoiseshell combs she found in the bottom of her jewelry box. Just like going to visit Grandma, or to church, she thought, remembering the days when she and her parents used to worship every Sunday.

As she pushed open the heavy glass doors and paused to get her bearings, Simão Freitas rose from his seat in the lobby to greet her.

"Good evening. You look very nice tonight." His smile was warm, but his voice was husky with nerves.

"Thank you." You too, she thought, admiring his well-cut suit and his tanned, chiseled face. But where was the meeting? A handful of people sat on the tattered lobby chairs speaking Portuguese. Beyond the lobby she saw empty desks and closed doors.

As three men gazed curiously at her, a young, dark-haired woman alone on the sofa smiled up at her hopefully.

"Where is everybody?" Chelsea asked. She had expected to sit in the back of a crowded room and take notes.

44

"It is a board meeting," Simão said, quickly turning to the others. *"Este e a sinhorita Faust de Silveira."*

Standing awkwardly in the doorway with her notebook sticking out of her purse, Chelsea felt very tall and very American. "Hello," she said, hoping the rest of the board members spoke English.

"Welcome," said a slender man with glasses. The scowling bald man next to him merely nodded.

"Sit down, please." Simão pointed to a plastic chair near the door and took his place on the couch next to the young woman. So, he has a girlfriend, Chelsea thought. That's the end of that.

"We are glad to have you here," said the third man, salt-and-pepper-haired and stocky, with a booming voice and a manner that indicated he was in charge. "I am Eduardo Gomes. I hear you are a writer."

"Yes." Her palms began to sweat.

Gomes seemed to be waiting for more. "What do you write?"

"I work for the South Bay Weekly Times, doing mostly features, some news, lots of photos. I've also published some national magazine articles, and I've worked in Sacramento and Washington, D.C."

"What were your articles about?" asked the kind-faced man with glasses. He didn't seem to have a Portuguese accent.

"For *Woman Today*, I wrote about nuns and how their role has changed in recent years. I also interviewed members of Congress as part of my fellowship."

He nodded, smiling. "How interesting. I would love to see some of your work."

"I can get you copies," she said. Out of the corner of her eye, she saw Simão beaming, as if he had captured a rare prize.

"So, you are Portuguese," Gomes interrupted, his voice a challenge.

"Half. My mother's family is from the Azores."

"Ah. And your father?"

"He's of German descent."

Chelsea could feel all the muscles of her body clenching under this inquisition. It was time to change the subject. "So, now that you know all about me, I came to find out about you. My publisher. . ."

45

"Can we begin our agenda, Eduardo?" interrupted the scowling man, his eyes narrowed to slits in his fleshy face. "This is supposed to be a formal meeting."

Eduardo Gomes sighed. "You have no manners, Miguel. All right, with our visitor's kind consideration, we will talk about her publisher under New Business. I declare this meeting open. António, will you read the minutes?"

As the spectacled man who was interested in her articles began to read, Chelsea sat against the plastic chair-back and tried to relax. She noticed an empty coffeepot, drained during the day by the Portuguese seniors who came for meetings and services. Next to the coffeepot was a paper plate littered with bread crumbs. Sweet bread?

Over Gomes' head hung a painting of a harbor scene labeled "Faial," similar to the one in Simão's office. On the shelf to his left perched a doll with a black hooded cape, another doll in bright red, green and yellow skirts, a few books and more pictures.

Chelsea noticed the young woman looking at her. She smiled and the girl smiled back, unconsciously smoothing her blue skirt. Why hadn't Simão introduced them, she wondered. As the meeting progressed from the minutes to Miguel's treasury report and then news about the upcoming scholarship dinner, the girl seemed to take no part.

Suddenly Eduardo turned to her. "Rosa, you will do the flowers, yes?"

Her cheeks turned pink as she nodded. "Yes. Okay." Her accent was thick.

Simão spoke for her. "Rosa will do the decorations, as she did last year."

"Fine," Miguel said. "But no gardenias this time. They stink up the place. *Compreende?*"

Rosa blushed even deeper. "*Sim*, Miguel, no gardenias."

Chelsea watched the clock on the wall opposite her seat as it passed 8:00, then 8:30, then 9:00. They hassled over whether to serve pork, beef or fish, who would set the table, who would do the dishes, who would receive certificates.

Her hips and back grew stiff and sore from the hard chair, and her throat felt parched in the overheated lobby. Two hours sitting here, and she didn't have much of anything for her article. Mel expected her back at the office in 12 hours. She raised her arm slightly and stared at her watch.

"It is getting late," Simão said, taking her cue. "This could all be taken care of by the scholarship committee. We have other business."

"All right," Eduardo said. "Since Erlinda Soares didn't show up to talk about our cultural arts program, let's hear from our visitor."

Chelsea swallowed. The pressure was back on. "After we published our article about the--the *festa*, my publisher decided we needed more coverage of your area, so. . ."

As she talked about the planned feature on the Portuguese in San Jose, Simão nodded encouragingly. António and Eduardo seemed interested, but Miguel's scowl deepened. Finally he burst in.

"They come in here one time, write a few stories, get us to buy advertising and then we never see them again. This has happened before, Simão. Even the San Jose Mercury wrote one big story, full of mistakes. Then when we called about our symposium, they had no time to talk to us. Once they got our money, they didn't care no more."

"But this is good publicity, Miguel. It will help our businesses, and our cultural organization, too."

"You have only been here three years, Simão. It is not what you think."

Chelsea's head was beginning to ache. "No," she began, "We're trying--"

"To make money," Miguel finished.

Simão stood and waved his hand at the unruly Miguel. "You like money, do you not? Why should they not make money? Why should we not all make money? Whatever happened before does not matter. This is a different newspaper, and we have a reporter here who is one of our own. She is Portuguese, her family comes from the same islands ours did, and she will treat us fairly. Did you see her article on the parade?"

"No." Miguel squinted at the floor, breathing hard.

"I did," said António, pushing his glasses up. "It was very nicely done."

"Thank you," Chelsea whispered.

"I have a copy," said Simão, opening his briefcase. "Look. This is

47

good work. Here are the bands and the women. She talks about our traditions. She names some of our businesses. Look at the photographs. She did those, too. Here is your store, Miguel."

"Hmm," Miguel said, scanning the page and handing it back. "It is blurry."

It's background. You can't focus on everything, Chelsea thought, staring at Simão's strong hands.

Simão folded the paper carefully and sat back down. "This will be a big story. And afterward, we will have a contact at the paper. We can call whenever we have news and make sure it gets published."

Chelsea uncrossed her legs and re-crossed them. What if she couldn't get their stories in? They might not be deemed newsworthy or there might not be space. . ."Well, I don't--" she began.

Miguel looked up, like a bull ready to charge at anything she said.

António jumped in to save her. "I think we should help Miss Faust in whatever way we can." He smiled warmly at her.

"I agree," Eduardo said.

"All right, I give up," growled Miguel.

"Good," said Simão. "Chelsea, how do you want to proceed?" He said her name with a soft "C", like Shell Sea. She liked the way it sounded.

"Well, first tell me about your organization."

By 10:30, her head was pounding, she needed a restroom and she longed for something cold to drink, but she had enough notes for a story on the cultural center. She also had an appointment with António to talk about his Portuguese bookstore and promises from Eduardo Gomes and Simão to introduce her to other members of the Portuguese chamber of commerce.

As they rose, stretching and yawning, Miguel pulled Eduardo off to the side, saying something to him in Portuguese. Chelsea must have looked worried because António patted her shoulder. "They're arguing about the scholarship dinner invitations again."

"Oh." António was the only one there besides Simão who was as tall as she was. But he lacked Simão's broad shoulders. "It was very nice to meet you," she said. "I'll see you tomorrow."

He nodded. "Yes. I look forward to it. Now I must go home and get some sleep.'

As António walked out, limping slightly, Chelsea turned to Rosa. "I'm glad I met you," she said, even though they hadn't really met.

"You, too. This, this, your work, sounds very interesting."

"Sometimes it is."

Rosa grinned. "Mine, too. Sometimes interesting, sometimes just hard work."

"Flowers, you mean?"

Simão shook his head. "No, Rosa thinks she is an artist. She did our brochure."

"Oh?" Chelsea looked with interest at the slick folder Simão handed her. On the front was a striking sketch of a Portuguese fisherman and his wife and children, all looking out to sea. At the bottom, it was signed Rosa M. Freitas. Chelsea looked from Rosa to Simão. "So you two are married?"

Simão laughed. "Oh no. Rosa is my sister. No, you keep it," he added as she held the brochure out to him.

"Thank you."

"Rosa," called Eduardo from the other side of the room.

As she went over, Simão said to Chelsea, "I will walk with you to your car."

"I'm fine."

"No, I do not let ladies walk alone in the dark in this neighborhood. Back where I come from, you would never have been allowed to come here by yourself."

"I'm 28 years old."

"And an unmarried woman," he said as he held the door for her.

Chelsea stared at him, but decided not to pursue it. She breathed in the cool air outside. "So this was just a board meeting?"

"Yes. We have about 60 members, but they do not get together except for big events. The important ones were present, and you got a story, did you not?"

"Sure, it's a start."

"You parked way over here?" Simão asked as they rounded the corner. Her truck was the only vehicle in the section of the county lot closest to the Portuguese center. A dozen identical white county cars were lined up at the opposite end of the lot.

49

Chelsea could feel Simão eyeing her truck. "Well, thank you again," she said, holding out her hand.

"You are welcome." He shook her hand warmly. "Get in. I will watch to see that you get started safely."

She climbed aboard, conscious of her skirt riding up high on her thighs. She pulled her skirt down and started the engine.

Simão was still watching as she drove out of the lot onto Santa Clara Street. Roaring through the intersection, she rolled open the window and felt the air on her face. Finally free. Her headache began to ease a little as she left Simão and Little Portugal behind.

Chelsea hunched over her desk, staring at the blinking cursor on the blank computer screen and sipping coffee so hot it scalded her tongue. She was still bleary-eyed after last night's meeting. As she looked at her notes, she realized she didn't have much of a story yet.

She had forgotten to set the alarm clock. Pressed for time, she threw on jeans and a white cotton shirt and pulled her hair back into a ponytail. She skipped her usual light makeup and went to work feeling as if she looked about 13 years old, except for the tiny crow's feet around her eyes.

Mel looked up from the story he was editing. "Tough night?"

"Yeah, I spent three and a half hours in a room full of Portuguese men," she growled.

"Must have been good."

"Oh, shut up, Mel."

"Okay," he said. "I know when to leave Ms. Faust alone." He looked at the craggy police reporter sitting with the telephone against his ear, on hold. "Sarge, don't talk to Faust today. She had a hard night."

Sarge nodded. "Sorry to hear that." The edges of his lips tilted up in a barely suppressed smile.

Fine, she thought, typing "Portuguese Cultural Association" on the screen. She held her hands poised over the keyboard, then let them drop to her lap. "You got anything else for me to work on, Mel? I can't face this right now."

The police radio jabbered, "See the man at 1193 Mission. He says somebody spray-painted his fence last night."

50

"Here," Mel said, punching keys on his computer. "Edit the calendar for me, okay?"

"I meant photos or an interview."

"Nope, I need the calendar. Besides, I wouldn't want to take you away too long from your big Portuguese feature."

Sarge strangled his guffaw into loud throat-clearing as Chelsea hit the escape key so hard she bent her fingernail under. "Damn it," she hissed.

"It's under Junecal," Mel called.

Chelsea silently shook her head. More intern work. Back on her old beat, she could have gone to the capital and found a real story. Like the time she walked in just as the four-term assemblyman from Fresno announced his resignation. That was news, and it didn't have anything to do with advertising. She remembered the feature she did on the first woman assistant director of transportation. It won second place in the California Press Awards that year. Sighing, she typed Junecal and watched the familiar listings pop up on the screen. Toastmasters, 7 a.m. Monday; Las Madres, 10 a.m. Wednesday; Rotary. . . Maybe it was time to follow up on some of the resumes she had sent out when she first came home.

It was almost noon when Berta buzzed her. Mr. Dunning wanted to see her in his office.

Chelsea felt last night's headache returning. What now? She rarely talked to the publisher, letting Mel do all the high-level interfacing, but she knew Dunning was a non-journalist, a corporate manager who consistently failed to understand the difference between a newspaper and an auto manufacturing plant. Somehow everything he said made her crazy, even when he seemed to be trying to be nice.

She rubbed her forehead wearily. Of all days for him to summon her. Well, this is how photographers dress, she told herself, storing the few paragraphs she had written on the Portuguese group.

She paused at the editor's desk. "Dunning wants to see me."

Mel nodded. "I know. It's nothing bad, Chelsea."

"If you already know what he wants, why do I have to talk to him?"

He shrugged. "He said, 'I want to meet with her myself.' I said, 'Okay, fine.' "

Her phone buzzed again. "Chelsea, better get going," Berta said. "Dunning's got a lunch meeting at 12:15."

Chelsea grimaced at Mel and walked down the long beige-carpeted hall to George P. Dunning's paneled office. She knocked lightly on the door frame. "Mr. Dunning?"

He was on the phone, but beckoned her in and motioned to one of the leather chairs in front of his desk.

She sat, feeling small in the oversized chair, and studied Dunning's office. The wall behind the publisher was covered with plaques, awards the Weekly Times had won from various civic and journalistic organizations. There were pictures of Dunning with Congressman Norm Mineta and Mayor Susan Hammer and one with Clint Eastwood, taken at the Pebble Beach golf tournament in Carmel.

Near her on the corner of Dunning's massive mahogany desk was a photograph of his wife and three teenage daughters, all redheads. Next to the photo, in a marble ashtray, Dunning's pipe sat in a pungent pile of ashes. Chelsea's full-page feature on the Portuguese *festa* was spread out on the desk. She could see notes he had made on a yellow pad.

She was trying to read those notes upside down when Dunning hung up the phone and studied her with a bemused grin. "I remember when I used to be able to dress like that for work. On you it looks good."

Fire began to burn in her cheeks. "You wanted to see me?"

He patted the yellow pad. "Yes, I did. I've been thinking about this Portuguese thing, and I've decided we're not playing it up big enough. Our ad people tell me those Portugees have bucks, and we've barely tapped the potential sales there. They can afford it, Fred says. So. . ." He reached for his pipe, filled it with tobacco from a silver canister and lit it, puffing several times to get the fire going. "So, I've decided to do a whole special section on the Portuguese in San Jose. And of course, since you're Portuguese and you have connections in that community, I want you to write it."

"I. . ." she began, but didn't know what she wanted to say. The work would be interesting, but she didn't really have any Portuguese

52

connections, except Simão. It would also be obvious to everyone she talked to that the paper's only motivation was money. She heard Miguel's words again. "They do one story and hit us up for advertising, then we never hear from them anymore."

"What were you going to say?" Dunning said, his blue eyes fixed on her face.

"Well," she replied, matching his stare. "These people are not rich. Most of the businesses are mom and pop affairs. There's some concern that all the paper wants is their advertising money, and that once this is done, we'll never publish anything about them again."

Dunning glanced away from the direct challenge in her dark brown eyes. "Unfounded. When it's newsworthy, we'll write about them. We don't discriminate. Okay?" He tore off the top sheet and pushed it toward her. "I've made some notes on the sorts of places you might want to include. I want you to work on this exclusively for the next couple weeks, really show them we're interested."

"But what about the other things I've been working on?"

"I've already talked to Mel about that. There's nothing on your agenda that can't be put on hold or delegated to the intern. What's her name, Mandy?"

I don't get a vote in any of this, Chelsea thought, noticing a tiny hole in the left leg of her jeans.

The telephone buzzed. Dunning picked it up. "He is? Already? Yes, I guess it is that time." He pulled his gray suit jacket over his white shirt. "I've got to go. Read my notes. If you have any questions, talk to Mel. And, um, you might want to put on a dress for your interviews."

He waited for her to go through the door first. She felt his eyes on her back all the way down the hall until she turned into the newsroom.

"Good stuff, huh?" Mel said.

"Yeah, great. I'm going to lunch."

"Portuguese food?"

She stifled a curse. "No. I have to go home and put on a dress."

As she slammed out the door, she heard Mel and Sarge chuckling behind her. Even Mandy was smiling. To hell with them all, Chelsea thought, stomping all three blocks to her apartment.

53

She was still fuming as she grabbed the mail out of the box next to her door, noticing a small white envelope sticking out between the VISA bill and the Safeway circular. It was written in a familiar scrawl and had a Washington, D.C. return address.

"Jeffrey," she whispered. She hadn't heard from him in months. When she left Washington, they had agreed they probably wouldn't have time to write and it was better they let each other get on with their lives, without a lot of phone calls and letters to make them feel bad.

Now as she studied the envelope, she felt her heart lurch. It was the right thickness and size for a wedding invitation. She had no more claims on him, but . . .

She slit the envelope with her fingernail and pulled out a card. She let out her breath. It wasn't an invitation at all, but a pretty, flowered greeting card with a clipping from the Washington Post classified section tucked inside. Jeffrey had circled an item that read: "Government reporter. Experienced. Help us find the real stories the officials try to hide, the humanity behind the images, the truth behind the governmentese. Degree, experience required. Salary negotiable." The ad gave a post office box, but didn't name the publication or list a telephone number.

She turned to Jeffrey's note. "His handwriting's not getting any better," she muttered.

Dear Faust:

Saw this ad and thought of you. I'm told this is a new paper put out by some guys--and gals--who have decided the Washington Post has gotten too tame since its Watergate days. It's going to be quality stuff. I hear they're looking for a woman. To be politically correct, of course. I think it ought to be you. Your previous work makes you super-qualified, and I wouldn't mind having you within touching distance again.

She squinted to read the last lines, which Jeffrey had started and crossed out twice before ending with "I was a jerk. I miss you more than I thought I would. We could be a great team again. Jeffrey."

P.S. I borrowed this frilly stationery from the wife of a friend. She thought you'd like it. Call me. 202/555-9099.

Chelsea sat back, her hand over her mouth, feeling an ache in the back of her throat. After all this time, he wanted her to come back. And this job sounded great, especially after her morning at the Weekly Times. Of course, any new publication was a risk. She would never forget how quickly the first paper she worked on in San Francisco folded, or the sting of losing her job in Sacramento, but this sounded pretty safe.

To move to Washington, 3,000 miles from her parents and friends. . .No Portuguese there, but she would be writing about other things that mattered, not just serving the advertising department. However, it wouldn't be just a job. She would be going back to Jeffrey, too, and she wasn't sure that was such a good idea. All the reasons they had had for breaking up were still true. Plus her father's depression worried her; maybe she should stick around. But this was a great opportunity--

The telephone rang, startling her so badly she dropped the card on the floor. "Hello?"

"Chels, it's Mel. Your 3:00 appointment wants to know if you can come at 2:30 instead. I said I thought so, but if you can't, you'd better call him."

"Sure." António from the cultural association was her only appointment that day. The one for whom she was putting on a dress. Which she had planned to do anyway, even without Dunning's wisecrack. "I can make it."

"You okay? You sound funny."

"No, I'm fine, just, you know, eating lunch."

"All right, I'll see you later."

Chelsea glanced at the clock and stuffed Jeffrey's card into her purse. She set water on the stove to boil for instant soup and raced to the bedroom to pick out a dress.

Chapter Four

"Chelsea, come on in," António said, greeting her at the open door of Maria's Bookstore with a warm handshake. "Thanks for coming earlier. I thought the afternoon was clear, but my wife set up a meeting with a distributor at 3:30 and forgot to tell me. Come sit down."

She followed him to a squared-off office area behind the counter and sank into a low-slung orange armchair.

"I brought copies of my articles for you," she said.

He took them from her, smiling as he paged slowly through the folder. "Oh my, these look very nice. You did the photographs, too?"

"Most of them, yes."

"Very impressive. You have a good eye."

"Thanks." Chelsea sat quietly as he continued to look at her work. Something about António's bookstore was soothing to her. Perhaps it was the cool air or the classical music in the background or just being surrounded by books neatly arranged in alphabetical order. Most likely it was António himself, so calm and content, unlike most people she met. Everyone always seemed to be in a hurry and angry about it.

António looked up. "If you ever write a book, I want some copies for my store."

"But I thought you sold only Portuguese books."

"That would cut my business in half," he said, smiling as he nudged his glasses back into place. "Most of my customers do read English."

She felt her cheeks turning red. "Oh, of course."

"Well," he said, glancing at his watch. "I guess we'd better get down to business. Would you like some coffee or a soda?" When she shook her head no, he leaned back in his chair. "How shall we proceed? Do you have questions for me?"

Chelsea pulled her notebook out of her purse. "Yes. First of all, how did you get started in this business?"

Again that gentle smile. "I did it for my mother. She came from São Jorge in the early 1900s, in the big wave of immigration. She was just a young girl, only 15, but she was already married to my father, and they were both eager to come to America. You see, São Jorge is very beautiful, but there is no way to make much money. When you come from a big family, as my father did, there is only so much land, and the older brothers inherit what there is, so what was my father going to do? Plus, it was the law that he would have to go into the Portuguese Army when he turned 16. That's why many of them emigrated. Why go far from home to fight for a government that had little to do with the islands where they lived?

"Like many other young men, my father got on a ship in the middle of the night and left for America. It was over a year later before he had enough money to send for Mama. She came by herself, all that way."

"Wow," Chelsea said. "So young."

"Yes. Just children. When my own daughters were that age, I wouldn't even let them go out at night by themselves. But things were different then."

Chelsea leaned forward, fascinated. António's story reminded her of what she had heard about her great-grandparents.

"You're wondering what this has to do with the bookstore," António said, absent-mindedly smoothing his thin white hair. "I know. Well, Mama never got to go to school. There weren't many schools in São Jorge then anyway, and her parents, like many, decided she should stay home and take care of her younger brothers and sisters. There were nine, and so much work. No washing machines or dishwashers or anything. She always talked about sweeping the dirt floor and feeling like she could never get dirt clean. She worked, that's all. It wasn't much better here in America. My dad bought a dairy farm, and she had to milk cows and plow alfalfa fields just like him because they couldn't afford to hire any help. Plus she had three kids to take care of.

"When my brothers and I started going to school, Mama kept looking at our books, curious, you know. One day I found her crying. I was just a little boy, but I loved my mama so much it hurt me to see her that way. I said 'Mama, why are you crying? Is something wrong?' She said, 'No, it's just that I am so glad you are learning to read. I always wanted to do that.' 'You can't read?' I said. Because I assumed all grownups knew how. I had never noticed that there were no books in our house except the ones my brothers and I brought home.

57

"'No,' she said, shaking her head so sadly. 'Well,' said I, a big guy of seven years old, 'I will teach you.' And I did. Whatever I learned in school each day I came home and showed Mama. She was very smart. My brothers started teaching her, too. By the time I got to fourth grade, she was way ahead of me. Every two weeks, she went to the library and brought back more books. And she read them for hours. She did her housework as quickly as she could so she could return to her books. Papa thought she was wasting time, but Mama always said Heaven for her would be a building full of books and plenty of time to read them.

"She made me love books, too. She helped me get all the way through school in an age when lots of boys, including my brothers, were quitting at 14 to go to work. Later, when I said I wanted to open a bookstore, she gave me enough money to get started. I had been in the Navy and Papa had died while I was overseas. I got hurt on the ship and couldn't do any physical work. So she took the money out of what Papa had left her. 'I want people to be able to read and fill their houses with books,' she said. 'No one should be ignorant like I was.' "

He pulled a white handkerchief from his pocket and wiped a tear from under his glasses. "She was quite a lady. She died just last year. I named the store for her."

Chelsea blinked back her own tears, hastily writing down António's last words. "That's beautiful. What a tribute to your mother." She stretched her aching hand. "So, how did you decide what kind of books to stock?"

"I wanted both English and Portuguese and as many books in both languages as I could find, so nobody would be shut out because of not knowing a language, you know. And then I wanted lots of simple books, easy ones that people like Mama could pick up and read while they were learning, so they wouldn't get discouraged. I use some of them to teach English at the Portuguese senior center."

"Wonderful," she said, quickly making a note about his teaching.

"I enjoy it. To see people begin to understand is like magic." He checked his watch again, and Chelsea looked at hers. It was 3:10. "Sometimes I get on my soapbox. What else do you need to know?"

She scanned the list of questions she had prepared in advance. "Basic information, like how long you've been open, your hours, any special activities, books you want to feature. And then I just want to nose around and look. I might even buy something."

"No problem." Patiently he filled her in on the store and gave her a guided tour of the shelves, then let her photograph him surrounded by books. She noticed again that he limped when he walked.

"I had no idea there were so many Portuguese books," Chelsea said, scanning the shelves full of Portuguese titles.

"Mostly from the mainland. We have a big university, you know, at Coimbra."

"Oh. Yes." She didn't know.

They were standing by the cash register when a tiny dark-haired woman came out, looking curiously at Chelsea. "It is almost 3:30," the woman told António.

"Yes, I suspect it is. We're nearly done. Alma, this is Chelsea Faust. She's the one who is writing about the Portuguese. Chelsea, this is my wife, Alma."

Her hand was so small, Chelsea thought as she shook it.

"Who else you going to interview?" Alma asked in an accent so strong she had to be a recent immigrant. Chelsea wondered if she met António in one of his classes.

"I'll be talking to as many of the merchants as I can."

"Oh, watch out for Miguel at the hardware store," she said. "He can be so rude, especially to women."

Chelsea looked at António. "The same Miguel from the cultural group?"

António chuckled. "They already clashed, but I think Chelsea can hold her own."

"She is taller than he is anyway," Alma said, with a low sexy laugh.

They were all laughing as the bell on the door jingled and a fat yellow-haired man with a huge briefcase staggered in. He was sweating and tense.

"Harry, come in here before you collapse," António said. "Alma, get him something to drink, please." He turned to Chelsea, holding out his raw-boned hand. "Thank you so much for coming. I look forward to seeing you again. And I'll be watching for your articles."

59

Chelsea was still smiling as she came out into the warm afternoon. She had gone only a few steps when António leaned his head out and beckoned her back. "I was thinking. If you want to talk to somebody interesting, interview Simão's grandmother. She's very old, but she has got some great stories to tell."

Having thanked António, she sank into the seat of her truck with a sigh and looked around, thinking she should make a list of the businesses in this area. As she reached for her pen, something hard nudged her hand. Jeffrey's card.

"Damn," she whispered. For the past hour, she had forgotten all about it.

She shoved the card back into her purse. This was no time for Jeffrey to complicate her life again. No matter what she decided about the job or about him, she had to do this assignment. It would be easier if she got to the merchants before the ad sales staff did. Resolutely, she started making her list.

Back at the Weekly Times office, Chelsea found the newsroom a warm haven in a crazy world. Things were simple there; write the stories, meet the deadlines.

Mel looked up. "How was the interview?"

She plopped into her worn swivel chair, crossing her legs. "He was very nice, and he told a charming story about how the bookstore was named for his mother."

"Great. Do you have more interviews set up?"

"Not yet." She pointed to the list she had just set by the telephone. "That's what I'm going to do now."

"Good. Dunning says the ad guys will start knocking on doors as soon as this week's paper is done."

"Ugh." She dialed the number at the top of her list. She might as well get Miguel's hardware store over first.

"*Sim*," he answered curtly.

Chelsea put on her most upbeat voice. "Hi, this is Chelsea Faust from the Weekly Times. I met you at the cultural center meeting the other night. My publisher has decided to expand the article into a whole section on the Portuguese. I need to interview many of the merchants in the area, and I wondered if I could talk to you."

"I do not think so."

Her smile faded, but she persisted. "It's wonderful publicity for your business, and I'm certain it would make a great story."

"No interviews. Good-bye."

She heard another line ringing in the background, then silence.

"He hung up," she said, but Mel was busy on another line and didn't hear her. She dialed the number for Francesca's Flowers.

"*Bom dia. Quem fala?*"

"Oh hello, my name is Chelsea Faust. Do you speak English?"

"*Não.*" And she hung up.

After six more calls, she had one interview set, at the bakery. Of the others, two were not interested and three claimed they didn't speak English.

She decided to try the church. Five Wounds seemed to be the center of the Portuguese community. Maybe the pastor could give her some insight into the people and the culture.

When the receptionist answered "*Cinco Chagas,*" she wondered if she had dialed the wrong number.

"Is this Five Wounds Church?"

"*Sim.*"

"Do you speak English?"

"*Não.*"

"I'll try again later."

Chelsea sighed. It was five o'clock. She closed her notebook, slung her purse over her shoulder and started out of the newsroom. "I'm gone for the day," she told Berta, who was all in black again, except for a chartreuse streak in her hair and matching chartreuse fingernails.

"Wait. This call's for you, I think. I'll send it through."

Chelsea raced back to her desk. "Chelsea Faust."

"Did you look up Slater yet?"

It was the same voice from before, raspy with a Southern accent. "No, I've been very busy."

"You're missin' the biggest story of your life."

She pulled a blank piece of paper out of her desk drawer. "Why don't you tell me a little more about it."

61

"Can't do that. You're the reporter. You find out."

She glanced toward Mel, who was on the phone. "Look, I'm on a special assignment for a couple weeks. But I could pass the information on to one of the other reporters. If you'll just give me your name and number."

"Nope. It has to be you." He hung up.

"Nuts." Maybe she could squeeze in some phone calls tomorrow when the others were at lunch.

Twenty minutes later, Chelsea was in shorts and tee shirt, jogging around the perimeter of the San Jose Municipal Rose Garden. She took deep breaths of the warm, rose-scented air and felt herself beginning to relax as she moved easily around the park on her long colt's legs.

She had discovered running back in high school. While the other girls grumbled at their teacher's requirement that they run a mile three times a week, Chelsea loved it. With her feet skimming along the path, her muscles working and her hair flying in the wind, her frustrations faded away. She focused on the purely physical pleasure of running.

Usually she did four laps around the park. Today she went for six. This Portuguese assignment was starting to drive her crazy. It was as if she were blocked by a giant concrete wall with no footholds to help her get over. Once the ad staff descended on Little Portugal on Wednesday, there would be no way she could convince the Portuguese people that her own motives weren't strictly monetary. Maybe she could ask António to introduce her around, serving as an interpreter if necessary. Dunning had no idea what this culture was all about. Shoot, she didn't either, even if her ancestors did come from the same place. That was a hundred years ago.

The Slater call bothered her, too. Why did he specifically want her to investigate it? And why wouldn't he tell her who he was or what he suspected? This was one of those times she was glad she had paid extra for an unlisted home telephone number. At least he couldn't bother her there.

She was also trying to run off her frustrations about Jeffrey and his Washington job offer. If she took it, she would also be taking Jeffrey back, which was probably a mistake. He would always be addicted to his work. For that matter, so would she. Someday he would run for office. Talk about conflicts of interest. It still hurt to remember how he treated her that night at the campaign party.

She shook her head and ran a little faster. Forget all that. Just run. She smiled at a husky man passing her. He nodded back. This time of day, the park was crowded with joggers. Inside the fence, workers still in their suits and dresses strolled through the pampered roses or sat around the concrete fountain, relaxing before facing the evening commute. Neighborhood kids played Frisbee on the big lawn, screaming as they threw the whirling blue disk.

As Chelsea approached the gate for the sixth time, she slowed to read a pink flyer dangling from the post.

The flyer advertised a July 17 10K run, sponsored by the San Jose Mercury News.

"Hmm." She trotted to her truck to get the little notebook she always kept on the dash and jotted down the information, glad for something new to think about.

A half hour later, Chelsea tossed her keys on the kitchen table, opened a bottle of cherry-flavored mineral water, and stretched out on the couch with a contented sigh. It was true what they said about endorphins, those mood-brightening hormones produced by exercise. She had decided to ignore Jeffrey's letter for a day or so. As for the Portuguese stories, she would call António in the morning. Obviously, she needed help with this project. And she'd ask Sarge about Slater. Maybe he knew something.

Lying back against the granny square pillows her mother had crocheted for her, Chelsea looked out the front window and watched her neighbor Angie, the policeman's wife, playing with her two-year-old on the front lawn. Would she ever do that herself? It became less likely every day. Anyway, it wasn't bad having a cop downstairs. It made Chelsea's mother less antsy about her living alone in what she saw as a crime-ridden neighborhood. Of course, anything downtown was bad to her.

As Chelsea glanced back into the room, she noticed the red light on the telephone answering machine. She had forgotten to check for messages when she got home. Now she stared at it. Jeffrey, looking for an answer already? He would be like that, impatient, demanding instant action. It could be her mother, checking up on her. Or maybe Mel with a hot news flash. Maybe Dunning had decided to start a whole new paper, the Portuguese Weekly Times, and make her the editor. Or perhaps the Slater caller had found her number somehow.

She slipped off the couch, crossed the linoleum on bare feet, and pushed the playback button.

"Hello, this is Simão Freitas. Your editor gave me your number. I wanted to know how you are coming with your writing. Perhaps you would have dinner with me--to discuss the articles. Please call at 264-9988."

Chelsea stared at the telephone. Simão Freitas. Asking her on a date. She pictured his tanned face with the thick mustache and soft sensitive lips. Yes. Why not? Then she remembered how he had ignored his sister and had told her the women in his country would not be allowed to go out alone at night. No. Forget it. But he could help her with her stories, breaking down that wall. He knew everyone in Little Portugal. Yes.

Simão, dapper in a blue pin-striped suit, beamed at Chelsea through her screen door. "Ah, *tão linda.* So beautiful."

"Thank you. You look nice, too." Her face felt hot as she let him in. Why should I be blushing, she asked herself. It's just dinner. He's a source.

She had gone shopping at lunchtime and brought home a soft purple knit dress cinched at the waist with a wide leather belt that flattered her trim frame. She wore her hair pushed back with silver combs. At her ears sparkled tiny amethyst earrings she had borrowed from her mother, enduring an hour of teasing about going out with a Portuguese man.

"Finally you're looking in the right place for a good husband," Mom said, grinning. "Didn't I always tell you to marry a nice Portuguese boy? Right, Carl?"

Sitting in his easy chair by the window, Dad looked up from the newspaper he was reading and shrugged. "What does that say about me, Louise? I'm not Portuguese."

"I don't know. I've been trying to figure it out for 31 years."

At the door, Chelsea's mother grabbed her hand. "I know you think you're a very independent young woman, but try to keep your feminist ideas to yourself tonight. Portuguese men don't like that stuff."

Chelsea stared into her mother's dark, serious eyes. "I'm going to be myself, Mom. If he doesn't like it, too bad. It's mostly business anyway."

Her mother shook her head. "You'll be a lonely old lady with that attitude."

"Give me a break, Mom. Thanks for the earrings." She called, "Bye, Dad" and went out, letting the door slam behind her.

Chelsea hadn't mentioned Jeffrey's letter. She knew what her folks thought of him. If they weren't going to get married, then she should forget about him. She'd heard enough of that when she first came back to San Jose. Why start it up again?

In fact, she wondered now, why had she made such a big deal out of this date, with a new dress and everything? Simão Freitas was just someone she was writing an article about. Or was she trying to prove to herself that she didn't need Jeffrey McNeil?

She had rushed around cleaning her apartment, expecting they would talk a while before they left for dinner, but Simão lingered in the doorway.

"Would you like to sit down?"

He looked at his watch. "Thank you, but we have reservations for 9 o'clock. Are you ready to go?"

"Sure." She grabbed her purse from the table by the door. It was already 8:30, and her stomach was growling. Simão had explained that he had a meeting in the early evening and besides, the Portuguese usually ate dinner later than most Americans did. "Things are just getting started at 10 o'clock back home. I do not understand how people can eat at 5 and then stay up for so many hours afterward. I get hungry all over again."

Okay, eating late is part of the culture, Chelsea told herself. She could put it in her story, but her American stomach was screaming for food.

65

They went to Sousa's, parking in the tiny lot the restaurant shared with the Portuguese bakery. There was room for about eight cars and a huge garbage dumpster that smelled of rotting fish.

As they walked around to the front of the restaurant, Chelsea realized it had been months since her last date. Lately all she did was work, exercise and sleep. This isn't a date, she reminded herself.

In her two-inch heels, Chelsea was almost as tall as Simão, but his broad shoulders and erect posture made her feel small. They were a handsome couple, she thought, both dressed up, their coloring similar. Simão's eyes glowed in the street lights as he caught her looking at him and smiled. She smiled back, then turned away, embarrassed. Why are you making so much of this, she asked herself again.

"Here we are." Simão pushed open the glass door and gently nudged her inside. Chelsea hesitated, wishing he would lead the way.

"You go ahead," she said.

He raised his eyebrows but went in first.

As they passed a flowered screen set up in the doorway, a short man with an apron over his clothes came rushing out. "Simão. *Amigo.*"

The two embraced and talked in rapid-fire Portuguese. Chelsea heard her name and smiled at the other man, but they did not include her in the conversation. She stared at Simão, feeling suddenly invisible, just like that night with Jeffrey. Stick to business, she told herself.

Their host led them through an opening shaped like a giant guitar to a table in the inner room. Great photo possibility, Chelsea thought, wishing she had brought her camera. Simão pulled out her chair, then seated himself across from her, taking his napkin out of his water glass.

"*Obrigado,*" he said to the host. The man nodded and retreated to the other room.

"Well," Simão said," spreading his napkin across his lap. "That was Manuel Sousa, the owner. He says you are very pretty." He folded his hands atop the table and beamed at her. "He is right. Even when I first saw you in your jeans, with cameras hanging all over you, I thought you were very attractive."

"Thank you," Chelsea said, feeling the heat rise from her neck to her cheeks. She looked for a menu. She saw none.

Simão noticed. "I told him to bring you a typical Azorean meal. Everything here is very good. You will enjoy it."

"Oh, I--" Should I mention that I don't eat red meat or fried foods, she wondered. No, she heard her mother saying, one meal won't kill you. She sighed. Okay. Typical Azorean food. "Thank you."

Chelsea hung her purse over the back of the chair, conscious of the notebook that threatened to burst the clasp. "I don't know much about Portuguese cuisine, I'm afraid. Just linguiça and beans."

Simão chuckled. "That is not all we eat. We would have such stomachaches."

"I know what you mean."

A young woman dropped off a basket of hard rolls and butter. Chelsea grabbed one, famished. The rolls were as big as grapefruit, dry and crumbly on the outside, soft inside. Following Simão's example, she tore off a little piece at a time, buttering it and eating it. Crumbs showered onto her purple dress.

"Good, no?" Again that smile.

"Yes, very good." But embarrassing, she thought, brushing crumbs to the floor.

The waitress returned with wine, a thick, dark red that she knew was going to give her a headache. She took a small sip and looked around.

There were no other Anglo-Americans in the restaurant. Portuguese conversations floated across to them. Occasionally as someone came in, Simão nodded a greeting. He seemed to know everybody.

Chelsea cleared her throat. "I was hoping you could help me with the stories I'm working on."

He set down his glass and leaned toward her. "More than one story?"

"Well, my publisher wants a whole section on the Portuguese now, but everyone I call either doesn't speak English or doesn't want to get involved."

Simão buttered a piece of bread. "Most of them do speak English, at least a little. They are just shy about it. They are also a little suspicious of people they do not know. I will call some of my friends. If you want, I will even go with you as an interpreter."

"I can't ask you to give up that much of your time."

He reached across the table to squeeze her hand. "It would be my pleasure." Their eyes met again, and Chelsea felt herself stop breathing. Quit it, she told herself, you just haven't had a date in a while.

Simão sat back as the soup arrived. "Helping you with your articles is good for my business," he said.

"What kind of soup is this?" Chelsea pulled up a spoonful of stringy green strips that fell off her spoon and splashed back into the milky broth.

"Koyvhs," she heard.

"What?"

"Kale soup. C-o-u-v-e-s."

"Why isn't it coo-vez?"

He grinned. "That is how we say it. We eat a lot of kale in the Azores. It is very good for you."

She nodded, struggling to eat the soup without getting it all over her dress. She already had a lapful of bread crumbs. She set down her spoon and sighed. "It tastes good." It was warm, comforting, somehow reminding her of her grandmother.

Simão spooned his soup deftly and neatly into his mouth. When the bowl was empty, he shoved it aside and looked up. "My mother makes it better, but this is not bad."

"Your mother? Is she here in San Jose?"

"Yes. She lives with me."

"Oh. Does your grandmother live with you, too? António said I should meet her because she has had a very interesting life."

"No, she lives elsewhere, and her life is not very interesting." He shrugged. "She is like other women. Just a wife and a mother."

Chelsea winced. Here was that sexist attitude again. "Women's lives are often more interesting than it appears on the surface."

His jaw tightened. "My grandmother is not a merchant. You do not need to interview her."

"No, not for this section, but. . ." She could hear her mother saying, "Shut up, Chelsea," but she refused to let him dismiss women as inferior.

"I will give you better people to interview. Would you like more wine?"

68

"Okay, thanks," she said, letting him add to her still half-full glass. This isn't going well, she thought. She reached into her purse for her notebook and pen. "I made a list of businesses in the area that I want to write about."

He pulled the notebook toward him, frowning at the names on the list. He grabbed her pen. "You do not want to talk to this guy," he said, crossing out the third name. "All he does is complain. Oh, and this flower shop. It is just women's stuff."

"It's a business," Chelsea protested.

"But not an important one."

"I think I should choose--" she began, feeling her temper rise, but the waitress arrived then with the main course. Her heart sank as a plate of fried pork, French fried potatoes and rice was placed in front of her. Simão's dinner was some kind of white fish, also with potatoes and rice. Too much grease, she thought.

"*Obrigado,*" he said to the waitress, then turned to Chelsea. "If you want me to help you, you must listen to what I say. I know my people. Now let us eat this good food."

Chelsea took a big swallow of wine, feeling as if she had been scolded. What ever made her think she was attracted to this man? Even if he was good-looking, he was a sexist jerk.

Simão went on with the conversation as if their argument had not happened. "So, why is a beautiful woman like you not married?"

She stared. Was he serious? It was a line from a B movie. But at least it was conversation. She would answer a cliche with a cliche. "I never found the right man."

"How do you know when you have found the right man? In my village, girls were engaged at 13 and married at15. By 18, they had three children. They do not ask is this the right man. They ask is he a good man who will take care of them."

"What about love?" She could feel the wine loosening her tongue.

"It comes with time. My mother's parents arranged her marriage to my father. They barely knew each other, but they grew to love each other so much my mother swore she would never marry again after he died."

"Oh, I'm sorry."

"It was a long time ago. But if they had waited for love, they would never have been married. My mother might not have made such a good choice on her own."

"Yes, but Simão, this is 20th century America. People don't do that here."

"And look at the divorce rate."

"Well. . . " She poked at her food, eating the rice, shoving the strips of pork around on her plate. Fifty percent of American marriages failed. She had written about it last year. "I know there are a lot of divorces, but here we are free to admit our mistakes and move on. People who get married as teenagers are the most likely to get divorced. They grow up and realize they committed themselves to the wrong person." Before he could respond, she added, "So, why have you not married?"

Simão set down his fork and looked straight at her, sudden pain in his eyes. "I was married. She died two years ago." In that moment, his bravado vanished. He looked young and vulnerable.

"I'm sorry, Simão. I had no idea." Chelsea started to reach for his hand, but Simão gazed over her head and waved his fork toward the tiny stage behind them. "We are going to have music tonight. Have you heard of the *fado?*"

"No. What is that?"

"You will like it. *Fado* is pure Portuguese music, from the heart. The best singers are in *Lisboa,* but the ones they have here are very good."

Thank God, Chelsea thought, something to distract them from this awkward conversation. Between his views on women, his wife's death and their differing ideas about whom she should interview, there seemed to be nothing neutral to discuss. They didn't even agree on the food.

Dessert came just as the music started. Chelsea took a bite of cinnamon-coated flan--Simão called it *pudím*--and felt her face pucker at the overpowering sweetness. She gulped more wine, noting that she was getting tipsy.

As two men in black pants and white shirts played a mournful guitar backup, a plump woman with curly hair and a strikingly unlined face began to sing in a voice strong and full of emotion. Although

70

Chelsea couldn't understand the words, she drank in feelings so deep she felt tears filling her eyes, especially when she thought of Simão losing his wife. She wondered how it happened. She was sad for herself, too, suddenly feeling terribly lonely. Why hadn't she found someone by now? Besides Jeffrey McNeil, who was married to his career.

"Come over here so you can see better," Simão whispered, helping her move her chair closer to his. "She is singing of her home in the Azores. The feeling is something we call *saudade*. There is no English word for it, but we all feel it; it is a big part of who we are. Sort of homesickness and longing and love for what we have left behind."

Chelsea smiled through her tears. "It's beautiful."

"Yes." He sighed and she felt his breath on her cheek. For a man to admit to this *saudade,* maybe he wasn't so macho. It was just his culture that made him act like a rooster in charge of the henhouse.

The music went on. Simão quietly ordered more wine. Chelsea drank and began to feel more kindly toward her date. He was going to help her with her story, so she didn't have to worry about that anymore. She sat back and watched the singer, lazily thinking she ought to do a story on her, too. If Simão said she wasn't a merchant, she would counter that *fado* was a big part of the culture. Hadn't he said so himself?

They stayed until the last song was finished, applauding loudly with the half dozen other people who remained. As the men laid their guitars in their cases, Chelsea rose on unsteady legs and moved forward.

"That was wonderful," she told the singer, who was busy unplugging her microphone and coiling up the cord.

"Oh, thank you very much."

"I-I never heard that kind of singing before."

"It is *fado,* that is all, very Portuguese."

Simão came up behind her. "Amalda, this is Chelsea Faust. She works for the newspaper."

Chelsea nodded, swimming in a sea of red wine. "I want to interview you," she said, certain her words were slurred.

"Not now, I hope," the singer replied with a weary smile.

71

"No, no," Simão said, nudging Chelsea back toward their table. "She will call you. I will ask Manuel to give her your telephone number."

"Okay. Sure. Nice meeting you, Chelsea." She turned to her accompanists, who stood waiting. *"Prontos?"*

"I will take you home now," Simão said to Chelsea, slipping her light jacket over her shoulders and handing her her purse and notebook.

On the way to the parking lot, he put his arm around her and she leaned on his shoulder. He pulled her closer. "I think you are a little drunk. I thought reporters were all big drinkers."

"I usually don't drink at all. It's not healthy."

"You did not eat enough."

"Yes I did."

"Shh," he whispered, chuckling. "You will learn to like our food. It is in your blood."

"Not that pudding stuff."

Simão laughed out loud. "That is the best part."

"Too sweet. Ugh."

"Well, maybe you are so sweet you just cannot take any more sugar."

Chelsea giggled. "You must be inebriated, too. That's the most disgusting line. . ."

Simão helped her into his Buick, got in on the driver's side and pulled the seat belt across her. "Mm," he said, leaning toward her and kissing her. His lips were warm and full, and Chelsea felt a charge of electricity that made her sigh and reach for more, but Simão pulled back and started the car. "This is why we have chaperones in Portugal," he murmured.

Chapter Five

"Oh, no," Chelsea moaned, opening her eyes a crack and closing them again. Blinding sun poured through the bedroom window. She rolled over and peeked at the clock. It was almost 9 on Saturday morning.

She had planned to go running, training for the 10K coming up. But when she tried to sit up, her head hurt so bad, she lay back down again with a groan.

"I'll never drink red wine again," she muttered, remembering last night as if through a fog. Vaguely she recalled driving home and Simão kissing her at the front door, a very chaste kiss. When she leaned toward him for another kiss, he had shaken his head and pulled back.

"Call me on Monday, and we will talk about your interviews," he said, leaving her swaying in the doorway as he drove away.

She fell into bed feeling slightly disappointed and was soon deep asleep.

"God, what did I do?" she thought now, rubbing her throbbing temples with her fingertips. With most American men she dated, things progressed quickly from gentle kisses to necking and even into bed. Apparently either Simão wasn't interested in her or disapproved of such things. Probably the latter.

"Then he shouldn't have gotten me drunk. He should have let me order my own food. I should have insisted." She slid her feet to the side of the bed and stood gingerly.

In the bathroom, she held a wet washcloth over her face and sank onto the edge of the tub. All this in the interest of a story. Well, it wasn't as bad as the time the llama bit her at the children's zoo or the day she got sunstroke following a hiking trail in 105-degree weather in search of an ancient Indian cemetery that turned out to be just an unmarked piece of ground.

She tossed the washcloth into the sink and went for her robe, pulling it over her Mickey Mouse nightshirt. She was pouring orange juice into a glass from the big bottle in the refrigerator when the telephone rang.

"Don't tell me he's up and at 'em already." It had to be Simão. Who else would call her this early on a Saturday morning?

73

"Hello," she croaked.

"God, Faust, what happened to you?"

Jeffrey. He sounded so cheerful. And so American.

"I just got up."

"What? It's noon, baby, time for lunch, time for getting out and doing things."

"Not in California."

There was a pause. Chelsea could hear an old Beatles song in the background get quieter. "Okay, now I can hear better. Chelsea, are you all right?"

Her throat tightened. Something about that so-familiar voice would always tug at her heart. Especially at times like now. "Yes. I just was out too late and drank way too much red wine."

"I thought you gave up drinking. Being an athlete and all."

"I did. I was having a 'typical Portuguese meal,' part of a story I'm working on."

"What'd you have?"

Chelsea's stomach churned. "I can't talk about food right now, Jeffrey."

"Oh, sorry. So, how's the weather?"

"I-um," she looked out the window. Sun beamed on the lawn out front and reflected off the windows across the street. "Sunny and clear. No clouds."

"Great. It's raining here. Everything that I can see over the tops of the buildings is gray. Makes you want to move right back, doesn't it?"

"Not really."

"So, did you sleep with him?"

"Jeff!"

"I'm kidding. And jealous."

She sighed. "No, I did not sleep with him. In fact, I seem to remember, he didn't even want to kiss me good night."

"What is this guy, gay?"

"No, Portuguese. From Portugal."

"Of course. Anyway, when are you coming back? I told the publisher of that new paper about you, and he's waiting for your call."

"Jeff. . ."

"I know. You like to make your own decisions. But I really want you back here."

"Oh." She stared out the window, watching her neighbor John pull in, just getting home after working the night shift. Angie and the baby came out to greet him with hugs and kisses.

"Chelsea?"

"Don't pressure me this morning, okay?"

"Fine. So how's work?"

"Ugh. Dunning's got me doing this special section on the Portuguese in San Jose. Which could be all right, but his only motivation is to sell ads, which makes me sick. Plus these people are like, no interviews, no interviews, and half of them don't speak English. Or won't," she added, remembering what Simão had said.

"Could be a book in it."

"You and my Aunt Julia. I can't even do these articles." She reached for her juice. She was starting to feel better. "So what are you up to, Mr. President?"

"Oh, please, just senator this week. Believe it or not, we're starting to get ready for the next election. I'm putting together a staff and campaign itinerary for the senator, hiring speech writers, screening lobbyists, the usual stuff."

"So early."

"Yep. You know what they say about the early bird."

"What?"

"He calls his friend Chelsea on Saturday morning but wishes she were right here so he wouldn't have to spend so much money on long distance calls."

"Jeffrey. I thought we were going to go our separate ways and just be friends, and maybe I'd write your official biography after you left the White House."

"I still want you to do that."

"I will. I promise."

"But it's lonely out here, Chels."

"Surely there are other women in Washington."

"Politicians. And black women who work at the Shop and Drop and have 12 kids at home. Pass."

Chelsea finished her juice and started thinking about heating a bagel for breakfast. "I might become a nun. It sounds so peaceful."

"Poverty, chastity and obedience? No way, Faust. Not you. Besides, you don't even go to church."

"I could start." She opened the toaster oven and tossed in a blueberry bagel.

"Chelsea, I wish I could kiss you."

"Stop," she said, feeling lips on hers, but realizing with a jolt that she was thinking about Simão, not Jeff.

"A guy can fantasize."

Silence. Nothing left to say, Chelsea thought, watching the heating element in the oven turn red. They both knew she was dodging the question.

"Will you call my friend the publisher?" Jeffrey said, sounding tired now.

"I'm not sure. I have to think about it some more."

"I really believe you'd like the job."

"Maybe I would. But it's not just the job."

He cleared his throat. "Call me either way. And don't let this Portuguese guy sleep with you. Tell him you're a nun."

"Too late. He knows I'm a reporter."

"Right. Take care. Call me."

"I will. Good-bye."

"Chels?"

"Hmm?" She was getting the cream cheese out of the refrigerator.

"I still love you."

She winced. "Jeffrey, please don't. Bye." She gently hung up.

She sliced the hot bagel in half and spread cream cheese on it, watching it melt. How could he tell her he loved her after all this time? What happened to their agreement to just be friends? How could he disrupt her life when she thought that part of it was settled?

Maybe she was just lonely. Around Jeffrey, she felt like herself. With Simão, she didn't know who she was.

The bagel tasted good. Something healthy for her tortured stomach. If she had the energy, she might go running after breakfast. Or maybe she'd go to the beach. She could just lie on a blanket on the sand, soaking in the sun. The weather was wonderful, and there were no telephones on the beach.

It was so hot inside the Portuguese bakery Chelsea wished she could turn around and walk out again, but the bell on the door had already given her away.

"Good afternoon," said the aproned woman with gray-streaked hair who came out to greet her. "Are you Chelsea?"

"Yes." Chelsea held out her hand, ignoring the sweatiness of Anna Silva's childlike hand. The woman couldn't have been more than 4 foot 10. Chelsea felt like a giant beside her.

"I am so glad to meet you," Anna said. "Simão spoke very highly of your work. I saw your piece on the *festa*. It was terrific. Do you know, I found myself in one of the pictures. And my daughter. We were so exited. We had to show everybody." Her scratchy voice almost disappeared as it rose in excitement. Her accent was subtle, her English near perfect.

Chelsea took a breath and prepared to start her interview, but Anna kept talking. "I'm sorry about the heat. The damn air conditioning is broken again. I told my husband, but he said he's too busy to fix it today. I told him, 'Then you come and bake all these loaves of bread.' Come here, I'll show you something."

Anna led the way into the back room. Round loaves of sweet bread filled three huge ovens and covered all the counters.

This will make great photos, Chelsea thought, raising her camera and clicking off several shots of Anna surrounded by bread.

The baker laughed. "I look so bad to have my picture taken. Oh well. We have to make 2,000 of these by Saturday for the Fremont *festa*. Can you believe it? Last year, we made 1,600. They want four hundred more this year. My husband Pedro told them 'okay, no problem,' he didn't even ask me. I tell you, these men sometimes they don't think. My daughter helps me after school, but you know we've got the store to run and other orders, cakes and things. I got a wedding on Sunday. I don't know when I'm gonna do that cake, and these are important people."

Chelsea smiled. Her notebook was still blank, except for a few questions she had scrawled.

"I'm sorry, I talk too much," Anna said. "Pedro tells me that all the time, 'Anna, you talk too much, you need to stop and listen.' What do you want to ask me?"

A chuckle escaped Chelsea's lips. Anna laughed, too. "I know, it's crazy, I talk so much." They laughed until Chelsea wondered what they were even laughing about.

Sweat was beginning to gather under the arms of her silk blouse. She leaned against a rack of bread. "Okay. How long have you been in business here?"

"Oh, just four years. You want me to tell you how I got started?" Anna raised her eyebrows and giggled. "It's a long story."

Chelsea choked back a laugh. "Go ahead. I'm ready."

"You should have brought a tape recorder, huh?"

She nodded. "Yes." She had thought these stories would be so short and easy that she could get by with just her notebook. Next time she'd know better.

"Well," Anna began, "We were in Massachusetts--my family emigrated from Pico. My dad got laid off, and they said there's lots of jobs in the United States, so the whole family, we had to go. Well, 10 years later, I was working at a school in Boston, and my dad and mom decided to go to California. It was too cold in New England, they said."

Anna must have read the look on Chelsea's face. "Don't worry," she said, "This really does have something to do with the bakery. I mean it."

I love that scratchy voice, Chelsea thought, writing "talkative" in her notebook. "Okay, I believe you."

"Have faith. You got to have faith. So my dad bought this fish business, and pretty soon he got my brother into it, and they were doing pretty good, so he wanted another business. That's how the Portuguese men are, they want to make lots of money."

Like Simão, Chelsea thought.

"Anyway, Dad saw this bakery for sale, and he wanted to buy it, but he didn't want to run it himself. So when my husband and I were here for Christmas that year, he says, 'Hey, come with me and look at this bakery. I think it's a good deal.' Well, my husband sees it, and he says, 'Yes, it's a very good deal.' My father says, 'I will give you the money, or we can each pay half, and you and Anna will run it.'

"Now I'm thinking, wait a minute, I like it here. I love my job, and all my friends are in Boston." She pulled a wad of dough out of a giant bowl and started kneading, her tiny hands moving rapidly, pushing the dough, turning it, pushing and turning with a force that showed how upset she was at the time. "What do I want to move everything and work in a bakery for? You know what I mean?"

Chelsea, startled by the question, looked up from her paper. "Yes. I can imagine how you felt."

"Well, do they listen, no, men don't listen. So pretty soon, my husband goes back down to California, for a visit supposedly, and when he comes back, he says, 'Hey, Anna, we bought the bakery, quit your job.'"

"Wow," Chelsea said. "What did you do?"

"Ah! Now I'm working with all these you-know liberated women, and they say, 'That's crazy, just tell him no, you won't do it. Divorce him if you have to.' Can you believe it, that's what they said, divorce him.

"But I couldn't do that. I thought about it and I prayed about it a lot, and finally I said to myself, well, what can I do? When my grandfather left Faial for Pico, my grandmother went with him. When my father left Portugal for Massachusetts, my mother went with him. I should go with my husband to the California. It would be good to be near my mother and father and my brother, I thought, and the weather is warmer, and we can have a business for ourselves.

"I was head secretary at the school, in charge of all the office work. I loved watching the kids grow up from little freshmen to adults graduating into the world. But I said goodbye. I went to this baking school and learned all these fancy French frostings and pastries and stuff, you know, but when I got here, all they want is the stuff from the old country, the breads, the *filhós*, the *biscoitos*, all that stuff. The only time I get to do anything really interesting is when I do cakes. That's kind of fun. But all these loaves of bread, Santa Senhora. And now the air conditioning doesn't work. What else do you want to know?"

79

Chelsea's hand ached from trying to get down everything Anna had said so far. But there were still lots of questions. "Where did you go to school?" she asked, glancing at the clock and mentally abandoning her afternoon schedule.

"Near Boston." Anna opened the oven and pulled out three loaves of bread, nudging several others over to make room for them on the cooling racks. She wiped her sweaty forehead with her arm. "God, it's hot. You want a soda?"

"Sure." By now her blouse was soaked. She could feel sweat in her underwear and her stockings and her shoes. But Anna's story was a gem. She was sure Simão would disagree with everything Anna said, but she was the writer, not Simão.

"I didn't know a word of English when I came over to the United States," Anna said, wiping her hands on her apron and popping open frosty cans of Coca Cola for herself and Chelsea.

"Really? You speak so well now."

"Well, I went to school and I studied hard. Where we first lived, sort of out in the country, there were no other Portuguese. The high school didn't know what to do with me. They were good though. They found a lady who knew some Portuguese, and she taught me English after school. A lot of people I know, they didn't get any help, they just sat there and didn't understand anything, but I was lucky. Later we moved to a neighborhood where half the people were Portuguese, but I already knew English by then.

"Anyway, I went to this bakery school. . ."

It was 4:30 when Chelsea left the bakery. In that time, only two customers came, buying bread and hurrying out. After Chelsea slipped her notebook into her purse, Anna reached up and hugged her. "Oh no, I got flour on you," she said, brushing it off Chelsea's jacket. "Oh, golly, I'm sorry."

"Don't worry about it." Chelsea squeezed her hand.

"Oh, here, take a loaf of bread home to your family."

"I--" Chelsea stopped herself. Maybe she could take it to the office. "Thank you. That's very nice. How much is it?"

"No, no, it's a gift. Don't worry. I'm so glad you're writing about us. I'll let you come back another time and buy something."

"I will," she promised.

Chelsea was still smiling as she walked out into the fresh air, where the temperature was 20 degrees cooler. It wasn't often that an interview brought her a new friend, but this one had.

Happily strolling toward her truck, glad the workday was almost over, she didn't see anyone else in the parking lot until she heard her name. She turned and saw Simão striding toward her.

"Hello," he called. He was dressed as usual in a gray suit. "You have been talking to Anna?"

"Yes." She grinned as she brushed at the flour on her sleeve. "She's great. Did you know she didn't even want to work in a bakery? But her husband bought the business and told her she had to come."

"No, I did not. But that is not important for your story, is it? What counts is their success, their role in the community. You must know it is really her husband's business. Maybe I should have had you talk to him."

Chelsea frowned. "No, Simão. She's the one who does the work."

"But he is the one in charge. Anyway, I convinced Miguel to talk to you."

"Oh," she said, not sure that was good news. "When?"

"Right now. I will go with you. I thought you would be earlier, but you did not come out."

"You were watching me?"

"I noticed your truck and asked Manuel from Sousa's to keep an eye on the parking lot to tell me when you came out."

Chelsea swallowed, her good feelings from the interview fading. "That's like spying on me, Simão. You could have just called me on the telephone."

He shrugged. "You are here. He is waiting. You are lucky to talk to him. Let us go now. We can go in my car."

"It's only half a block away. Why not walk?"

"No. We will drive. It is faster. Get in, please."

She left the bread in her truck. Simão moved his briefcase off the passenger seat of the Buick, and she reluctantly got in, vaguely remembering when he had kissed her Saturday night. It must have been the wine, she told herself.

81

Massaging her aching hand, she opened her notebook to a fresh page and wondered what on earth she could ask Miguel about a hardware store. He already thought she was an idiot, and she was afraid she was about to confirm that impression.

"I really--" She stopped and took a breath as Simão pulled up in front of the hardware store, parking in a yellow zone. "I really wish I had some time to prepare for this interview. I don't like to go in cold."

"What is to prepare? He is waiting."

Chelsea hesitated. What if she just told Simão no, she wouldn't do it right now. She was sweaty, tired, and unprepared. She didn't have to do what he said when he said it. But she did need to do the interview, sooner or later. Obviously Miguel had some influence in the community.

She thought about Anna moving all the way across the continent to work in a bakery because her father and her husband decided that's what she should do. I'm going to write Aunt Julia's book, she decided. For Anna. And for me.

She opened the car door and followed Simão to meet Miguel, who stood scowling in the doorway.

"You're late," Miguel growled.

"I was at another interview. I didn't know about this." Is he going to invite us in, she wondered, or would she have to interview him standing in the street?

"She was talking to Anna," Simão said.

"Oh, Anna." Miguel said something in Portuguese which Chelsea didn't get, and the two men chuckled. It would help if she understood the language, Chelsea thought, plans for her book in the back of her mind. She should take a course. Maybe António could help her find one.

"Can we come in?" she asked.

Miguel shrugged and led the way. The tiny hardware store was icy, the air conditioning struggling against the heat coming in the open front door. Chelsea smelled perspiration, grease and fertilizer.

"What do you want to know?" Miguel asked as he walked behind the counter and opened the cash register. He took the bills out of their slots and began counting.

Chelsea wished with all her heart that she was on her way home, where she could take off her sweaty suit, put on her running clothes and head for the park. She gazed at the rows of tools, light bulbs and pipes and decided to ask the same questions she had planned to use for Anna's bakery. Most would apply to all stores. Maybe she could run a big photo and a short story. "How did you get started in the hardware business?"

"I bought it from a friend."

"Had you worked with hardware before?"

"No. I fished."

She watched as he counted ten $20 bills, eight tens, two fives and 18 ones and wrote the numbers on the back of a receipt. She raised her camera and clicked off two shots.

"What would you say is your specialty here?"

He looked up at her with his eyes narrowed. "Hardware."

This was going to be a very short story, she thought. "Okay, what hours are you open?"

"It is on the door." He dumped the coins on the counter with a great clatter and started pushing the quarters into a pile with his fat sausage fingers.

Chelsea sighed and glanced at Simão. He stood with his arms folded over his chest, tapping his fingers against his sleeve. Great. She was making a fool of herself as Simão watched. But what did he expect, hauling her here with no advance notice?

"Miguel," she tried again, "you need to tell me something about yourself and your store. I've only got half a page of notes so far."

He shook his head. "There is nothing to tell. I run a hardware store. I sell hardwares."

"Okay. Do you have any hobbies?"

"What has this got to do with my store?"

"Nothing. But maybe people would like to know about you."

Simão put his hand on her shoulder. She looked up and saw him smiling gently. "Miguel does not like to talk much. But he loves to play cards. Poker, rummy, especially Pedro. He wins all the time. He is a very rich man now, not because he sells so many pipes and doorknobs but because he wins at cards every day. That is why he is in a hurry to

83

leave now. There is a game at the I.E.S. hall."

"Oh," said Chelsea. "I didn't realize." She turned back to Miguel. "So, you're a gambler."

Unexpectedly, he grinned and nodded. "Yes. Just like in the cowboy movies."

"Well, since we're in a hurry, I'll ask a couple more questions and take some pictures of the store, and we'll be out of your hair."

Simão laughed and said something in Portuguese. Miguel laughed, too, rubbing his nearly bald head. Chelsea looked at them questioningly.

"He says he does not have any hair," Simão explained.

"*Não*," said Miguel, adding something else.

Simão guffawed. "He says he is more sexy without hair."

Chelsea smiled with them, but was thinking of something else. "Is it hard for you to talk in English?" she asked.

Miguel nodded. "I know English pretty good. But it is not the same as talking your own language. I always feel like I cannot quite say what I want to say, and it takes too long to think of the words. So I do not say much."

"I guess I'd feel the same way." Finally. That was the longest speech he had made yet.

Miguel spoke again in Portuguese, and Simão translated. "He says such a beautiful woman makes him nervous, and he does not know what to say and he does not trust newspapers anyway, but he will buy a big advertisement in your paper because he needs more customers. Now he has to finish counting his money because it is getting late. Go ahead and look around the store."

"All right." Chelsea held out her hand. Miguel took it in his big paw and shook it.

When they were out on the street, she turned to Simão. "Thank you."

"Miguel is all right, if you know how to talk to him." Simão opened the car door for her again and got in on the other side. "The others will be easier."

Chelsea felt a hint of panic. "No more today, I hope."

"No. I have a list back at my office of people I talked to, but I will let you call them. I did not know your schedule."

"Thank you."

He hesitated before starting the car. "You look very pretty today."

"No, I feel all worn out and ragged."

"No. Not at all. Not to me."

"Thank you very much." As their eyes met, she swallowed, feeling again the electricity of that night after dinner when they kissed in this same car. This time they were sober. She cleared her throat. "That list is at your office?"

As they climbed the rickety steps to Simão's office, Chelsea thought of the ratty old sofa just inside the door and how they would be alone together in that small space. She remembered that kiss.

But Simão left the door open. He plucked a sheet of yellow paper off the top of his desk and handed it to her. "Please call me when you know what times you will be interviewing."

With that, he opened his briefcase, pulled out his datebook and studied the page for that day. "I am late again," he mumbled to himself as Chelsea stood waiting and realized their visit was over.

"All right. Thank you. Good night," she said and went down the stairs, shaking her head at her silliness. Maybe it had just been too long since she'd had a serious relationship with a man.

In a half hour, she was running around the park, breathing the scent of roses and wishing she dared sprint through the fountain to cool off. How many days would this Portuguese madness go on?

Chapter Six

The best interviews turned out to be the ones Simão did not attend. When he was there, she was always conscious of his nervous foot tapping, and the people talked to him instead of to her. Too often, they would lapse into Portuguese and she'd be left out. So she didn't call Simão for several days. As her notebook filled with stories, she began to think this special section would be a real showpiece for her. Then she returned from an interview to find an urgent note from Simão on her desk.

"What's this?" she asked Mandy.

The intern looked up from the newspaper she was reading. "Oh, I don't know. This guy was in here. He asked if he could leave that on your desk. I said, 'Sure, why not?'" Mandy, clad in tee-shirt, jeans and leather vest, shrugged her slender shoulders and turned back to her paper.

"Where's Mel?"

"He's not in. He got a call from his kids' school and booked out of here. I don't know what it was about. He just said he wouldn't be back today."

Mel's computer was on, a half-edited story still on the screen. "I hope everything's okay."

"I don't know. He seemed upset."

Chelsea dialed the number on Simão's note. As she listened to the phone ring, she heard the chatter of the police radio and felt a wave of longing for the hard news she used to cover before this Portuguese thing took over her life.

"Simão Freitas," he answered.

"Hi, this is Chelsea. Sorry I missed you. I was talking to Floralinda at the dress shop."

"We have a problem."

"What's that?" She reached up and crossed Floralinda's name off the list on her bulletin board. There were only three names left.

"The Portuguese Chamber of Commerce met today--"

Damn, she thought. "I wish I had known, Simão. It would have been helpful for me to be there."

Simão ignored her interruption. "They met today, and they

86

discussed your newspaper. Your salespeople have been talking to everyone about buying advertising."

"Yes. I told you they would."

"They voted not to buy any advertisements until they see what you are writing about them."

"But--" Chelsea took a deep breath. People she interviewed often asked to see articles before publication. She always told them no, that it was against company policy, and there wasn't time anyway. But to tie the stories to their ads. . . She knew what Dunning would say if she presented this to him. Show them the copy. To him, money was always more important than journalistic ethics.

"Chelsea?"

"Simão, this puts me in an awkward spot. It is against our editorial policy to show articles in advance. Besides that, I don't want these stories to have anything to do with the ads. I don't care whether you buy ads or not. I want to write good, honest stories."

"But your employer cares about the money."

She nodded, chewing on her lip. "Yes," she said quietly. "I'm sure he does." That's why he's doing this section; she thought, not because he gives a damn about the Portuguese. He'd probably do every ethnic group in town if they'd buy ads.

"Are you there?" Simão prodded as the silence dragged on.

She took a deep breath. "Simão, you have to trust me. These stories won't hurt anyone. If anything, they will help their businesses."

"I know your articles will be very good," he said, his voice soothing over the phone. "So why not show them to the people?"

"What about Miguel? He already said he would buy an ad."

"He voted with the others."

She glanced across the room at Mel's empty desk. "I'm going to have to talk to my editor. You have to realize that some of the stories are not written yet. I'd have to finish them. Meanwhile, if there are no ad sales, my publisher might cancel the whole section, wasting all of our work."

"I understand. But we are not like presidents and business executives who are in the newspaper every day. We want it to be just right. You could fax the articles to me. Let me give you my number."

"No, not yet. I'll talk to my editor and let you know."

As they hung up, Chelsea stood, grabbed her wallet and headed for Ed's Liquors down the street for a diet soft drink. How did she ever get into this mess? She hoped Jeffrey didn't call tonight. It would be too easy to say, "Yes, I'm coming to Washington."

When she returned, Berta waved another pink message slip at her. "He called again. That guy with the Southern accent and no name?"

"Damn." She still hadn't done any research on Councilman Slater. It was intriguing, but this Portuguese section was taking up all her time. "What did he say?"

When Berta spoke, Chelsea could see the green gum in her mouth. "He said, and I quote, 'Slater don't live here anymore.' Then he hung up."

"Swell." Chelsea crumpled the message and hurried to her desk. This story couldn't wait much longer.

Mel wasn't back the next day. Chelsea sat at her desk, staring at the list on the bulletin board, and didn't know what to do. Was there any point in continuing work on these Portuguese stories? Reluctantly she opened her notebook to the interview with Floralinda and started a new file on the computer. Floralinda was a delightful person, and her shop was full of dresses she had designed herself. If her story never ran in the paper, maybe Chelsea could use it in her book.

She shook her head. What book? At this point, she had no proposal, no outline, no contract, just a bunch of Portuguese people who didn't trust her. Meanwhile Jeffrey was waiting for an answer.

"Chelsea."

She looked up at the towering figure of George P. Dunning. "The ad people tell me the Portugees are stalling."

Here it comes, she thought.

"They want to see the stories in advance before they'll buy ads, Mr. Dunning."

"That's the problem? Show them the stories."

"But that's--" She spoke slowly. "That's not usually our policy. I wanted to talk to Mel about it, but--"

Dunning picked up her stapler, clicking it open and closed. "Mel's not going to be here for a couple of days. His daughter had some kind of seizure and crashed her bike at school. She's in the hospital."

"How bad is she hurt?"

"I don't know. Not too bad, I think, but they're checking out her head to see why this happened. Bottom line, Mel is not here. Sarge and I are dividing his work. We need to get this special section done and get you back to general assignments. So this is the deal. I want you to fax copies of your stories to every Portugee that wants one and make the changes they ask for."

"But--"

"Ms. Faust, we've invested too much time in this to let it go down the tubes now. You've already been on this for over two weeks."

"I know." It was your idea, she thought. "I haven't written them all yet. And I still have a couple more interviews to set up."

"Don't do any more interviews. Write the stories you have and fax them out. I want to see some signed ad contracts by Friday. All right? Are we clear?"

"Crystal clear," she said, turning away so he wouldn't see how red her face was getting.

When Dunning was gone, Sarge looked up. "It's the pits, isn't it? Ads running the paper. In the old days, this never would have happened. The founder didn't believe in letting advertising influence editorial."

"I know." I don't either, she thought. What happened to those great ideals I learned at Berkeley?

The old Mel would have told Dunning to shove it. Now she wasn't sure. "I have to get out of here for a while, Sarge."

"Berta, I'll be back in a half hour," she said, letting the door slam behind her.

Or never, she added to herself as she headed for her truck.

Councilman James Slater's official address was on California Avenue in Willow Glen. The broad boulevard was shaded with old willow trees, and the pampered lawns were velvet green despite the heat. Red, pink and yellow roses bloomed in lush rows around large, ivy-covered houses of wood and brick.

Chelsea slowed as she approached 3575 California, Slater's address. The house looked deserted, with no cars in the driveway, no knickknacks in the windows, no furniture visible through the open curtains. In the yard, the petunias were wilting, and the lawn was starting to turn brown around the edges. A sheet of yellow paper was posted on the front door.

Parking a couple houses away, she looked around to see if anyone might be watching, then got out and walked up to the door, moving quietly in her rubber-soled sandals.

"Foreclosure," the notice proclaimed in tall black letters. It gave information about an auction scheduled later in the month. Chelsea memorized the date, location and the names of the bank and auction company and peeked in the front window.

The only furniture was a brown easy chair with stuffing coming out of the seat. A six-pack of empty Coors beer bottles sat beside it, and in the corner was a pile of rags. The peach-colored walls had big discolored rectangles where paintings had hung. A broom and mop leaned against the sliding glass door to the back yard.

"Well, they're certainly gone," Chelsea said to herself. She tried the front doorknob. It turned easily and the door opened. She was about to go in when she heard footsteps behind her and felt the muscles in her back tense as someone stopped in front of the house.

She turned and forced a smile at a dark-haired man in a white tee shirt and red shorts. "Nobody home."

"No, they're gone," he said, running in place. "Too bad."

"Do you know where they moved to?"

He was panting. "No idea. Sorry."

"Okay, thanks."

He waited for her to leave. Reluctantly, she walked back to her truck.

She drove to the shopping center at the corner of Hamilton and Meridian and wrote down everything she had seen. This was starting to look like a real story. But who was her informant? Why did he call her? Why hadn't the Mercury News printed anything about this?

There was a pay phone in front of the grocery store. She took her file with her and called Slater's business number. He operated a headhunting firm.

A recorded voice said Mr. Slater was out for the rest of the week; leave a message at the beep.

Chelsea hung up and headed for the office. This could be her ticket to the big time. As soon as she got past the Portuguese mess.

That afternoon she called Simão for his fax number. He agreed to distribute the articles among the merchants. She wrote and faxed for hours, staying at the office until almost midnight. Just finish it and get it over with, she decided.

She took the next morning off, grateful Mel didn't hold her to a fixed schedule. As she parked outside the office at 1:00, she dreaded what might be waiting on her desk: Angry messages from Simão and the others, ultimatums from Dunning, more bad news about Mel's daughter?

"Hi Chelsea," Berta said, her kiwi-green contact-lensed eyes twinkling. "How are you?"

Chelsea looked at her, puzzled. "Just fine."

"Good. I'm glad," Berta smirked as the phone rang. "Weekly Times," she said. "No, he's not in today."

"Mel?" Chelsea mouthed.

Berta nodded and turned to her message pad.

Sarge and Mandy watched Chelsea.

"What--?" she began. Then she saw an immense pink and white bouquet of roses and carnations in a fluted pink vase on top of her desk. "Oh my gosh." Her first thought was Jeffrey, although he had never sent her flowers. Perhaps Floralinda? She read the note tucked into the leaves, knowing the others were waiting to hear what it said.

"Holy shit." She sank into her chair and reread the note.

"Dear Chelsea: Your articles are very good. We will gladly sign advertising contracts. Please accept these flowers in appreciation for your hard work and your caring about your fellow Portuguese. P.S. Will you eat dinner with me tonight? Simão Freitas."

"Well?" said Sarge. "Judging by the grin on your face, it must be a love letter."

91

"She's turning red," said Mandy.

"Yes, she is. I've never seen you blush so often, Faust."

She shook her head, unable to stop smiling. "No, I was lying out in the sun this morning, and I guess I got a little burned."

"It's cloudy," said Mandy. "Besides, I hear you spend all your spare time in the darkroom."

"No, really. These flowers are just from a source who liked what I wrote."

"Oh. Sure. I get roses all the time," Sarge said, chuckling as he turned back to his computer. "Of course, a lot of the guys I write about are in jail."

Chelsea took a deep breath and opened the folder that lay next to the flowers. There were very few changes. She could enter them into the computer in less than an hour. She pushed the flowers gently to the side of her desk. First she had to tell Dunning.

The publisher was standing with his back to her, legs spread, a golf club in his hand. As she watched, he putted the ball easily into an automatic golf machine.

"Mr. Dunning?"

He turned. "Oh. Ms. Faust. How's it going? Do we have contracts?"

She stayed in the doorway. "We will soon. I got the corrected stories back, along with the first contract. They all liked the articles and are ready to talk money now."

"Excellent. I'll tell Fred. Thanks."

As he turned back to his putting, Chelsea hesitated. "Um, should I do any more Portuguese interviews?"

He waved his hand. "No. We have a representative sample. We don't want to make this the Portugee Times. Ask Sarge for something else to do."

Let it go, she warned herself as she felt her temper rising. "Okay. Thanks."

She heard him hit the ball and curse as it missed its mark.

Sarge was on the phone when she returned. She booted up the computer and started entering the corrections from the faxes. Each time she read Simão Freitas Enterprises at the top of a page, she felt a little glow and wasn't even sure why. He could be so arrogant and sexist. Yet it was there.

When Sarge hung up, she cleared her throat. "Sarge, I'm going to need some assignments. I'm back among the living." She would tell him about the Slater story later, when she had more information.

"Hallelujah."

"Just let me get these corrections done, and I'm yours."

"I've got a list a mile long for you, girl."

"Great." She sighed and continued typing. As she flipped the page and saw that letterhead again, she hit the save button and picked up the phone.

"Simão Freitas," he answered.

"It's Chelsea Faust. Thank you so much for the flowers. They are gorgeous, and everybody here at work is jealous."

"Well, you did a good job. I know you didn't want to let us see your stories, but now that we did, we look forward to reading them in the newspaper."

"Thanks."

"Will you have dinner with me tonight?

"Yes, I'd like that."

"Sousa's again?"

"How about someplace American?"

"American like Chelsea Faust, huh?"

"Exactly."

"All right. What time should I pick you up?"

"7:00." No more of this starving until bedtime business. "Let's eat on American time."

"All right, American girl. 7:00 at your apartment."

"Great. I look forward to it."

She caught Sarge winking at Mandy. "Hurry up and get those corrections done, Faust. I've got serious business for you," he said as she hung up. "I think we should have you cover the planning commission tonight."

"Hey!"

"Okay, okay, I'll let the kid do it."

"Give a guy a little power. . ." she muttered, wondering what to wear to dinner.

She looked in the mirror and nodded. Just right. She topped her black slacks with a pink blouse, a delicate necklace of pink and white flowers, and matching earrings. She let her long hair hang free, ending in gentle curls.

She had just shoved her wallet, lipstick, pen and a spiral notebook into a tiny black purse when the doorbell rang.

"Oh, jeez." She surveyed the bedroom, smoothing the comforter and kicking her running shoes under the bed, and glanced at the living room on her way to the door. Her apartment was as neat as it ever got. Boxes she had brought from Washington were still stacked in the bedroom and kitchen. Her furniture was a hodgepodge of hand-me-downs from Mom and Dad and from garage sales. Someday she'd buy new furniture--when she settled down. But now wasn't the time, even if she could afford it, which she couldn't.

Simão had his hand poised to knock when she opened the door.

She swallowed. His perpetual three-piece suit was gone, replaced by an open-necked green polo shirt and gray slacks. She stared at his bare arms, muscled and covered with soft brown hair.

Simão smiled, showing deep dimples. Sparks zinged through Chelsea's stomach. "Hi. Come on in." She held the door open for him, and he followed her into the living room.

"Sit down. Can I get you a drink? Beer? Wine?"

He sank into her overstuffed sofa. "A little wine would be very nice."

"Okay." She rushed into the kitchen, feeling unaccountably nervous. Relax, she told herself. You've been going out with guys since you were 16. All nationalities, all colors. What's the big deal about this one, even if this is definitely a date, not work?

She carefully uncorked the *pinot noir* she had picked up at Ed's Liquors on the way home and poured the wine into two glasses.

It was strange to see Simão leaning back on her sofa, his arm draped over one of Mom's crocheted pillows. He had been looking at her Popular Photography magazine. Now his eyes followed her across the room as she fumbled in a drawer for coasters and set down the wine.

She joined him on the couch, conscious of their knees only a few inches apart.

He raised his glass. "Here's to your hard work and your great talent as a writer."

"Thank you very much."

He waved his glass toward the magazine. "Very nice pictures."

"Yes."

They fell silent. What do we talk about besides my work?

"How is your business going?" she ventured.

He set his glass on the coaster. "It is going very well. I have a possibility of buying an office building. I am just waiting to hear about the loan. I will be able to rent out space to other businesses, and soon I will make a profit."

"Where's the building?"

"Not far from my office. Just down Alum Rock Avenue. They say it is not a good part of town, but I do not believe that. I can work with the Portuguese, the Mexicans or the Vietnamese. We are all just people."

"I agree."

Again silence. I should have gotten some chips and dip or something, she thought. She set her half-full wine glass on the table. "Are you getting hungry?"

"I am fine. I usually eat later, you know."

"Yes. But how do you sleep with all that food in your stomach?"

He grinned. "Very well. My mother says sometimes I sleep so soundly she has to watch me breathing to know that I am still alive."

"Oh, not me," Chelsea said. "Everything keeps me awake." The telephone rang. "Excuse me."

Simão picked up the magazine again as she hurried to the kitchen. "Hello?"

"Chels, what's the verdict? There's like this big silence between California and Washington. Your nation's capital needs you."

"Jeffrey."

"Uh-oh, what's going on? You don't sound thrilled to hear from me."

"No, I--um, I have company right now."

"Your folks?"

"No."

"People from work?"

"No. It's just somebody I've been working on some stories with."

"The Portugee guy."

"Portuguese."

"Sorry. Does 'Portugee' bother you now? You used to use it all the time."

"It's starting to. I guess it's the way Dunning says it, like we're dirty or something."

"Don't take it personally. Now, why are you dodging your best friend and former lover's phone calls?"

"I'm not. I didn't get any messages."

"Hey, if the phone rings three times, you're not there, so I hang up. It costs money to talk to machines. Anyway, you can't put off this decision forever, Chels. They're getting ready to hire somebody, and if your resume isn't in the pile, forget it."

"I know."

"You're not interested."

"Not true."

"You love your job there so much you can't bear to leave."

"Yeah, right. Sometimes I do like it, but Dunning is an ass. He doesn't know the difference between editorial and advertising. He's ethically empty."

"So come to Washington."

"Jeffrey, don't push."

"Is it me?"

"What do you mean?"

"You'd come back and take this job if I weren't here?"

"No. I--hell, I don't know." She noticed Simão listening from the living room. "Jeffrey, I can't talk about this now. I've got company, remember."

"Is he good-looking?"

"Yes, if you must know."

96

"Damn." His voice hardened. "Chelsea, you do what you want. It's your life. I can't save your career for you. Have a nice evening."

"Jeffrey--." He was gone. She hung up, staring out the back window at the fence between her house and the one behind it. "I just don't know," she muttered.

Back in the living room, Simão was standing. "Is something wrong?"

"No." She shook her head and drained the rest of her wine. "Let's go eat. I'm starving."

Chelsea led Simão into the foyer at Marie Callender's. Ribbons dangling from the blue and yellow helium balloons clinging to the ceiling tickled their shoulders as the gingham-aproned hostess led them to a booth in the back of the restaurant.

Simão looked around at the old books, washboards, kettles and farm tools hanging on the walls and said, "This is a cowboy restaurant."

"No. Country, I think is what they call it."

"Country. Like rural, right?"

"Yes." She opened her menu, trying to avoid Simão's laughing eyes. "It's very popular."

He shook his head. "Where I come from, this is poor people's things. We all want to escape this." As the waitress handed them menus, Simão said, "Red wine, please."

She looked at Chelsea, who shook her head. "Just water for me."

Simão studied the menu. "What is the most all-American dish on the menu?"

"Hm." Chelsea looked at the familiar listings. This was her favorite place, and she had tried just about everything. "Ah. The beef stew. Served in a big hollowed-out loaf of French bread. It's great."

"I will have the stew. And you?"

"Quiche."

The waitress set a glass of red wine in front of him. "Thank you," he said.

Chelsea saw Simão open his mouth to order for them both and jumped in before he could speak. "I'll have the quiche. With salad. Italian dressing on the side."

Simão's eyes narrowed, but he said nothing, just waited for her to finish before he ordered his stew.

As the waitress walked away, he said, "American women, so independent."

"That's right," Chelsea said, challenging him with her eyes. They both laughed.

The food was good, and Chelsea began to enjoy herself. Simão talked about his business and about his home in Faial, an island of green fields divided by rows of blue hydrangeas that grew so abundantly they were used as fences. He loved the marina, working on the boats, going out to fish, but he also had to work on his father's farm.

Chelsea listened, fascinated by his gentle accent and eyes full of dreams.

"What made you come to America?"

"My grandfather came here as a young man. After he returned to Faial, he always talked about America as the land of opportunity. My father wanted to come here, but he had too many obligations back home. A man could make his fortune here, he used to say. He could get away from this life of hard physical labor that left him as poor as he started and old when he was 50. Unfortunately, my father died before he could come to the U.S."

"I'm sorry."

"Yes, it was very hard. But I vowed to make his dreams come true. I brought my grandmother, my mother and my sister with me. We've been here almost four years."

"Did you know anyone here?"

"My uncle had a house in San Jose. He let us stay with him until I could find someplace of our own."

"How did you make a living?"

Simão shook his head. "You wouldn't think it to see me in my fancy suits, but I work in the mornings at the fish store, unloading the fish, cleaning it, setting it up to sell. See, I still know a lot about fishing. I work there, then I shower and go to my office."

"I thought you lived there."

"Oh no. I just rent a little space in the front. Another man lives in the back part. This stew is very good," he said, taking a big mouthful. "Very American."

She laughed. "Yes. How did you learn English so well? And how did you get to be such a big shot in the Chamber of Commerce?"

He guffawed. "Big shot? No, I am the one who is willing to do all the work. Everybody else is too busy. They all say, 'Let Simão do it, he is young.' But look, I am getting gray hairs." He bent his head, and Chelsea looked for gray among the black hairs.

"Where? I don't see any."

"They are coming. Anyway. My English. I learned a little in school in the Azores; it is required now. And when we moved here, I read, watched TV and listened to the radio. I just buried myself in English. If you want to succeed in a country, you must speak the language as well as you can."

"Yes, you're right."

"People hear you talk with an accent, having trouble with the words, they think you are ignorant. So I try very hard to speak good English."

"Your English is excellent, Simão, probably better than mine."

She watched him scoop out the last of his stew and tear into the bread. She was only halfway through her quiche.

As he paused for a sip of wine, he sighed. "You are so pretty."

She blushed. "Thank you. You embarrass me with so many compliments."

"It is just the truth." He smiled gently. "You know, I heard you on the telephone, I shouldn't listen, but I am interested to know who that man was and what you were arguing about."

She shook her head. "It's just somebody I used to, um, to date." To live with, you mean. "He's got a job possibility for me to consider. I don't know whether I want it or not."

"Where is it?" He looked anxious.

Chelsea stared into his caramel brown eyes. "Washington, D.C."

The waitress returned. "Would you like some dessert? We have a special on our apple pie tonight."

99

Simão looked at Chelsea. "Yes?"

There goes the diet, she thought. "Okay."

"Would you like ice cream with your pie?" the waitress asked.

"Why not?" said Simão. As she left, he leaned across the table toward Chelsea. "Washington, D.C. That is on the other side of the country, very far away."

"Yes, very far."

"But it is a good job?"

She nodded, sighing again. "It sounds like it."

"Well, I am being selfish, but I hope you stay here." He raised his wine glass in a toast and drank the rest, his eyes still on Chelsea.

She felt that zing of electricity again. What was this?

After dinner, Chelsea watched guiltily as Simão paid the bill. She had started to argue, but he was almost huffy about it. "You are my date. I pay," he said, setting $32 cash on the tray.

Outside in the car, they leaned back against the leather seats. "I'm so full," Chelsea said.

"I have an idea for something to do now," Simão said.

Chelsea bit her lip. Did she have a vote? At this point, most men would want to go back to her apartment. But this was Simão. He started the car and headed in the opposite direction.

Chapter Seven

Chelsea's alarm clock startled her awake. Sun peeked through the blinds, promising a warm day. She slid out of bed in her blue nightshirt, ran her fingers through her tangled hair and went into the bathroom.

The evening had turned out differently from what she expected. Simão's plan was simply a drive down Winchester Boulevard into Los Gatos, where they parked and walked along the rim of Lake Vasona. He talked about his home and his plans, and she shared stories of her work and her family, carefully avoiding her life with Jeffrey.

Then they were quiet, looking at the stars mirrored in the smooth water of the lake. The scents of pine and eucalyptus trees mingled with Simão's pleasant musky cologne.

As they walked, Simão took her hand in his strong callused fingers. She smiled in the dark. It had been a long time since she had felt so peaceful.

At the end of the path, Simão pointed to a large flat rock. "Would you like to rest?"

"Sure."

He sat beside her, staring into the water. "You know," he said quietly. "In my country, a woman would not be allowed to go out alone with a man like this unless they were married. Always there would be a chaperone."

"But I'm 28 years old."

"It does not matter. She must be protected from the uh, the urges of the man."

She laughed. "Why?"

He shook his head. "Ah, America is so different. But big cities in Portugal are different from my village, too. The girls go to school, they drive cars, you cannot keep them home."

Chelsea was silent, dangling her long legs from the rock.

It was so still she heard Simão swallowing.

"My problem now is that I want to kiss you. I want to make love to you, but it is not proper."

"It's all right," she whispered, reaching for his hand.

"No." But he didn't pull his hand away.

The darkness made it easy to talk. "Simão, I sensed the other

101

night, even though I was drunk, that maybe you thought I was a little forward. I'm used to American guys who just assume that sex is part of the date. Sometimes I like it, I can't pretend I don't. But I hope that doesn't make you think I'm a bad person."

Simão rose and walked to the edge of the water. "Why are you 28 years old and never married?"

Chelsea sighed. He had asked the same question before and she'd dodged it. "I never found the right man," she said softly. "I had a long relationship with a man I met in Sacramento, but we decided not to get married. And then I've been so busy with my career. Twenty-eight isn't old. You're about the same age, aren't you?"

"I am 33."

In the silence, she asked softly, "Have you thought about getting married again?"

He shook his head. "I have been occupied with my business, and I have my grandmother, my mother and my sister Rosa to take care of. But someday, yes, I suppose I will. A man needs a wife."

"I guess so." It was all just talk, Chelsea thought. They were dancing around what they were really thinking. Her eyes fixed on his, she ran her finger along the soft hairs on his muscled arm.

Simão pulled her close then, and they kissed. Chelsea opened her mouth and his tongue pressed hungrily in. Her head spun as she felt his chest against her breasts and his hips against hers. She felt her body opening to him.

But Simão brushed her cheek with his hand and pulled back, breathing hard. "*Ai, Deus*, you are such an exciting woman. But we must wait."

For what? "That's not easy."

He nodded. "Yes, it is very difficult. Come on, let us walk back."

In the car, he paused before starting the engine. "Chelsea Faust, I feel something very important happening between us."

"I know," she breathed, thinking, but we are so different. Our families speak different languages. What if I decide to move to Washington, D.C.?

She hadn't noticed the red light shining on the answering machine last night. She had floated into bed feeling like a high school girl experiencing her first crush and slept deeply and soundly, dreaming of stars, trees, a lake and a handsome man.

Now she frowned at the machine and punched the button reluctantly, not anxious for reality to intrude on her dreamy mood.

"Chels," said Jeffrey's urgent voice. "I know it's late. It's even later here, but my friend at the paper called to tell me he's going to start setting up interviews on Monday. If you want that job, you'd better hustle. I mean fax your resume now. I don't have to be part of the package, Chelsea. Maybe that will help you make up your mind. Hope you had a good time. G'night."

"Oh God," she sighed, holding the coffeepot under the faucet. "Give me a break, McNeil." It was Friday, and her schedule was packed with interviews. When would she have time to type a letter and fax it with her resume to Washington?

She spooned coffee into the basket and flipped the switch, listening to the water start to bubble through. Time to decide once and for all. But she knew in her heart it was already decided. Sometimes no decision is a decision. She thought of last night with Simão, the book she was thinking about writing, the Slater mystery she still needed to resolve, her father's depression, her ambivalence about Jeffrey. "I'm not going," she announced and went to the bathroom to shower.

One more lap, Chelsea told herself Saturday at the Rose Garden, just one more. If I go beyond 10K, the race will be a breeze.

But it was already summer, and the temperature had stuck around 90 all week. Her tank top and shorts were soaked with sweat. She could feel it running down the backs of her knees and taste it on her upper lip. Her legs had gone on automatic pilot a couple laps earlier. It was as if she were detached and floating somewhere above them and didn't dare stop or she would never start again.

Up ahead she saw a man whose curly hair, white skin, and the cocky way he held his head looked familiar. As he jogged toward her, she smiled at city councilman Mike Peterson, wondering if he would recognize her from the recent press conference on plans for the sports arena. She wondered, too, if he knew what was going on with Slater.

"Hello," she said, fighting for breath.

103

He nodded, too winded to speak. As he passed, he looked back over his shoulder, suddenly remembering where he had seen her. He raised his hand in greeting. Maybe he's running the 10K, too, she thought. Politicians often used events like this for publicity.

The encounter had broken her concentration. She aimed for the gate and started slowing down, forcing her breath in and out in a steady rhythm, telling her legs to stop running and walk, letting her muscles cool.

In front of the wooden platform in the center of the park, a wedding party was gathering, the bridesmaids in pink satin gowns, the ushers in white tuxedos.

Chelsea skirted them and went for the fountain, leaning in to dash cold water on her face and arms. She sank wearily to the stone bench, breathing in the roses, which were beginning to wither in the heat.

As the sweat cooled on her body, she lay back, looking up into the cloudless sky. This morning she felt 12 years old. No deadlines, no responsibilities. The physical demands of running pushed concerns about money, boyfriends and work out of her mind.

A pink-clad bridesmaid came toward her, walking carefully with her pink shoes and white stockings in the spongy grass. Chelsea sat up, pulling her top down over her waist.

"Can you tell me where the restroom is?"

"Over there," she said, pointing back toward the stone building near the stage.

"That's it? It's locked."

"Oh. Sometimes they do that. Afraid of vandalism, I guess. Sorry."

The girl grimaced. "But I really need to go. They told us it would be open."

Chelsea shrugged. City budgets. If they left the park restrooms open, kids broke the toilets and sprayed gang symbols all over the walls. If they locked them, the public complained. She had listened to a three-hour public hearing on that very subject last month. Nobody came away happy. "There's a deli up Park Avenue a block or so," she said. "I'm sure they have a restroom."

"Thanks." The bridesmaid walked away, lifting her feet like a cat trying to stay out of the mud.

In a minute, Chelsea saw the bridesmaid and one of the tuxedoed men get into a red Camero and drive toward Park Avenue.

She sighed. Time to get out of here.

It had been a week since she had talked to Simão. The special section on the Portuguese was coming out Wednesday. The deadline had passed for the Washington job, and she had heard nothing more from Jeffrey.

Mel had come back to work, but he didn't smile much these days, and he never stayed late. Chelsea ached for him. Carrie, his oldest, was so precious to Mel. She had been born five weeks early and spent nearly a month in an incubator in intensive care before Mel and Kathy could bring her home.

Up to now, Carrie had been an energetic, normal preteen, but those early problems had always lurked in the back of her parents' minds. Mel often shook his head over news stories telling of children's deaths or serious illnesses. "They are such a gift from God," he would say. "You never know when God might take them back."

Devoted as Mel was to his job at the Weekly Times, nothing took precedence over his wife and daughters. That's why he'd never moved on to a bigger paper, while Chelsea, unfettered, had only stayed in San Jose, working at the now-defunct Palo Alto Times-Tribune, for a year before zooming off to the state capital. Unlike Mel, she figured her current stint on the Weekly-Times was just a temporary stop until she found a better job. Meanwhile, she could devote nights and weekends to work because there was no one waiting for her at home. Well, almost no one. Jeffrey had been there for a while, but he was always busy with fundraisers, speeches and meetings.

It was as if one made a choice of family or career. Chelsea still hoped she could experience both. But the door was closing a little every day.

The following week, she was gazing out the Weekly Times window, thinking about her life, when Dunning walked in.

Now what, she thought, straightening up.

"Chelsea, I hear you're running in the Mercury News 10K."

"Yes." Where did he hear that, she wondered. Mel was the only one she had told. "I thought I'd try it."

He pulled up a chair and sat, his bulk straining the aluminum frame. "You know the sponsors are a competitor of ours."

"Yes. But I don't see how this--"

He raised his hand. "What you do in your private life is your business. It's not as if you're writing for them. But I was thinking if we could send a photographer to shoot some pictures of you in the race, it could be good publicity."

"What do you mean?"

"You know, 'Chelsea Faust, one of the Weekly Times' finest, runs with the best.' Or, 'We give our all so our readers can have the best.' Or, 'We're number two, but we try harder.' Something like that. We could run it in the paper, put it on billboards."

Chelsea stared at his pudgy white face, feeling a little sick. Did he have to turn everything into advertising?

Dunning was staring at her legs. "How good are you anyway? Is there a chance you might win?"

She chewed on her lips, wondering if she dared tell him to go to hell. "I don't know. Maybe. Maybe not. I don't know about the competition."

"Well, try to win. That would be the best. I can see the headline: 'Weekly Times reporters get there first.' What do you think?"

Chelsea sighed, smoothing her long skirt over her knees. "I don't know, Mr. Dunning. I'm not very comfortable with the idea of having a photographer along. When I run, I need to concentrate on what I'm doing."

"Oh, I'll send Marty, the sports guy. He knows how to get action shots. You won't even know he's there. In fact, he's already agreed to do it."

Swell, she thought, thanks for asking me first.

"Wonderful," she said, her voice laden with sarcasm the publisher didn't catch.

"This'll be great," Dunning said, slapping her on the knee. "You're doing super work these days, Chelsea. We're lucky to have you."

When he went out, she lay her head on her desk. Why does he

have to spoil everything? If I win, he's going to take credit for it. As if that bucket of lard could run from here to Ed's Liquor Store.

Sarge strolled in, still scanning the pages of his notebook after his biweekly visit to the police station. "What's eatin' you?"

"George P. Dunning."

"Oh, is that all? There's a guy here who says somebody barbecued his pet chickens and left the bones in his back yard. Now that's awful."

Chelsea couldn't help giggling. "Yes, it is awful. Good lord, I'm glad I don't have your job."

"Beats writing about lady's tea parties."

"I don't write about lady's tea parties."

"Oh no? Where were you Friday?"

"Well, not all the time. Sometimes I get to cover the water board, you know. Or even city council. Speaking of which, have you heard anything about Councilman Slater--?"

She stopped. Sarge was already on the phone. "Hey, Tim, about this chicken story. Is this on the up and up? Yeah, it'd make a great short item, one of those weird things readers love. 'Robbers Leave Bones Behind.'" He chuckled.

Nuts, Chelsea thought. She turned to her computer and reread the first line of her story: "The theme was 'Spring into Summer' at Delta Chi's annual tea and fashion show."

Copies of the special section were stacked on her desk Wednesday morning. Chelsea, dressed in a white suit for the annual YWCA Women in Business luncheon, sank into her chair and stared at the picture of Anna Silva on the cover smiling and holding up a loaf of sweet bread. "A Taste of the Old Country," said the headline, with the subhead, "Portuguese Businesses Cater to All-American Clientele."

Slowly she turned the first page and stared at back-to-back full-page ads. Page four was also ads. Finally on page 5, she found Anna's story, squashed into the top third of the page above still more ads. Other stories were wrapped around ads on the following pages: Miguel's hardware, António's bookstore, Floralinda's dress shop, Oliveira Travel. In typical Dunning style, the ads dominated the publication. The copy in those ads seemed corny and patronizing to Chelsea. At least the photos looked good.

As Chelsea skimmed the section, Mel sank heavily into his squeaky wooden swivel chair, uncharacteristically late.

She looked up from her paper. "How's Carrie?"

He shook his head. "A zombie. The damn drugs they give her have turned her into a little ghost with no life, no energy, no joy."

"How long does she have to take them?"

"I don't know. Maybe forever." He rubbed the sagging skin under his eyes.

"Jeez, Mel, there must be something else they can do."

He shrugged. "Not according to the doctors. We've got to drive her everywhere. We can't let her ride her bike, and she's too muddled to even walk to school by herself. That's why I'm late. She forgot her homework, so we had to go back."

"It's only 9:20."

"I don't like to be late. I'm the editor. It looks bad." He frowned at the mail piled on his desk.

"It's okay, Mel. Hey, do you want to go out to lunch or something?"

"Thanks, but I can't. I've got to put in as much time as I can before I have to go pick Carrie up at school."

"Can't Kathy do it?"

"No, she's trapped at her desk at Intel. They've got her on a time clock. Besides, I'm closer."

"If there's anything I can do. . ."

"Just keep up the good work. Did you buy that suit in Washington?"

Change the subject, she thought. "Yes, I did."

"Ever want to go back?"

She stared at him. She hadn't told anyone about Jeffrey's calls and the job he wanted her to take in Washington. "No," she said. "So, what do you think of this Portuguese section?" Change the subject again.

"I haven't even looked at it yet. How do you like it?"

"Too many ads. It looks like a shopper. Other than that, it's not bad."

"It's money," Mel said. His phone rang. "Oh, hi Mandy. I'm sorry to hear you're not feeling well. No, that's okay, I'll do the calendar."

Chelsea turned back to her desk. With the paper out, it was time to get organized for the next week. She was just listing the assignments she planned to work on, not sure what to do about Slater, but knowing she had to act soon, when Simão walked in.

She set down her pen. "Simão."

The receptionist was behind him. "Sorry, Chelsea, I was on the phone. I had four lines going at once."

"It's okay, Berta."

Simão had a copy of the special section in his hand. "Good morning," he said, surprising her with a kiss on each cheek. "You look beautiful."

"Thank you." She was blushing again. Mel was ostensibly going through the mail, but she knew he was listening.

Simão held up the paper. "This is fantastic. I have been getting calls already from people wanting me to tell you how much they like your articles. The whole thing looks good. These nice big advertisements will promote our businesses, and your stories tell about the people. It is very good."

"Thank you again," she said. Mel was watching her now, looking from her to Simão and back.

"I was going to come in this morning anyway. I wanted to give you this."

"What is it?" She took the stiff white envelope he offered and pulled out a gold-embossed invitation.

"We are having our annual chamber of commerce dinner dance, and I want you to be my guest."

"Oh?" She opened the card and read the date, July 17, next Saturday, the same date as the 10K run. But the dinner didn't start until 8 o'clock. Portuguese time.

Simão's dark eyes were anxious. She felt a tug at her heart.

"I, um, yes, I'd like to go."

He nodded, smiling. "Good. I will put your name in with mine."

"Great. Thank you."

109

He looked at his watch. "I must go. I have an appointment at the bank."

"Would you like some more copies of the paper?" she said, giving him a handful.

"*Obrigado*." He kissed her on both cheeks again and left, whistling softly as he went out the door.

"Isn't that shindig the same day as your race?" Mel asked. "I think I got a press release on it."

"Hush." Chelsea stared at her story list and willed herself to stop blushing.

Chapter Eight

Coastal fog turned everything gray-white and softened the edges of the buildings as Chelsea jogged into the warm-up area in front of the Fairmont hotel. She stretched each leg, bent forward, sideways and back, circled her arms in big loops, and rolled her head around.

At 7:30 a.m. on a Saturday, only runners, media and homeless people occupied Market Street. Everyone else was sleeping. She noticed Channel 4 and Channel 7 cameramen already setting up by the finish line. Marty, the Weekly Times sports photographer, had shown up early but dashed into a nearby espresso shop to get a bagel and coffee. She could see him now through the window, huddled in his leather jacket and jeans, staring sleepily at the gathering crowd of runners.

Coffee would be great. Chelsea was too nervous to be sleepy, but the fog buried the usual summer warmth in cold air. She jogged in place, trying to keep warm, and noted the mayor arriving in burgundy sweats, joining a cluster of men and women that included council members, the city manager, and several of their aides.

Her heart jolted as she saw Councilman Slater join the group. She watched him affix the paper number to the back of the mayor's shirt. Apparently, he was acting as his coach. Free publicity, she thought. But where has he been the last few weeks? Like everyone else, he was wearing sweats, and his graying hair was windblown and shaggy, but he looked thinner as he headed for the espresso shop where Marty still lingered. Noticing her staring at him, Slater frowned and walked more quickly.

The aides hanging around the city council group reminded her of Jeffrey. He was an aide to a senator now, at his side for every press conference, photo opportunity or speech. Someday Jeffrey would be a senator himself or maybe even be appointed to a cabinet post at the White House. The press would follow him wherever he went.

"You gonna wear all that?" The photographer surprised her by showing up at her elbow.

"No, I've got shorts and a tank top underneath. Why?"

"If you show a little leg, it'd probably be more sexy."

Chelsea glared at him. "Marty, If I show my legs, I'm doing it

111

because I'll run better, not so jocks like you can stare at them."

"Jeez, I'm sorry. Don't sue me for harassment, okay?"

"Just stay out of my way."

"Oh yeah, Dunning clued me. When that gun goes off, I'm invisible."

"You'd better be."

A bullhorn squawked and Chelsea turned toward the sound. All she could hear was noise and static, but she saw the runners gathering behind the starting line. Quickly she unzipped her jacket and slipped off her sweat pants with a warning look at the photographer. She joined the group at the line, edging in about three from the front.

Things happened quickly. A few announcements, the gunshot, and they were off.

Too fast, Chelsea thought, watching the runners in front of her sprint down Market Street at top speed. They'll burn out. She slowed to a comfortable pace, letting those in a hurry get past her, and settled into the route.

Marty had been right. She couldn't tell where he was. Good.

This was different from running around the Rose Garden. The paved surface was harder, but the view was more interesting. She passed the art museum, St. James Park, a French restaurant, the old courthouse. The normally crowded streets were blocked with sawhorse barricades so the racers could run on the asphalt.

Her moderate pace paid off. Gradually most of the leaders fell back, weary already, and Chelsea moved toward the front of the pack, speeding up a little.

I could really win this thing, she thought, pushing on, her legs going on automatic again. She passed the mayor and his aide. Way ahead she could see a long-legged, muscular man in green shorts sprinting down the sidewalk, his legs kicking high, his arms tight at his sides. There's the winner, she thought. Five paces behind him, a short, balding man in red held second place. Chelsea, 100 yards back from the leading pair, realized she was third.

Her legs were beginning to ache, and she was sweating despite the fog, but by the time they reached the final kilometer, the winners were set. Unless she fell, she would place.

In the distance, she heard a camera motor drive whirring. Marty.

112

Ignore it, she told herself, and kicked into a higher gear. Ignore him and Dunning and Jeffrey and Simão and all the other men who complicated her life. Just run for the finish line.

People began to cheer as she turned the corner from San Carlos back onto Market Street. A roar greeted the first- and second-place men. Then she heard a shout over the bullhorn: "Here comes first place in the women's division. Can it be? Yes, it's number 63, Chelsea Faust from, oh my, our competition, the South Bay Weekly Times. Let's hear it for Chelsea!" Shutters clicked. TV cameras followed her movements.

Everything was a blur as she crossed the finish line. She passed the tape, someone marked down her time. She went on, slowing to a walk, almost stumbling, hands on her hips, breathing hard. Dunning had his wish. She had won. But it was her wish, too.

Behind her, people were running into the arms of husbands, wives and friends who had come to cheer for them. Chelsea felt a pang of loneliness. She hadn't brought anyone except Marty, who was more interested in the looks of her legs than in whether she could run.

As her breathing slowed, she walked toward the spot where she had left her clothes. Her legs felt like painful shafts.

"Chelsea," said Morgan Caldwell, the afternoon news anchor for Channel 11. "Congratulations. How does it feel?" She held a microphone up to her face and the cameraman next to her started taping.

Chelsea stared at the camera, wiping the sweat off her forehead with the back of her arm. "Good," she gasped.

"What factors do you think led to your victory?"

"Oh," she said. It was odd to be on the other side of an interview. "I don't know. I trained a lot, and I ran hard. It was a faster group than I expected. I had to really work at pacing myself."

"Well, that certainly paid off. Thank you and congratulations to our women's winner and third place overall, Chelsea Faust."

I'll have to tell Mom and Dad I'm on TV, she thought, smiling as the reality began to sink in. I won. I actually won.

In the recovery area, a volunteer handed her a towel and a cup of fruit juice. "Thank you," she said, wiping her face, arms and legs.

The fog had broken. Summer warmth penetrated the wispy white

113

clouds that remained. She put on her sweats and sat on a bus stop bench, sipping her juice.

Runners were still coming in, moving slowly, fighting for breath as they crossed the finish line. The TV crews were already moving to the awards area, not interested in the non-winners.

Someone slapped her on the back, and she saw the mayor smiling down at her. "Good job."

"Thanks."

He moved on to join his cronies. A white-haired woman whose knobby knees jutted out of her baggy sweatpants collapsed onto the bench next to her.

"How'd you do?" asked the woman.

"Oh, pretty good," Chelsea said, smiling to herself.

"That was a hard race. I didn't think I was going to make it."

"But you did."

"Yes, I did. I don't think I'll try it again though. Once was enough."

Chelsea stood. Her legs were starting to freeze up. "If I sit still too long, I'll never get up."

"Yes. Me too," said the woman, massaging her legs. "See you later."

Afterward, at home on her sofa with her feet up on a pillow, she called her parents.

"Dad, guess what? I won the Mercury News 10K women's division."

"Hey, that's great, honey," Dad said. "Let me tell your mother."

Soon they were both on the line congratulating her.

"I'm going to be on Channel 11 tonight."

"What time?"

"6:00, I think."

"Why don't you come over and watch it with us? We could have dinner afterward," Mom said.

"No, I can't, Mom." She chuckled. "I have a date to go dancing."

"Tonight?"

"Tonight. At the Portuguese hall."

"Oh my. Brush up on your *chamarrita*."

"My what?"

"The *chamarrita*. It's a dance. Every Portugee knows how to do that one."

"Not me."

"Better rest those legs, honey," Dad warned.

"I'm resting, I'm resting."

Simão held her hand as they moved into the crowd at the Portuguese Athletic Club, upstairs in the I.E.S. hall next to Five Wounds Church.

She noticed people looking at her curiously as they greeted Simão in Portuguese and urged him toward the front of the ticket line.

All around her, people chattered in Portuguese. Chelsea felt as if she had suddenly gone deaf and mute, unable to speak or to understand what anyone was saying. I have to find a Portuguese class, she told herself.

She was glad she had decided to pull one of her Washington reception dresses out of the closet. A black off-the-shoulder sheath, it made her look tall, slim and elegant, she thought. She wore the pearl earrings and necklace Jeffrey had given her for her 26th birthday. In his tuxedo, Simão was as dashing as a prince, and she knew they made a striking couple.

However, her legs ached standing on the hard floor waiting to get into the main hall. An afternoon of relaxation with a mystery novel had done little to ease the strain of the morning's race on her legs and feet.

When Simão had come to her door, she had greeted him with the news.

"I won!"

"Very good. Won what?"

"The race. The Mercury News 10K race through downtown San Jose. I came in first in the woman's division."

"Running?" He seemed confused.

"Yes. I told you I like to run."

"But I didn't know you competed in races."

"Oh yes. Look, here's my trophy." She grabbed it off the coffee table to show him.

Simão nodded. "Very impressive. We should get going."

115

"Okay." Chelsea's forehead wrinkled in puzzlement. "I'm ready."

She let him help her on with her beaded red and black bolero jacket. "I was on the 6 o'clock news tonight."

"Yes? I did not see it."

So now she stood mute as Simão chatted with the heavyset woman at the reception table. Apparently he had introduced her. The woman looked at her and said "Please to meet you."

"Thank you," said Chelsea, her mouth dry and stiff.

The woman turned her attention back to Simão. Chelsea wondered what they were chuckling about. Her? Something related to the dance? Did he tell the woman she was a reporter? She remembered that last party she attended with Jeffrey. At least here nobody would have to worry about her quoting them in the newspaper. She didn't understand a word anyone was saying.

When Simão finally broke free, two dinner tickets in his hand, they headed into the main room. "I think I need to learn some Portuguese," Chelsea said. "Do you know of a class somewhere?"

Simão shrugged. "You don't need to study Portuguese. I will translate for you."

"Yes, but I feel left out. Like just now."

"Do not let it bother you. *Olá*, Manuel," he said, greeting a man with bushy black eyebrows and white hair. "*Como está?*" And they were off in conversation as Chelsea stood, feeling hungry, thirsty and footsore. Would it be like this all night?

More men joined their group, and Chelsea found herself pushed aside. She spied the bar in the far corner of the room and tried to get Simão's attention, but he was looking at a Portuguese newspaper one of the men had handed him. He had raised his voice, protesting one of the articles.

What was I thinking coming here, she wondered. If this had been an American gathering, her date would have introduced her to everyone and included her in the conversation. If he were busy, she could break off and talk to someone else. Here, she was trapped by her lack of language.

Looking at Simão almost shouting over the roar of the crowd, she walked away from the group, across the room toward the bar. She felt many eyes watching her in her slinky dress and shoes that felt like nails going up her feet. At the bar, she reached into her tiny beaded bag and pulled out $5, then tried to get the bartender's attention. He was busy serving a line of men.

She waited until every man was served, including several who had come after her, before the bartender looked at her. By then, she had lost her patience. "Could I have a beer, please, if it's not too much trouble?"

The bartender stared at her, then shrugged and reached below the bar. He pulled out a bottle, opened it and poured the contents into a tall glass. "Two-fifty."

She left $3 and turned away, sipping at the foam in the top of the glass, sighing as the beer slid down her dry throat.

She was in the middle of the dance floor when a woman in a blue satin gown with huge cloth flowers sewn to the hips rustled toward her. "Chelsea," said Floralinda, almost making her spill her beer as she bussed her on both cheeks. "How are you?"

"Good. And you?"

"Terrific. Your story was wonderful. I am so glad you take an interest in us Portuguese people. Are you working on a story tonight?"

"No," Chelsea said, glancing toward Simão. "I'm here with Simão."

"Oh," Floralinda said with a knowing nod. "He is a good man, that one."

"Yes."

"Are you going to be writing any more stories about the Portuguese?"

Simão interrupted. "Chelsea. I was looking for you."

"I'm right here."

"Yes. What are you drinking, beer?"

Floralinda touched Chelsea's hand and rustled back to her table.

Simão shook his head. "I would have bought you a drink. It is the man's place."

"That's okay. I have money."

"But it does not look right. You see no other women at the bar."

Chelsea looked at her handsome dark-eyed date and wondered where he had learned such things. He was clearly embarrassed. But this

117

is America, she thought. A woman can buy herself a beer if she wants to. "I didn't mean to cause a problem. I just--"

"Come with me. I want a drink for myself. And then we will find our table."

He's annoyed, she thought, following him back to the bar, watching as he got his whiskey sour right away. He's actually angry because I bought myself a beer.

Long tables covered with white cloths were arranged in rows along the sides of the immense hall, with the center left empty for dancing. From behind the curtains on the stage, she could hear shuffling sounds as the band moved their instruments into place, and soon she heard random toots and bits of tunes from the horn players warming up. Through a door to the left of the stage, she saw the kitchen, where several women prepared the food. Teenage girls in white blouses and black skirts waited to start serving. Fish smells blended with the cigarette smoke that hung like a cloud over the room.

Simão led her to a table near the door where they had come in. He sat at the end, motioning for her to sit to his right. She gazed at the people sharing their table: two 50ish men in black suits and their wives in glittery formals and stiff hair and a young man with hair slicked back like Simão's sitting with a tiny white-haired woman in black.

Simão greeted everyone, and Chelsea heard her name in the middle of a stream of Portuguese. The couples nearest them nodded in greeting. The old woman stared at her, suspicion in her dark eyes.

Simão and the men to his left began to talk, leaving Chelsea staring at the balcony opposite them where the Athletic Club had its library and photo gallery. Books lined the shelves, and the walls were covered with photographs of what must have been the club's past officers. Red velvet wing chairs circled the oval mahogany table. Portuguese, Azorean and American flags sat on tall brass stands along the paneled wall.

What sort of meetings went on up there, Chelsea wondered. Perhaps there was a story in this club, which no one had mentioned while she was interviewing the businesspeople. Judging by the lavish hall and the wardrobes of the guests, they didn't lack money. She could hear Dunning saying, "Those Portugees have bucks. . ."

118

At a lull in the conversation, she touched Simão's hand. "Tell me about this athletic club. What do they do?"

He brushed at the air with his hand. "It is just a big club. They sponsor soccer teams, and they show games on television from Portugal. They host dances and things."

"They seem to have a lot of money."

"Enough." He leaned left to hear what his neighbor whispered in his ear, then burst out laughing.

"*Sim, verdade.*" He turned to Chelsea. "He says it is a bunch of men who do not like cards, but do not want to go home to their wives and listen to their nagging."

The other man was still laughing. Chelsea looked to the wives at her right. They were busy talking to each other, ignoring the men.

Simão rose from his chair. "Excuse me. I have to talk to someone. They want me to make a little speech tonight."

Left alone with her Portuguese neighbors, Chelsea looked back toward the kitchen. Her beer was gone, and there was only wine and bread on the table. The girls were still clustered near the door, waiting.

She looked at her watch. 8:45 and still no dinner. She resolved to eat something at home before her next Portuguese-time dinner date. The excitement of the morning and her aching muscles left her feeling exhausted and anxious to be home in bed.

"You are a writer?" The woman next to her addressed her in English.

"Yes, I am. I work for the Weekly Times."

I have seen your stories. Very nice."

Chelsea leaned closer, fighting to be heard over the crowd. "Do you have a job outside the home?" She was sure the answer would be no.

"Oh yes." The woman opened her purse and handed her a business card. "I own a chain of flower shops, mostly in the East Bay."

"That's wonderful." And I thought she was a housewife, she chided herself, admiring the white card with gold roses twined around the name Gloria's Flower Shops. Gloria Souza, owner.

Gloria motioned toward the woman next to her. "Maria is my partner. We are cousins. Our husbands brought us here from Terceira

119

and went into the plumbing business together. When our kids grew up, we wanted to do something, so we started our own business. Now we have three stores."

"Great." Even more so, she thought, in a society where men don't even want you to buy a beer for yourself.

Someone was blowing and tapping on the microphone, then she heard, "*Atencão.*" The word was repeated several times before the crowd quieted down.

The speeches began. The plumbers turned around to watch. The old woman reached for another roll. Now would be the time to take out her notebook, Chelsea thought, but not tonight. The speakers' words were masked in Portuguese.

When it was Simão's turn, she sat tensely watching. He was so handsome and spoke with such confidence she felt her frustration with him subsiding. She couldn't help being proud that he had chosen her for his date. This was their third dinner together. It was becoming a relationship, although she had no idea where it was going. Half the time she couldn't stand him.

"He speaks well, no?" said Gloria at her right.

"Yes, he does. I wish I understood what he was saying."

"Oh, you don't speak Portuguese? I thought you were Portuguese."

"I am part Portuguese, but I don't speak the language at all."

"That's too bad. You should learn. I think some of the colleges have courses. When Maria and I came, we had to learn English by ourselves. It was difficult. But Portuguese is not so hard."

Chelsea filed it away in her mind. Check the local colleges for Portuguese courses. She couldn't depend on Simão to translate all the time.

He returned to the table just as the girls began serving the salads.

"*Muito bom,*" said one of the plumbers as Simão sat down.

"Speak English," scolded his wife Maria. "Chelsea does not understand Portuguese."

"Bah," he said, waving his hand at her, but for the rest of the evening he spoke mostly English, and Chelsea knew she'd be forever grateful to the cousins Gloria and Maria with their flower shops.

The main course was salmon with a dab of hollandaise on top, served with new potatoes, and sauteed vegetables. Very American, thought Chelsea, relieved to have a meal she could enjoy. When the *pudim* appeared for dessert, Simão ate his and silently switched plates with Chelsea to eat hers, too.

"That is how she stays so skinny," Maria said, winking at Chelsea.

Simão filled her wine glass, and Chelsea sipped at it, trying not to drink too much. She refused to get drunk this time.

The serving girls took their empty plates and cleared the tables. The curtains opened on the stage, and the band, seven men in white dinner jackets and black tuxedo pants, began to play. The music was subdued, the kind her parents listened to. As couples moved onto the dance floor, Simão held out his hand. "Do you want to try it?"

"All right."

Soon they were dancing, surrounded by other couples. Chelsea noticed they were both taller than many of the women and men there. Simão held her tightly against him. He was a good dancer. She felt as if her feet knew exactly where to go as he whirled her around the floor and guided her through the steps.

"You dance well," he murmured, resting his head against her cheek.

"Thank you. It's because you lead so firmly I don't even have to think about what I'm doing."

"That is the way it should be," he said, surprising her with a gentle kiss. "Are you having a good time?"

"Yes. Thank you."

"I am glad."

She closed her eyes and let herself get lost in the music and feeling close to Simão. She had never danced with anyone like this before.

It was almost 2 a.m. when they finally strolled out into the cool darkness and walked arm in arm to Simão's car.

Weariness combined with wine and the magic of the music and dancing left Chelsea ready to collapse, yet she was reluctant to part with Simão.

121

In the car, she sat close to him, and he put his arm around her, driving with one hand. Too soon, they were at her apartment.

He came to the door with her, and they kissed under the porch light. As he leaned into her, she opened her mouth and felt his tongue probing hers gently. She could taste the wine. His hands came up under her jacket, moving along her waist, grazing the bottom of her breasts.

She shivered and whispered, "Come in with me."

He leaned his head against hers and sighed. "Not yet. It is too soon."

No, it's not, she thought, but it was late, and she was exhausted.

Simão stroked her hand. "Will you come to my house tomorrow? Please. I want you to meet my mother and have dinner with us."

"I'd love that."

He hugged her and kissed her again. "Goodnight, my beautiful American writer."

"Goodnight."

He made sure she got safely into her apartment then walked down the sidewalk to his car, his hard shoes tapping on the pavement.

Chelsea stood at the door and waved.

"Oh my God, " she whispered as she shut the door and kicked off her painful shoes. He was taking her home to meet his mother!

The room was spinning slightly as she dozed off to dream of a dark-haired prince with a mustache. She had no idea evil forces were on their way to storm the castle.

Chapter Nine

Emerald lawn edged with scarlet geraniums lined the brick walkway to Simão's white house on 33rd Street in Little Portugal. The roof was pink-tiled, and the front door was bright green. Purple, yellow and red pansies and petunias filled the planters under the windows. To the right of the door, six mosaic tiles formed an image of the Virgin Mary. All was neat and pretty, like a fairy tale cottage, Chelsea thought.

Fuchsias hanging from the porch eaves touched her hair, and an orange butterball of a cat rubbed against her legs as she followed Simão onto the porch that sunny Sunday afternoon.

"This is wonderful," she said, breathing in the geranium smell and bending to pet the cat. "It reminds me of my grandmother's house."

He smiled. "I am glad. I want you to feel comfortable in my home."

As he opened the door, heavy footsteps hurried toward them. "Simão, *onde estavas? Tão tarde.*"

He held up his hand. "Mama, I am not late. This is Chelsea."

"Oh, hello," she said, coming forward to kiss Chelsea on both cheeks. Chelsea thought she smelled lavender and cumin. Simão's mother was short and wide, dressed in a dark blue dress with a hand-knit blue sweater over her shoulders. Her hair was streaked with gray. Her accent as she spoke was thicker than Simão's but took the same dips and turns. "I am happy to meet you. *Tão linda*, Simão."

"She says you are beautiful."

Chelsea clasped the older woman's gnarled hands. "Thank you. I am so glad to meet you, Mrs. Freitas. Your house is delightful."

"Oh." She waved away the compliment. "Come in, come in."

The simple comfort Chelsea had felt surrounding her outside was echoed inside. The furniture was old, upholstered in cocoa brown velvet and corduroy, with crocheted covers on the arms and backs. A flowered beige and maroon rug covered most of the polished oak floor. Vases of fresh flowers and photographs decorated the mahogany end tables. Chelsea's eyes were drawn to a large portrait of a man with a black mustache and dark eyes that reminded her of Simão's.

"Is that your father?"

"Yes. That is Papa, the year before he died."

"You look like him."

"I know."

A smaller photograph caused her to stare. Simão, looking boyish, posed with a slender dark-haired girl in a lacy white dress. His wife?

"Sit down," Simão's mother said, waving impatiently toward the sofa. "*Dê-lhe doces. Tenho que cozinhar.*" She bustled toward the kitchen as Chelsea looked questioningly at Simão.

He shrugged. "She has to do something in the kitchen. She says I should give you some candy."

Chelsea sank into the deep sofa cushions with a sigh. Simão held out a dish of fudge. "You must have some. Mama made it for you."

"Oh God, no," she protested mildly, but took a piece anyway. The chocolate was rich and creamy. "Umm." Somehow in the peace of this house, with Simão and his mother, her diet didn't matter. Neither did work or anything else. She was a little girl enjoying Grandma's Christmas fudge again. She could almost picture the big Christmas tree in the corner of her grandparents' living room with the toy train running around the heaps of presents.

Simão sat in the wing chair at her right, studying her. Chelsea crossed her hands over her flowered skirt and stared back. "What are you looking at?"

"You look good in my house."

"I don't know what to say." She felt herself falling into something soft and wonderful that she had no desire to escape. From where she sat, she saw lace curtains on the windows, a rose garden in the back yard and a patio with a redwood table, a brick barbecue and lounges padded with forest green cushions. "This is a great house."

"Like your grandmother's."

She closed her eyes, remembering. "In a way, yes. There's that same feeling, I don't know what it is. Maybe it's the old-fashioned furniture. But I always felt at peace there. And I always felt like a little girl, not a woman, even when I was older." She shook her head. "When I was little, I thought Grandma knew everything there was to know. She was as smart as God."

Simão grinned. "Maybe she was." His face saddened. "You are lucky. I missed a lot of years with my mother's mother. We lived too

far apart. I brought my father's mother here with us, but she is in poor
health and has to live in a nursing home."

"Oh, Simão, I'm sorry. Is she around here?"

"*Sim.* Yes. Not far."

His mother beckoned from the dining room. "*Vamos comer.*"

"I really need to learn Portuguese."

"It is time to eat," Simão said, rising. "You don't have to learn
Portuguese. Mama needs to learn English."

Still, Chelsea stored up the words she had heard and was eager to
learn more. As soon as she was alone, she would write them down.
Perhaps she would buy a Portuguese-English dictionary at António's
store.

The big table was covered with an embroidered white cloth and
set with rose-edged plates, thick-handled silverware and cloth napkins.
Simão sat at the head and gestured to Chelsea to take the seat at his
right. Chelsea thought about what she had seen and what Simão had
said and wondered how he could possibly make enough money to
support all this and his grandmother in a nursing home.

Her thoughts were interrupted by another arrival. "Rosa," she
said, rising to greet Simão's sister.

Chelsea was surprised to hear Simão scold his sister in
Portuguese, then noticed her rubbing at a purple paint spot on her wrist.

"I am sorry," she said to Chelsea. "I was painting, and I guess I
did not get it all off. Simão says I insult our visitor."

"No, that's all right," Chelsea said with a shrug. "I almost always
have ink on my hands." As their eyes met, Rosa smiled then looked
away. Chelsea realized Rosa's was the voice on Simão's answering
machine. She was his "receptionist."

"Bread?" Simão passed her a straw basket of hot rolls.

I'm going to get very fat if I keep eating here, Chelsea thought,
filling her plate with roast beef, mashed potatoes, gravy, yams and
homegrown tomatoes. I'll never win another race. But right then it
didn't seem to matter.

Simão did most of the talking that evening. Mama was shy about
her English, and every time Rosa spoke, Simão frowned at her. Chelsea
didn't know whether to encourage her or not.

125

"Tell me about the painting you're working on," she ventured.

"Oh," said Rosa, "it is my cousin's children playing in the park. I am working from a photograph. You know how kids are. They do not sit still, but--"

"She does not want to hear about that," Simão interrupted.

"Sure I do," said Chelsea, casting a puzzled look at her date. "Rosa, do you work in oils or acrylics or what? I'm afraid I don't know much about art."

Rosa darted a look at Simão and then back at Chelsea, who was nodding to show her interest. "Acrylics. I started with oil, but it was so expensive, and it, I don't know, the acrylics just feel more right to me. I like the colors better. I also do a lot with pen and ink in black and white. Some things are better that way."

"I'd love to see your work."

Rosa glowed. "Thank you. Maybe after dinner. . ."

Simão was frowning into his roast beef.

"Have you sold any of your paintings?" Chelsea asked.

"It is just a hobby," Simão growled. "Mama, we need more gravy. *Molho.*"

"Oh." She set down the roll she was eating and hurried into the kitchen.

She is not a slave, Chelsea thought, watching Simão continue eating. Her contentment faded.

After dinner, Chelsea and Simão went for a walk. In the twilight, the weather pleasantly cool, families had gathered on their porches or front lawns, the adults talking, children playing ball or chasing moths across the grass. It was a familiar scene that reminded her of own childhood days and those summer evenings when she and her friends had roller-skated and played badminton until they couldn't see the birdie anymore. She missed those days, she realized now. How had she gotten to be 28 years old living alone in an apartment without husband or children?

But she was more troubled by Simão's attitude.

"Why do you treat your sister that way?" she asked as they crossed the street and started the second block south on 33rd Street.

"It is my duty." He stared straight ahead as he walked, hands in the pockets of his gray slacks.

"I beg your pardon?"

"She wastes all her time on her 'art' when she should be helping Mama and me and finding herself a husband."

"Couldn't she do both?"

"No."

Chelsea felt the words forcing themselves out. "Simão, I don't understand your ideas about women. We can have a career and a husband at the same time. There's more to life than cooking and taking care of children."

"You don't want to cook?"

"No, that's not it. I like to cook. And I like kids. But there are lots of hours between meals, and there are years between children. If a woman has a talent, she ought to use it."

"Like you." He stopped at the end of the street and faced her.

"Yes. Exactly. Writing and photography are part of who I am. I wouldn't be completely myself if I didn't do them."

"Ah, but you are very smart. And you are American."

"Yes. So?"

He threw up his hands. "I don't know. American women are different."

"We're all just people."

"In Portugal, the man is in charge. There is no question."

"Here we share responsibility."

"Hmm."

"It's easier for the man, too, Simão. He doesn't have to take everything on his shoulders."

"We have strong shoulders."

Chelsea didn't reply. She was thinking that she was probably as strong as Simão.

They walked in silence and were nearly back to Simão's house when he sighed and reached for her hand, folding her fingers into his.

She found him staring at her, a longing in his dark eyes that made her swallow nervously. "What?"

"You are crazy, but I like you," he said as they turned up the brick walk. "Will you come to church with us next Sunday?"

She looked directly into those *saudade*-filled eyes and nodded. "Yes. That would be nice."

On Wednesday morning, Chelsea stared in horror at the three-column photo on the front page of the Weekly Times. In the long vertical image that ran from just under the masthead to beneath the fold, the most prominent feature was her nipples showing through her sweat-soaked tank top. Her clothes were plastered against her skin, her hair was wet and stringy, and she had an idiotic grin on her face.

"Weekly Times Stands Out from the Crowd" proclaimed the headline. The caption told briefly of her victory in the 10K race.

Instinctively Chelsea pulled her loose-knit green sweater across her chest, wishing she could run away and hide.

She was alone in the newsroom. Mel hadn't come in. Sarge was at the police station, and Mandy was out sick again.

"Oh my God," she muttered. "My parents are going to die when they see this." She reread the headline. "Those bastards!" she exploded. "Those sexist macho bastards!" Clutching the paper in her hand, she charged into the next room, where the sports staff worked.

Marty was leaning back in his chair, the front legs tilted dangerously in the air. He grinned around his chewing gum, and Chelsea was tempted to push him over.

"Good morning, Chelsea," he said, smirking at the two interns who shared the sports office. "How are you this fine morning? You're looking especially . . ."

"Can it, Marty! How could you do a shot like this?"

"Like what? What's wrong with it?"

She slammed the paper on the desk in front of him. "You know damn well what's wrong with it. Take another look."

He shrugged. "Looks good to me." He turned to the two other guys sitting there, chuckling. "Don't you think so?"

They both smiled and nodded, barely stifling their laughter.

"Oh, you guys think it's so funny. We're supposed to be a serious newspaper, not Playboy."

Mike, the San Jose state intern who was covering baseball for the summer, put on an innocent smile. "Oh, were you in Playboy, Ms. Faust? What month was it?"

128

The others guffawed.

"Jesus. You're just a bunch of little boys getting your kicks off my body."

"It's a very nice body," said Marty.

"Well, it's private property. You shouldn't have taken a shot like that."

The photographer brought his chair down and sat up straight. "Look, Faust, you won the race, and I took the picture. I didn't realize your nipples would show. They were pretty small on the proof sheet. You should have worn a better bra, I guess. Anyway, I didn't pick out the shot or write the headline or put it on the front page. Actually there was another less provocative shot that I thought was better."

Chelsea closed her eyes. "I can't believe Mel chose this shot."

"Naw, he wasn't here. Dunning did it, I think. He had final approval on the pages."

Chelsea opened her mouth to protest, then closed it. Dunning probably did do it.

She turned and walked out, holding her sweater tight around her, feeling her skirt swish against her legs.

The publisher wasn't in his office. She thrashed back to Berta. "Where's Dunning?"

"He's going to be out all day at some meeting somewhere."

"Oh, swell."

Back in Dunning's office, she left a note on the top page of his yellow pad: "I need to talk to you right away about this week's cover. Chelsea Faust."

In the newsroom, Chelsea paced, not ready to face the minor stories she had waiting for her to write. Her first impulse was to quit her job. How could she work for a jerk who would embarrass her like that? What a rinky-dink tasteless stunt. I should have gone to Washington, she thought.

But what about Simão?

Back and forth she walked across the office, her skirt rustling, her canvas-soled shoes chuffing on the thin gray carpet. There was no way she could settle down and work. Not now. She grabbed her notebook and went out. It was a good day to go to the library for that research piece on government finance she'd been putting off. Maybe she'd glance at the want ads while she was there.

Newspapers in Tampa, Cleveland, Ohio, Santa Barbara and Seattle were looking for advertising salespeople, editors and sports reporters. She bent closer to read a listing in Editor & Publisher for a lifestyle writer in Salt Lake City.

She sighed. Did she really want to move to any of those places? Especially Utah? They were all so far from anybody she knew. Besides, the way she felt today she wanted to do nothing but news from now on, serious investigative pieces, not the sexist, ethnocentric, advertising-motivated fluff that George P. Dunning thrived on.

She closed the magazine and tossed it onto the reshelving tray. The air in the library was stifling. She couldn't possibly work on a story for the Weekly Times right now. Besides, she might not even be employed there after today.

Hurrying back past the counter and out the double doors, she headed east toward Santa Clara Street and Simão's office. Nobody at the paper knew where she was. She had been so angry she didn't sign out. But what did they expect when they put that photo on the front page?

Part of her knew she was overreacting, making too much of this, but she was so embarrassed she felt feverish, as if she had the flu. She had never realized how she looked when she ran.

Parking near the bakery, she passed a newsstand on the way to Simão's office. There she was, nipples and all, 50 cents a copy. She started to go by, then returned, took two quarters out of her wallet, opened the news rack and turned the copies over so no one could see the front page.

Floralinda's dress shop was across the street. She thought about going to her. But she wasn't that close a friend. Besides, she might not understand. Anna the baker either, nice as she was.

Simão would sympathize, Chelsea thought, climbing the rickety stairs, inhaling the sewage smell again, knocking on the door. Maybe he would confront Dunning for her. It would suit his macho self-image.

"*Um momento*," she heard him call. He sounded cranky.

She waited, holding her sweater around her, feeling the whole

Portuguese world watching her. The air was hot. It smelled bad, and she wondered what she was doing here in the middle of a work day.

Two minutes passed, and she was still waiting. She was about to knock again when Simão opened the door a few inches.

"Oh," he said. "It is you. Do we have an appointment?"

Appointment? "No. I just needed to talk to you."

"I am very busy today. I am sorry."

"But Simão--"

As he started to shut the door, she saw a copy of the Weekly Times on his desk.

He opened the door again. "I was going to call you. We cannot go to church together this weekend. I am sorry. Good-bye."

With that, he shut the door, gently but firmly.

Chelsea stood at the top of the stairs, her throat aching with tears, her lips quivering. By the time she got into her truck, tears were streaming down her face. She had promised herself after breaking up with Jeffrey that no man would ever make her cry again.

"It's not fair. It's not fair." She almost hit a passing car as she pulled away from the curb and jammed on the brakes just in time. "Oh God, why do I keep winding up with these pig-headed men? I thought Simão cared about me. To hell with them all." Not knowing what else to do, she drove home, called the office and told Berta she was sick.

She put on her strongest bra and her baggiest sweatshirt and went running, hoping she would never have to stop and decide what to do next.

She called Mel at home that night. "I'm going to quit."

"Over the picture?"

"Yes. That and everything else."

"What else?"

"I don't know. Personal stuff. I want to write hard news. I need more money. I want some respect."

"Is there something else? Trouble with your new Portuguese friend maybe?"

"No. That was never really anything. Just business."

"You sure, Chelsea?"

She swallowed and watched the neighbor's little girl playing out in the yard. "Yeah."

"Chelsea, I really don't want to lose you right now. You're the only reporter I've got who can cover news and features. And we need your photos. Mandy's worthless, and frankly Sarge is getting old. He barely handles the cop beat. I can't seem to find time to write anything these days, and Dunning won't authorize any new hires."

"You'll find a replacement for me. There are lots of reporters looking for jobs."

"But you're special. Besides, I like having you there. I thought we were friends."

She felt tears coming again. "We are friends, Mel," she said, her voice a croak.

"Chelsea. I am so sorry about that photo. I would have been there, but Carrie had another seizure. If I hadn't been stuck at the hospital. . ." He sighed. "If you need more money, I'll talk to Dunning. But to be honest, the budget is really tight right now."

"I know. It's not just the money."

"If you want to do more news, you can do it. I'll get some freelancers for features. Don't leave because of this stupid photo. I'll talk to Dunning, get him to run an apology. Hell, I'll just put it in."

"No, don't draw any more attention to it."

"Maybe you're right."

She reached for a tissue and blew her nose.

"Chelsea, has somebody offered you another job?"

"No. I turned down a possibility in Washington recently."

"Thank God. But you don't have any leads now?"

"E & P has lots of jobs. I can find more through California Newspaper Publishers. I want to start fresh, Mel. I can't have people ogling my breasts everywhere I go."

"They'll forget by next week."

"Not everybody." In her mind, she saw Simão's stern face and the newspaper lying on his desk. "I've got to go, Mel. I'll write up my resignation tonight."

"Come on. Let's go get drunk at El Torito's like we used to. We both need a night out. Kathy can watch the kids. We can talk about our troubles, and things will look better in the morning."

"Mel, you're a good friend, but you can't fix this with three margaritas and a basket of tortilla chips. I'll see you tomorrow."

She hung up and rested her head on the table. The cool wood was soothing and tangible. Everything else was smog.

If anything called for getting drunk, surely this was it. In one day, her job, her reputation, and her love life had turned to garbage. Chelsea opened the cabinet above the refrigerator and took down the bottle of Scotch she had gotten from George P. Dunning last Christmas. All the employees received the same gift, whether they drank or not.

She poured the Scotch over ice and went into the living room, still in her running clothes. The liquor made her throat hurt. She flinched at the first sip, but forced it down like medicine, taking several big gulps. It warmed a path through her chest to her empty stomach, where it sat like a comforting campfire.

"Maybe I'll become an alcoholic and live on the streets with my shopping cart." But right away, she thought about how she would want to take pictures of street life and write about it. Maybe she could do a book: Homeless Women. To live without working was unthinkable.

But that picture.

She took another sip and got up wearily. She had run 12 miles before she stopped, and now her legs felt weak and watery. The Scotch was already making the room spin. She got the Weekly Times off the kitchen table and unfolded it to stare at herself.

"You know, I don't look too bad," she said to the air. She smiled at the slightly bulging biceps from her workouts at the gym, her trim legs, and flat stomach. "Look at those breasts. Too many athletes don't have any boobs. Well, I've got 'em, and here they are for all the world to see."

She chucked the paper onto the floor and lay back against the pillows. "Maybe I'll get a husband out of this. Mom would like that." She could imagine the phone call. "Hi, my name is Alfonso, and I saw your picture and fell in love right away. Can we go out and maybe get married?"

"Ha," she laughed, "Right. I spend years working at my career, and all he'd care about was my breasts. Which will start to sag in a few

133

years, and then what? He'll find somebody else whose knockers are still perky and leave me alone, this bitter old divorced ex-newspaper reporter who can't get a job because she mouthed off to George P. Dunning, whose company now owns every newspaper in the world. All hail, George P. Dunning." She tilted her head back and emptied her glass, rising to fix another drink.

The telephone rang. "Oh, great," she said, her words a little slurred. "Who is it now? Mel again? Dunning? Jeffrey to beg some more? Simão to tell me what a slut I am? Maybe it's Alfonso."

She slid in her socks across the linoleum and collapsed onto a kitchen chair. "Hello?"

"Hi, sweetie," said her mother, her voice cheery.

"Mom?" She struggled to sound sober. "What's up?"

"Just wanted to know how you're doing."

"Oh, fine."

"That's nice. Your father and I took a trip to Monterey today. The weather was beautiful. He's feeling a little better this week, and he had the day off, so we thought we'd go for a ride. It's so crowded on weekends, you know."

"Yes. I know."

"How's everything at the paper?"

Chelsea closed her eyes. The room seemed to be swaying slightly. "Fine. You didn't see it this week, huh?" Please say no, she prayed.

"No, we were gone. In fact, I think the boy forgot to deliver it."

Perfect. "Well, you didn't miss anything."

"Are you all right, honey? You sound different somehow."

"Oh, I'm okay. I've just got some film in the developer. I've got to get back to it before the timer goes off."

"Gee, you're always working. Well, I won't keep you. Come over this weekend if you're not busy."

"Right," she said. Not busy then or ever. "I will."

"Bye now."

And Mom was gone. Chelsea went back to the counter for her glass. Her father would have been too embarrassed to mention the photograph, but her mother would have reacted the same way Simão did. She hoped they never saw it.

"Oh shit," she said, drank another sip, then poured the rest of the

Scotch down the sink. "How can I drink this junk? It came from George P. Dunning himself."

This was the kind of day when she wondered why she didn't have any female friends to talk to.

She thought of Rosa. Now Simão's sister would be turned against her, too. All the Portuguese women would think she was a whore. It wasn't just the picture in the paper. Why did she appear in public that way in the first place? They wouldn't understand that she was an athlete.

So much for her book on Portuguese women.

Chelsea stood in the kitchen, not sure what to do next, then walked over to the phone, dialed the area code for Washington, D.C. and Jeffrey's number. It was 10 o'clock there. She listened to the phone ring four times, then heard a hissing sound and Jeffrey's muffled voice. "I can't come to the phone right now. . ."

"Damn," she whispered. After the beep, she said, "Jeff, it's Chelsea. I'm in a jam. Please call. Even if you hate me."

Chapter 10

Summer heat pressed at the blinds the next morning as Chelsea looked at the clock and groaned. "How could it be 8:30 already?"

There was no way to make it to work on time. But did it matter? She was going to resign anyway.

Tiny doubts began to creep in under the resolve. What about the stories still on her list to do? What about the rent?

"Oh God," she muttered, washing her face with cold water and remembering the note she'd left on Dunning's desk. That showdown hadn't happened yet. It was hard this morning to feel as angry as she had when she first saw the paper. Yet he had to know he couldn't run pictures of her nipples on page one and not hear about it. Especially if he planned to use the photo again as advertising. That was harassment, wasn't it?

Dunning was a sly guy. No pats on the butt from him, just a look, a sneer, a failure to promote women, and a deep-down belief that they existed for only one purpose.

Hell, she thought, sitting on the bed in her nightshirt. If nothing else, I need to try to set him straight. You can't change a guy like that, but you can let him know when he steps over the line. Maybe he could at least use a more innocuous photo for his ads.

Perhaps she wouldn't quit immediately. She'd warn him and start looking for another job.

She picked up the cordless phone she kept by the bed and punched in the Weekly Times number. "Hi, Berta, this is Chelsea. I overslept. I'll be there in about 45 minutes. Is Dunning in?"

"Just walked in."

"Try to hold onto him till I get there. I really need to talk to him."

"It's that picture, huh?"

"Yep."

"I can't blame you, Chelsea, but you know, you look really cool, like those chicks in the Olympics."

Chelsea shook her head. "Thanks. I wish everybody saw it that way."

"Oh, I've got another call. See you in a little while."

Chelsea had oatmeal with sliced bananas for breakfast, showered,

136

put on her navy blue "power" suit, took a deep breath and walked the three blocks to the office.

Berta waved her down at the door. Chelsea stared at the receptionist's new hairdo. Slicked straight up in black spikes, it had a fuchsia streak down the left side. She wore a black leather skirt and jacket with fluorescent pink earrings, necklace and bracelet. Her two-inch fingernails were also pink, and there was a tiny pink bead attached to her left nostril.

Despite her appearance, Berta was efficient. She had cleared a path to the boss for her this morning. "Mr. Dunning said for you to go right in when you got here."

"Thank you." This is it, she told herself. Be calm but firm. No tears, no yelling.

"Good morning, Chelsea," said Dunning, looking up from his Wall Street Journal. "Sit down." His tone was formal, his expression sober. "I hear you have a problem with our cover this week."

"Yes." She perched on the edge of the high-backed chair opposite the publisher's desk. "Mr. Dunning, I don't know if you realize how embarrassing that kind of photograph can be for a woman. I mean, my breasts are the prominent feature. I'm blushing just to talk about it. The guys in sports are laughing over it. People on the streets are staring at me. And, um, the person I've been dating won't even talk to me now. I'm shocked that you allowed this picture to run, especially with that headline. The prurient angle negates my accomplishment in winning the race."

"Oh now, aren't you overreacting just a little bit?" He set down his paper and looked over her head at the plaques on the opposite wall.

Chelsea clenched her hands into fists to keep from screaming. "No, I don't think so, Mr. Dunning. I mean, I was very relieved that my parents didn't get their copy of the paper this week. They would have been humiliated."

"What if the picture was of somebody else?" he said, linking his fingers together and fixing a half-smile on her.

He's trying to trick me, she thought. "I would hope you would never run that kind of photo of any woman." She smiled nervously. "What if this were a guy and his, um, his erect penis showed through

137

his shorts? Would you run that picture?" Now she was sure her face was glowing red.

"I don't think this is the same thing."

"Would you run it?" she repeated.

He placed his hands flat on the desk and looked away from her. "We'd probably cut him off at the waist."

"Of course you would. You might snicker a little in the composing room, but you'd never let that picture run."

Dunning looked at his watch and stood up. "So what do you want me to do now? The paper is already out."

Chelsea stood, too, and leaned over his desk. "I want you to swear that picture will never appear anywhere ever again, and I want to see any photo of me that you plan to publish before it goes to press."

"Okay. We'll try. I suppose you want a printed apology on page 1, too."

She shook her head. "That would just call people's attention back to the photo. Those who didn't catch it before would look for this week's paper to see what we were apologizing about."

Dunning shrugged. "Fine." He started toward the door, but Chelsea raised her hand.

"One more thing. If you ever embarrass me or any other woman like that again, I'm out of here. I almost turned in my resignation this morning, but I've still got stories I want to write."

The publisher turned, his eyes hard and cold. "If you're not happy here, you're welcome to go work elsewhere. I will run my paper as I see fit, and if it bothers your feminist sensibilities, maybe you can go find a job at Ms. Magazine. Or didn't they go out of business?" With that, he walked out, strode down the hall and slammed the door of the restroom. Chelsea stood staring at his big desk, empty except for the Wall Street Journal.

"You bastard," she whispered. She walked slowly to the newsroom, conscious of Berta's anxious gaze and Sarge, Mandy and Mel watching her as she went to her desk and sat down. From the reception area, she heard Berta whispering to one of the ad salespeople.

She tried to ignore them all and logged onto the computer, ready to start the stories piled on her desk.

A "message waiting" notice flashed at her from the bottom of her screen.

The message was from Mel. "You still quitting?"

"No," she typed back. "Not yet."

"Good," he returned. "Let's go to lunch."

"Okay." Tears tried to force their way out, but Chelsea squelched them back. She had work to do. Crying was for little girls.

"How long has it been since you got out of here for a real lunch?" Chelsea asked. She was squeezed into the front of Mel's Volvo. She had had to push the seat back and move a pile of newspapers and a brown teddy bear before she could sit down.

"Sorry for the mess," Mel said. "I seem to spend more time in this car than I do in my house these days."

"No problem."

As they turned onto Santa Clara Street, Mel punched on the stereo, and an old Bon Jovi tune poured out. Chelsea smiled and settled back against the velour seat. It reminded her of the old days when she and Mel were both students at Berkeley and used to share rides home to San Jose on weekends.

"You up for Mexican? I'm in the mood."

"Sure." She watched an old man push a shopping cart across the street against the light. Maybe it was time to bring her camera down here again to take pictures of the homeless people.

"So what did you end up doing last night?"

Chelsea chuckled. "I drank Dunning's Christmas Scotch."

"But you hate Scotch."

"I know."

"Then my mom called, and I was drunk, and I felt like I was 16 getting caught being bad. Not that I ever did anything wrong when I was 16. My folks rarely let me out of the house until I escaped to college. Maybe that was the Portuguese influence."

"Yeah?" Mel slid the car into a metered space at the curb in front of Mexico Lindo. "So what about this Portuguese stuff? You going to pursue it?"

"What do you mean?"

139

"I know you. I know you were thinking about doing a book, or at least some freelance pieces. That's why you took all those extra pictures."

"Well, yeah, but the nipples picture kind of squelched that. Simão won't even talk to me. I can just imagine what people like his mother will think."

"Give them some credit."

"Mel, it's like 1948 with those guys. A woman is supposed to be quiet and submissive and let the men be in charge. She must dress like a girl and never ever show her breasts on the front page of a newspaper."

"You talk like you were nude."

"Just about. It was the wet T-shirt look. Sexy but inappropriate."

"You looked good to me."

"Mel!" She punched his arm.

"But I wouldn't have run it on page one." He grinned, shut off the stereo and opened his door. "I might have hung it over my desk thought. Come on, I'll buy you a margarita."

Over a strawberry margarita and chicken tostada, Chelsea told him about her meeting with Dunning. Mel shook his head.

"You shouldn't have pushed him so hard, Chelsea. He's under a lot of pressure right now."

"You're siding with him?"

"No, of course not, but some of what you said could be misconstrued. You don't want to be enemies with him, even if he is a creep, which he is."

"What are you trying to say?"

Mel mashed his refried beans with his fork. "Nothing. Just now that you've said your say, try to be as accommodating as you possibly can for a while. He won't run another picture like that, but he will remember that you threatened him, and that could backfire on you in the future."

"You mean like I might not get a raise."

"Yeah, something like that." He hailed the waiter. "Can I get another margarita?"

"Will you be able to edit this afternoon?"

140

"Sure. Besides, your stories don't need much editing anyway. If you'd just get `lay' and `lie' straight."

"I thought I did. Besides it hardly ever comes up."

She sipped the melted ice at the bottom of her margarita and pondered Mel's warning. What was he not telling her?

A week passed with no word from Simão. Chelsea focused on her work, avoided Dunning as much as possible, and ran or worked out at the gym every night. Her notes and pictures on the Portuguese sat in a pile on the floor of her bedroom. Someday she'd file them away.

It was late Tuesday afternoon when Rosa called.

"Chelsea, hello," she whispered. "I am so sorry to bother you at work, but I have to call when Simão is not here."

"Why?"

"He thinks you are a bad influence on me. Filling my head with foolish ideas."

Chelsea rolled her eyes. "When did he say that?"

"After you were here that night."

"Oh. Has he said anything about me lately?"

"No, nothing. He was very angry about something, but I do not know what it was."

"Oh, Rosa. There was this picture of me in the paper, and I'm sure he thought it was very, well, improper."

"I did not see it. But it cannot be that bad."

"It is. I was very embarrassed, but I didn't do it on purpose. You must believe that. Anyway, what can I do for you?"

Her voice became quieter still. Chelsea strained, but couldn't catch the words. "Rosa, I'm sorry, I can't hear you."

Rosa cleared her throat and started again. "I want to work as an artist. Maybe you can help me. I could draw for the newspaper. Illustrations of articles, charts, anything. I need to make some money."

"Oh, gosh, I don't know." She looked out the window at the sparrows playing in the eaves. "Tell you what. Why don't you put together some samples of your work. Include that brochure from the cultural society. I'll set up a meeting with my editor."

"You are very kind to me."

141

"Rosa, I like you. And you're a good artist, from what I saw. Hold on just a second."

"Mel. What's your schedule like tomorrow?"

"Huh?" He jolted awake and rubbed his eyes. "Why?"

"I've got a friend who's an artist who'd like to do some work for us. Can she come show you some samples?"

"Well, we don't buy much art, but what the hell." He studied his calendar. "Tell her 2:00. I have to leave at 2:45 to pick up Carrie."

"Great." She spoke into the phone. "Rosa, can you come at 2 tomorrow?"

"Yes. Oh, thank you. You are so good."

Tell Simão, she thought. She gave Rosa directions, wondering as she hung up if Rosa had a car. Oh well, if she really wanted to, she would find a way to get here .

"Who is this friend?" Mel asked, pen poised over his calendar to note the appointment.

"Simão's sister Rosa. Rosa Freitas."

"Oh boy. Trying to get him back through his sister?"

"Hardly."

Chelsea was in the middle of a telephone interview with the new recreation department director when Rosa walked in the next day. Busy taking notes, she watched out of the corner of her eye as Rosa took a newspaper off the pile on the counter and studied the front page. Rosa glanced at Chelsea, then back to the page, her eyes serious.

After a minute, Rosa set the newspaper down and sat in the chair by the door, a cardboard portfolio beside her. She held her hands twisted tightly together in her lap.

"I'm sorry. What was that last sentence?" Chelsea realized she had stopped paying attention to the man on the other end of the line. She focused her eyes on her notebook and wrote, wishing she didn't have a dozen questions to ask before she could hang up.

She was still on the phone when Mel went out to greet Rosa and led her back to his desk.

It was hard not to listen in.

Rosa had dressed up in a silver-gray dress with a white collar and white buttons. Her shoes were gray pumps. Her short curly hair formed a dark cloud around her tanned face, accented with red lipstick.

Chelsea wondered if Simão would approve of his sister's stylish look. But then again, he wouldn't even have approved of her being here.

Mel caught her watching and shook his head at her.

Back to her interview. "So, what you're saying is that this new park you want to build will be a positive influence in a neighborhood where too many kids tend to join gangs instead of more wholesome activities?"

"Yes," the recreation director responded. Just try getting the money for it, Chelsea thought. Parks were always at the bottom of the city council's list.

Finally she reached her last question. "When would be a good time for me to come out and take a photo?"

She wasn't prepared for the answer: Right now. He was going out to the park site and she could join him. He was leaving town tomorrow and wouldn't be back for a week.

She hung up, gathered her notebook and camera and stood.

"Heading out?" said Mel.

"I have to shoot Francisco at the park today or not at all."

"All right. Rosa's got some pretty good stuff here."

"That's great." Chelsea moved toward Mel's desk, looking at the drawing that sat on top. It was a sketch of Simão on the steps at the Holy Ghost festival. She had never realized Rosa was there. But they hadn't met yet.

"I got the same shot with my camera."

"I know," she smiled. "I drew this from your photograph."

"Oh. Well. . ." She grabbed a pen off Mel's desk and scrawled her telephone number on a scrap of paper. "Call me at home, okay? I want to know how you make out."

"Thank you very much," Rosa said, folding the paper carefully.

Chelsea left, grumbling to herself on the way to her truck about having to run out to take a picture of a fat ugly old man standing in an open field next to a sign.

When she called that night, Rosa was practically screaming in her excitement. "He said I could do one illustration a week, for things you couldn't get pictures of, and to dress up feature stories. He is going to pay me $50 for each one."

Chelsea sat back in her kitchen chair and pushed away the empty plastic plate that had held her Weight Watchers lasagna dinner. "That's fabulous. Have you ever sold your work before?"

"No! I've done paintings for gifts, and I do all the brochures and flyers for Simão's groups, but nobody ever paid me money. Money of my own, Chelsea! Of course, much of it will have to go to help pay Avó's hospital bills, but--"

"Avó?"

"My grandmama. In the nursing home. She is very old, 86 this year, and it costs so much money. Simão, he is trying to do everything by himself. He is too stubborn to admit he cannot do it all. Mama is too old to work, but I can help."

"Of course you can. You know, if you took some courses in graphic arts, you could probably get a regular job at the Weekly Times or another newspaper."

"Simão would never allow that."

"School or the job?"

"Both."

"You're an adult, Rosa. Why do you let him tell you what to do?"

"Oh, he is impossible when I--" Her voice lowered suddenly. "He is home now."

"So what? Can't you talk on the telephone?"

"Yes, but if he knew I was talking to you. . . Let us talk about something else so he will not know. Tell me about your family."

Chelsea described her mother and father, noting her half-Portuguese/half-German roots. She told her about going to college in Berkeley and living in Sacramento and Washington with Jeffrey.

"You were in love?"

She closed her eyes. "I guess so. Jeffrey and I were best friends, you know, but we were also lovers."

"But you did not get married?"

"No, we were both too involved in our careers. Now sometimes I wonder if we should have gotten married anyway and forced it to work. But I don't know. With Jeff, it was always Senator somebody or

144

Representative somebody who came first. I was somewhere down the list. How about you? What are you, 24, 25?"

"26. I--Simão had this friend he wanted me to go out with, so I did. He was nice, but I did not feel anything. I kept looking around, and every other man I saw was more interesting. I do have this friend now. . ." Her voice got even lower and Chelsea wished she could turn up the volume. "He is an American. From Texas. He works at the airport. Very handsome. We have gone out three times when Simão did not know."

"Rosa!"

"He is a very good kisser, Chelsea." Rosa giggled.

"Is this serious?"

Chelsea heard a commotion in the background and Simão's voice speaking Portuguese. He sounded angry. Suddenly he came on the line.

"Do not talk to my sister, please. You are a bad influence. You pose for dirty pictures and then you promise her a job at that same filthy place where you work."

"Simão!" Chelsea protested. "That is not fair!" But he had hung up.

"Damn it!" she screamed, pounding the table so hard her plate flew off and landed upside down on the floor in a smear of tomato sauce.

Was it just Portuguese men or were all men crazy, Chelsea wondered at Danny's Gym the next night as she pedaled the exercise bike up an imaginary hill. Her eyes were on the red and amber lights that charted her progress, but her mind was miles away.

Simão really did seem to hate her, and the only reason she could guess was that picture in the paper. It came out, and boom, he wouldn't talk to her, wouldn't give her a chance to explain. She supposed he hadn't heard about the American legal system's view that one is innocent until proven guilty.

The way he wouldn't let Rosa speak to her was absolutely medieval. She wondered if he would prevent Rosa from working for Mel. It would be criminal if he did.

"God, your heart rate's up to 145," said Stacy, a young aerobics

145

teacher who was warming up on the bike next to hers."

"I'm fine," Chelsea responded, feeling as if her mind and body were not in the same place.

Stacy dismounted and stretched her arms over her head. "It's almost time for class. Why don't you rest a few minutes and come join us?"

Chelsea shrugged, her eyes still on the lights on the computer display. The little heart sign came on and showed her rate was up to 151. She sighed and eased back. Stacy was probably right. Usually she did 20 minutes, then went to the weights. She feared if she picked up the free weights tonight she might throw them at somebody.

In the big exercise room, the rock music got louder, and she heard Stacy shouting. "All right, are we ready? Let's go! To the left, two, three, four. . ."

Chelsea slid off the bike and stretched. Heading for the locker room, she glimpsed herself in the mirror. Her gray leotard was streaked with sweat. Standing in the cool air pumped out by the oversized fans that stood in every corner, she shivered and noticed those rebel breasts standing out again.

Armor. I need a bra made out of iron. She changed into her bathing suit and plunged into the lukewarm water of the lap pool. She swam the length of the pool freestyle, back and forth, listening to the aerobics music thump through the walls. When she couldn't swim anymore, she would sit in the hot tub for a while. Then she'd shower and go home to bed, get up in the morning and go back to work. What else was there?

She floated, staring at the blue ceiling. "I need a vacation," she decided. "It's summer. Why not?" As soon as she figured out where and when she wanted to go, she would talk to Dunning. Or maybe she'd ask Mel to talk to Dunning. The farther she stayed from that creep the better.

Two men came into the room, their voices echoing off the brick walls, their faces blurred in the mist rising from hot tub. They stood flexing above the water for a minute, then dove in, their wakes dashing water into her face. Chelsea swam toward the ladder. Time to go home.

Hours later, she lay awake in bed, staring at the moon through the gap in the beige curtains, and knew she would never sleep until she talked to Simão.

Jeffrey hadn't called back, she noted. Men were all scum. Maybe she should go work for Ms. The magazine had gone out of business, but it had been resurrected in a new no-advertising format. Maybe Dunning didn't know that. New York wouldn't be so bad. After all, it was supposed to be the Mecca for writers.

She sat on the edge of the bed and dialed Simão's number. It was only 11:30. Judging by how late he had dinner, he'd probably still be up.

He answered on the first ring. "*Boa noite.*" His voice was stern and tired.

"Simão, please don't hang up," she said, unconsciously pulling her nightshirt down toward her knees. "We have to talk."

"I do not think there is anything to talk about."

She switched on the lamp next to the bed. "Yes, there is. We were becoming good friends, and then suddenly you won't speak to me. I suppose--"

"You know--"

"Let me finish before you tell me what a whore I am. I suppose that picture on the front of the Weekly Times is what turned you against me. And that is not fair. I had no idea that picture had been taken or that it was going in the newspaper. I had no say in it. Nobody showed it to me. My publisher is a sleazeball who thinks he can sell more papers if he runs sexy pictures."

"Yes, but--"

"Simão, let me talk. I was incredibly embarrassed. I almost quit my job, and I told my publisher I would if he ever did this again. I did not mean to do anything to offend anybody. I just wanted to run the race. And I am proud that I won. That's a pretty good accomplishment, and I needed something to feel proud of lately."

She stopped and felt her body shaking.

"Are you finished?"

She took a deep breath and let it out slowly. "Yes."

"You must understand that I have a position to uphold in the

147

Portuguese community. I cannot be attached to a woman who appears half naked in the newspaper. Not only that, but everyone who was at the race saw you that way."

"That is how runners dress. You must know that."

"Then you should not be a runner. You are a woman, almost 30 years old. You should be someone's wife and mother, not racing like a child."

"Oh, for God's sake. Haven't you ever watched the Olympics?"

"No, I have no interest in this."

"Does Portugal even compete?"

"I do not know. In the Azores, we have only *futebol*--what you call soccer, and it is played by men."

"Simão, this is America. Grown women run races and are proud to do it. I'm sorry if that picture embarrassed you. As I said, it embarrassed the hell out of me. But I can't do anything about it. And if you cared about me, you would at least talk to me before you shut me off completely."

Simão said nothing. Chelsea pictured him standing very tall in his three-piece suit beside the lace-covered dining room table in his old-fashioned house.

"Simão?"

"I do not know what to say. I do not know how to understand what you do."

"You don't have to understand it. Just accept it. I'm a runner. Hell, even the president runs."

"He is a man. Does his wife run?"

"I don't know. She's--never mind. Before you hang up, can we talk about your sister?"

"No. I have plans for her life. I do not want you to get in the way."

Chelsea gasped in frustration. "I'm not getting in her way. She told me she needs to make some money because you can't afford to support your whole family by yourself."

His voice was frosty. "That is my affair. What does Rosa know about money?"

"Practically nothing. Thanks to you."

"Women do not need to know about financial matters."

Her head felt like it was about to explode. The words tumbled out of her mouth before she had time to think. "Simão, you are a conceited macho jerk." She hung up and hurled the portable phone across the room. It crashed against her old pine dresser.

"Shit!" she hollered, picking up the phone. She was relieved to hear a dial tone.

She was still sitting on the side of the bed in her nightshirt when she heard a gentle knock on the front door. "Aw jeez, now what?"

Halfway hoping it would be Simão come to apologize, although he couldn't be here this soon, she looked out the peephole and saw John, dressed in his police uniform and ready for work.

She opened the door a crack. "Hi."

"You okay? I heard a crash and shouting."

"Oh, man. I'm sorry if I worried you. I'm fine. Just furious at this guy. I was so mad I threw the telephone across the room."

He chuckled. "At least you took it out on an inanimate object. You sure you're okay?"

"Oh, yeah, I'm fine. But I don't think I'll ever get to sleep."

"Try a hot toddy, my mother's remedy. Of course, my wife swears by Tylenol. Says it puts her to sleep even though there's no logical reason for it."

"Maybe I'll try both. Hope I didn't wake up the baby."

"She's already up. We couldn't get her to sleep. She and the wife are watching an old movie. Well, I've got to go to work."

"Okay. Thanks for looking out for me. I'll throw something softer next time."

She watched him drive away, then went into the kitchen, flipped on the light and started a pot of coffee. She had to put her energy to use somehow and she knew what she wanted to do. She pulled out her notes on the Portuguese and started making an outline. She was going to do that book to vindicate women like Anna Silva and Rosa Freitas to show how they persevered despite the macho jerks they were married or related to.

She would find a Portuguese teacher. Maybe she'd even start going to the Portuguese church. She didn't need Simão to lead her by the hand or give her permission. She was Portuguese and Catholic, too.

This weekend she would sit down with her mother and make her tell every last detail about the women in her family.

Chapter Eleven

Chelsea found her father digging a ditch around the blackberries in the back yard. He looked up, nodded and focused back on the earth beneath his big wrinkled hands. "Couldn't get any water in here anymore," he said. "It all just ran right off."

"How are you?" she asked. His shovel barely nicked the earth. There seemed to be no strength behind it.

"I'm okay." He moved a clump of dirt onto the dam he was building around the berries.

She watched him pat the dirt in place, then struggle to his feet with a groan. He leaned the shovel against the fence and walked toward the faucet, his lean body sloped forward as if he were being pulled by a chain around his neck toward the ground.

In a minute, water hissed through the hose and filled the ditch with a chocolate milkshake of water and dirt. Dad stood with his hands on his hips staring at the water. He worked his lower lip in and out of his teeth as the water seeped into the ground, leaving a dark wet spot around the berries. He turned off the tap, coiled the hose and carried it back to the rack behind the faucet.

"Time to rest now?" Chelsea asked, forcing a smile. She had never seen her father look so worn out. It frightened her.

"I've got all the time in the world to rest," he said, bending to pluck a weed out of the mud.

"You can fight this, you know."

"Honey, I'm almost 60 years old. I'm washed up."

"I think you have grounds for a lawsuit."

"I don't want to sue them. If they don't want me, they don't want me."

"You can't just give up."

He fixed his hazel eyes on her. His cheeks were haggard, stained with red from hours working in the sun. "It's my business, little girl."

He started toward the house, then turned back. "I need a beer. You want one?"

"Sure. Thanks, Dad."

He trudged up the steps, clumping his shoes on the porch, slapping the dirt off his hands.

151

Chelsea had come armed with notebook and tape recorder to interview her mother. But Mom had greeted her at the door raging about her husband's former employers. "Do you know what your father's boss just did?"

"No.

"He fired him. Said he didn't fit into their new management plan. What he really meant was he's too old. Well, that's discrimination. I told your father to call a lawyer. They just can't do this." Mom's voice lowered. "Can they?"

Chelsea shook her head. "Well, I'm not a lawyer, but I don't think they can. They have to have a lot more substantial reason to get rid of someone."

"They said they were reorganizing their staff and there just wasn't a place for your father. That's bull. He's the best they ever had."

"I know, Mom. Maybe he can find something better."

"At 58? He might as well be a hundred years old."

A buzzer went off in the kitchen. "Oh, that's the apricot pie. I made it to cheer him up. Not that anything will. Go see your father while I get it out of the oven."

Now the pie was cooling on the counter as Chelsea and her father came in the back door. Dad took his beer to the den and slumped in the recliner. Chelsea lingered in the kitchen, where her mother was tearing up lettuce for a salad.

"Can I help?"

"No, no. You just relax. You work hard all week. Sit down, enjoy your beer."

Chelsea pulled out her chair by the stove. "I'm going to do that book, Mom. About Portuguese women."

Her mother reached for a tomato and sliced it into narrow rings. "I guess that boyfriend of yours will be a big help."

"We're, um, not together anymore. So I need to talk to you about Grandma and Aunt Julia and all the rest."

Mom slammed the knife onto the cutting board. "What did you do, chase him away?" She picked up the knife and started another tomato. "Never mind. I don't want to know. This thing with your father's got me crazy enough."

"I know." Chelsea stared into her Budweiser can, thinking.

"Mom, do you have enough to live on without Dad working?"

"I don't know. We've got some savings, but it's going to be tight. He can't collect Social Security yet."

"He could take them to court."

"Your father won't even discuss it." Mom chopped both ends off a fresh carrot, peeled it, and grated into the salad. "He doesn't care. It's his ego, you know. It really hurts to be told you're too old, even if it's just implied. He loved his job. Now what's he going to do?"

She shook bacon bits into the salad, poured in a dollop of bottled thousand island dressing and covered the bowl with plastic wrap. "There, that's done. We'll just wait for the ham to be finished."

From the other room, Chelsea heard a sonorous voice narrating a nature show. The TV was turned up so loud she could hear the rushing of a river and the chattering of wild birds. As she passed, she saw her father sitting with his elbows on his knees, his head bent toward the TV. The afternoon light coming through the gauzy curtains made his wispy hair look white and thin. He didn't even glance up as she passed.

At dinner, she looked around the cheery kitchen with its yellow walls and cross-stitched pictures. Outside, pale pink roses bloomed, and she could see a squirrel perched in the walnut tree in the twilight. Nothing had ever changed in this house. But what if her parents couldn't afford to stay here anymore? She wanted to ask about a pension or severance pay, but her father was picking at his ham, shoving it from one side of the plate to another, and she didn't want to anger him again.

It would be hard, maybe impossible, for him to find another job. If he couldn't work, what would they do?

And what would happen when her parents got older and maybe started having serious health problems?

She thought of Simão supporting his sister, mother, and grandmother on dreams and whatever he made at the fish market. All her life, she had never had to worry about taking care of another person. Now she felt a shiver in the warm breeze that waved the yellow and white curtains on the window over the sink.

To think she had almost quit her own job in a snit, with nothing to fall back on.

Silence hung over the table. Mom spoke first. "Chelsea's going to do that book, Carl."

"What book?" He didn't look up.

"The one about the women in our family and other Portuguese women," Chelsea said.

"Waste of time," he growled.

Chelsea's jaw dropped. Her father had always backed her, no matter what she did, even when she moved to Sacramento to be with Jeffrey and later went on to Washington, D.C. He was always excited about her work. He's just depressed, she told herself, but it still stung. She watched him roll his baked potato over and set down his fork.

"The sonogram showed your cousin's having a girl," Mom said.

"That's nice."

Her plate was empty too soon, and she wasn't hungry for more. Nobody was. The heap of brown sugar-glazed ham sat almost untouched.

That night as she was brushing her hair, she noticed a gray strand among the brown. She bent closer to the mirror to be sure. The hair was long, must have been there a while. How had she not noticed it before?

She studied her face. Crow's feet had sneaked in around her eyes when she wasn't looking, and there was a tracing of lines along her forehead. Of course the years were beginning to show. Her parents were almost senior citizens. No wonder Mom was anxious for her to marry and have a family.

Why was it that Simão's house came into her mind now? She felt again how cozy it had been sinking into that plush sofa, eating his mother's chocolates, looking at the faces in the family photos while Simão sat nearby admiring her. What would it be like to have children and grandchildren, to line up their photos on the mantel and feed them fudge and roast beef on Sunday afternoons?

Going for a glass of water, she looked around her kitchen with its tiny table for two, the computer set up in the corner, the tripod and boxes of photos in the pantry where another woman might have stored cake mixes and canned goods. The cupboards and freezer contained only instant food. Nothing in the apartment showed the touch of loving hands making a home for someone else, except the few things her mother had given her, like the pillows on the sofa and the pink and white afghan across the foot of her bed.

Her life had always been about work. What if some day she got hit by a bus and couldn't work anymore? She'd be alone in this apartment, starving because nobody except her parents cared and going crazy because she had nothing else to do.

"I never planned it this way," she said to the walls. She went into the living room and ran her fingers over her portfolio on the coffee table. "My clips look good. But they're only stories and pictures."

She heard a wail as the baby downstairs started another tantrum. "A human being. That's an accomplishment."

She kicked off her sandals, trading them for running shoes. "I'm losing my mind."

When she returned from her run 40 minutes later, she threw open the windows, took off her shoes and sat down at the phone, holding her breath as she dialed. "Please, please," she whispered.

Rosa answered, and she let the air out in relief. "Rosa, it's Chelsea. Can we get together tomorrow?"

In the silence, Chelsea heard her neighbor's child still shrieking.

Then Rosa answered, her voice determined. "Yes. Tell me where to meet you."

Chelsea waited nervously outside the nursing home. Through the glass doors, she could see three old women in wheelchairs lined up in the hallway. She was struck by a skinny lady with pearly white hair who sat bent over, staring at the floor. Something about her face reminded her of her father's mother, Grandma Marie, who had died when she was little.

In the next chair sat a fat, toothless Japanese woman with just a few strands of dark hair curled over her bald head. She stared at the door as if she were waiting for someone.

The third woman was all in black. At first Chelsea thought she was a nun. But the black scarf she wore around her wizened face was not that of a nun but a Portuguese widow. Was this Simão's grandmother?

Chelsea looked down the street for Rosa. She didn't have a car.

She had planned to take the bus and walk the last two blocks. They had agreed that it would not be a good idea for Chelsea to pick her up. If Simão found out, he would be furious. Chelsea didn't want to see him anyway.

Maybe this is a crazy idea, she thought, aware of a nurse studying her from inside, no doubt wondering what she was doing loitering outside the door.

At the far end of the block, Rosa turned the corner and walked toward her. Her plaid skirt, white blouse and green sweater reminded Chelsea of Catholic school uniforms. Of course, she wasn't much more stylish herself today. She'd put on a navy blue dress for this visit and pushed her hair back with big flowered barrettes.

For a minute, she let herself wonder what it would be like to be sisters-in-law with Rosa, dutifully visiting their grandmother on Sunday afternoons. Afterward they would go home, and she could help her mother-in-law make dinner. Maybe there would be children to watch over, to put to bed early. . .

"*Olá*, Chelsea," Rosa greeted her. She surprised her with a hug and a kiss on each cheek. "Avó is just inside. I see her."

"I thought that might be her." Chelsea glanced in, feeling nerves dancing in her stomach. "She doesn't speak any English, right?"

"No. Not a word. Well, no, that is not true. She knows "Yes," "No" and "It is time for supper." Rosa chuckled. "I will translate, do not worry." Rosa pushed a buzzer beside the door, and a young Filipino man in a white uniform unlocked the door. "Let's go."

Chelsea followed Rosa hesitantly into the dimly-lighted hallway.

"*Avó. Como está?*" said Rosa, kneeling before her grandmother, grasping her hand.

"Ah, Rosa," said the grandmother, launching into a stream of Portuguese that Chelsea couldn't understand. Her voice rose in anger, and Rosa patted her shoulder, responding in soothing tones.

"She wants to go home," she explained to Chelsea. "She hates the food here, the workers are rude, and the only nurse who spoke Portuguese has left to have a baby."

"Oh," said Chelsea, aware of the Japanese woman and the white-haired one staring at her.

Rosa told her grandmother, "*Esta é a minha amiga Chelsea que é uma boa escritora.*"

Grandma looked up. "*Escritora?*" She reached for Chelsea's hand and held it tight in her gnarled fingers. "*Muito linda.*"

Chelsea had heard those words before. "Thank you, Mrs. Freitas."

"Avó!"

"Hm?" Chelsea turned to Rosa.

"Call her Avó. Grandmother," she says.

"Oh. Thank you." The old woman was still gripping her hand, and Chelsea's back was beginning to feel the strain of leaning over. "Can we go someplace to talk?"

"Yes, there is a sitting room or the dining room, or we can go to Avó's room."

Avó was looking up, waiting for an explanation. "*Aonde vamos, Avó?*" said Rosa.

"*O meu quarto,*" said the old woman without hesitation.

"Her room. It's just down here to the right."

Rosa pushed the wheelchair down the long hallway, nodding at the nurses they passed. Chelsea noted the faint smell of urine. In one of the rooms, a woman hollered, "Help me! Help me!" Chelsea wanted to run for help, but Rosa said she yelled that way all the time.

Cardboard signs on the doors named the patients and labeled the restrooms for men or women. In a sitting room on the left, a shriveled black man was asleep sitting up in front of the TV. They passed a room where an attendant was changing a diaper on a bony old woman. Chelsea looked away, pressing her lips together.

"It is not a very fancy place," Rosa said, as if reading her mind. "But the people who work here give a lot of love to the residents."

"How did your grandmother wind up here instead of at home?"

"She broke her hip, and it did not heal right. And then she has some other problems, diabetes and her heart. Mama wanted to keep her at home, but Simão said no, it is too hard. I think he wanted to show off his money, too, by giving her professional care."

"Money certainly is important to him."

"Yes. But he is a good man, Chelsea. Just stubborn. He was so happy while he was seeing you. I think you were good for him. Then I do not know what happened."

"That picture in the paper. . . "

Rosa shook her head. "That? That was nothing."

Chelsea stared at her.

"Okay. It was sexy. But Simão is being foolish. It is not the first time."

Grandma looked up at Rosa and complained.

"She says we are talking as if she isn't here. The nurses do that all the time. She hates it. Avó, *sabemos que está aqui, e este é o seu quarto.*"

In the afternoon sun, muted with light cotton curtains, Avó's room was as sweet and comfortable as Simão's house. An orange and black afghan, the same pattern as her own pink and white one, lay across the puffy beige comforter on her bed. Photos of Rosa, Simão, and others Chelsea didn't know were arranged on the dresser. On the nightstand, she saw a statue of the Virgin Mary at Fatima, a red votive candle with the wax half melted down, a tiny black prayerbook and a string of amber rosary beads. The room smelled faintly of lavender and roses.

Rosa rolled her grandmother's wheelchair next to the bed and gestured to Chelsea to sit in one of the brown easy chairs nearby. They matched the sofa at Simão's house, and Chelsea guessed they had been brought from home.

Rosa took a brush out of the dresser drawer, removed Avó's scarf and started to work on the old woman's bristle of gray and white hair. She spoke softly into her grandmother's ear and the woman looked at Chelsea with sudden interest.

"I told her you want to interview her and to write about her. She likes that idea, wants to know how soon she can see it."

"Can she read English?"

Rosa shook her head, smiling. "She can barely read Portuguese. But she is still excited about being in a book. What do you want to ask her?"

Chelsea pulled her notebook out of her purse and fixed her eyes on the old woman's as Avó sat letting Rosa brush her hair. Without looking away, Chelsea reached into her purse and switched on a miniature tape recorder. "What is your first name?"

"*Quer saber o seu nome.*"

"Maria Dolores Gomes Freitas." The woman said the words slowly, wonderingly, as if she rarely heard them anymore.

Chelsea repeated the name as she wrote it.

Avó looked at the notebook and nodded. "Ah." She grinned, showing a row of perfect plastic teeth that looked too big for her mouth. Chelsea noticed faint dark hairs on her upper lip and chin. It was a plain face that had probably never worn makeup. She was conscious of her own carefully applied eyeliner, blush and pink lipstick.

"How old are you?"

"*Quantos anos tem?*"

"86."

"Tell me about your life." Avó spoke rapidly, leaning forward in her wheelchair, as Rosa translated for Chelsea.

"Maria Dolores Gomes grew up in a dirt-floored cottage on the coast of Pico island. She was married at 14 to Pedro Freitas. She didn't even know him. Her father had arranged the match. Pedro, only 15 himself, came from another village. His family supposedly had money and would take good care of Maria Dolores. With nine brothers and sisters left at home, her parents were anxious to marry her off and ease the burden a little, although they would miss her help sweeping the floors and holding the twin baby boys when they cried.

"The Frietases talked big, and they gave a lavish wedding, with days of feasting and dancing. Maria felt like a commoner marrying a prince. She knew her in-laws had many cows, and their house was bigger than the Gomes'. She would not have to scrimp as her mother had.

"But Maria quickly discovered Pedro's family had told many lies. They were not nearly as rich as they claimed, and worse, they did not get along with each other.

"She and Pedro were sent to live in a one-room cottage down the coast in the middle of the fields. The father had quarreled with Pedro shortly before the wedding and would give him no money. Live off

159

your own labor, he told him. After that, Pedro was mean to everybody, but especially Maria Dolores.

"'I don't need a wife,' he told her on their wedding night. 'I only do this because they make me. I want to go to America. How can I save my money and leave on a boat if I have a woman holding me back? If you have a baby, I will not help you. I am leaving in one year, when I am sixteen.'

"With that, he turned his back to her and went to sleep, snoring from all the wine he had drunk that day. Maria Dolores cried and lay awake all night, missing the sounds of her little sisters and the twins, wishing she could run back to Mama. But her family must never know this wasn't the best thing for her. They would be heartbroken, and besides, there was no divorce in those days.

"Pedro had said nothing about taking Maria with him to America. What if he went alone, she worried. He might slip away in the night like so many young men did, leaving her to explain the disgrace of a husband who didn't want her. She would be forced to lie, to say he was coming back for her."

Chelsea relied on her tape recorder, taking only a few notes. Staring at the old woman, she saw the girl she had been and felt her pain at being so young and unloved.

"What happened?" she asked.

"*O que é que aconteceu?*"

Avó stared into space and talked on, her throaty voice a soft shushing and jhhzing.

"For one whole week, she and her new husband had not slept together as husband and wife, and Maria grew more and more anxious. She cleaned the filthy little cabin until it shone. She mended Pedro's shirts, pants and socks, even his old leather shoes. She cooked the best she could with the vegetables she could gather from the garden and the rotting meat left over from the wedding. She gave Pedro the biggest portions and took little for herself, still hungry when she went to bed. But nothing pleased Pedro. His temper grew worse with each day.

"Then on the seventh night, a Sunday after they had gone to Mass and Pedro had been drinking *vinho* and playing cards with his friends till late, he came home, pushed her into the bed and tore her clothes off. 'You are my wife,' he said. 'You must do your duty.'

160

"She was terrified. When he entered her, she felt as if she were being torn apart, and she prayed to the Virgin Mary for strength. Pedro didn't care that she cried out in pain or that there was blood on the sheets afterward. 'Clean it up and be quiet,' he said. Oh, he was a bad one. She cleaned it up and said nothing.

"That night, she ran all the way from that village to her home, waking her mother and father late in the night. She didn't dare stay with Pedro for fear he would kill her. She told them what a monster her husband was, how he had hurt her, how she had to live alone with him in this horrible little cottage.

"Her papa cried to think what he had done to his oldest daughter, how he had ruined her life because he wanted money. But now that she was married, he didn't know what he could do. She didn't care, she said, she was not going back. After all, she was only 14." Rosa turned to Chelsea. "Think about when you were 14."

Chelsea sighed. At 14, she was a gawky adolescent, still getting used to having periods, in love with rock stars and movie actors, playing badminton in the back yard. "What happened?"

"The worst possible thing. Maria got pregnant. From that first awful time. There was no choice. She had to go back. But her papa talked to Pedro's father and insisted Pedro and Maria be taken back into the big house. So it was better. Pedro's mother looked after Maria Dolores and scolded Pedro when he was mean. There was no private place to have sex, even though their house was bigger than Maria Dolores' father's house. They slept in the living room. As Maria's stomach got bigger, Pedro didn't want her anyway. He was gone all the time, working in the fields or playing cards and drinking with his friends."

Chelsea shook her head. "This is so sad."

Rosa nodded. "It is. I never heard all this before."

Avó was staring out the window at the tops of pine trees that swayed in the schoolyard next door. She began to speak again.

As Chelsea listened, her eyes widened. How could anyone be so cruel, she thought. "The night Avó gave birth to her son, Jose, Pedro left. It hadn't been a full year, and he wasn't quite 16, but she heard

161

later that three of his older friends had arranged to meet a whaling boat, and he went along. Not a word of goodbye.

"Of course Maria Dolores was hurt by this, but it was a relief to have Pedro gone. He was so cruel. Never a kind word or touch. He called her stupid and ugly. He hit her for no reason. Deep in her heart, she was glad he had left. But of course, now she was only 15, and she had a baby and no husband. He'll come back or send for you, people said, but she didn't want him to do that." Avó's voice lowered and she bent closer to Rosa. "Secretly, she hoped he would drown. Then she would be free of him forever. May God forgive her these evil thoughts."

"Mrs. Freitas," a voice interrupted from the doorway. "It's almost time for supper."

Avó smiled suddenly and nodded at Rosa. "*Jantar*," she said.

"Okay." Rosa turned to Chelsea who still sat spellbound by Avó's tale. "It is time for supper." Rosa got up and started to swing the wheelchair toward the door.

Chelsea hesitated. "But. . ."

"We'll have to get the rest of the story next time. Avó doesn't want to miss dinner."

Avó said something else, and Rosa laughed. "She doesn't want any of those old busybodies to know her secrets."

"Oh," said Chelsea, switching off the tape recorder. She stood, stiff from sitting so long in the chair. The tufts of upholstery had made a bumpy pattern on the backs of her legs. She bent toward Avó. "Mrs. Freitas, Avó, I am very interested in your story. You've had a fascinating life."

After Rosa translated, Avó stared at her for a minute, then barked a question at Rosa.

"She wants to know, aren't you the girl that Simão was going out with?"

Chelsea nodded, startled. "Yes. I was, but . . ."

Avó spoke again. "Good, she says. She likes you."

"But. . ."

Rosa waved her hand at her and shook her head. She bent and kissed her grandmother on the top of her hair, now combed into a neat bun. "*Até terça-feira.*"

"Goodbye," Chelsea said, patting the old woman's hand.

Avó pulled her down for a musty kiss. *"Obrigada, linda. Adeus, a minha Rosa."*

On the way out, Rosa said, "Please don't complicate things by talking about your quarrel with Simão. Avó would just get upset. Besides, I feel you two will get back together."

"I don't see how."

"We Portuguese women have a lot of, what do you call it, where we know things before they happen."

"Intuition?"

"Perhaps that's it."

"I think you're wrong on this one, Rosa."

As she held the door and they went out, Rosa smiled. "Not me. I know that for all your American ways, you have a Portuguese heart and it is tied to Simão."

"I don't know whether I want you to be right or wrong."

"He is not like Pedro," Rosa said. They had reached Chelsea's truck. "I promise."

She dropped Rosa off at the bus stop, leaving her still waving as she drove toward her apartment, her head full of the story of Maria Dolores and Pedro, wondering about the story of Chelsea and Simão.

Chapter Twelve

Chelsea sprinted up the stairs at Mission College, thinking the building looked more like a shopping mall than a school. Classrooms surrounded a broad open space where tee-shirt-clad students who looked like they were barely old enough for high school sipped colas and pondered their schedules for the fall semester.

Still in her slacks and blazer from work, Chelsea felt more like a teacher than a student and she was baffled by the numbering system which labeled the rooms north, east, south and west. She paused at the top of the stairs, looking for S233.

She started to her left, then heard voices behind her. A heavyset woman with an unruly brush of gray and black hair panted as she talked to a tall young man on her way up the stairs. They were speaking Portuguese. Chelsea wheeled around.

"Excuse me, are you by any chance going to the Portuguese class?"

The woman nodded. "God, these stairs. I always ask for a classroom downstairs, but no. Anyway yes, I am Gabriela Machado, and I am the teacher for beginning Portuguese." She turned to the young man. "Could you get me something to drink? I can't do these stairs again, and I am suddenly very thirsty."

Her accent was like Simão's. Chelsea swallowed the wave of longing that rose from her stomach. Simão always said she didn't need to take Portuguese. She would show him he was wrong. "I'm glad I ran into you. I'm Chelsea Faust, and I'm in your class, but I can't find the room."

"I'll show you." Gabriela looked her over and nodded. "I like the older students better. They want to learn. They're not just filling up a list of requirements. Why do you want to study Portuguese?"

"Well," she began, "I'm half Portuguese, on my mother's side, and I've been doing some research on my roots for some writing projects, but I find myself left out of too many conversations because I don't speak Portuguese."

"I see. Your mother doesn't speak any Portuguese?"

"None. She never learned."

"That is too bad. It happens a lot here in America. My own

164

children don't want to speak Portuguese either. But I make sure they know how. If they want to ask me for something to eat or for permission to go out on a date, they have to ask me in Portuguese." She held up the silver-dollar-sized watch hanging from a chain around her neck. "I am late again. These damn stairs."

Chelsea and her teacher walked together into the small wedge-shaped classroom where a dozen students sat waiting, notebooks open.

"*Boa noite,*" Gabriela said as Chelsea took a seat close to the door.

They stared at her.

Gabriela shook her head. "No. I want you to repeat what I say. *Boa noite.* It means good night or good evening." She scrawled it on the blackboard.

Chelsea repeated the words with the class. She had heard that one before when she was out with Simão, but she copied it onto her notepad, then pulled out her tape recorder and turned it on.

An hour and a half later, she had filled several pages with Portuguese words and information about her fellow students. The man up front was marrying a woman from the Azores. The gray-bearded professor type was taking a sabbatical in Brazil next summer. The pretty woman in white needed Portuguese for her work as a nurse at San Jose Medical Center. When Chelsea said she was a writer, several, including Gabriela, said they had seen her special section on the Portuguese in the Weekly Times.

At the break, Gabriela approached. "So, you are not finished writing about us Portuguese yet."

Chelsea smiled. "No. I'm working on a book on Portuguese women.. Maybe I could interview you."

"Sure. Any time. But right now, I must find the restroom."

As Gabriela rustled out, Lyle, the English professor from the University of California at Santa Cruz, lingered at Chelsea's side. "I'm interested in your book," he said "Have you written others?"

"No, but I've published many articles." Other students leaned closer to listen, and she told about her Washington stories.

Her celebrity soon faded when class resumed. Gabriela pointed at Chelsea and asked, in Portuguese, "*Onde mora*? Where do you live?"

165

Chelsea couldn't remember how to say "I live." "*Bebo em San Jose?*"

Several class members giggled, and Gabriela guffawed. When she caught her breath, she said, "No, no. *Bebo* is 'I drink.' I don't care where you drink. It is "*Moro em* San Jose." She pronounced the j with a soft zhhh and the e with a lilt off the end of her tongue--zzho-SEH. "Sit down, listen again."

Gabriela went over the verbs on the board one more time as the class repeated them, and the three-hour session passed quickly. Chelsea slipped out as Gabriela was signing forms for students hoping to add the class.

Outside, the cool air felt good. Portuguese words kept repeating themselves in her mind. *Boa noite. Bom dia. Boa tarde. Faz favor. Obrigado. Moro, bebo, como.* So much to learn. She climbed into her truck. An old Beach Boy tune blasted her ears as she turned the ignition. She searched for the radio station the teacher had told the class about. Soon a soft voice murmured in Portuguese, and Chelsea wished with all her heart she could understand some of it, any of it. She smiled then as she heard *"boa noite."* Already she had at least two words she could use.

She thought of Miguel and how he couldn't always say what he wanted to say in English. The same would be true for her in Portuguese. It would take years to learn to express herself clearly. But she had made a start.

The next day, a hot August Tuesday, Chelsea took a long lunch break to go to António's bookstore. She would need a good English-Portuguese dictionary for her classwork, and so far she hadn't found any in the other bookstores. They all had Spanish and French. Some had German and even Japanese, but no Portuguese books.

António was reading when she walked in. Cool air and soft music contrasted with the noisy, exhaust-scented street outside. She hesitated in the doorway, looking for the dictionaries.

"*Boa tarde,*" António said, then saw who it was and set his book down, beaming. "Chelsea. I haven't seen you in a long time."

"I know," she said. "I've been working."

He came around the counter to stand beside her. "Your section on the Portuguese was top-notch. I bought several copies."

"Thank you." He stood smiling at her, waiting. "Well, I finally started taking Portuguese."

"Really? Congratulations. Where?"

"Mission College. Gabriela Machado. I don't know if you know her."

"Oh sure. She's from São Jorge. She is good."

"I like her. Anyway, I need a dictionary, a good, complete dictionary that has everything but isn't so heavy I can't carry it around."

He led her to the shelves along the window. "I recommend this one. It's a little expensive, but it's the best one."

Chelsea shrugged. "Okay. So long as I can get beyond *boa tarde* and *obrigada*."

"You will. Especially with Simão and his family to help you."

She pretended to study the words in the dictionary he handed her. "I don't see Simão anymore."

António looked worried. "No? You're just so busy, I guess."

"No, we kind of had a fight." Why are you telling this man about this, she asked herself.

"Oh, I'm sorry."

"It's my fault, I suppose. I ran in the Mercury News 10K, and my publisher had one of the sports guys take pictures. They ran a photo on page one that was embarrassingly sexy. Simão took one look and broke up with me."

"Oh." António leaned against the counter, rubbing his chin. "I see."

Chelsea felt herself blushing. What was it about António that made her spill her guts? Now she wanted to run and hide. "I'll take this one," she said, closing the dictionary.

"Good."

As he punched numbers into the cash register, he spoke softly. "It's none of my business, but I hate to see you and Simão break up over such a little thing."

Chelsea shrugged. "It's over. We move on."

167

"No, no, no. $29.55."

Chelsea started writing a check.

"He told you about his wife, didn't he?"

"That she died? Yes."

"Do know how she died?"

She tore out the check and stared at António. "I figured she was sick."

"No. Come over here and sit down."

Mystified, Chelsea came around the counter to the chair where she had sat to interview Antonio what seemed like years ago. In reality, it was only a couple weeks.

António crossed his legs and folded his hands over his knee. "Simão's wife was killed outside a bar on Story Road."

Chelsea stared. "How?"

"She was stabbed."

"My God."

"Fátima--that was her name--changed a lot when she came to America. She was a beautiful girl, and Simão worshipped her. But he's an old-fashioned man, as you know, and Fátima got caught up with new friends and new ideas. While Simão was working, she would dress up and go out shopping or to shows or sometimes dancing at the bars.

"One night, this man was drunk, and he thought she was a, how do you say it politely, well, a hooker. She never was, it was all show, and she never missed Mass on Sunday, but the man wouldn't take no for an answer. He forced her outside and when she fought back, he stabbed her. It was a terrible scandal. The man was Mexican, and with Simão so popular, it practically caused a war. It was in the papers."

Chelsea swallowed. Tonight she would go to the library and look up that story. "I had no idea," she whispered.

António patted her hand. "I know. Simão never talks about it. Rosa either. Oh, I know you two girls are friends. I've seen you together. Anyway, the family almost went back to Portugal when that happened. But Simão couldn't afford it, and he didn't want to disturb his grandma in the nursing home."

"Oh boy," she said, shaking her head. "No wonder Simão is so overprotective of the women in his life."

"Including you," António said.

168

"But I have to live my life. I'm not hanging out in bars. I just like to run and be independent."

"I know." An elderly woman in black came in, heading for the greeting card rack in the middle of the store. "*Boa tarde, Sra. Costa, como está?*"

The woman sighed. "*Bastante bem.*"

António rose. "That means 'well enough.' You'll find the Portuguese never say they're feeling wonderful. It's like tempting fate. You say you're so-so, then you don't sound so cocky."

Chelsea shook her head. "I have so much to learn. António, thank you for telling me about Simão's wife. He never gave me a clue."

"I know. It hurts him to talk about it. But have faith. He will return to you."

"I'm not so sure. But thank you."

"Come back again."

On the sidewalk, the heat seeming to press her into the ground, she looked down the street toward Simão's office. His Buick was parked out front. She could go there now.

But she remembered the morning he shut the door in her face. No. Go back to work, she told herself.

That night, Chelsea found a vacant computer terminal in the library reference section, called up the Mercury News data base, and typed in Fátima Freitas.

"Searching" said the label at the bottom of the screen. Two Vietnamese girls sat at the next terminal, giggling as they punched random keys. Not far away, a harried-looking man held a telephone to his ear, but he was watching the kids, ready to scold them as soon as he got free. At the big round table near the counter, a black man in a Navy foul weather jacket sat hunched over the newspaper classified section. A pudgy white guy perused the consumer guides, and a college student was making photocopies from a stack of reference books. Typical evening at the main library, Chelsea thought. Just the place for people without a social life.

The search yielded five references. Two were identical obituaries: Fátima Marie Gonsalves Freitas, age 25. Wife of Simão, beloved

169

daughter-in-law of Elena E. Freitas, daughter of Jose and Filomena Gonsalves and sister of Maria, Anna, Jose, Leonel, and Manuel of Pico Island in the Azores. Mass of Christian burial at Five Wounds Church, followed by interment in Calvary cemetery.

Chelsea shuddered as she read the headline on the small item that ran the morning after Fátima was killed. It was as António said. She was stabbed outside a bar on Story Road, died at Alexian Brothers Hospital a few hours later. Suspect arrested that morning. Husband Simão said he did not know the suspect, had urged his wife not to go out at night without him. He had to go to a meeting. She had said she was staying home, but apparently changed her mind.

"Oh my God," she whispered as she reached the second column of the article. Fátima was three months pregnant, said the doctor at Alexian Brothers. Simão hadn't known. The suspect, an unemployed Hispanic man, said he had seen her in the bar with her female friends. They were all pretty girls, dressed like prostitutes, and he assumed that's what they were. Otherwise, what were they doing in the bar?

Chelsea clenched her teeth, imagining how Simão must have reacted. She read on. Friends of the victim said the suspect, Hector Garcia, had approached Fátima, proposing they have some fun together. She tried to tell him no, she wanted to hear the music. "Come on," said Hector, "Let's go." When she tried to run, he grabbed her. She fought back, scratching him with her nails. He got angry and carried her outside, where he stabbed her. He never thought she'd die from it, he told the police.

One of Fátima's friends, Nazaria Silva, told the court the bandleader had said he could get Fátima into his band, that she could be the lead singer. That's why she was there so late. All she could see was the stars in her eyes, said her friend.

When Simão testified at Garcia's trial, he fought to control his tears and his anger. Fátima wanted to be a singer, he confirmed. She was always talking about it. She knew this guy with a band and kept following him to gigs because he told her if she learned all the band's songs he would let her sing with them. She was an immigrant, she was young, she didn't understand that you can't trust everybody.

Chelsea swallowed. Poor Simão. No wonder he was so protective of his sister and so resentful when Chelsea's sexy picture came out in the newspaper.

The next story gave the verdict. Hector Garcia was found guilty of manslaughter. There was no premeditation or intent to kill, the jury decided. He would go to jail, but only for a few years. And Fátima was gone forever.

Chelsea printed out the articles, then sat back, thinking. What a dreadful thing, no doubt made worse by the language and cultural differences. Their mother must have felt completely lost, not understanding anything. And Rosa must have ached for Simão and her lost sister-in-law. . .

"Are you done?" asked a woman standing behind her, waiting for the computer.

"Oh, I'm sorry."

Chelsea gathered her papers and her purse and strolled toward the escalator. It had all happened while she was in Sacramento. She wondered if she would have paid any attention if she had been here. The killing itself was just a small item in the back of the local section. The trial got more coverage, but it wasn't front page news.

She sighed. Fátima wanted to be a singer. Rosa wants to be an artist. Chelsea wants to be a writer. And Simão wants to keep them all home, frustrated but safe.

The library was closing. It was almost dark. Chelsea walked quickly toward Fifth Street, passing a homeless woman pushing a shopping cart full of empty soft drink cans, three teenage boys in baggy jeans and backwards baseball caps, and a well-dressed couple on their way to the Fairmont Hotel.

She kept a speedy pace, wary of her surroundings, thinking about Fátima being stabbed outside a bar at night. An immigrant from a tiny village in the Azores where the only creatures moving around at night were cows, where everyone who lived there was a brother or a cousin, would be dangerously trusting when she was thrust into the whirlwind of San Jose. She would be excited by all the new fashions and freedoms she found here, and she would believe a stranger who said he could make her a star. She would think she was safe on the streets.

Chelsea was almost home when she passed a figure on Santa Clara Street who looked familiar. He was a bulky man, dressed in a suit, but he wore a fedora pushed down over his forehead, and he stared at the ground. Before she could figure out who he was, he disappeared down an alley.

At last she reached her apartment. She was glad to see John's truck parked out front. She hurried upstairs, locked the door behind her and turned on all the lights. Tonight she wished she lived someplace like Simão's house, surrounded by family and comfortable old furniture. She remembered Fátima's photograph. She looked so young, so vulnerable. She had lived in that house, and it didn't give her what she needed.

Chelsea was different. She wished Simão would see that. She could take care of herself.

She was alone in the newsroom Friday afternoon when the call came. The man with the southern accent said, "I know where the councilman is. This is a story that will blast your socks off. Ain't no other paper got this story. I want you to have it."

She squirmed in her chair, doodling on the blank back of an old press release. How could she know whether this person was crazy or telling the truth? But he had been right about Slater's house. "Can you tell me your name please?"

"Don't matter, ma'am. What matters is that somebody exposes this story."

"But I have to know if my sources are reliable."

"You can trust me. I know what I'm talking about. And after I tell you what I'm gonna tell you, you can check it out for yourself. It's all there, if somebody would just look. Now the Mercury, they couldn't be bothered. Channel 11 either. But I know you used to work in Washington, D.C., so you know something about government and corruption. And I know a pretty girl like you can talk some secrets out of people."

Chelsea stopped doodling and stared at the phone. How did he know she had worked in Washington? How did he know what she looked like? The picture from the race?

172

"I really would like to know who you are. Off the record, of course."

"No, ma'am. I can't risk it. I got a business and kids to support. Now listen to what I'm gonna tell you." The informant's voice lowered to a whisper. "Slater is sleeping under the Guadalupe Bridge these days because he lost his home to gambling debts."

Chelsea's eyes widened. "What?"

"That's right. The man who makes such a big hoorah about not allowing bingo at the churches and about sheltering the homeless lost his shirt betting on horses at Bay Meadows. He even put in a little city money, I hear, and now he's sleeping under the bridge. His wife went back to her people in Illinois, and his grownup kids don't want nothing to do with him. It's been goin' on for weeks."

Chelsea glanced out the window, watching two paperboys chain their bicycles to a post in front of the office. "Supposing this is true, how do you know about it?"

"I seen him camped out with the other bums. And a friend of mine seen him at Bay Meadows raising hell because he says he got gypped in a race. It wasn't no gyp. He just bet on the wrong horse. Anyway, I think it ought to be published that our high and mighty councilman is a gambler and a bum. Hell, I don't even know if he's qualified to be a councilman if he don't have a home no more. Check it out. It'd be a hell of a story. I gotta go now. I'll call ya again."

Chelsea heard the phone click off and sat thinking. If it were true, this was a hell of a story. Slater had been a loud crusader for morality in San Jose, proposing ordinances against everything from bingo to women's halter tops. She had written several stories about his battles with the other, more liberal council members.

This is crazy, she thought. But then how would anybody think of this stuff if there weren't some basis for it?

The voice on the phone bothered her. It seemed slightly familiar yet she couldn't connect it with a name or a face.

She went out to the reception area to look through some of the back issues bound together on a spindle on the front counter. Berta glanced up from the phone, waved a handful of blue fingernails at her and kept talking while Chelsea read.

The homeless had long camped in the dry area between the trickle of a river and the railroad tracks. Several city cleanup campaigns, including one led by Slater, had only deterred them for a few days before they returned and set up camp again. Even during the coldest days of winter, when the city set up a shelter in the old armory building a few blocks east, some of the homeless insisted on staying under the bridge. Chelsea and Sarge had both written articles about the situation. She remembered meeting with Slater in his office, listening to his pompous pronouncements about how if these homeless guys would just get sober and take whatever jobs they could find, they wouldn't be out there. . .

Brow furrowed in concentration, Chelsea read the articles and tried to picture Slater in the gravel and dirt under the bridge in his tweed suits and shiny shoes. "It's crazy," she muttered. "Just a crank call from somebody who's got a gripe against him." She didn't like Slater, but she had never doubted that he was honest.

Mel came up the hall from the pasteup area. "You got time to help with some headlines, Chelsea?"

"Sure." Chelsea let the pages flop closed and followed him into the newsroom.

Mel looked tired, his eyes red, his forehead wrinkled, unconsciously breathing rapidly in his deadline haste. He scribbled a half dozen filenames and headline sizes on the back of a message slip and passed them to her. These go on the Lifestyle page."

"Okay." Chelsea glanced at the clock and sat down at the computer. They had an hour to finish the last pages for the issue in time for Mel to pick his daughter up after school and take her to the doctor.

She called up the first story, typed in the headline code and stared at the blinking cursor. The story was about a charity ball, but all she could think of was James Slater living under the Guadalupe Bridge.

It was a lead she knew she wasn't going to be able to resist.

Chapter Thirteen

Avó poked the woman beside her as Chelsea and Rosa walked in. The nursing home residents were finishing supper in the dining room, eating tiny wedges of apple crisp on paper plates. *"As minhas netas,"* she said, but the woman beside her just stared at her uneaten dessert.

Rosa hugged her grandmother. *"Boa noite, Avó, como está? A Chelsea vai comigo."*

"Sim. Bom." Avó reached around Rosa to pull Chelsea down for a kiss.

"Did you hear what she told the other lady?" Rosa asked Chelsea. She said her granddaughters were here. Plural."

Chelsea shook her head. "That's sweet. You don't think she's got me confused with Fátima, do you?"

"No, you look totally different. Besides, Fátima spoke Portuguese and you don't."

"Of course." Chelsea hadn't told Rosa what she had learned from António and the newspaper articles. Why bring up painful memories?

Orderlies were wheeling the residents out of the dining room one by one. They tactfully left Avó until last because she had visitors. Finally the tiny Filipino nurse asked Avó, "Do you want to go to your room or watch TV?"

Avó said something in rapid Portuguese to Rosa.

Rosa patted her hand. "She hates it that nobody speaks Portuguese," she told Chelsea. "I know she understands what Nita wants, but would she give her a break? No. She is like Simão, stubborn. *Avó, vamos para o seu quarto?"*

Avó shrugged. Rosa took that for a yes, and Chelsea followed them to the comfortable room again, sitting next to her as she had last time.

"Can I continue my interview, do you think?"

Rosa translated, and Avó nodded, her oversized false teeth showing as she grinned. "She would like that."

"Okay, when we talked last time, you told me about your husband Pedro and how he left on a whaling boat the night you had your baby."

Avó sighed and was quiet for several minutes. Chelsea's eyes met Rosa's.

"Wait," Rosa whispered.

Then Avó started to speak rapidly, her voice low. Rosa translated.

"Avó--Maria Dolores--wanted to go home to her parents after that. But there wasn't room. The twins were getting big, and another baby was coming. Besides, her in-laws were very upset about Pedro's leaving. They were sure he would come back soon. Also, they did not want Maria Dolores to take the baby away. He was their first grandson, and they insisted she name him Pedro after his father. She did not want to honor her cruel husband this way. She secretly called him João--John--after her mother's father.

"A long time passed. Her mother-in-law was good enough to her, but Maria missed her own family. Pedro's mother taught her to make lace and to crochet and sew. She made clothes for all the family, helped in the garden and took care of Pedro's four brothers and sisters. She rarely left the house except for church on Sunday. Whenever she went out, people asked her about Pedro.

"'He is on a long journey,' she would say, 'but he will be back soon.'

"In truth, she did not know if he would ever return. She hoped he would not. But she did not want to stay with his parents forever. She longed for her own home and family or even the little cabin where she had stayed with Pedro when they were first married. With no money of her own, there was no way she could leave. She could only do what she was told."

Avó's jaw was tight. She stared at the darkness outside, shook her head and went on.

"A letter came from Pedro once. It was addressed to his parents. He did not even mention Maria Dolores, his wife! He did not care. He boasted of the money he was making, of how he had seen Hawaii and Canada and San Francisco and was thinking of living in California."

"He didn't even mention her?" Chelsea asked.

"Not a word," Rosa replied.

"How painful that must have been."

"Yes." Rosa relayed to Avó what Chelsea had said. It was awful, Avó replied and went on. "Her heart was broken. But time passed. Her younger sister got married. Her husband was tall and handsome, and Maria Dolores felt even worse. There were other men at the wedding,

176

and she thought of how she could have married one of them, but now she was married to Pedro, and he had left her. Her life was ruined."

Chelsea shook her head. "If they lived here, she could divorce him. Abandonment is always grounds for divorce."

"No divorce in Portugal. Not in those days. Now, yes, it happens."

Avó interrupted, nudging Rosa to keep telling her story.

"Her father-in-law, he got hurt, got his arm caught in the tractor, almost torn off. He could not work, and his sons were too young. Maria Dolores and her mother-in-law had to milk the cows and work the fields. Meanwhile, they tried to find Pedro, sending letters everywhere. No reply.

"Surely, thought Maria Dolores, this was the worst time of her life. She brought her baby to the fields with her, carrying him on her back or letting him sleep in a basket while she weeded and plowed, getting dirt all over herself, straining her muscles, burning her skin in the sun. Sra. Freitas was old, weak from female problems from too many babies, and she worked slowly and had to rest a lot. Only Maria was young and strong.

"The women could not keep up, and they were afraid the crops would spoil before they could harvest them. Pedro's father was proud and stubborn like his son and would not ask for assistance, but the neighbors could see. Men from the village came to help. One, Martin Goulart, was very handsome, and Maria Dolores used to blush when he came to work. He had worked all day at his own farm, but he was strong. His muscles when he took off his shirt were big and manly, and Maria Dolores felt for him things she had never felt for Pedro. All day long she brought him water and bread and cheese. He smiled, and she smiled, and when he went home she could hardly wait to see him the next day.

"Sra. Freitas saw all this, of course. 'Maria Dolores,' she said, 'you have a husband. He is coming back. You have his son. Do not behave like a whore.' 'I am not,' said Maria Dolores. You have to understand she was still only 16 years old, very young, and it was so hard.

"Anyway, the crops were done, the ground prepared for next season, and Martin had no reason to come anymore. Maria Dolores tried to think of chores he could do. 'Mama, he could fix the roof,' she suggested, 'or build an extra room for me and the baby, so I don't have to sleep in the living room.'

"But Sra. Freitas just shook her head. 'I know what you want. I have seen you. Your husband is coming home. Besides, Papa is stronger now, and little Manuel is almost 13. They can do these things.'

"So winter came, and Maria Dolores stayed home, sewing, cooking, watching the children. She went out when she could, but Sra. Freitas was always watching her.

"One day, Sra. Freitas was taking a nap, and Rosa decided to go to the market. There, standing in front of the *taverna*, talking to Martin Goulart, was her husband Pedro. He was taller, had a beard, much more handsome, but his eyes were still mean.

"And she could tell he didn't even remember who she was. She too had gotten older. Her figure had filled out, she was taller, and her long hair was wrapped around her head like the older women's now. Pedro stared at her, said something to Martin, and they both laughed.

"She felt like she couldn't breathe, like she would die it hurt so bad. Suddenly she lifted her skirts and ran as fast as she could, far out into the fields. There she threw herself down on the ground and cried. She prayed, 'God, how could you make me be married to a man like this? I am young. Let me be free.' I am not going back to that house, she thought, but what about João, Pedro's son?"

Avó brushed tears from her wrinkled cheeks and fumbled in her pocket for a white handkerchief with pink crocheted edging. Chelsea squeezed Avó's hand.

"What did you do?"

Avó shrugged, as if to say, what else could I do?

"It was getting dark. She walked slowly back to the big house. Pedro was there, holding her baby, and everybody was acting as if he were a king. They looked at her like she was dirt, and she wished she could die."

"Mrs. Freitas," said Nita from the doorway. "It's time for bed."

"Avó," Rosa began, but her grandmother nodded sadly. She understood. "Well, Chelsea, I guess we'll have to wait for the rest. I know some of it, but not all of it."

"It's fascinating. And so sad."

178

As they rose to go, Avó grabbed Chelsea's hand. *"Linda, tem cuidado."*

"What?" She looked at Rosa.

"She says to be careful. I don't know what she means. *O que é que acontece, Avó?"*

"Alguma coisa má vai acontecer a ela ."

Rosa looked puzzled. "She's says something bad is going to happen to you."

"O que, Avó?"

"Uma coisa muito mal."

"Something very bad."

"Why does she say that?"

"I don't know, Chelsea. Sometimes she has premonitions, but I think she just worries about everybody. Don't let it bother you."

Chelsea stroked her wrinkled hand. "I'll be fine, Avó. *Não se preocupe.* Don't worry."

As they left, Avó's warning echoed in her mind. Chelsea was still thinking about what had happened to Fátima, but in real life, what could happen? She might die of boredom or frustration, but she was safe. After all, she had a policeman living downstairs and her parents checking up on her every other day.

She dropped Rosa off and drove home, her mind full of Avó's story. What a book this would make, she thought. She popped a Portuguese tape into the cassette player, eager to learn more words.

Late Friday afternoon, when Mel was gone, and the feature pages had gone to press, the Weekly Times reporters relaxed before the crush of the news and sports pages on Monday. Chelsea pulled her chair over to Sarge's desk.

He looked up with an amused smile, ignoring the chatter on the police radio. "Getting friendly, are we?" His craggy face was scarred around the chin from a car accident years earlier, and his nose had been broken when he boxed in the Marine Corps. No one would call the old bachelor handsome, but Chelsea knew he had a warm heart and he loved chasing a good story.

"Yes," she answered, winking. "Actually, I got a call that I can't get out of my mind. This anonymous guy with a southern accent was telling some pretty wild stories about James Slater."

Sarge raised his eyebrows. "Like what?"

"Like his wife left him, and he lost his house, and he's living under the Guadalupe Bridge. All because of gambling debts."

The older reporter chuckled. "Well, I'll be."

"What, do you know something?"

"Aw, hell, I don't know anything for a fact, just that he's been missing a few meetings and looking a little disheveled lately. I figured he was having an affair with some young woman."

"Really." She studied the yellowing certificate from the San Jose Police Department honoring Sarge for "honest and accurate reporting." "I suppose that could be it. But I went to his house a while back, and it was empty. Then I called his business, and he wasn't there. Now this guy says he's living under the bridge. I'm not sure what to do next."

"I still think a woman is involved." Sarge slapped the desk with his meaty hand. "I'm sure that's it. A guy'll say anything to cover his behind on something like that."

"But what about this guy who keeps calling?"

"I don't know. Could be a jealous husband. Check it out if you want. But don't tell Dunning. He and Slater have been playing golf together."

"Oh, Jeez. Hasn't that guy ever heard of impartial--"

The phone buzzed. "Chelsea, you have a call," Berta said over the intercom.

She rolled her chair back across the carpet. "Okay, I've got it."

Her mother's voice grated in her ear. "Are you coming for dinner tomorrow night? We're having chicken Parmesan, and I don't want to buy too much if you're not coming."

Chelsea rolled her eyes at Sarge. "Yes, Mother, I'll be there. But you don't have to make a big fancy dinner. I'm family."

"I need something to give me a little pleasure these days."

Chelsea formed her thumb and forefinger into a gun, pointed it to her head and shot it. "Come on, Mom, it's not that bad, is it? How about if I bring a great gooey dessert?"

"You'd bake?"

"No, but I'd pick something up at the market."

"That's what I thought. Do what you want."

"Mom, you can't count on me for your entertainment. Why don't you and Dad go to a movie or something? You could practically walk to the Century Theaters and you never go."

"He wouldn't go. Besides, we can't afford it."

Another call interrupted the conversation. "Mom, I have to go. Please try to cheer up. Say hi to Dad. Bye."

She punched the next button. "Chelsea Faust."

"Have you looked into Mr. Slater's activities yet?"

Her southern informant was back.

"No, I've been on deadline. Why don't you tell me your name and how you know about these alleged activities?" She could tell Sarge was listening.

"Oh, they're not alleged; they're true. I can't tell you how I know. But I can tell you that another paper is interested, and I would hate to see them get the story first. Better jump on it." He hung up.

Chelsea gritted her teeth.

"Same caller?" Sarge asked. "Be careful, Faust. You have to think about why this guy is so interested in what Slater's doing."

"I know."

She heard Dunning's voice just outside the newsroom door and turned to her computer, but her mind was still on Slater.

These August nights were long, light till almost 9 o'clock, and Chelsea was restless. It was one of those times when she wished she had a group of friends to hang out with, like she did when she was in college. She had taken a chance earlier and phoned Rosa's house, grateful when Simão didn't answer. Using the few words she had mastered in her Portuguese class, she asked their mother if Rosa was home, thanked her when she said her daughter was out, and said goodbye without leaving a message.

So now she sat staring out the front window at the purple and green Victorian across the street and thought about James Slater. If she were to catch him living under the bridge, it would have to be at night. The homeless scattered during the day. Neither Mel nor her parents

181

would approve of her going to look for him, but if the charges were true, the citizens deserved to know.

Anyway, she had heard the Guadalupe Bridge dwellers were peaceful people, helping each other survive without money. She pictured it in her mind as a campground, with people sitting around fires playing music and telling stories.

She could already see the headline: Councilman Living Under Bridge. And the subhead: Gambling took everything I had, Slater says.

Changing from her shorts to jeans, putting a gray sweatshirt over her Cal tee-shirt, she got out her camera and filled her pockets with film. Her notebook went in the back pocket with her driver's license and a five-dollar bill. She added a few coins for phone calls.

Coiling her hair on top of her head, she hid it with a baseball cap, grabbed her keys and went out into the twilight.

It took only a few minutes to get there. She walked along the bridge, peering into the gloom below. After five years of drought, the river was nothing but a trickle in the center of a wide wash of gravel and dirt. Scrawny trees waved in the warm breeze.

It was 8:30, and the light was fading. Chelsea could see vague shapes below. It would be difficult to take pictures in this light, but it might be her only opportunity--unless she came back at dawn, and then Slater might be gone.

Nerves jangled her stomach. She read Sarge's cop stories. She knew about the beatings, shootings and rapes that happened downtown at night. But she could take care of herself, and she needed this story.

She edged carefully down the embankment, cradling her camera against her ribs with her right hand. Five feet from the bottom, she lost her footing and slid on her rear end the rest of the way.

As she sat on the ground putting her hat back on, a rotting smell filled her nostrils. It was like a blend of old rags, human waste and beer. I should write that down, she thought, then realized how conspicuous it would look. It would be safer to pretend she was homeless, although her jeans were too new and her tennis shoes too white.

She moved forward slowly, gravel crunching under her feet. With a gasp, she pulled back just in time to avoid a prone figure next to a trash-bag-laden shopping cart. She shot a picture of the snoring man,

182

her flash blinding in the dusk, and went on, wondering where Slater would be.

Up ahead at the opposite end of the bridge from where she had come down, she heard voices. It sounded like a party. She moved in that direction, passing a couple sitting in a lean-to made of dirty tee-shirts and Hefty bags, an old man sitting alone talking to himself, a woman in torn jeans weeping. She took pictures of them all. The woman suddenly reared up and came at her, wielding her fingernails like claws.

"You don' take my picture, bitch. Who are you?" she shrieked.

"No, no, I didn't," Chelsea lied, glancing nervously toward the big group under the bridge. "I was just testing my flash."

"I don' b'lieve you," the woman growled.

"It's true. Why would I take your picture?" Chelsea whispered, hurrying away.

It was getting truly dark now. The crowd ahead was gathered around a garbage can from which flames lit their faces orange and yellow.

Chelsea stood still 50 yards away, hoping the darkness would cover her. Young, old, male, female, it was hard to tell. Their faces and figures were hidden in layers of grime and thick clothing despite the warm autumn weather. Slater would be bigger than the others, she reasoned, scanning the group. She didn't see him, but she could hear a voice, more resonant than the rest, apparently leading the conversation. It could be him.

She raised her camera, carefully switching off the flash so it wouldn't give her away. The fire would provide an interesting illumination.

The shutter echoed in the darkness, and Chelsea held her breath. But no one appeared to have noticed. She took a couple more pictures, unconsciously moving closer in her excitement. What a spread this would be.

A man separated from the group and headed off to the right, disappearing in the dark. A minute later, she heard him urinating on the ground.

That explained the smell.

183

Chelsea tiptoed closer, placing each step carefully to avoid dislodging the gravel, until she was only about 20 feet away. In the opening left by the man who had gone to urinate, she saw a bulky, wavy-haired man perched on a wooden camp stool. He wore tweed pants and a blue windbreaker over a white shirt. My God, she thought. That's Slater. Holding court like some kind of royalty. She raised her camera and clicked off one prize-winning shot before the man who had left the group came rushing at her like a raging bull.

"Get the fuck out of here!" he yelled. Before she could move, he jumped at her, knocking her down.

Desperately grabbing for the camera, she fell hard. She felt a sharp pain in her side as she landed on a rock. But she clung to the camera strap.

"Get the camera," Slater ordered. Before she could move, the man flashed a knife, swiftly slicing Chelsea's Nikon off the strap. She heard it fall to the ground with a dead clunk. Still fighting for breath, she struggled to her feet.

"Give it back, you creep," she said, but the knife in her face stopped her.

"Get out of here," the man ordered. "Now!"

Chelsea stared at him. He wasn't even 21, good-looking through the dirt, but his eyes bulged dangerously.

"Let me take my camera," she said, her heart pounding and every instinct telling her to run. "Even if I don't have pictures, you know I'm going to report what I saw."

The man picked up her camera and hurled it across the river wash. "She's a reporter," he called to Slater. Without warning, he kicked her hard in the shin and she crumpled to the ground, holding her right ankle as pain blazed down to her toes and up to her groin.

Suddenly Slater was standing over her, huge and ominous in the dark. "I don't remember what paper you work for. I don't care. You saw nothing here tonight except a councilman exploring the homeless situation. No big story. Not a photo opportunity. We are discussing what we can do to make these fine people's lives better."

"Then why did you have this big goon attack me?" She hated that she sounded like a scared little girl.

"Charlie just gets a little nervous sometimes. He's had a hard life," Slater said. "It really isn't safe here for a young woman like yourself. I suggest you go home right now."

She forced herself to sound tough. "I'll go straight to the police."

Slater shook his head, looking past her with a smug smile. "I wouldn't. There are nervous people like Charlie all over town. You just get into your nice little car and go home to your cozy apartment and mind your own business. We'll call you when we have a story for you."

She caught her breath as Charlie moved closer, waving his knife. "Okay, I'm going."

She got up slowly, wincing at the pain in her ankle. Could it be broken with just a kick? She glanced at Charlie's steel-toed shoes. "I don't know if I can walk."

"Go," Charlie hissed. "Crawl if you have to, but go and don't come back."

The group had scattered. Only Slater and Charlie were still watching her.

Each step was torture. Her ankle bones felt like they no longer meshed, and her side throbbed. She moved slowly, looking back often, until she could no longer see anyone, then fell to her knees and crawled, dragging her battered ankle. Her hands touched rags, rusty cans and excrement. In the dark, she heard a woman wailing to herself. Somewhere a deep voice chuckled. Her hat fell off. Her hair came loose and cascaded around her shoulders.

Something glittered in the dark. She grunted, losing her balance as she reached for her camera. Broken glass rattled inside, but maybe the film could be saved.

She was almost to the bank when her hand landed on something soft, and she realized it was a human body. There was no reaction, even though the skin was warm. She went on, not daring to look back.

The bank was steeper than she remembered, with nothing solid to hold on to. Trying to ignore the pain in her ankle and her ribs, she pushed and pulled against the dirt until at last she reached the solid cement of the sidewalk and hauled herself up.

The streets were busy. Cars passed. Someone pushed a shopping cart along the opposite sidewalk. She sat on the pavement, leaning against the bridge, wondering what to do now.

Chapter Fourteen

A man approached the bridge, jingling a set of keys and whistling.

Chelsea started to stand, but her ankle wouldn't hold her. It hurt so bad she sank to the ground, clutching her leg. The man rushed over. *"Menina, o que é que está a fazer aqui? Está ferida?"*

Although she rarely cried, Chelsea felt tears coming to her eyes now. A Portuguese man. "Do you speak English?"

The man shook his head. *"Não. Não Inglês."*

"Oh God," Chelsea said, searching for words. "Okay. *Eu--falo--um--pouco Português. Preciso, uh, preciso médico."*

The Portuguese man immediately helped her up and leaned her against the bridge. *"O meu carro está perto d'aqui. Espere."*

She nodded. She gathered he was going to get his car. Hers was just down the street, but how would she drive it without her right foot?

The man sprinted away to the right. In a minute, he was back with a white Pontiac, opening the passenger door, helping her in. She couldn't keep from moaning as she jarred her ribs getting in. He gently shut the car door and raced back to the driver's side.

"Eu so Joaquim. Ah, menina, o que é que aconteceu?"

Tears streamed down her face now as she pictured again the man with the knife and Slater standing over her, threatening her.

"Um," she began, *"Os homems,* um, I don't know how to say it in Portuguese. *Não sei como dizer."*

"Não faz mal. Vamos para o hospital."

Chelsea rested against soft crocheted seat covers, fighting to stop crying. Gradually anger took over. You stupid idiot, she told herself. What a dumb thing to do. She looked down at her ankle swelling tight against her jeans. So much for her running career.

"Não se preocupe," murmured Joaquim.

Soon they were at San Jose Medical Center emergency.

Joaquim waited the three hours it took for her to see a doctor, have x-rays and have her fractured ankle cast. The pain pills the doctor prescribed would help her bruised ribs, too. A nurse helped her wash her hands and face and swabbed antiseptic on long scratches on her chin and arm.

Chelsea also had to speak to the police officer called by the emergency room nurse. "Do you want to press charges?" asked the stocky female officer.

Chelsea shook her head. "I don't know." Lord, she thought. I was going to uncover a scandal and now I could wind up in the middle of it. "I guess I should, but--I don't know." She cradled her head in her hands. "I don't know anything tonight except I hope the pain pills start working soon."

"Do you have somebody I can call? A husband? Boyfriend? Parents?"

Her parents didn't need any more grief right now. Her mother would demand that she quit her job and move in with them. Obviously she didn't know how to take care of herself. Maybe they were right.

She could call Mel. Or Sarge. But they would scream at her for being so stupid. Dunning would defend Slater. Simão hated her. Rosa couldn't get away at this time of night. "No," she said. "Nobody."

It was nearly 1 a.m. when the nurse rolled her out in a wheelchair and handed her a pair of crutches. Joaquim was dozing in the mauve and gray waiting room.

Chelsea sighed. "Joaquim."

He sat up, rubbing his eyes, staring at her in the light. *"Já conheço à menina. É amiga do Simão."*

She bit her lip. Everybody knew Simão. *"Sim. Estou pronto. Vamos?"*

The crutches were torture. Each step pulled at her ribs. She was grateful to sink into Joaquim's car. Then came the struggle to tell him where she lived--in Portuguese. But she managed and let him help her up the stairs and into her apartment.

At the door, Joaquim handed her her extra shoe and her camera, and she forced a weary smile. "I don't know how to say anything but *obrigada*, thank you very much."

Joaquim shrugged, squeezed her hand, and backed down the stairs.

Chelsea went straight to bed, not stopping for anything. She pulled the covers over her face and fell asleep, grateful for the codeine-laced painkiller the doctor had prescribed.

Tomorrow she would have to figure out a way to get her truck

187

back and explain to her mother why she couldn't come to dinner, but tonight nothing mattered except that the doors were double-locked and she was home safe.

I spoke Portuguese, she mused as she drifted off. Simão said I didn't need it. What does he know?

The light was hazy from an early morning fog when Chelsea opened her eyes, moaning as she remembered the events of the night before. The pain pills had worn off, and it hurt just to breathe.

But she had to go to the bathroom, and she was hungry. Her crutches leaned against the wall. She sat up slowly, brushing her hair out of her face. "Ohhh," she groaned, "What was wrong with covering ladies' luncheons and water board meetings? Even Sarge wouldn't have done this for a story."

Or would he? She smiled. Yes, he would. Twenty years ago, he would have done exactly what she did. Only maybe he would have taken a gun.

Her broken camera sat on the dresser.

"Okay, up," she said, grabbing one crutch and hopping on her good left foot to the dresser. She inspected the camera. Despite the battering, the back was still closed. However, the winding mechanism was broken. She would have to lock herself in the darkroom to unload the film and put it in the developing tank so the light wouldn't hit it. As for the camera itself, she would take it to Dave at Camera Tech and see if there was any hope at all.

But not today. For now, it would be challenge enough to dress and make breakfast.

An hour later, she opened her front door and stared down the stairs. They suddenly looked like the 20-foot high-dive platform at school. Except the bottom was cracked cement, not cool blue water.

Fourteen steps.

She started down, planting the crutches on the step below, swinging herself to meet them. Three steps down, a crutch slipped and she fell hard onto her seat. Pain streaked from her ribs through her whole body.

Downstairs, the door opened, and John looked up. When he saw the crutches and cast, he dashed up the stairs.

"What the hell happened to you?" He glanced toward the driveway. "Where's your truck? Don't tell me you crashed it."

Chelsea shook her head. "No. It's parked by the Guadalupe Bridge. At least I hope it's still there. I went down there last night working on a story, and I got beat up." She pulled herself back against the wall, wincing, holding her side.

"Broken ribs?"

"Bruised."

He sat down beside her, his leather gunbelt creaking. "Jeez. I was on duty last night. I heard something about a fracas near the bridge, but I didn't think much of it. Stuff happens out there all the time."

"Swell."

"What kind of story were you doing?"

She raised her hand to rub the scratch on her cheek then forced herself not to touch it. "I got an anonymous call that a city councilman was homeless and living down there. I checked out his house, and it was empty. Foreclosure sign on the door. He hadn't been to work. I decided to see if I could find him."

"Did anybody know what you were up to?"

She frowned. "Nope. Pretty stupid, huh?"

"Damn stupid, Chelsea. You could have been killed."

"I know. The guy had a knife." Her voice shook at the memory. She cleared her throat. "I got some pictures, I think. They broke my camera, but I still have the film. Slater was there, just like the guy said."

"James Slater?"

"Umhm. Said he was doing a study of the homeless, but I don't think so. He would have welcomed publicity if that were true. Instead, he ordered this goon to attack me."

"Wow. Big scoop. But not worth your life."

She stared down at the lawn. John's wife Angie was outside now with their little girl, looking up at them, her hand shading her eyes. "What happened?" she called.

John answered. "Ace reporter got herself beat up."

"Oh my God." She joined them, pulling the girl behind her. The child stared at Chelsea as Angie asked, "Are you okay?"

189

"Yes," she said, swallowing back tears.

"Bullshit," John said, patting her bare knee. "How do you plan to take care of yourself?"

She wiped her face with her hand. "I'll figure it out. I've got to go to work on Monday."

"Oh, sure," said Angie, eyeing the cast on Chelsea's leg.

John looked at his watch. "Shoot. I have to go. I'll swing by the bridge area tonight. If Slater's there, I'll make a report. Then you have documentation for your story. But once you turn it in, you'd better lay low. You get worker's comp, don't you?"

Chelsea stared, still thinking of the story. "It would be great if you could check out Slater. He's probably gone though. He knows somebody in the media has seen him now."

"Yeah, but he's pretty cocky. He probably thinks he scared you off."

"He might be right."

"Meanwhile, what are you going to do?"

She shook her head. "I don't know. I just wanted to come out and get some air. I need to get my truck back. I--"

"I'll get the truck. Don't even worry about it."

"Thank you, John. I really appreciate it."

He shrugged. "No big deal."

"So, I guess I'll sit around and read, watch TV and try to figure out some excuse for not going to my parents' house for dinner tonight."

"How about telling them the truth? You need somebody to help you, Chelsea. You'll be laid up for a few weeks, and you'll need food and clean clothes and all that. Pretty hard to do on crutches. Besides which, you're in pain. I can see it in your eyes."

She shrugged even as her ankle throbbed. "I'll get past it. I've got work to do."

"Yeah, right. I suggest you find somebody to stay here with you or you go stay at somebody else's house. I'd offer our place, but--"

"No, that's okay. I know you don't have room."

John went down several steps. "You know, if Slater really feels threatened, you could still be in danger. He could find out where you live pretty easily and send somebody here. Don't stay here alone, Chels."

"I have a cop living downstairs."

"Yeah, and he's gonna be gone for the next nine hours. Promise me you'll call somebody."

"I will."

The child was pulling at Angie's jeans. "Mommy, I have to go potty."

She rolled her eyes. "Call if you need help. Okay?"

Chelsea watched as her neighbors kissed and John drove away. The door below closed softly, and she was alone on the stairs.

The fog had started to burn off. It was a beautiful morning, just warm enough to feel good. Perfect for running. Chelsea looked ruefully at the cast on her ankle. No more running for her. She was amazed she had walked as far as she did. The bone was fractured in two places. Her toes were swollen and bluish purple. Her ribs ached, the scratches on her face and arms burned, and she felt exhausted just from the effort of getting dressed.

Yet while it was fresh in her mind, she had to write what she had seen and heard last night and take her camera to the darkroom to develop the film. Please let the pictures be good, she prayed. It was her proof that Slater was really there. Without pictures, she had only words he could easily refute. Especially with her publisher as his golfing buddy.

Behind her, she heard the telephone in her apartment begin to ring. She looked at her foot and the crutches and realized she'd never get there before the machine took over. Besides, if it was Mom, she didn't know what to say yet. She was afraid she'd burst into tears and beg to be taken care of. Just what they always wanted.

No, let the machine, with its calm, businesslike message, tell the world everything was just fine.

"San Jose City Councilman James Slater is living among the homeless, an anonymous source told the Weekly Times last week. Evidence makes it appear likely.

"The Weekly Times learned last week that Slater's home is vacant, under foreclosure by Bank of America. The whereabouts of the councilman's wife and children are unknown. Nor has the councilman been at work the last few days. Other sources note that he has been missing official meetings and appears disheveled and out of sorts.

"Slater was discovered camping among the homeless under the Guadalupe Bridge Friday night. Although he maintained that he was involved in a city study, he refused to answer questions and was hostile to a reporter investigating the story."

Chelsea sat back and reread the words on her computer screen. She sighed. "Not one single named source. No facts. Dunning will never allow it to run. Even Mel isn't going to put it in like this. A picture would help, but who could say Slater wasn't holding court as a city councilmember? Ignoring the fact that normally he'd have all the press out and be surrounded by aides . . . He'd sue me for libel. Truth is a defense, but I have no proof."

If John could make a report, it would help. But she needed more. Maybe Slater had confided in somebody on the council or on his staff. Would they speak to her off the record? Could she get information on his alleged gambling? Would the bank talk about the foreclosure?

"Shoot. All my phone numbers are at the office, and most of these people won't be available until Monday. Meanwhile Slater has two whole days to make it look as if nothing is out of the ordinary."

Reaching for her phone, she punched in Sarge's number.

The old reporter was watching football. She could hear the announcer and the crowd noise in the background.

"Sarge," she said, "It's Chelsea."

"Who?"

"Chelsea. From the paper."

"Wait. I can't hear."

The TV noise decreased. "Okay. Chelsea?"

"Yes. I hope it's okay to call."

"Sure." He sounded reluctant to talk.

"Sarge, I did something stupid."

Suddenly his voice was louder, more interested. "What do you mean?"

"Last night I went looking for Slater. I found him under the Guadalupe Bridge."

"No kidding. So it's true."

"I think so. His house is foreclosed, empty, sign on the door. He

192

hasn't been at work, and there he was in the dark with all these homeless people, holding court like royalty."

"I'll be damned. Did you talk to him?"

She hesitated. "Sort of. One of his goons beat me up. After I took his picture."

Sarge whistled into the phone. "Sweet Jesus. Are you hurt?"

"Bruised ribs, broken ankle, cuts and scratches. Broken camera, too, but I think I can save the film. I crawled out of there and got picked up by this Portuguese guy who took me to the hospital."

"Were the police called?"

"Yes. I had to make a report, but I didn't know whether to file charges or not."

"I wouldn't. Faust, that was really dumb. A girl like you going down there alone."

"I know, I know. I didn't realize. Anyway, I want to nail him with this story, but I don't have any proof of anything, and I can't drive with this cast on my foot."

"You want me to take it over?"

"I don't know. I guess I just needed to tell somebody what happened."

"I'm honored," he drawled.

"Yeah."

Silence. Was Sarge watching the game again or thinking?

"You'd think Slater'd know better than to beat up the press," he mused.

"He couldn't remember where I worked."

"Doesn't matter." The TV went silent. "This isn't much of a game. I'll check some of my sources. It doesn't sound like you're in any shape to work."

"I'll be there Monday. It's still my story."

Sarge chuckled. "You just said you couldn't drive. How can you work? If I get anything, I'll share the byline. Then they can come blow up my house, too."

"Thanks."

"Keep your foot up. Helps the swelling."

As soon as Sarge hung up, Chelsea dialed her parents' house.

193

"Mom, I can't come tonight. I have to work."

"Work? On a Saturday night?"

Chelsea searched for an excuse. "Rotary club dinner. And fashion show. You know, with the big hats and all."

"You could have told me yesterday. Now I have all this chicken."

"I'm sorry. They just called me. The intern has the flu again."

"Well," she said, sounding pouty. "Can you come tomorrow?"

Lies on top of lies, Chelsea thought. "No, I've got a date. You can freeze the chicken."

"Not after I already defrosted it."

"I'm really sorry, Mom.. It sounds delicious." She was starting to feel hungry. Maybe she could send out for pizza or Chinese food.

"I guess we'll just have to eat it. Your father was looking forward to seeing you."

"I know. I'll come during the week or something."

Yeah, how, she thought.

"Well, at least you have a date. So, you've made up with your Portuguese friend?"

Lord, it's getting deeper. "Yes," she lied. "We're back together. I've gotta go, Mom. My film's done."

She switched off the phone and dropped her head into her hands. It was going to be a very long weekend.

Monday morning, she rose early, had coffee and instant oatmeal for breakfast and struggled to find slacks that fit over her cast.

Her side was greenish black with bruises, and it still hurt to breathe. Fighting to hook her bra took so much energy she sank onto the bed, exhausted. Maybe John and Sarge were right. She wasn't ready to go to work. But what else could she do?

The weekend in this apartment had seemed eternal. She soon tired of reading and watching old movies on TV. Her usual escape, running, was impossible. When she went to process her film, she remembered she was out of fixer and had planned to buy more this weekend. But the photo shop was a couple miles away.

Already she was feeling stir crazy and counting the hours until she could go back to work and feel like a real person again.

Carefully putting on a loose blouse and a long flowered skirt, she

194

stuffed her notebook, camera, brush and pain pills into a backpack and went out the front door. At the top of the stairs, she hesitated, then tossed the crutches down and went down the stairs on her rear end, arriving at the sidewalk sweaty and wrinkled.

John had left her truck in the driveway. She patted the hot steel bumper. "Tomorrow," she said. She smiled, glad to be back in the real world, planted a crutch on either side and started toward the newspaper office.

As she moved slowly toward work, her ribs aching with each step, she puzzled over how she could drive with her right foot encased in plaster. If she had a truck with an automatic shift, she could learn to brake and accelerate with her left foot. But with a clutch, she needed both feet.

She reached the Weekly Times door and was struggling to reposition her crutches so she could open it, when Berta sprang to her aid.

"Oh my God, what happened?" she screeched, holding the door as Chelsea hopped in on one foot.

"Shh." said Chelsea. "I got mugged downtown."

"Oh man. What a rotten city. I swear I'm moving back to Montana. Now you're a statistic. How did it happen? How bad are you hurt?"

Chelsea winced. Why hadn't she figured out what to tell people? "Just a broken ankle and bruised ribs. I need to go sit down."

"Oh, yeah. Let me help."

"I'm okay."

"You sure?" She watched Chelsea work her way toward the newsroom. "Some guy called. Wouldn't leave his name. Weird accent."

"When?"

The phone buzzed, and Berta punched the button, still shaking her head. "This morning. Weekly Times."

Her eyes fixed on the blue swivel chair at her desk, Chelsea didn't see Rosa coming toward her until they crashed into each other.

Rosa gasped. "*Ai, meu Deus, o que é que aconteceu?* You are hurt."

Chelsea nodded and collapsed into her chair. "Yes. Somebody

beat me up while I was trying to get a big story. Why are you here?"

"Oh, I was waiting for your editor. I brought some pictures."

"I see." Chelsea stared at the story list on her bulletin board, wondering how she would cover the AIDS walk on crutches.

Rosa was still waiting as Sarge came in.

"I'll be damned. I didn't think you'd make it, Faust. You look even worse than you sounded on the phone."

"I'm fine." But her ankle was throbbing and so was her side. In fact, her whole body hurt. Chelsea fumbled in her pack for her pills, found them, then realized the water cooler was at the back of the building. "Rosa, could you get me some water?"

"Of course. Where?"

"Down the hall. By the restroom."

"Hope you've been here long enough to have insurance," Sarge said, turning on his computer.

"Just barely, Sarge. So what'd you find out?"

He pulled a tiny wrinkled notebook from his shirt pocket and flipped through the pages. "On the record, nada. Nobody knows nothing. Off the record, yeah, he's living out there. Official word is he's doing a first-hand study of the homeless. But he's totally broke, his business is bust, and he's getting his meals by attending every official function he can find. Breakfast meetings, luncheons, dinners, charging it all to the city."

Chelsea leaned forward, forgetting her pain. "Ooh, if we could prove that. . ."

"Tricky stuff. Libel and crooks. Say the wrong things and we're dead." He glanced at Chelsea's cast. "So to speak. You don't look so hot, kid."

"I'm okay, but I really want to get this guy now."

"I hear ya. But I think you're gonna be benched for a while."

She grunted as she adjusted in her seat. "What for? I can type, I can talk on the phone. I'll figure out how to drive."

Rosa returned with the water and waited as Chelsea took her pill.

"Those things'll make you sleepy," Sarge cautioned.

"I'll drink more coffee."

Sarge nodded toward the door. "Let's see what the boss says."

196

Mel's face paled when he saw Chelsea. "Oh God, Chelsea. What happened?"

"She got mugged," Berta called from the reception area. "What a city. I'm gettin' out of here as soon as I can afford it."

"What does she mean, mugged?"

Chelsea stared at her cast. There was no way she could lie to Mel, not without losing the story. "I got an anonymous tip that James Slater was living among the homeless, that he had lost his house and his wife to gambling debts. I went down there to see what I could see and take some pictures--"

"Oh my God," Mel said, sinking to his chair, dropping his head into his hands. "Did you find him?"

"Yes, I did. He was sitting there giving a speech like the king of the bums."

"She snapped a picture, and a friend of Slater's took offense," Sarge put in.

"Oh shit. Police report filed?"

"Yes, the hospital insisted. But I didn't press charges."

"Doesn't matter. It's on record now. Chelsea, why are you so damned independent? Dunning's gonna--"

He stopped and sighed.

"What happened with the film?" Sarge asked.

Chelsea frowned. "I was out of fixer, so I thought I'd do it here. Mel, my camera got broken. I don't know if the pictures survived or not."

"Let me see the camera."

"I'll take care of it."

"No."

Chelsea stared at her friend and employer. "Why not? It's my personal camera."

Mel pressed his lips together and looked around at the walls. "Chelsea, you have to go home. Medical leave. Workers' Comp. Whatever you want to call it. You can't be here like this. We'd be responsible if you didn't heal properly." He sounded as if he was making it up.

197

"Hey, that's my problem. I can do the work. I'll die of boredom at home. I've got things to do here."

Mel walked over to the newsroom door and pulled it shut. He glanced at Sarge and Rosa. "Maybe we should talk privately."

"No, I have nothing to hide from Sarge or Rosa. Jeez, I don't understand your attitude, Mel. Don't I get at least one bravo for extra effort?"

"Not this time. What you did was foolhardy, stupid, and dangerous. Not to mention that you were acting on an anonymous tip from somebody who's probably a wacko. Maybe he even planned for you to go out and get hurt."

"But what he told me was true."

"Maybe. Anyway, aside from that, Slater is a friend of Dunning's. A close friend. You probably didn't know that."

"No, I knew. Sarge told me."

"Then use your head!" The editor's voice rose, and he struggled to rein it in. "Chelsea, Dunning does not like you. I didn't want to tell you, but he has informed me that due to budget constraints, I have to cut one permanent position from the newsroom. He wants it to be you. He says you are a troublemaker. This would prove it."

"What?" Chelsea rose to her feet, struggling to stand straight. "Are you kidding? You told me yourself I'm the best reporter you have. Oops, I mean next to Sarge."

"Don't worry about it, kid," Sarge said quietly.

"You are good, but you consistently refuse to cooperate with other people. You're a loner, and Dunning hates loners."

"Well, that's his problem."

"No, it's my problem, and yours. And this whole paper's problem."

"I don't believe this." She sank back into her chair. When she reached for her cup, her hand wobbled and some of the water spilled out.

His voice softened. "I'm sorry, Chels. Look at you. You're obviously in no shape to work anyway. I want you to go home, file for Worker's Comp and stay gone for at least three weeks, till the end of the budget period. No one in this room is to utter a word about Slater and his shenanigans."

198

"It's a hell of a story, Mel," Sarge said.

"It's poison," Mel countered. He rose. "I'll get you the forms. You give me your camera, and I'll see if it's fixable and if the film survived. You go home. Now."

"Shit," Chelsea said, afraid to look at any of them.

Berta knocked on the door. "Mel, you've got a call."

"We're in a meeting!"

Rosa squeezed Chelsea's hand. "I have Simão's car. I will drive you home."

Silently Chelsea laid her camera on the desk, put her pills and notebook back in her pack and stood. "Thanks, Rosa."

"Good luck, kiddo," Sarge said. "Get yourself a pile of books and movies."

She nodded and slowly followed Rosa out the door, the crutches hurting at every step. She had already seen all the movies she ever wanted to see.

They were at the car when Berta dashed out with a fistful of forms. "Here, Mel says you need these. I hope you feel better. Oh dang, the phone again. Bye."

Chelsea leaned back against the soft seats of Simão's car, fixed her eyes on the Weekly Times sign, then closed her eyes. Portuguese music played softly on the car radio. She clenched her teeth and cursed to keep from crying.

199

Chapter Fifteen

Rosa was a godsend. A mother without the nagging. When they reached Chelsea's apartment, she declared she would stay with her all day.

"You cannot be using crutches with bruised ribs," she said, hands on hips as they stood in Chelsea's tiny kitchen littered with newspapers, clothing, dirty dishes, and empty instant food packages. "I cannot believe the hospital sent you home like this."

Chelsea shrugged. "I wouldn't have stayed anyway. Besides, I can hobble around. Hospitals are for sick people."

Rosa shook her head. "I will make you some tea, okay? And then I will clean up this mess."

"Rosa, you're not the maid. I just appreciate your company."

"So I keep busy while we talk. You sit. In the comfortable chair with your foot up. I will get a pillow."

Chelsea had no choice. Rosa soon had her established in her one easy chair, her leg cushioned on a pillow atop a kitchen chair. A TV tray beside her held tea, that day's Mercury News, the TV guide and the remote control.

Chelsea sat back and gazed out the window. Only a small black cat across the street stirred. She watched it bat a candy wrapper then trot across the lawn and over the fence.

From the kitchen, she heard Rosa bustling around, stacking papers, washing dishes. After a few minutes, Chelsea grew impatient.

"Rosa, stop working, and get out of there. Come talk to me."

Her friend appeared in the doorway with a dish towel wrapped round her skirt. "Just let me finish this little bit."

"Five minutes. *Cinco minutos.*"

"I am so pleased you are learning Portuguese."

"Yes, but I don't know how I'm going to get to class now. I'm not going tonight, that's for sure."

"I will take you next week when you feel better."

"Rosa, you can't--" she started to protest.

But the water was running, and Rosa couldn't hear.

Finally Rosa came out, folded the towel neatly and sat primly on the couch. "Are you comfortable?"

"Yes," Chelsea said. "Thank you. I keep getting rescued by Portuguese people."

"What do you mean?"

She told her about the man who took her to the hospital.

"He said he knew Simão, and he knew we were dating."

"I know Joaquim. I wonder if he told Simão what happened. My brother did not say anything to me."

"He probably doesn't care."

"Oh no, Chelsea. He cares. He is so stern since you two disagreed."

"I tried to talk to him."

"My brother is very stubborn. And he also has pain from--no, never mind."

"What?"

"I think I will get some more tea." As she rushed away, Chelsea watched the mail carrier, a skinny woman in blue shorts, drop letters in the boxes across the street. What had Rosa been about to say? Why wouldn't she talk about Fátima?

Rosa returned, mug in hand. "I don't understand about your job, why you had to go home."

Chelsea shifted her weight, struggling to get comfortable. "Me either. Apparently I need to stay away for a while because Dunning--the publisher--hates me and wants to fire me, and because I made a friend of his angry. Because I'm not a team player. Because I got hurt and I'm an insurance liability. It's all politics. I could work. Most likely things will be back to normal by the time I go back. As long as I squelch the Slater story."

"You think so?"

"Sure." Chelsea stared into the cold black tea in her cup. She wasn't as certain as she sounded, but why should Rosa worry about it?

Rosa began writing a grocery list. "You know, this is fun," she said after a while. "I never had my own home to take care of. Mama does everything."

"Believe me, it gets old." Her mind elsewhere, Chelsea sighed. "I wonder what's going to happen with my film. I hate to say it, but I

201

don't even trust Mel. I'm afraid he'll just throw it away so there's no evidence."

Rosa looked up from her list. "I could draw what happened."

Chelsea stared at her. "You could, couldn't you?" She had seen Rosa's pictures in the last few issues. Most were for advertisements, but she had done some very accurate illustrations for a court case Sarge was covering. "That would be great."

"This afternoon. After lunch. After I buy groceries."

"You're amazing. Doesn't Simão need his car back?"

"No. He spends all day in his office. He can walk home from there."

Chelsea remembered the day Simão insisted on driving the block from the bakery to the hardware store and smiled. "Are you sure?"

"He cannot expect me to take the bus everywhere. I spend all day waiting. And some of the people who ride make me very fearful."

Chelsea realized guiltily that she hadn't ridden a bus in years.

"You need your own car."

"I have no money."

Rosa scribbled away at her list.

"What all are you planning to buy? I don't eat that much."

She grinned. "Oh, just things."

Chelsea looked around her clean kitchen in amazement as she forced down the last cool, sweet bites of cheesecake, pressing her fork into the graham cracker crumbs on her plate. "This is so good, almost as good as sex."

Rosa gasped, then giggled. "I do not know about that."

Chelsea set down her fork. "What, you don't know about sex?"

She blushed. "Oh, I know about sex, but . . ."

"You're not a virgin, are you?"

"No." She stood suddenly, picking up the empty plates, turning to the sink to start washing dishes.

"But Simão thinks you are, right?"

"Of course." She turned the water on hard, its splashing drowning out all possible conversation.

Chelsea contemplated Rosa's stiff linen-clad back and shrugged. Her sex life was her business. When the water was finally turned off, she changed the subject. "I never had chicken like that. It was great."

"Oh, thank you. Mama taught me how to make it a long time ago. It is very easy."

"Well, I appreciate it. I hardly ever get real food unless I go to my parents' house, and then they're watching every bite. Eat, eat, you're too thin, they say. When are you going to get married? Why don't you come to visit more often? Why do you have to work so much?

"*Ah, os pais.*"

Chelsea watched as her friend washed the dishes, dried them, and put them away.

Rosa wiped her hands on the towel and sighed.

"Time to relax," Chelsea said.

"I--" Rosa began, but the telephone interrupted. Rosa blanched.

Chelsea, feeling nerves stir in her own gut, motioned for the phone. "Hello?"

"Chelsea," said Mel. "Bad news. Light got into the camera and fogged the film."

"It's Mel," Chelsea whispered. Rosa had sunk into a chair, looking frightened. "Gee, Mel, why am I not surprised? But we may have an alternative. Rosa drew up some pictures based on my descriptions of the area and what happened."

"No. The subject is dead, Chelsea. As far as the Weekly Times is concerned, you were in an auto accident, and you'll be out for a month."

"A month! You're going to spread a lie about this? Mel, I'm amazed at you. This is a big story you're killing."

"I'm saving our asses, Chelsea."

"Your ass, you mean. You think Dunning wouldn't bask in the glow if we exposed Slater and won some more plaques for his wall?"

"Chelsea, you're not listening. As I told you before, you're skating on thin ice. Just sit back and relax for a while."

"And do what?"

"Nothing. Rest. Read. Write a bestseller."

"Sure." When did Mel sell out, become an editor instead of a friend, a corporate lackey instead of a journalist?

"Are you still there, Chelsea?"

"Yes."

"Did you finish those insurance forms?"

"Not yet."

"Better do it. There's probably a waiting period. I'll pick them up tomorrow sometime. You got food and all?"

"Rosa's been taking good care of me."

"Well, I'm glad of that. It'd be just like you to hole up there alone."

"Probably. Bye, Mel."

As she hung up, Rosa stood. "I have to go. I was so afraid that was Simão."

"He doesn't know you're here, does he?"

"No. He will be looking everywhere."

"You've got to stop letting your brother run your life."

"I know. But it is the Portuguese way. First your father and brothers. Then your husband." She stared out at the twilight. "I must go."

Chelsea stood, leaning on one crutch. "Thank you so much for everything."

"It was fun. But now I missed dinner, and Simão will be angry."

Too bad, thought Chelsea. "You're an adult, Rosa. You didn't do anything wrong."

"I know." But as Rosa went down the stairs to Simão's Buick, her furrowed brow and slumped shoulders showed she clearly thought she did.

Chelsea limped to her easy chair and switched on the television, but she found it hard to concentrate on the sitcom that came on. She leaned her head back against the cushion and closed her eyes. Weariness, good food, and a pain pill combined to make her sleepy. Soon she was dozing.

A knock on the door startled her. Before she could get up, the front door opened and her neighbor poked his head in. "You doing all right?"

"Oh, John." She rubbed her eyes. "Come on in. I'm fine."

He stood in the doorway, smelling of sweat and leather. "I just wanted to see if you were okay."

"I'm fine. A friend came and babied me all day. Cleaned house, bought food, and cooked dinner. She just left a few minutes ago."

"Great. So you didn't go to work."

"Oh, I went. Crutched all the way there. They sent me home."

"Told you. Nobody wants a gimp around. Well, I've got to go. Angie's holding dinner for me. Just wanted to check. You shouldn't leave this door unlocked."

"I know. I guess Rosa didn't think about it."

"Well, I'm going to lock the main lock. You shut the dead bolt. And go to bed. You look beat."

"Right. Thanks."

She listened to John's heavy footsteps going downstairs and switched off the TV. Pulling herself up on her left foot, leaning on her crutch, she locked the dead bolt, turned out the light and went to the bedroom.

Rosa had cleaned in there, too, hanging up the clothing she had tossed on the bed and floor in her haste to dress this morning. The bed was made, with fresh sheets neatly turned down.

"All I need is a mint on the pillow," Chelsea thought, going to wash up.

Soon she was in bed, the sheets smooth under her arms. She turned out the light and lay on her back, listening to cars outside. Inside, it was so quiet she could hear her own heart beating. She didn't dare move for the pain in her ribs. The cast on her foot stuck up awkwardly under the sheet.

Reaching an arm toward the other side of the bed, feeling nothing but an empty pillow, she sighed. It was going to be a long, lonely month.

The pain pills wore off about 4 a.m. Her ankle and ribs throbbing, Chelsea lay in the dark waiting for dawn. After a while, she fumbled with her clock radio and turned it on for company. A DJ joked about insurance forms. Not funny, she thought.

She stared at the digital clock, willing the numbers to change from 4:16 to 4:17. One minute seemed an eternity.

Finally she switched on the light and took another pill. That would dent the pains in her body, but it wouldn't stop her mind from

205

leaping into a disastrous future with nothing to do for weeks and a job that might not be there when she recovered.

Why did I move back here anyway, she asked herself, plumping the pillows behind her and sitting up against the headboard. At bigger newspapers, there was room for advancement and most of the bosses were journalists, not glorified salesmen with no imagination.

Sure, it was good to be in her home town, living near her parents, and she had thought it would be great to work with Mel. It had been. Until recently.

Lights played across the wall as a truck passed on the street below. Somewhere a few doors down, somebody started a car, revved it a few times, and drove away.

She would try the closest papers first. The San Jose Mercury News, the San Francisco Chronicle, the Oakland Tribune, the Santa Cruz Sentinel. Yes, it was a recession, and they were all laying people off, but she had experience, good references, great clips. While she was laid up, she could send out resumes, make phone calls, get herself into something better. Then she could tell George P. Dunning good-bye.

Or maybe it was time to write a book. She could squeak by on Worker's Comp and unemployment for a while.

Pain blotted out her thoughts for a minute. She turned up the radio and tried to enjoy the rock song blaring against the dark outside, but it just gave her a headache. She switched it off and studied the clock again. 4:28.

Without thinking, she was figuring the time difference. In Washington, D.C., it was 7:28. She dialed Jeffrey's number.

"H'lo," he said. Probably somewhere between shaving and moussing his hair, she thought.

"Jeff. It's Chelsea."

"Well, well, Ms. California," he said. She could hear him running water as they talked. Putting in his contact lenses?

"I needed to talk to somebody."

"Jeez, Faust, I've got an 8:30 meeting, and traffic's gonna be a bear. Construction on the parkway again."

"I thought they finished that."

"Ha. They did something wrong. It melted in the last heat wave. Big mess. So, what's up?"

206

"Oh, nothing. I just got beat up working on a story. The publisher wants to fire me. I'm lying in bed with a cast on my ankle and bruised ribs. Same old stuff."

He turned the water off. "Shit, Chels, what kind of story was this?"

"Councilman becomes homeless street person living under the Guadalupe Bridge. Lost his house, his wife, his business, all due to gambling debts. Taking his meals at public functions using city money."

"Ooh, juicy. Did it run yet?"

Chelsea eased down in the bed a little. She missed hearing Jeffrey's voice. "Nope. Mel killed it. Seems the councilman is a friend of the publisher."

"Damn. So who beat you up?"

"One of the councilman's new friends. I was exploring under the bridge Friday night and--"

"You went there alone? Faust, you're crazy."

"I know, I know. I took a picture, he took offense. Kicked me up and down the street, trashed my camera."

"Wow. You going to be all right?"

"Sure. Just bored crazy and lonely."

"Chelsea, Chelsea. Well, I wish I were there, but--What? Hold on." Chelsea heard a woman's voice in the background, saying something about dinner.

A hard lump rose in her throat. Of course. Jeffrey had somebody else at his apartment. Why wouldn't he after almost a year? Especially when she kept turning him down. But somehow she'd always thought he was still hers.

He came back on the line. "Chelsea, I have to go. It's like five to eight already, and I--well, I have to go. You take care of that ankle."

"Sure. Bye."

Chelsea hung up and turned the radio back on. Outside, the traffic noises were increasing, and the darkness seemed to be lightening.

It didn't matter. She switched off the light, pulled the covers over her head and hoped the pill would put her to sleep soon.

207

Surely this was the longest day of her life. Chelsea watched TV talk shows and caught up on her newspaper reading. She tried to get interested in a romance novel her mother had passed down to her because the main character was a reporter. Soon she tossed the book onto the coffee table in disgust.

"This author has no idea what real newspapers are like," she complained. "Not a clue."

By 11:00, she was hungry but forced herself to wait until noon to reheat Rosa's leftovers from last night. Soon lunch was over and it was back to her chair.

She was surprised Rosa hadn't called or come over. They hadn't made any arrangements, but she had thought her friend would be around today. It was awfully quiet without her. She was restless, but every move hurt.

At 2:30, Mel pulled his car into the driveway and got out, leaving the engine running. She could see his daughter Carrie in the passenger seat.

Opening the door before he could knock, she leaned against the doorway, balancing on one foot. "Hey, other human beings. Thank God."

Mel didn't smile. "You got the forms?" he said from several steps down.

"Yes." She hopped back to the coffee table and returned to the door. "Here they are, all signed and filled out in triplicate. I wasn't sure what to say since you seemed so adamant about not telling the truth. I said I was taking pictures and fell down an embankment."

Mel closed his eyes, breathing hard. "I said you were in a car accident."

"They won't pay off for that, will they?"

"I don't know. Well, maybe Dunning won't look at the form. I have to sign it off."

"Good." Chelsea nodded at the car. "Got your daughter with you."

"We're going to counseling."

"Sounds like fun. So, how's the paper?"

"Surviving. I assigned Mandy to the water board and planning commission while you're--uh, gone."

"Okay. Has she ever done anything like that?"

208

"No. But I was running out of bodies."

"What did Dunning say?"

Mel glanced back at the car. "I've got to go, Chelsea. We're due there in 10 minutes."

She watched him run down the stairs and into the car. Gears crunched and gravel flew as he sped away.

She sighed. "Didn't say what the boss said, did he?" She hopped to the landing and sat on the top step, dangling the cast over the stairs. "Guess I'd better polish up my resume."

She leaned against the warm wooden wall and watched an ant parade climb down the top two steps and up the drain spout. Each ant followed the leader exactly, even going around a bit of leaf in precisely the same way.

Chelsea placed her finger across the ant stream and watched the insects scurry in a confused mass until they found the path again and started toward the spout. She herded one away from the crowd and watched it look around.

"That's me. Chelsea the ant. Never following the crowd. Sometimes you get lost."

She was still watching the ants when a chorus of barking dogs heralded the arrival of the mail carrier. Chelsea smiled and waved down at her. "Hi."

"Hello," said the girl, wearily climbing the steps. "You have to sign for this one."

Chelsea stared at the return address: Weekly Times Publishing, Inc. "G.P. Dunning" was typed underneath. Her heart started to pound.

As the girl went back down, Chelsea set aside the grocery ads, Visa bill, telephone bill and a letter from a friend in Sacramento and opened the certified letter.

The single sheet of gold-embossed letterhead read:

Dear Ms. Faust:

Due to financial considerations, we are forced to eliminate several positions on our staff. Unfortunately yours is one of them. You will remain in our employ until Sept. 15. In consideration of your hard work, benefits will continue through November, and you will receive two weeks severance pay.

We regret the need to lay off good people, and we hope that in the future, our situation will change and we can hire you back. In the meantime, our staff will be happy to assist you in finding alternative employment."

George P. Dunning's signature was at the bottom.

Chelsea stared, her hands shaking. Then anger surged through her. "Those bastards! Chicken shits! Mel included. He had to know. Why don't they just talk straight to me instead of sending me a letter while I'm home in a cast. That's real noble. I should hobble over there right now and tell them what I think."

But she knew she couldn't manage it again. They knew it, too. "Damn." Her time off would end just about Sept. 15. So what they were saying was, don't come back at all.

"Those dirty bastards." Was anybody else really laid off or was it just verbiage? "I want a list," she said through clenched teeth. "Show me a list and a budget. Show me this isn't just a ploy by that creep to get rid of me."

She reread the letter. So impersonal. Why didn't Mel just tell her? He had to have known. What were they saying at the office about her?

Looking back through her open door, she scanned the room, looking at her sofa, TV, coffee table, framed Monet prints on the walls. Rent was $600 a month, plus utilities, food, car expenses, insurance, credit cards. . .

"Can one collect Worker's Comp and unemployment at the same time?" she mused.

She ought to file tomorrow at the unemployment office. "That should be fun, standing in line for an hour on one leg, and how the hell would I get there anyway? It's way out on Bascom. Man, they've got me screwed every which way." She threw her mail inside as hard as she could, watching it scatter across the floor.

"No wonder Mel needs to go to counseling. He has lost his mind."

As her temper eased to a slow simmer, she made a mental list of all the places she would apply for jobs. She should have gone for that position in Washington that Jeff was pushing so hard. What an idiot. I stayed here because of Simão. Next time I won't let a man run my life.

The telephone rang. She started to rise, then sank back to the step. "Let it ring."

When she finally went in, the sun had moved to the other side of the house, and the porch was cold. She stood, feeling sweaty and shaky, and hopped slowly around the scattered mail to her chair.

In the kitchen, she could see the light on the answering machine. After a minute she grabbed a crutch and hobbled in to push the replay button.

"Chelsea," said Rosa's voice. "I am so sorry I could not come or call today. Simão is furious at me, and he said I had to work with him in his office until five o'clock. I don't know if I mentioned I am sometimes his secretary. I hope you are all right. Simão is gone for a few minutes if you want to call. *Adeus*."

"Tell Simão to buzz off, Rosa," she told the air, then went to her computer.

She punched the on buttons for printer, monitor and computer and listened to the hard disk whine as it booted up.

Chelsea Anne Faust, she typed at the top of what would become her new resume. "Those bastards," she kept muttering under her breath. "They're all bastards."

211

Chapter Sixteen

Chelsea dozed in front of a TV talk show the next afternoon. Envelopes addressed to all the major Bay Area newspapers waited for the mail carrier. She would show Mel and George P. Dunning that she didn't need them.

That morning Angie had come upstairs with coffee, bagels and strawberry jam. "Hope you like bagels," she had said, holding her squirming daughter with one hand and the bakery bag with the other.

"That's my favorite breakfast. Want to come in?"

"No thanks. I can't. But let me know if you need anything else."

"No, no, I'm fine, thank you."

Now when she heard footsteps on the stairs, she assumed it was either Rosa or the neighbors coming to check on her again. She opened the door. "Dad!

Her father stood, a camera case looped over his shoulder, car keys in hand. "I knew something was wrong," he said.

"I was just--busy," she tried, her voice falling into a near whisper. "I didn't want you to worry."

"It's our job as parents." He looked past her to the easy chair and the TV tray full of the remnants of her breakfast and lunch. "Looks like you'd better sit back down."

They sat. Dad set the camera case on the coffee table. "Now, what happened, and let's have the truth."

The stern set of his narrow lips reminded her of those nights when she was a teenager and stayed out past her midnight curfew. Her father would be waiting just inside the door, demanding an explanation.

She sighed. "You make me feel like I'm 14 years old."

"Sometimes you act like it."

"Want a bagel? A beer? Coffee?"

He waved his hand. "Later. Tell the story already."

"Okay, okay. I got this anonymous phone call. . ."

As she talked, his thin lips grew narrower still. When she finished, he removed his glasses and massaged his eyes. Chelsea noticed the deep lines underneath.

"You know that was absolutely stupid of you." His voice shook.

Her throat was dry. After all these years, it still hurt to have her father angry at her. "Yes, I know."

"Even more stupid is that you didn't call us right away to help you."

"I figured you had enough trouble."

Dad was silent, rubbing the leather strap on the camera case. Chelsea heard a motorcycle rev and another one echo, then both shot down the street with a roar. Dad pushed himself back against the couch. "To be honest, part of me wishes I had been there to take those pictures."

"There is a thrill to it, Dad. It would have been such a great story."

"But you shouldn't have gone alone."

"I know, I know."

Dad slapped his knees and stood. "I will have some coffee. Don't move. I'll get it."

"It's ready. Just turn it on."

He started the pot then returned and passed the camera to Chelsea.

"I planned to give this to you anyway. Looks like you need another camera now."

Chelsea swallowed. This was the camera Dad had used when she was first starting out, when they used to go on shooting expeditions together. His trusty Pentax. Nothing automatic, but it was solid and dependable. He had other, newer cameras, but this had always been his favorite. "Dad, are you sure?"

"I'm sure. I don't need half a dozen cameras. Now that I have time, I figured I might as well take some pictures. I was cleaning out my camera gear, and well, I decided I didn't want you to have to wait till I died to get this old gem. Besides, with my old eyes I need auto-focus these days."

"Wow." She opened the case, which still smelled of leather after all these years. "It looks great. Any film in it?"

"Yes. Tri X inside, couple rolls of Kodachrome in the holders."

She aimed the camera at her father and studied his weary face through the viewfinder. Turning the focus ring until the stripes on his shirt were clearly defined, she set the exposure and clicked the shutter.

213

"I will think of you every time I take a picture."

"Good. Maybe you'll use your head about where you go with it."

"I will. How's that coffee coming?"

As they sipped together a while later, Chelsea wondered whether to tell her father about her job. But he looked sad enough. It could wait.

"What are you thinking, Dad?" she asked softly.

His eyes were a gentle gray. "I was thinking how young you look. How could an old guy like me have such a kid for a daughter?"

"You're not old, and I'm not such a kid."

He glanced out the window. "Your mother's at the hairdresser. She thinks I'm at home as usual. But I have to get out sometimes or I'll go crazy."

"Dad, I'm sorry about your job."

He drank the last of his coffee. "Ah, don't let it bother you. Anyway, I'm going to have to tell your mother about you being hurt. I know why you lied. But she is going to want you to come home until you heal."

"No, I can't."

"Honey, look at you. You need help."

"I have help. John and his wife from downstairs are here a couple times a day. My friend Rosa cooks and cleans and does all kinds of stuff for me. I'm fine."

"You can't expect your friends to wait on you indefinitely."

"I don't. I expect to be out in the world next week. I'm not hurt that bad, and I need to work."

"How much time do you have off?"

Gulp. "I'm supposed to stay home for three weeks and collect Worker's Comp. But I'm thinking about looking for another job." At least that part was true.

"Your mother will want you at home."

"I know. But I'd go nuts."

The phone rang.

Rosa, sounding out of breath, said she would be there in an hour to make dinner.

Chelsea smiled at her father. "See, Rosa's coming to cook dinner. I'm fine."

He shook his head. "Well, I'd better get home before your mother arrives with her new hairdo. Take good care of that camera."

She stood at the door and watched him take the steps slowly, carefully. When he was gone, she returned to her chair and picked up the camera again. It had been babied for 30 years. No smudges or nicks. Like new. Clean and proper like Dad's photos.

Giving her the camera was like giving away part of himself. "Damn," she whispered, gently snapping the camera case shut.

"Avó is asking to see you," Rosa said later as they sat together over shrimp salads. "She wants to finish her story."

"I'm eager to hear the rest." Chelsea speared a shrimp, dipped it in thousand island dressing and put it in her mouth. "Shoot. How am I going to get there?"

"Maybe I can borrow Simão's car." But Rosa looked doubtful. "He doesn't like me to do that. Says I do not need to drive. "Take the bus," he says. He needs his car for his big business deals, he says."

"Speaking of big business deals, does he pay you for your time?"

"Oh, not exactly, but he pays for the house and the food and the car and Avó. . ."

"I know, but you could do the same work somewhere else and get actual money."

"She shrugged. "I'd rather be an artist."

"Do you like what you're doing at the paper?"

She sipped at the white wine she had brought and nodded. "Yes, I like it very much. Simão, he thinks it is foolish, but when I see my name under the picture, Rosa M. Freitas, oh, it makes me feel important, special."

"You are, Rosa."

They clinked glasses and toasted each other.

"I suppose you are anxious to go back to work."

Chelsea sighed. "Oh, Rosa. They're laying me off."

"Firing you?"

"Sort of."

"Because you got hurt? I thought, in America--"

"It's a complicated country. Anyway, I mailed resumes today to all the major newspapers in the area. I should have a new job before the old one expires."

"That is good." Rosa half-smiled, her eyes worried.

"I'm sure this will turn out to be the best thing that could have happened. I'll be forced to go to a better job at a bigger paper with managers who have some moral strength."

Rosa narrowed her eyes, pondering, then pushed her chair back and collected the empty plates. "I thought we might see Avó on Friday. I will get the car. 10 o'clock?"

Chelsea watched her scrape leftovers into the garbage disposal, rinse the plates and set them in the dishwasher. "What's the rush, Rosa?"

"You need to practice your Portuguese before you forget," she mumbled, turning the water on so high and scraping so vigorously at the frying pan they couldn't talk over the noise.

As soon as the dishes were done, Rosa put on her sweater. "I cannot stay. I have to go home," and Chelsea found herself alone in front of the television again.

"Ai, Deus," Avó cried when she saw Chelsea coming on crutches, her face scratched, pain in her eyes.

Chelsea smiled and started to reach out her hand to reassure Avó, but she almost lost her balance. She forced a laugh. "Avó, I guess your prediction was right."

Rosa translated and Avó nodded. *"Ah, sim. Sabia."*

"She knew," Rosa said.

Suddenly Avó burst into tears. *"Ah, minha pobre Fátima. Minha neta."*

"Avó, não," Rosa begged, kneeling in front of her grandmother's wheelchair. *"Não chore."* She turned back to Chelsea. "I'm afraid you have reminded her of what happened to Fátima. Someday I will tell you--"

"I know. Antóio told me, and then I looked up the old newspaper clippings."

"Oh. So you understand why Simão. . ." She let the words drop.

"Sort of." Chelsea leaned over Avó, patting the heavy shoulder.

"*Estou bem,*" she said, reaching for Portuguese words. "*Isto não é nada. Sou--forte.* Strong. Yes.*"

After a while, Avó looked up, dabbing her wrinkled cheeks with her handkerchief, and nodded. "*Sim. A minha escritora. Vamos falar mais.*"

"My writer. Let us talk more," Rosa translated.

They went back to Avó's room with its smells of powder and potpourri. Rosa pushed the wheelchair slowly, Chelsea hobbling behind.

After they were seated, she pulled out her tape recorder and set it on the dresser between them. She opened her notebook and looked at Avó.

Rosa translated as before.

"When we talked last time, you were in a bad fix. Your husband had come home after being gone for years, and he didn't even remember you. Everybody treated you as nobody. What happened?"

Avó's eyes teared up again. Chelsea looked at Rosa, anxious. Her friend shrugged.

The grandmother's voice came out low and quivery. Rosa bit her lip as she listened. "My God, Chelsea. She says her husband Pedro got drunk that night, very drunk, and forced himself on her. He didn't care who she was, she was just a woman, and he wanted a woman. She remembers the baby was crying while it happened, and she was crying, too. Surely Pedro's parents will hear and stop him, she thought. His father looked in the doorway, but he just smiled, as if everything was the way it was supposed to be. But it wasn't.

"She got pregnant again right away, but this baby was doomed. It died in her womb. Pedro's family blamed her for losing this son. It had to be her fault, they said. It was her cold attitude that killed the baby.

"The priest was no help. He agreed with them. She did not welcome her husband or the baby, and that is why the infant died."

"That's awful," Chelsea whispered.

Rosa nodded. "Years passed. She had one more baby, a girl, whom she loved very much. It was like she finally had a friend. Meanwhile Pedro was teaching his son, Pedro Jr., whom Avó called João, all about farming and sailing. He filled his head with stories of

217

America, and little João was always talking about going away on a ship just like his papa. It broke Avó's heart to hear that. But it was a man's world. She was just like a servant. *Como?*"

Avó shook her head and waved her hand in the air.

"She wants to skip the next few years. Nothing to say. Same thing except that something went wrong inside her so she could not have any more babies. She thanked God, even though the priest told her it was a sin to be glad about that.

"Her mother-in-law died, and her father-in-law became an invalid, and she had to take care of him. Her own mother died, too, and she never got to say good-bye. João got big, as did his sister Cristina. And then--*o qûe? Ai Deus.*"

"What?"

"A big volcano eruption shook the whole island. Lava came down from the mountain and covered many houses. People were running away, getting into boats and going to Pico or Terceira and from there to America. 'We must go, too,' Pedro's father said, but he was too weak to help. Pedro was out somewhere, Avó didn't know where. He had not been home since the day before. João, he was stubborn like his father, he refused to leave his home or even to help pack. Cristina did what she could, but the lava was coming, and Pedro's father was too heavy for Avó and the little girl to carry. It was coming, it was coming--"

Avó's eyes were far away, seeing the destruction again.

"It was like black tar flowing over everything, steaming hot. It reached the doorway. Cristina and Avó screamed and pulled at Pedro's father. The old man yelled at them, 'Leave me here. You run. I am dying anyway.'

"'No, Grandpa,' said Cristina, 'we cannot leave you,' and she pulled even harder.

"'Stop,' he said, 'You are just hurting me and yourselves. It is God's will.' Then there was a scream from outside. João had been trying to free the donkey, and the lava had come over his feet, burning them. With just a look back at her father-in-law, Avó hurried to her son, pulled him away and they both ran toward the ocean. They thought Cristina was behind them. But she was still inside the house, not willing to leave her grandfather."

Avó fell silent. Chelsea heard a robin singing outside. Down the hall, a worker was talking to someone.

"*Mortos*," Avó said softly.

"Dead," Rosa echoed, but Chelsea understood.

"Oh, Avó," Chelsea said, grabbing a tissue from the box beside the bed. "How awful. What about Pedro?"

"*Morto, também.*"

"I've heard this part before," Rosa put in. "Pedro was downtown at the *taberna* trying to find a buyer for the land. He claimed the lava would make it the richest farmland around. He was still talking when the bar collapsed on top of him."

"Good Lord." Chelsea set down her pen. "We should stop for today, shouldn't we?" She looked anxiously at Avó, who seemed to be seeing something far away.

Avó shook her head and continued the story.

"Horrible as it sounds, Avó's life got better after that. She missed her daughter terribly, but she was finally free of Pedro and his parents. She took João home to her family, and he grew up a better man than he would have with Pedro around. He still dreamed about going to America, but he never had enough money to actually do it. He was 18 when he married and became the father of Simão and me. When we grew up, Simão fulfilled his father's dream of coming to America, and here we are."

"I feel like I missed something in between," Chelsea said.

"Maybe next time. Avó is tired, and they are about to serve lunch."

Chelsea put out her hand. "Avó, thank you for sharing your story with me. Um, *muito obrigada dizerme a sua historia.* Is that right?"

Rosa laughed. "She understands. Thank you for listening to her story. We have nothing from that time, no pictures, no written records-- nobody could write. Now we will have something."

Avó suddenly seemed to notice Chelsea and Rosa again. She pointed to Chelsea's foot in the cast. "*O que é que aconteceu?*"

"I fell down taking pictures," she said, patting her shoulder, "but it's not too bad."

219

The sunlight was bright after the gloom of Avó's room. Chelsea shielded her eyes with her hand and looked up and down the street. "I'm hungry. How about you?"

"Sure." Rosa smiled. "I can make you lunch."

"Nonsense. You've slaved enough for me. Let me take you to one of my favorite restaurants."

"Here?" Rosa looked anxiously in the direction of Simão's office.

"Oh no. How about Mexican food?"

Soon they were eating tortilla chips and drinking sangria at Mexico Lindo. Chelsea's mind was still on Avó's story.

"A lot of years have passed since all that happened," she mused aloud. "I mean, she's an old lady now."

"Yes. She is 86 years old."

"But what did she do in between?"

Rosa shrugged and dipped a chip into the salsa. "I don't know. Just life, being a mother and grandmother."

"Yes, but everything is so different for her from where she grew up. The language, the clothing, the food. The transition must have been hard for her."

"Ask her next time you visit." Rosa suddenly started choking on a tortilla chip. Her dark eyes were fixed on a tall blond man coming in the door.

"Who is that?"

Her cheeks scarlet, she rasped, "It is Mark. My American friend."

"From the airport?"

"Yes."

Mark came toward them, smiling. "Ah, Rosa, *como está?*"

"*Estou bem,*" Rosa said

"I'm glad." Mark leaned over and kissed her, stroking Rosa's hair. "I really enjoyed last night."

Chelsea looked from one to the other, grinning. So that's why Rosa was in such a hurry to leave after dinner.

"Oh, Chelsea," said Rosa. "This is Mark. Mark, Chelsea is a friend of mine. She works at the newspaper."

Worked, thought Chelsea, past tense.

"Really? I think I've seen your byline. In fact, weren't you on the cover a few weeks ago?"

It was Chelsea's turn to blush. "Yes, I'm afraid so."

"Well, congratulations on the race. Listen, I wish I could stay and talk, but I just came to pick up some takeout. We've got two guys out sick and I can't afford to be gone very long."

"Of course," Rosa said, nodding vigorously.

"Nice to meet you," he said to Chelsea before kissing Rosa again, a long slow kiss that was embarrassing to watch. "Call me," he whispered.

As he went to the cash register for his food, Chelsea grinned. "Pretty handsome."

"Well, yes."

"And he likes you."

"Yes." Rosa poured more sangria into her still half-full glass. "So tell me about this book you want to write."

Chelsea sighed. "All I know right now is there are stories to be told. I'm not sure how I should tell them. But if I don't get a job, I'll have plenty of time to figure it out."

Chelsea sat back and stretched her cramped fingers as the computer printed out Avó's story. Sunlight poured through the kitchen window, lighting up the stacks of papers, books and photos around her and glinting off the glass of iced tea next to the computer.

Her crutches lay against the wall. She had been so involved in her work she had completely forgotten her injuries. The ribs still ached. Her ankle didn't hurt much anymore, but the cast was heavy and in her way. She couldn't take a real shower, and she still hadn't figured out how to drive with it.

The breeze gently stirring the leaves on the twin cherry trees out back, the puffy white clouds, and the clear air made her want to get out and run. What a perfect day to go to Alum Rock Park, she thought. Or camping on the coast.

Five more weeks. The doctor had said on Tuesday that everything was healing fine. He had given her a walking cast, making it easier to get around. She would have to start slowly, building up the strength before she could run again, but by Christmas, she would barely remember she had had a broken ankle.

Christmas. She leaned back against the wall. If she kept at it, she could have her book done by then. Then would come the challenge of trying to sell it. Her mother would probably still think it was a foolish waste of time.

Was it? Chelsea picked at a loose thread on the binding around her cast. She still felt like an outsider among the Portuguese community. It simply wasn't her world. She had grown up completely American and had gotten plunged into Portuguese society only because her publisher wanted to sell advertising.

She saw good stories in the lives of the Portuguese, but was she sharing her own heritage or just taking advantage of the connection to further her career? She could just as well write about German women, using her father's side of the family. All immigrants had things in common.

A heavy knock on the door startled her out of her reverie. She hobbled slowly across the kitchen and into the living room.

It couldn't be Rosa. Her knock was light, feathery. Maybe John, although he wasn't usually so ham-handed.

More knocking.

"I'm coming!" she called. "Give me a break." This had better not be a salesperson. The "no solicitors" sign on her door discouraged a few peddlers, but most ignored it.

She looked through the peephole and gasped.

Slater's bulky body filled the whole view. Her heart pounding, she went to the window, but saw no one else around. She dialed John's number downstairs. "Just a minute!" she called toward the door.

Angie answered the phone.

"Ang, the councilman who got me beat up is here. Can you get John?"

Flustered, Angie stuttered, "Uh, n-no, he-he's at work. Is that the guy knocking?"

"Yeah. I don't know what to do."

"Oh Jeez. I'll page him . . ." The baby cried in the background.

The knocking stopped. "Wait. He stopped. I'm going to leave the phone off the hook and see what he wants. If I holler, call 911."

Chelsea opened the door a crack, looking around the security chain. "Mr. Slater?"

222

Slater took in the cast and the fading scratches on her face and shook his head. "Broken ankle?"

"Yes, from where your friend kicked me. Bruised ribs, too."

"You shouldn't have been there."

"That's no excuse for violence. Now what do you want?"

"Can I come in?"

"No."

His fat face seemed to cave in on itself as he struggled with his words. "You have to understand what your pictures and article would do to me. My position in the community is all I have left. I have no family, no house, no money."

"I'm sorry, but that's not my problem."

"If you could write about how I'm trying to help the homeless, how I've been studying their situation close-hand--"

"Mr. Slater, I'm not writing anything about you."

His eyes lit up. "You're not?"

"My publisher is a buddy of yours, or used to be. The story is dead."

"Thank God."

"But, if I ever get another chance, I will expose you for what you are. They can take away my space in the paper, but I know what I know. That doesn't change."

Slater shook his head. "You reporters have no hearts."

"Sure we do. We just believe people have a right to know when their politicians are ripping them off."

"So what do you want?"

"What do you mean, like money? You can't bribe me. Just don't bother me. Don't threaten me, don't send your goons after me, just leave me alone."

He shrugged. "Fine. Besides, it's a dead story. I'm staying with a friend now."

"A lady friend? Great. Thanks for coming. Good-bye." And she shut the door in his face. Shrieks from the baby downstairs reminded her the phone was still off the hook. "Angie?" she said into the phone. But there was no answer. She could hear Angie talking to the baby. Gently she hung up and sank into her easy chair.

223

Slater had cost her more than a broken ankle. Her job was gone, too. In fact, they seemed to have a lot in common. They were both unemployed, with no money. But he represented himself as a solid upstanding citizen when he was gambling city money away. Chelsea had just been trying to do her job.

Chapter Seventeen

A week later, she was watching three women argue about a family feud on the "Oprah Winfrey Show" when she heard the sirens.

Fire engines went by all the time; it was no big deal, but this time they seemed to go on forever. They headed east down Santa Clara Street, toward Little Portugal. Chelsea felt a chill run through her as she looked out her back window and saw a cloud of smoke in the distance. She switched the TV to the local station.

"Oh my God." On the screen, flames roared out the top of the I.E.S. Hall. In the foreground, a crowd was gathered, among them a tall man in a suit. Simão?

The I.E.S. Hall was where the Holy Ghost Festival concluded, where she went to dinner and danced with Simão, where the old Portuguese men played cards every day. Built by the community 60 years ago, it was the center of every major activity among the Azorean immigrants. The band practiced there. Couples held their wedding receptions and anniversary parties there. Dances, crab feeds, bingo games. It was constantly in use.

This was a huge story, and she was still technically a Weekly Times reporter for a few more days.

Without thinking, Chelsea switched off the TV, grabbed her father's camera off the coffee table and clunked down the stairs, leaning on one crutch.

At the truck, she paused. "Rats. Well, there has to be a way." She unlocked the door and got in, laying her crutch across the back seat. She clutched with her left foot, put the truck in neutral and turned the key. The faithful engine roared into action.

"Okay." She took off the brake, letting the truck coast down the driveway, turning the wheels to face south on Fifth Street. Now came the challenge. She touched her heavy right foot to the accelerator. The truck lurched forward. She stomped the brake with her left foot.

"Okay," she said, again. "Concentrate." She eased her plastered foot onto the accelerator, carefully letting out the clutch. The truck moved ahead slowly .

It was a slow, awkward process, but she made it onto Santa Clara Street, speeding through yellow lights, trying not to stop, thinking only of what lay ahead.

She saw the flames from several blocks away, rising up over the billboards, casting a pall of smoke over rush-hour traffic on Highway 101.

Fire trucks, police cars and hundreds of people blocked the road in front of Five Wounds Church and the burning hall next door. Chelsea parked a block away in a freight zone and stared at the blaze. Her hands were trembling. Several times the truck had jumped ahead, nearly hitting the vehicle in front of her, and she was exhausted from the effort after weeks of doing almost nothing.

As she opened the door of the truck, she could feel the heat of the fire, and smoke stung her eyes and nose. Grabbing her notebook, pen and her father's camera, she hopped out and began clumping toward the fire.

After a few paces, she cursed and returned, reaching inside to toss her press pass on the dash. Maybe it would help stop the truck from getting towed away.

She moved forward as quickly as she could, wincing as the camera banged her ribs.

A crowd had gathered on the sidewalk. Women stood weeping. Children clutched their mothers' hands and stared. Old men gawked, their wrinkled faces stark in the firelight.

Firefighters already had their hoses trained on the roof.

As she pointed her camera toward the flames, she heard a police officer with a deep voice yell, "Don't go in there anymore, sir. It isn't safe."

"We must go in," came the reply from a familiar voice.

She lowered her camera and stared as Simão and three other men disappeared into the smoke. "Oh no," she whispered. Her heart beat faster than usual, and she wanted to run in after him, but she was pinned in place by her broken ankle and the crowd that surrounded her.

"What are they doing?" shouted someone at her side. It was Paul Nixon, the lanky young photographer from the Mercury News.

"I'm not sure. Some guys just went inside. The police told them not to, but they went anyway."

"Fools," he said, clicking away. He glanced at her crutch, but didn't have time to ask.

As Chelsea took pictures, her mind was racing. What was Simão doing in there? Were there people trapped inside? Would he get out in time?

"That ceiling's going to go any minute now," the other photographer said.

"I hope not," she replied through clenched teeth. Oh please, she prayed. I'm not much on religion, but please. . . .

A shout echoed through the crowd as the four men emerged, their clothes and faces black with smoke. They carried band instruments and memorabilia. Simão held a tuba, a stack of framed photographs and an Azorean flag on a tall brass stand. Chelsea shot pictures as fast as she could advance the film and punch the shutter. Beside her, the other guy's motordrive was whirring. TV cameras along the chain-link fence caught the action for the late news.

The Portuguese men set the gear on the hot asphalt of the parking lot and started back in. A police officer grabbed Simão by the arm.

"That's it," the officer said. "No more."

"But there is still. . ."

"It's too late. I'm sorry."

The other men were similarly restrained. Cameras clicked and whirred amid the shouting of police and firefighters and distraught chatter and wails from the onlookers.

Suddenly, with a whoosh and a burst of orange flame, the roof fell in. The crowd shrieked and fell back, Chelsea with them as red embers landed around their feet.

Click. She had reached the end of her film. "Damn," she hissed, reaching into her pocket for another roll. But she was caught by Simão's face. He stood with tears rolling down his blackened cheeks, his shoulders bent, the flag still in his hand.

Chelsea felt tears come into her own eyes. Around her, men and women were holding each other, consoling each other in Portuguese. It was like watching their home burn down.

She put the unexposed film back in her pocket and limped toward Simão, conscious of stepping into the TV cameras' range. If her parents were watching the news, they would see her. So would George P. Dunning. She didn't care.

The hall was still burning. Police and fire radios blared, generators thrummed, and water sprayed from the fire department's cherrypicker truck onto the remains of the charred roof.

Behind her, a Mercury reporter was interviewing bystanders.

"We will build it again," she heard, and knew she should be asking questions, too. Her story would barely make this week's paper if she wrote it and developed the film tonight.

Simão saw her coming and brushed at his eyes with soot-covered hands. "The reporter comes to the fire." He stared at the flames, his voice raw with smoke and tears.

"The woman comes to her friend," she said, fighting her crutch to put her arms around him, oblivious to the soot getting on her white shirt. "I'm so sorry, Simão."

He shook his head, still fighting tears. "It started so quickly. We could not get many things out. There was an old man who wouldn't leave. I had to carry him out. He was burned pretty bad. I don't know. . ."

"Oh, Simão."

"At least the band can still play. There is a *festa* this weekend." He swallowed and looked over her head at the fire.

"I was so frightened when I saw you going in, Simão. It wasn't safe, you know."

"I did not care. I could not leave everything to burn."

She nodded. "You're braver than I am."

He shrugged and looked more closely at her. "I heard you were injured. Are you all right? I am surprised you are here."

"I had to come, Simão. I care about these people. I didn't think I did, but--"

He frowned. "You should be interviewing them. I can help you."

Simão translated as she leaned awkwardly on her crutch, struggling to write in the fading light and the thick smoke. Chelsea talked to an old man who had helped build the hall many years ago, to the leader of the Portuguese band, and to a woman who had just held her 50th anniversary party there. They all spoke of God's will, of fate, of how they would find the money to build a new hall better than the old one.

Some of the people drifted away, but Chelsea and Simão stood together with a core of Portuguese men and women, watching as the flames continued past sunset, shooting into the dark sky.

It was 10 o'clock before the firefighters packed up their hoses and drove away, their heavy trucks throbbing down Santa Clara Street.

"Let's go," said the last police officers. They had set up sawhorse barricades, stringing yellow tape around the charred remains of the building.

Chelsea's lungs were scorched and full of smoke. She felt sweaty and dirty, and her arms and legs ached from standing for so long.

"I guess it's over," she said, dreading the awkward drive back home.

Simão nodded. Most of the others had already left. The last stragglers were heading for their cars or walking home down the quiet smoky streets.

"It's too late to go back to my office," she said. She wasn't welcome there anyway. Mel might not even publish her photos, although she didn't see how he could resist. This was front page news.

"My office is nearby."

"Pardon?"

Simão clasped her hand. "If you like, we can go to my office and wash up a little, then I will take you to get something to eat."

"For an interview? Frankly, I'm all interviewed out. I'm ready to collapse."

Simão shook his head, stroking her hand with his rough fingers. "No, I do not want to be interviewed, and I am not very hungry. I just want to be with you tonight."

Surprised, Chelsea moved forward a few steps before Simão spoke again, his voice hoarse and so quiet she could barely hear him.

"When Joaquim told me what happened to you, all I could think of was my wife, Fátima, and what happened to her. And I knew then how much I cared about you." He swallowed. "Someday I will tell you how she died."

She stopped and reached up to touch his sooty face. "António told

229

me, Simão. It must have been terrible for you." In her weariness, tears came quickly to her eyes. "I have missed you, too, but I thought you hated me. We are so very different."

"Not so different." He pulled her close. She lost her balance, but Simão held her up. As they hugged, a renegade tear sneaked out and down her face. Rosa was right after all, she thought. The intuition of the Portuguese woman's heart.

Simão gently released her. She sniffed and dashed at the tears with her hand.

He pulled a handkerchief from his pocket and started to give it to her, but it was black with smoke.

"Never mind. I've got tissues in my truck. If it's still there." She looked into the distance and saw the truck where she had left it. She sighed and started toward it.

Simão stopped her. "I will drive you to my office. We will get your truck later. It will be okay."

She had no strength to fight. Leaning against his shoulder, she smoothed his hair out of his face and gently touched the dark stubble beginning to appear on his chin. It was impossible to have a relationship with this man; they were opposites in nearly everything, but her heart overruled her mind.

She kissed him on the cheek and let him help her to his car.

They took turns in the restroom, a tiny cubicle that smelled of strawberry air freshener and had a calendar from the Azores on the back of the door. Chelsea smiled at the crocheted toilet paper holder perched on the toilet tank as she washed her face in cold water. She brushed at the stains on her shirt, but they turned into a gray smudge. The shirt was ruined, but she didn't really care.

She was aware of Simão just outside the door, letting her have the bathroom first. She could hear him coughing. She could still taste and smell the smoke in her own mouth and nose, and her ears roared with the noises at the fire--the radios, the people, the water, the fire itself like an ocean wave constantly building and never breaking.

She saw Simão standing in front of the crowd clutching the Azorean flag, tears on his face, then felt his arms around her, tasted his lips on hers . . . She was staying in here too long. With a last look in the mirror, she opened the door.

Simão looked up from his desk and smiled wearily. "Even now you are beautiful."

"No." She bent to kiss him. The kiss was soft and sweet, their lips gently caressing each other. His lips tasted of smoke.

"Your turn," she whispered.

Conscious though she was of her deadline and the roll of photos waiting to be processed, Chelsea felt as if time had slowed to a dream pace, every moment to be cherished.

Simão changed out of his torn and charred suit into a pair of khaki slacks and a blue shirt he had left at the office. In casual dress with a hint of a beard, he looked more handsome than ever, Chelsea thought. The image he put on for the public was gone. She liked the real man behind it better. There was a vulnerability mixed with strength that she found very appealing.

They sat at a back table at Sousa's sipping *vinho verde*, Portuguese green wine, holding hands across the white cloth. This time Simão let Chelsea order for herself, and she chose the *camarão*, shrimp in a rich red sauce, while Simão had steak.

Despite all that had come between them, words seemed unnecessary now. Their hands clutched together wove ties stronger than language could.

Finally Chelsea cleared her throat. "Simão? That picture in the Weekly Times. . ."

"Let us not talk about it."

"But I don't want it hanging between us. I want to make sure we don't fight about this again."

Simão shook his head and chuckled wearily.

"What?" Chelsea said, leaning close.

"At first I was furious. But many of my friends said I was lucky to have such a beautiful woman with such a--" He grinned. "--a healthy, sexy body."

She stared, feeling a weight slide off her back. "Really?"

"*Verdad*e. True. Although. . ."

"I'll get a better bra."

231

Simão rolled his eyes. "You do have a beautiful body," he said in a quiet voice. "It makes me--I want to touch you and be close to you."

"Me too." She breathed it more than said it. The look in Simão's eyes sent a bolt of electricity through her entire body.

"But it is not right."

She pounded her fist softly on the table. "This is America, Simão."

"It is the same God telling us what is good and bad."

"And he brought us together, so it must be good, even if it doesn't make sense."

"Perhaps." He pulled his hand away slowly as the waitress came with their dinners. "I am very hungry," he said, more loudly than he needed to as the girl set down their plates. The waitress smiled and walked away.

"This looks great," Chelsea said, her desire making all her senses more alert.

"*Pudim* afterwards?" His eyes were dancing.

"Not a chance."

His smile faded as he looked out the window. More people than usual lingered on the streets tonight, too devastated by the fire to go home. "That building meant so much to our people. And it is completely gone."

Chelsea nodded sympathetically. "It was a grand hall."

"We will build it again."

"I know." If their romance could be resurrected, surely so could a mere building.

She looked toward the empty stage. There was no *fado* tonight, but she could swear she heard a Portuguese woman singing.

Chelsea smiled into the developer tray, watching another photo of the burning I.E.S. Hall grow more and more distinct. In the foreground stood Simão, clutching the Azorean flag, tears in his eyes, as a police officer gripping him roughly by the shoulders.

What a shot, she thought. Maybe someday this very photo would hang on their wall, where their children and grandchildren could see it.

She giggled, giddy at 3 o'clock in the morning from exhaustion and love. Thank God Rosa had replenished her darkroom supplies.

When the photo was fully formed, Simão's suit a deep black in the red darkroom light, she lifted it with rubber-tipped wooden tongs, let it drip for a few seconds, then swished it in the stopbath tray and slipped it gently into the fixer on top of three other fire photos.

They were good pictures, some of her best work. Flames shooting into the sky. Firefighters perched above the roof, their hoses raining water onto the blaze. Old women praying the Rosary. And Simão.

She set the timer for five minutes and sank onto the wobbly wooden stool with a sigh. Her story was almost done, drafted while the film was washing and drying. In the morning, she would have to add a few details--dollar amount of the loss, the exact date when the hall was built, the official word on the suspected cause. Some of the people she talked to thought it had been sparked by an electrical short on the top floor, where some remodeling had been going on.

It was a great story. Now all she had to do was get Mel to agree to run it.

She stared at Simão's picture. Worn out as he was, he had driven her truck home for her, trusting her with his automatic-shift Buick.

When she announced she was going to work in the darkroom, he offered to accompany her, but she could see he was ready to collapse. "No, you need to sleep. I'll be fine."

As it was, he had walked through the dark yard around her apartment, checking to make sure it was safe before holding her close and kissing her good night.

It was after midnight then. They had finished dinner and gone out to Santa Clara Street, now empty and quiet except for an occasional car passing on its way to the freeway. Standing on the sidewalk, arms around each other, they fell naturally into an embrace, their lips pressing against each other hungrily, their bodies squeezed together tightly.

As the lights went out in the restaurant behind them, Simão pulled away, breathless. "It is not right to do this on the street."

"No," she whispered, her face against his scratchy beard.

"Come." He helped her into his car and drove quickly to his office.

They walked the musty stairs together. As Simão unlocked the

233

door, she could see his hands were shaking. She felt herself shivering.

The red light on his answering machine glowed in the dark. He turned on a small desk lamp that was not much brighter than a candle and led her to the couch, pulling her down beside him.

She remembered she had quit the pill last month because she hadn't had sex in so long. "Simão," she whispered. "I have no birth control."

"It's okay," he said, his voice a purr in the dark. "I knew this would happen someday." She stared as he pulled a condom out of the bottom drawer of his desk.

Now was not the time to think about it. He pulled her legs across his lap and kissed her, slowly pressing her back onto the couch. His lips explored her mouth, her chin, her neck, nuzzling at the top of her blouse. Gently he undid the buttons and kissed the tops of her breasts.

"Oh God," she breathed.

"You are like an angel, Chelsea Faust."

"You are incredible." She struggled with the buttons on his shirt, plunging her hand into the thick hair on his chest, twisting to kiss him and touch him. Instinctively she reached out for the bulge in his pants.

He gasped as her fingers touched him.

Things progressed rapidly. He helped her out of her jeans and underwear, then pulled off his own shoes, socks and pants. They kissed and touched, trying to reach everywhere at once until finally he begged "Now, please," and entered her.

They came together quickly, crying out so loud Chelsea feared Simão's neighbors would call the police.

Afterward she lay limp in his arms, tears on her cheeks, naked except for the cast on her ankle. No one had ever touched her so deeply before. Simão sprawled beside her, his hot breath in her ear. "I could not resist you any more," he gasped.

"Nor I you."

Still inside her, his perspiration soaking her chest, Simão raised himself on his elbows, careful not to push against her ribs. "Chelsea Faust, you are a gift from God. I want you to be my wife."

Now as she slipped her photos into the sink, watching the prints dance in the current, she shook her head and sighed again. Everything

234

else in her life seemed to shrink in importance. Simão wanted to marry her. She had not given him an answer. "Not tonight," she said, kissing him again. She had only known him for a couple of months, and half that time they weren't speaking to each other. She lived with Jeffrey for almost three years, yet they had never reached this point.

It's chemistry, she thought, hormones, animal instinct. She chuckled. The Portuguese woman's heart.

Simão didn't understand her work or her American ways. He didn't even know about Jeffrey yet. For that matter, he didn't know that she and Rosa had become friends and had visited his grandmother. She didn't speak his language or understand his culture. So many differences.

What would her parents say? They hadn't even met him. Married? To whom? Are you sure, Dad would ask with that same worried look he had had when she announced she was leaving for Sacramento.

Others in the family would figure it was a good thing that she was finally going to settle down and have a family, especially since she had lost her job. But she would have to find another one. Simão wasn't making much money. He worked in a fish market to pay the mortgage. The rest was just dreams. Besides, she loved to chase a hot news story.

Don't do it, Chels, Jeffrey would say. You're married to your work, just like me.

Simão hadn't asked her to quit working, she thought, watching her photos swim in the washer. He knew her career was important to her.

Rosa would become her sister-in-law, and that comfortable white house in Little Portugal would become her second home. Her photograph would join the others in the living room. Her eyes closed as her daydreams faded into sleep.

The timer woke her. She turned off the water and flicked on the dryer. "This is crazy. I didn't even say yes. Yet."

As she squeegeed her photos and hung them to dry, she thought again of Rosa. Where had she been during the fire? All of Little Portugal seemed to be there, yet there was no sign of Rosa and her sketch pad. Another date with the airport man?

Chelsea sighed. So many secrets Simão didn't know about.

235

Chapter Eighteen

When the alarm shrilled at 7 a.m., Chelsea groaned and covered her eyes against the light pouring in the bedroom windows. Three hours was not enough sleep for anyone, but she wanted to get her fire photos and story to Mel before he assigned someone else to do a followup or designed the front page without it.

She threw on a robe, made coffee and showered. By 8, she was on the phone with the fire department spokesman, getting last-minute details. They were pretty sure an electrical short started the fire at the I.E.S. Hall, he said. Damage was estimated at a million dollars, a total loss, but the Portuguese were plucky people, he said. They were already planning to rebuild. Luckily, the hall had been well insured.

"Thanks," she said, hanging up and quickly plugging in the information. Then she called Mel.

"Chelsea, how's the ankle?"

"Buried in plaster. I think it's healing. But I didn't call about that. I have a story and photos for you on the fire at the Portuguese I.E.S. Hall."

"I thought you were on sick leave." His voice was brusque.

"That was your idea, not mine. Anyway, I was there and I want to bring you the scoop."

"I'm not sure--"

Chelsea didn't let him finish. "Listen, Mel, technically I'm still a reporter for the Weekly Times for a few more days. I'm being laid off for financial reasons, according to the letter I got. By the way, it would have been nice if you had told me about it in person, but anyway. These are some of the best photos I've ever taken, and this is a major story. I didn't see any other Weekly Times reporters there. All the other media covered it. Whatever you could get over the phone now won't compare to live coverage of the actual fire."

Mel sighed. "All right, fine. I need a cover photo. But after this, Faust, no more surprise stories."

"You've got a police radio. It shouldn't be a surprise. Unless you forgot to monitor it or decided Little Portugal wasn't of any more interest after they all bought ads." Lack of sleep was making her say things she knew she shouldn't.

"We're short-staffed, okay?"

"Not my fault, Mel. So why didn't you stick up for me with Dunning? You could still tell him you need me."

A long silence followed. Then Mel said, "Don't push me, Chelsea. What time will you bring the stuff in?"

"A half hour."

"I'll see you then."

Why is he being like this, she wondered. He should be glad to get the story. But she was feeling so content she refused to let Mel upset her. She decided to walk to the office, cast and all. It was a beautiful day, one of the most beautiful she had ever seen, and she was feeling invincible. Once he saw her photos, maybe even George P. Dunning would change his mind.

When Chelsea walked into the Weekly Times office, the phone was ringing, but Berta wasn't at her desk. As Chelsea reached out to answer it, the ringing ceased and the light stopped blinking.

In the newsroom, Mel bent over a sheet of paper, his head in his hand, a new pair of reading glasses perched on his nose. Sarge was typing his usual 100 words a minute, and Mandy was sitting at Chelsea's desk, staring at her computer.

Chelsea swallowed a sudden attack of regret and leaned her crutch against Mel's desk. She shrugged off the backpack and pulled out the envelope with her photos and story.

Mel looked up, taking off his glasses. "Hi. You're looking better." But his voice was a monotone, like a robot's.

"I feel good," she said. "And here's proof that I'm able to work." She slid the pictures and printed pages out and spread them on the desk.

"Nice." Mel pointed to a figure in the foreground. "Your friend Simão?"

"Yes. He went into the building several times to bring out band equipment--and he carried out an old man before I got there."

"A real hero, huh?" Still that noncommittal tone.

Sarge joined them at the desk.

"Best damn fire photos I ever saw," he said. "I bet it's a crackerjack story, too."

237

"Thanks, Sarge." She beamed at him. Sarge didn't give out praise easily, especially for work that infringed on his beat.

The old reporter shrugged. "We can hold my feature on the new fire truck," he told Mel.

"I suppose," the editor said, standing. He stacked the photos and put them back in the envelope. "Thank you for bringing these in. Excuse me."

Chelsea and Sarge stared as the editor hurried down the hall.

"What's wrong with him?" Chelsea asked.

"I don't know. Dunning, I guess, and problems with his kid. Maybe with the wife, too."

"Oh no."

"It happens. Anyway, you're gettin' a raw deal, kid."

"Thanks."

"It's their loss, Faust, and they will regret it." He looked away, his jaw twitching. "Well, I got a deadline."

As Sarge returned to his computer, Chelsea hesitated. Should she wait for Mel or what? She studied the bulletin board over her old desk. The story list from two weeks ago was still there. So was her photo of Mel Gibson as Hamlet, her list of rules for a good journalist, her award certificate from the last California Newspaper Publishers Association convention, and a photo she had taken at Alum Rock Park.

Mandy looked up. "How ya doin'?"

"Oh, fine," Chelsea replied. "You changed desks, I see."

"Yeah, I hope you don't mind, but my computer didn't work right, and Mel said you weren't coming back, so--"

The girl said it so glibly, as if she were leaving voluntarily. Chelsea cleared her throat. "Maybe I could just take a few personal things home while I'm here."

Sarge turned around. "Leave it, Faust. Maybe Dunning will change his mind after he sees your photos."

What little hope she began to feel evaporated when Mel returned, scowling. "You still here? I thought you'd be gone by now. Do you need a ride?"

She swallowed. "No. I can walk."

Taking a last look back, she shoved out the door, ignoring Berta's greeting.

The sky had turned cloudy. To match her mood, she thought. Raw deal is right. Best reporter they ever had, and they kicked me out. Already gave my desk to an intern when I worked half the night to get this story to them. She hobbled down the street, wishing she could kick stones and trash all the way home.

She was staring at her computer, trying to work up a proposal for her book, when the doorbell rang.

Simão stood there smiling in his blue suit, a huge bouquet of red roses in his hand. "Thank you," she said, blinking away tears.

"What is wrong?" He folded her into his arms, kissing her gently.

"Oh, it's not even worth crying about. I just went to the office, and somebody else was already sitting at my desk, and Mel was--never mind, it's stupid."

"Don't worry," he purred in her ear. "You don't need to work there anymore."

"I need to work somewhere," she replied, her voice hoarse.

"*Não, meu amor.*"

She pulled away and stared at him. "What are you talking about, Simão Freitas?"

"I will take care of you."

"Simão, you are a compulsive macho male, I swear. You can't afford to support the whole female world. I'll get another job."

"Perhaps," he said, kissing her again. "Can I take you to lunch now?"

His eyes were so brown and full of love she wanted to dive inside him and never come out. "Okay."

As she relaxed against the plush Buick seats, she thought how it easy it would be to let him support her all the time instead of fighting to meet deadlines, please impossible publishers and never have anything left over after she paid her bills.

"Where do you want to eat?"

"I don't know. I'm not very hungry. Whatever you want."

"How about all-American McDonald's?"

She looked at Simão's dancing eyes. "Perfect."

239

They sat on hard orange seats, holding hands across the tiny wooden table, feeding each other French fries.

"We have these in the Azores," he said, slipping a fry into her mouth.

She chewed for a minute. "Really?"

"Sure. Same thing."

"But not Big Macs."

"No. No Big Macs. We have better ice cream," he said stirring his chocolate milkshake with his straw. "Everywhere you go, you see cows. You must come to Faial. It is so peaceful. Green fields, windmills, the sea. We have so many flowers we use them as fences. The hills are lined with blue and white *hortênsias*--you call them hydrangeas."

"If it's so beautiful, why does everybody leave?"

"We all want more money. More opportunity. Better education. Our islands are pretty, but they are small. We have big families and not enough land to give a piece to every son. You can drive all the way across in a couple of hours. Here, you never run out of land."

"What happens to the daughters?"

"They marry. Move to their husbands' farms."

Like Avó, she thought. Chelsea tapped his brown hand. "What if they don't marry?"

"They become nuns perhaps, or they stay at home, taking care of their parents and their brothers and sisters all their lives."

"Don't any just leave by themselves?"

"A few. Some go to the mainland or to São Miguel, which is a bigger island with more opportunities. They become teachers or secretaries or they find a husband there."

"Some come to America, don't they?"

He wiped a blob of milkshake off his mustache with a napkin. "Yes. Usually they live with a cousin or a sister."

"Like Floralinda."

"*Sim.*" He turned her hand over and traced the lines on her palm.

She caught her breath as he reached the tender inside of her wrist.

He smiled. "Maybe I will take the afternoon off."

Chelsea had no trouble interpreting the look in his eyes. "How will you get rich?"

240

"Nobody gets rich in one day. Besides, I am the boss."

"Oh, yes." The boss who works in a fish market before he goes to his office to wheel and deal. She studied his hand, noting the rough calluses on his palm, a deep cut across his index finger. "How is the fish market?"

He shrugged. "It is all right. The people are good. The fish is good."

Chelsea chuckled. "Maybe they can find a job for me there, too."

Simão stared. "No women do this work."

"Why not?"

"It is just not right."

She punched his arm gently. "Simão, what am I going to do with you?"

He lowered his voice. "I have a very good idea. Are you finished eating?"

This time, their lovemaking was slower as they explored each other's bodies in the gray light coming through Chelsea's bedroom window.

Simão took her crutch and sat her down on the bed. "Let me help you," he said, and he started unbuttoning her blouse.

Sighing, she let him remove her blouse and skirt and slide her slip and bra down off her shoulders, baring her breasts.

"You are even more beautiful in daylight," he said, bending to kiss her nipples and circle them lightly with his tongue.

She moaned, feeling her legs start to shake. He gently shoved her backwards and began to kiss his way down from her neck over her nipples, her waist, her stomach, to where her legs parted. "Ohhhh," she moaned again, reaching up to remove Simão's shirt and slacks. His jacket and tie already lay neatly folded on the chair.

Chelsea felt the tension building higher and higher until just as Simão entered her, the world exploded in a roaring burst of light. With each thrust, it intensified until he cried out in Portuguese. Chelsea heard herself yelling "Oh oh oh!" and thought she should be quieter, but she couldn't. Simão had awakened a part of her that had long been asleep.

241

At last they relaxed, Simão still on top of her, both breathing heavily.

"Oh my gosh," she panted.

"Yes. My darling. You will marry me, won't you? We are meant to be together."

"Probably," she said, grinning into the pillow that had fallen over her face.

Simão traced the long lines of her legs and ran his hands along her stomach and breasts. "You should be in a painting."

"You too." She studied the dark hair that covered his brown chest and grew thick around his rosy penis, his firm legs and round buttocks. She touched the dark planes of his cheeks and chin, his Roman nose, the long thick lashes closed over his dark eyes. "You are built like a god."

"Me? No. That is crazy."

"I--um." She stopped herself. She was about to make a joke about how she had conducted a survey of naked men and that's how she knew Simão was the best. She thought of the others she had slept with. If Simão knew, would he be interested in her? She had known Jeffrey the longest. But there were others. Her high school boyfriend Doug, who was the first. Then Jerry, the drug addict she'd had a thing with in college, Stan, the married guy she dated briefly, and a couple other one-night relationships. Would she always have to censor her words with Simão?

Simão touched her cheek. "What are you thinking so hard about, *meu amor*?"

She shook her head. "Nothing. It's getting chilly, isn't it?"

He pulled the comforter up over her bare legs and torso. "I don't want you to ever be cold." As he kissed her, she pulled him down against her, feeling her breasts against his chest, his warm breath on her cheeks. Vaguely she thought that despite his old-country values, Simão must have had other women, too. She wondered what Fátima had been like and sighed.

Simão, his eyes closed, pulled her closer. Wrapped in each other and the quilt, still tired from the previous night, they dozed together.

When the telephone rang, Chelsea woke with a jolt, surprised at how dark it had gotten. She jumped out of bed, forgetting her cast until it hit the floor. "Damn!" she hissed into the receiver as pain shot up her leg.

"Chelsea?" said her mother in a worried voice. "What's going on?"

"Oh, Mom. Hold on."

She set down the phone and hopped to the closet to get her robe, then took the phone into the kitchen, closing the door behind her.

"Okay. Mom, hi."

"What on earth was that all about?"

Chelsea shook her head, staring at her reflection in the window-- tangled hair, robe open to the waist, her cheeks rosy. "Um, nothing. I was just taking a nap. When I went to get up, I forgot about my ankle and almost fell. But everything's under control."

"A nap? Are you all right?"

"Oh yes, I'm fine, Mom, but I've got to go. I have company."

"I thought you were asleep."

"I was, but . . ." She chewed her lip. If her mother knew that Simão was there, she would surely guess what they had been doing. But she was nearly 30 years old. Besides, she had told Mom that they were back together. This would make that lie into a truth.

"Simão is here." Before Mom could react, she added, "He and his sister have been taking turns helping me out."

Stony silence on the other end. Then finally, "I would have hoped you would call your own mother to help you."

"I didn't mean to upset you."

"Well I am upset. Is there anything else you haven't told me about?"

Chelsea rubbed her forehead. She was still half asleep and not sure what she was saying. But there seemed no point in holding anything back now. She took a deep breath and let it out in a rush of words. "I'm being laid off from my job."

"What? Oh my God. Carl!" she called, "did you know this?"

"Mom, Dad didn't know about it. Don't blame him."

Chelsea heard her father pick up the extension in the bedroom. "Chelsea, do you need any money?"

"No, no. Not right now. Thanks, Dad. I'm still covered for a few

243

weeks." They can't afford to help me, she realized with a shock.

"You'll have to move back home."

"Mom, I--no. I'll get unemployment, and I'll find another job in no time. I'm a big girl. I don't need to mooch off you guys."

"It's all right if you do," Dad said.

"We could use your company, you know," Mom added.

Chelsea felt the stabbing spines of guilt and wished her parents had had more than one child to pick on. "Maybe I'll have more time to visit," she threw out.

"Sure. What is your boyfriend doing while you're on the telephone."

"Oh, he's asleep, Mom. On the couch," she added quickly. "Did you hear about the fire last night?"

"I think I saw something on the news," Dad said.

"Simão was in the thick of it. He's exhausted."

"Well," Mom interrupted, "When are we going to meet him? Or is he another secret?"

Ouch. "Of course not. I told you all about him."

Her mother ignored that. "Well. I was calling to invite you to dinner next Saturday. Your Aunt Gloria is coming from San Leandro, and I thought you might want to talk to her for your book. You could bring your boyfriend, too."

So now Mom was taking this book seriously? Chelsea sighed. Somebody else must have convinced her. She heard Simão getting up, going into the bathroom. "Okay. That sounds good. I'll ask Simão if he can come."

"Why couldn't he?"

"Mom, he's a very busy man. He has two jobs, and he's president of the Portuguese Chamber of Commerce."

"Oh, really?" She finally sounded impressed.

"Yes, really. What time do you want us there?"

"5:00. Don't be late."

As she hung up the phone, certain her parents would be busy talking about her for the next couple hours, Simão opened the door and came to kiss her. He was wearing his trousers, but his chest and feet were bare. "*Bom dia.*"

She chuckled. "Yes, good morning. I hope the phone didn't wake you up."

"No, I noticed you were not there."

She kissed his warm face still red from the pillow. "That's sweet. It was my mother, driving me crazy. She wants us to come to dinner on Saturday."

Simão thought for a minute. "All right. That will be nice. But I am hungry tonight." He pointed to her ankle. "You cannot cook like this. Will you come to my house for dinner?"

Alternate waves of nerves and longing washed through her. Dinner again in that warm, comfortable house with the family photos and homemade candy. But how could she face Simão's mother and sister after having just been in bed with him? "Oh, I can cook," she ventured, knowing the cupboards were empty and the refrigerator had only a little cream cheese and some leftovers from Rosa's last dinner there.

"No. Let us get dressed. I will phone Mama to tell her we will be a little late and that you are coming."

As Simão spoke to his mother in Portuguese too rapid for Chelsea to understand, she stared at her closet. Should she put on a dress? For dinner at her own parents' house, she would wear jeans and a sweater, but this was Simão's house in Little Portugal. She reached for an old black corduroy skirt and a white blouse and wondered if it would always be this way, as if she were playing a role whenever she went near Little Portugal.

A light glowed over the porch as Chelsea hobbled up the sidewalk ahead of Simão. Before they reached the door, it opened and his mother came out.

"Oh, *pobrezinha*," she exclaimed when she saw Chelsea. "*Venha e sente-se.*"

"She wants you to come in and sit down," Simão translated.

"I know," Chelsea said, looking back. Tomato and oregano filled her senses as she moved into the warm entryway. The food was already on the table, and Mama beckoned them into the dining room.

245

"Where is Rosa?" Simão asked, purposely speaking English to his mother.

"*Não está aqui*," Mama replied, stubbornly sticking to Portuguese. "*Não sei onde está.*"

Chelsea was pleased that she understood. The class was helping. She was grateful to Rosa for getting her there. She hadn't mentioned it to Simão yet.

Simão was still thinking about his sister. "I must speak to her when she comes home. Lately she is gone almost every night."

"I'm sure she's okay," Chelsea said, taking the chair to which Mama pointed.

"*Meu amor*, it is not safe. Look at you."

"Yes, but I went into a dangerous situation alone. I should have known better. Rosa is probably perfectly safe."

Mama was smiling at Chelsea over the platters of chicken, potatoes and zucchini cooked with onions and tomato sauce. Clearly she knew what was happening with her and Simão and picturing her as her next daughter-in-law.

"*Come*," Mama said. "Eat." Chelsea helped herself to a chicken leg, a small serving of potatoes and zucchini. Simão handed her his plate. "*Faz favor*," he said. She filled his plate.

They were eating in silence, Simão already on his second helping, when a blob of tomato sauce dripped off her fork onto her blouse. Mama saw it fall and clicked her tongue.

"Oh, *a sua blusa.*" Suddenly Chelsea found herself at the sink with Mama, scrubbing at her blouse without success. Mama gestured that she should remove it and led her to her talcum-scented bedroom. She quickly took off her blouse and put on Mama's white sweater as Mama hurried the blouse to the washing machine.

"What a clutz," Chelsea told Simão when she returned to the table.

"Do not worry about it," he said. "Mama loves to help people."

She smiled uneasily. Most people would have let her swab off the top layer and wash the blouse at home.

Mama returned to her seat. "*Está bem*," she told Chelsea.

"*Obrigada*," she replied. Mama's smile broadened.

Mama's food must be cold, Chelsea noted, looking into the

246

kitchen for the microwave. But she didn't see one. Her parents had had a microwave for years, and a microwave oven was one of the first things she had bought for herself when she left home. But Simão's family seemed pretty old-fashioned.

When dinner was over, Chelsea followed Mama to the kitchen to help with the dishes. Mama waved her away.

"*Sente-se.*"

"No, no. Um, *vou--ajudar.*" She hoped that was the right word for help. "*Vou limpar.* I'll wash."

Mama laughed and threw up her hands. "*Obstinada como Simão.*"

Simão was watching from the doorway. "She says you are stubborn like me."

"Yes," Chelsea replied. "Now let's get those dishes in here. Where's the soap?"

Mama stood beside her and dried dishes. Chelsea thought of the many times she had done the same thing with her own mother. That was when they had some of their best conversations. She remembered Mom telling her about her grandmother's life as they washed and dried silverware. It was over dishes that she first told her mother about her plans to move in with Jeffrey.

Christmas and Easter at home brought all the women to the kitchen. She used to fight with her grandmother over who was going to dry dishes. Mom used to say the same thing Simão's mother had told her. "*Sente-se.*" Sit down.

But Grandma understood English perfectly well. Now Chelsea wondered what Simão's mother was thinking as she hummed a tune and dried the plates with a white dish towel covered with embroidered flowers she had probably stitched herself.

Or maybe Rosa had.

Growing up, Chelsea had learned to embroider, although she was more interested in photography and writing and going fishing with her grandpa. With many contributions from her grandmother and mother, she had filled a cedar chest with linens for her future home. A hope chest, Mom had called it, saying every girl should have one.

247

The chest sat in her apartment bedroom now, and the linens were still unused. But suddenly things were changing so quickly that maybe she would need them after all.

Simão had asked her again to marry him. She had said she probably would, but she knew she was just teasing him. Simão was serious. And so was his mother.

What am I doing? She kept her eyes focused on the bowl in her hand, scrubbing it way past clean as Simão's mother continued to hum. She was happy. Simão had found a new wife.

But what about her career? What about--everything?

As Chelsea sponged off the sink, Mama looked out the window. Suddenly she erupted in a volcano of words. Chelsea, a head taller, looked over her shoulder just in time to catch Rosa kissing her boyfriend on the sidewalk next to his Camero. Now it's going to fly, she thought to herself.

Simão hurried from the living room to see what his mother was chattering about. The car drove off as Rosa waved and walked slowly up the walk. Her hair was disheveled, and she moved, Chelsea thought, with the easy loose-limbed steps of a woman who had just had sex. She still had that feeling herself from her afternoon in bed with Simão.

His face was a thundercloud as Rosa entered softly, no doubt hoping no one would notice her. Chelsea watched Rosa's eyes cloud with fear as she saw her mother's and brother's faces and confusion at Chelsea standing at the sink, wearing Mama's sweater.

"*Boa noite*," Rosa said quickly, turning toward her room.

Simão blocked her way. "*Não, pára aqui.*"

Rosa stared at him, pulling herself up tall. "You are not my father, my employer or my Lord," she said in English, sounding as if she had practiced this speech before. "Simão, you do not have the right to command me. I am an adult woman, and I will choose my own friends."

"And lovers?" he challenged.

"*Sim.* And lovers."

Mama stood clutching her wrinkled hands together, looking from one of her children to the other, not understanding what they were saying.

"*Meus filhos, não disputes, faz favor.*"

Rosa looked past her mother. "Hello, Chelsea. I am surprised to see you here."

"Me, too," she said, feeling constrained with Simão listening. But when no else said anything, she added, "We, um, met at the I.E.S. Hall fire last night."

Simão pounced on his sister again. "Everyone was there but my sister. Either she did not care or she was doing something she should not have been doing."

"No more!" Rosa exclaimed, throwing her purse onto the sofa. "You want to know? I have a boyfriend. He is American, you do not know him. I love him, and maybe I will marry him someday, if I choose to. If not, I will enjoy his company. It is better than yours. *Oh mãe, desculpe. Este homem é um amigo. E um bom homem, e eu gosto muito dele. Você vai gostar dele também. Vou trazer-lhe a casa um dia quando o Simão não esteja aqui.*"

Now Chelsea was the one not understanding all that was said. As she watched, puzzled, Rosa translated. "I said I would bring him home one day when Simão is not here. I do not want my brother to abuse my friends."

Simão narrowed his eyes, ready to explode, but Rosa walked away, her heels thundering on the bare wood floor of the hallway.

"*Queres jantar?*" Mama called after her.

"*Não, já jantei.* I have already had dinner."

Rosa hurried into the second room on the right, shutting the door behind her.

Simão stared at the door as his mother turned away, heading back to the kitchen.

Chelsea put her arm on his. "Simão, she is an adult. You have to let her do what she wants."

"I am afraid she is getting American ideas from you," he grumbled.

She turned his face toward hers. "Is that so bad? I like being an American woman. It's as if anything is possible. We can do things today that even our mothers were not allowed to do. Women are police officers, judges, doctors, even priests in some religions."

"Nobody wants to be a mother anymore," he said.

"Of course they do."

He bent to focus his eyes directly into hers. "Do you?"

Chelsea swallowed. Her career had always come first, but she had always assumed that someday she would have children. It was just hard to see herself waddling around with a big belly or staying up nights mashing baby food. Although it would be fun to cheer them on at Little League or teach them to take pictures. "Yes. Someday. I'd prefer to win the Pulitzer Prize first." She smiled, but Simão's face was grim.

"But then you would be an old woman and unable to have children. Do you not see? A woman must choose work or her family. When she does not have to work--"

"Stop right there, Simão Freitas. I work because I enjoy it, because I'm good at it, because I have a gift which I believe it would be a sin to waste."

"Motherhood is a gift, too, and an even bigger sin to waste."

Chelsea rolled her eyes. Her ankle ached from standing, and she didn't want to fight with Simão, with whom she had just made love, who had asked her a few hours ago to marry him. She knew this argument would never be finished between them.

"I wasn't planning to waste it," she said quietly. "Until today, having children hasn't been a likely possibility. It takes a man and a woman, and I have never had a man who wanted to be a father. Maybe with you. . ." She stopped herself.

Simão sighed and pulled her close, stroking her hair. "Okay, I do not want to fight. But I suppose it is in our natures to argue. Come sit down. You have been standing too long." He led her to the couch, piling pillows behind her back and under her leg.

Chelsea sank into the soft pillows as Simão turned on the television, a news show. Soon he was sitting beside her with her feet on his lap. She held his hand, studying the dark hairs, tracing the deep lines and the cut across his index finger. A warm feeling spread through her. For the first time, she pictured a baby growing inside her, a son that would look like Simão. She smiled and surrendered.

"Mom, remember when I wasn't interested in learning how to cook? Teach me everything. Now."

Her mother burst out laughing as she packed deviled egg yolks into hollowed whites arranged on a ruby glass platter. "I can't believe it. Are you finally tired of frozen dinners? Or is your young man getting hungry? "

"Oh, Mom. You know I don't know anything about cooking. Last night, I thought I couldn't lose. I made steak, mushrooms, baked potatoes and a salad. The steak was hard as leather, the potatoes were mushy, and I forgot to buy dressing for the salad."

"But he's still with you. At least you told me that was him sitting out in the living room with your father."

"Yes. He said all the right things. 'It does not matter. It is fine. You should not cook with your leg in a cast anyway.' But I could see it in his eyes. Women are supposed to be able to cook, and I failed to get that part of my education. Remember my home economics class back in high school? I almost flunked. I would have if I didn't write such good papers for extra credit."

"I remember. I especially liked the green muffins and the runny omelet," Mom chuckled. "However, you won the top prize for high school journalists that year."

"Yes. But you can't eat words. I'm hopeless. To make matters worse, Simão looks around at all the stuff you made, your afghans and your cross-stitch pictures, ready to compliment me for my handiwork, and I have to keep saying, 'Mom made it, Mom made it.' I didn't make anything."

Her mother filled the last egg and handed it to her. Chelsea bit in, loving the combination of sweet and tart. "Mmm."

"You have other talents, honey."

"Sure. I can show Simão how I develop film. That'll fill him up on a cold night. When I was with Jeffrey, he didn't care. We ate out all the time. On the rare occasions we ate at home, he cooked. Usually pasta and salad, since we were trying to eat healthy. And it was cheap. But Simão is different. He expects a woman to be able to cook."

"Chelsea, anybody who can read can learn to cook. Do you still have that Betty Crocker book I bought you when you got your first apartment?"

"Somewhere. I couldn't find it last night."

251

"Well, dig it up and start on page one. From now on, when you come over, I'll let you help me. We'll get you trained."

"Thanks, Mom. Can we have knitting and crocheting lessons, too?"

"One thing at a time, dear." Mom spread a sheet of plastic over the eggs and put them in the refrigerator, then leaned her ear toward the door. "I wonder what those two men are talking about?"

"God only knows," said Chelsea. "When's Aunt Gloria coming?"

"About 7. Let's go sit down."

Chelsea went in ahead of her mother, and Simão patted a space beside him on the sofa. She sat with him opposite her parents, self-conscious about being part of a couple. Mom just kept smiling at her. Everything she had predicted was coming to pass, Chelsea thought. It was like going down a water slide. Once you started at the top, there was no way to stop sliding down to the pool below.

Chapter Nineteen

It was 7:30 a.m. The Weekly Times office was dark when Chelsea turned her key in the lock for the last time.

Despite the cast on her foot, she had walked all the way, feeling the need for fresh air and exercise. When Simão offered last night to drive her after he got off work at the fish market, she just shook her head. "No, I need to do this alone, preferably before anybody else is there. I hope you understand."

Simão shrugged. "I suppose so." He kissed her good night, leaving her sitting in her living room in her bathrobe. He still insisted on going home because it was "not proper" for unmarried people to stay together all night. Most nights Chelsea was reluctant to let him go, but last night her job was foremost on her mind.

She slept very little. Doubts kept her awake. If only she had not reacted so strongly to the race photo, if she had been more diplomatic with Dunning, if she hadn't gone after Slater by herself. She knew it wasn't the ideal job, but she could have stayed there while she quietly looked for another one. Or was the newspaper's budget really so bad that it wouldn't have mattered what she did?

She entered the office and flipped on the light, breathing the smells of old newspapers, tobacco and dust. Papers littered all the desks, including hers, no, Mandy's now. Indeed, Mandy had already claimed it. Pictures of rock stars and clips from the college paper now covered the bulletin board. Chelsea's things were stacked on the chair beside the desk. Under the chair, in a brown grocery bag, Chelsea found her stained Great America coffee mug, packets of instant coffee, rice crackers, and the chipped blue nameplate she had brought back from Washington. She rubbed the letters, Chelsea A. Faust, and sighed.

Suddenly she was nobody. She moved her papers off the chair and sat, covering her mouth with her hand, staring at the blank computer screen. It's a wonder they didn't just throw everything in the trash bin out back, she thought.

Something unfamiliar stuck out of the pile of papers. She pulled it out and found herself staring at an 8 x 10 blowup of the race photo that had offended her so badly. Attached was a note: "Bye, Chelsea. Thanks for the memories. The Jocks in Sports."

253

"To hell with them," she said, tearing the photo into tiny pieces and throwing them in the trash. She noticed a file folder on the parks and recreation department next to Mandy's computer.

My files, she thought. Glancing at the clock--7:45--she opened the big drawer and started taking out papers she wanted to keep. Everything on the Portuguese, on Slater, on her investigation of last year's scandal in the planning department. She stuffed them all into her backpack, along with the used notebooks at the bottom of the drawer. In, too, went the things from her bulletin board.

She zipped the bulging backpack and looked around the office, memorizing the scene. She remembered other leavings, the party they had given her in Palo Alto when she departed for Sacramento, the lunch in Washington. This was different. This was awful.

She heard a noise and saw Mel unlocking the front door. His cheeks were flushed, and when he came in, she smelled alcohol on his breath.

"Chelsea Faust, what are you doin' here?" he said.

Drunk? At 7:45 in the morning? "It's my last day on the payroll." she said. "I planned to clean out my desk, but it looks like somebody else already did it for me."

"Oh. Yeah." Mel reached for his chair and sat down hard, almost losing his balance. "I have a check for you." He pulled an envelope out of the top drawer of his desk and handed it to her.

Chelsea stared at it, telling herself this was the last one.

"Di' ya see your story? Page one?"

"Yes." Chelsea had bought a copy at the market on Santa Clara Street. Her photos dominated page one and the jump. The story ran above the fold, next to an item about the lawyer who committed suicide last week. "It looked good. Thanks. What did Dunning say about it?"

"Oh, Dunning said, I think he said, 'It's too bad we had to let her go,' and uh, he said--" Mel stopped and grinned.

"What?" Chelsea felt her cheeks burning. "What did he say?"

Mel sighed. "Don't hit me. He said, 'It's too bad that Portugee cunt had such a bad attitude.'"

Chelsea clenched her fists. Mel was right. She wanted to hit somebody.

"Count to ten, pal," Mel said.

"Yeah, count to ten, my ass. I ought to sue him for slander or wrongful termination, except I don't want this stinking job anyway."

"Chelsea, sid' down."

"Why?"

"'Cause you got a cast on your foot and you make me nervous. I wanta talk to you."

"Mel, you're drunk, and it's not even 8 o'clock yet."

"I know. I'm rotten." He took a deep breath. "Kathy left me last night."

"Oh, Mel, I'm sorry. What happened?"

"I don' know. Somethin' about how all I thought about was work anymore and she needed more attention, and then this guy came along--she met him at the grocery store--and--I don' know, I guess he was better in bed than I am."

"Where are you staying?"

Mel looked at her, his eyes red-rimmed. "I'm at home with the girls. She drove away. I think she's at his house."

Chelsea shook her head. "That's awful, but you can't come to work drunk."

"It's not the first time."

She stared at her old friend. "Oh, Mel, why?"

He pounded his fist on the desk. Chelsea saw tears in his eyes. "You think I like working for an asshole? You only see a little part of it. You get to leave. I have to stay."

"No, you don't. Get another job."

"Not now. They'll take the girls away if I don't have a steady job. I couldn't stand that." His head dropped to the desk.

"Mel, you need some coffee. You can't be sloshed when Dunning comes in."

"I know. Thanks. You're a better friend than I deserve."

"True." Chelsea limped down the hall to the back room where the circulation department inserted, banded and stacked papers for the carriers. In the corner were a sink, a refrigerator and a scratched-up Formica table. She put water in the stained Mr. Coffee from which she had drunk so many times. In a minute, the coffee was brewing, and she went back to Mel. He was staring at a story on the computer screen.

255

"This is Mandy's. I have to rewrite it," he said.

"It's that bad?"

"Yeah. She stinks." He whirled in his chair. "I tried to warn you about Dunning."

"Next time, speak plain English. I had no idea I was going to get fired. Why didn't you stand up to him for me?"

"'Cause I'm a worm, a louse, a spineless wimp. I can't even tell an intern to rewrite her own damn story."

"It's easy. Just say, 'Rewrite this piece of shit.' " Chelsea smiled, feeling dried tears on her face.

Mel burst out laughing. "I think I will." He typed Chelsea's words on top of the file.

"There you go. Now delete that and put something polite up there that gives her something concrete to work with."

"Oh, okay." As Mel typed, Chelsea noted it was almost 8:15. The whole staff would be there soon, possibly including George P. Dunning. She went back to the coffeepot and poured a second cup for Mel and one for herself.

"Cheers," she said, touching her plastic cup against Mel's newspaper association mug. "Mel, I'm going to miss this stuff, this place, and you."

"What will you do?"

"I don't know." She shook her head. "Simão wants me to marry him and let him take care of me forever after."

Mel nodded. "Typical man. Don't give up your day job, Faust. You never know when you might need it."

"I don't have one."

"You'll find one. At a better paper than this dump. And you'll write books and become famous. Just remember me when you do. Maybe we could have lunch sometime."

Chelsea saw Berta pulling up in her rusty VW Bug. "Any time. I've gotta go." She slung her pack over her shoulders, groaning at the weight, and bent to kiss Mel on the forehead. "Bye, pal."

When she reached the door, he called, "Will you invite me to your wedding?"

She nodded, tears choking off her voice. "Of course."

Passing Berta on the way out, she waved, unable to speak, and limped away until she looked back and couldn't see the Weekly Times sign anymore.

The backpack was heavy with files and keepsakes, but inside, she felt as if a large portion of her guts had been removed, leaving a monstrous hole.

"You DO know how to type?" the employment counselor asked. Ms. Pitts, it said on her name tag.

"Yes, of course, but I--"

"Good."

Ms. Pitts checked off "secretarial" on her form. Chelsea stared. She had already told the woman three times that she was a newspaper reporter and photographer, and that was the only kind of job she would be seeking. Obviously this bubble-haired blonde with the Midwest accent wasn't getting the message.

While standing in line for almost an hour, Chelsea had read the help-wanted notices on the bulletin boards as she passed. Secretaries, receptionists, delivery persons, assemblers. Nothing for someone like her.

After the first line, she'd waited again, this time with a group assigned to sit in a windowless room where a crewcut Mr. Takeda explained the unemployment process, guided them one line at a time through the forms and told them it would be two weeks before their first checks arrived. In the meantime, the applicants would be required to look for work and to show evidence of applications filled out and interviews conducted.

Chelsea sighed. Her fellow unemployed were mostly nonwhite, poorly dressed, uneducated. For them, the job-seeking process was clear: walk in, fill out an application, wait a few days, get a job or not. With newspapers, it could take months, and she might have to leave San Jose to find a good job. But she was a journalist, not a secretary.

The only good thing about this part of the process was that she got to sit for a while. How could they expect someone with a broken ankle to stand in line all this time? No one offered her a seat. At one point, she even went to the front of the line to ask if she could sit and be called when her turn came.

257

"You have to wait in line like everyone else," said the scowling man behind the counter.

Finally she had reached the last step in the process. It was almost 2:00. She was tired and hungry.

"So, I've got you down for secretarial, receptionist, typist, public relations, managerial, and journalist. Is that correct?"

"No!" Chelsea almost shouted. "You haven't been listening. I'm a reporter, period."

Ms. Pitts leaned forward, her thickly painted pink lips pursed into a frown. "Attitude is critical in finding a job," she said. "Now, if you're not willing to consider all the options, I'm not sure we can give you unemployment compensation. Do you understand?"

Chelsea rolled her eyes. "Yes."

"Now, our department says you must consider anything within one hour's drive. That takes us as far north as San Francisco, as far south as Hollister. Can you do that?"

Chelsea let out her breath wearily. "Whatever. If I get a job that far away, I'll move."

"Fine." Ms. Pitts pulled a blank payment book out of her drawer, stamped it and handed it to Chelsea. "Come back in two weeks for your first check."

"How much will that be?"

"Let's see." She looked at a chart on her bulletin board. "$431.95."

"For two weeks?"

"Yes."

"But that won't even pay my rent."

"Then I hope you have other resources."

Ms. Pitts stood, and Chelsea knew the interview was finished. As she limped toward the exit, the counselor called after her, "Will that cast prevent you from looking for work?"

"No, it won't," she said, letting the cast thump hard on the linoleum with each step toward the door.

The California Newspaper Publishers Association was easier. They would put her job-wanted ad in the bulletin that went to publishers all over the state. When Chelsea outlined her experience, the woman on the phone assured her she would have no trouble finding a job.

"You are willing to relocate, aren't you?" she asked.

"Sure," Chelsea said, swallowing thoughts of Simão and what he might say. Maybe, if she was lucky, one of the local papers would respond first.

She called every friend she had in the business. All greeted her warmly, but they knew of no openings. Every paper seemed to be laying people off. But they would certainly let her know if something came up.

Finally, having done everything she could, she sat down to start her book proposal, but it was hard to concentrate.

"This book will fill a serious gap," she wrote. "Where there should be 20 books in the library on Portuguese Americans, there are only two, and those barely mention the women. The struggles of Portuguese women have been every bit as dramatic as those of their male counterparts, yet they have not been acknowledged. Take the story of Maria Dolores Gomes Freitas, who was married at 14, only to have her abusive husband desert her to leave for America. When he returned, years later, she became virtually a slave in her in-laws' home, freed only when a volcano forced the whole town to evacuate. Her husband was killed, as was his invalid father. Then, when she came to America--"

Chelsea sighed. She didn't know much about Avó's life in America. Besides, this was going on too long. She needed to mention some other women, perhaps Anna Silva, whose husband bought a bakery and expected her to run it, or the women with the flower shops. Maybe Rosa, still struggling for the right to live her own life.

Chelsea let her hands fall into her lap. She and Rosa had not talked since that night her boyfriend had brought her home. Without Rosa, she had lost her link to Avó and other older Portuguese women. If only she could make Simão see the value of their stories.

She thought of her great grandmother, who scrubbed the church floors and worked at the cannery to support her eight children. There were thousands of women like her, leaving their homeland and their families to start at the very bottom in a new land in the hope of finding something better for their children. If she didn't tell their stories, who would?

And yet, she felt so far removed from the Portuguese side of her heritage. She was completely American.

She cleared the computer screen and started over. "I am an American. I look American, speak American, and prefer hamburgers to linguiça. But my dark eyes and skin, a deep loyalty to my family, and an unexplainable "saudade" link me to generations of women who grew up on tiny islands in the Atlantic ocean and came to America to follow a dream."

"Yes," she said, nodding. "That's better. Keep it personal. This could be the introduction. I can mention how strange I feel among the Portuguese, how hard it is to learn the language, how--no, I can't mention how it is to fall in love with a Portuguese man. Or how Rosa's life is complicated by loving someone who is not Portuguese." Oh Lord, she thought, I've lost my objectivity. I've become part of the subject instead of staying detached.

She got up and paced the kitchen, her cast thumping on the linoleum. It was 4 o'clock and she hadn't heard from Simão. Usually he called between leaving the fish market and going to his office. But today, the phone was quiet.

She dialed his number. If Simão was out, she could try to talk to Rosa. This silence between them had gone on long enough.

But no one answered at Simão Freitas Enterprises. She let it ring 10 times, hung up and tried again. No Simão, no Rosa, no machine.

She tried Simão's house. Not that she really needed him right now, but she was lonely and frustrated, and she had a feeling something was wrong.

Portuguese superstition, she told herself.

The phone was snatched up on the first ring. "Rosa!" screamed Mama.

"No," said Chelsea. "It's Chelsea."

"Oh." Mama sighed and let the phone drop. Chelsea heard her call Simão.

"Chelsea," said Simão, breathless. "Have you seen Rosa?"

"No, I--"

260

"She has run away. Please, I need to keep the telephone clear. I cannot talk to you."

"Okay. Bye."

She stood in the kitchen for a minute, staring out the window, then turned off the computer, grabbed her purse and limped down the stairs to her truck.

Nothing had changed outside the little white house with the brick walkway and the religious tiles beside the front door. Red geraniums waved softly in the autumn breeze, the scent of roses filled the air, bees buzzed in the bottlebrush. Yet the peace she usually felt there was gone as Chelsea parked her truck and walked toward the house. She had never driven herself to Simão's house before, she realized. He had always picked her up, even though it was out of his way. As if she couldn't get there on her own.

She was in an odd mood, angry, rebellious, nervous, suspicious. It could be just that she was due for her period, or it could be her maddening experience at the unemployment office. But it was more. Rosa had been forced to make a move. She was a grown woman in America, with every right to choose her own boyfriends and work at what pleased her, but Simão tried to control her whole life. Would he be the same way with her? Of course.

Only children "ran away," she thought. Adults simply moved out. Few lived with their parents or siblings at Rosa's age. I wouldn't, she thought. She pushed away the nagging thought of what she might have to do if she didn't get a new job before the rent money ran out. I'd take a typing job or wait tables before I did that.

She knocked gently at the door, received no answer, turned the knob and walked in. Simão and his mother were in Rosa's room, Mama sitting on the bed, Simão leaning against the wall, still in his grubby fish market jeans and sweater. The dressers were bare, stripped of Rosa's toiletries and keepsakes, only the embroidered bureau scarves left behind. On the walls, gray areas in the white paint marked where her pictures and her crucifix had been. The closet door stood open, revealing a plaid skirt, a white cardigan sweater and a sacklike black dress Rosa had rejected.

261

Chelsea cleared her throat. Simão looked up, frowning. "My sister is gone."

"So I see. I'm sorry. Um, *siento muito*, Mama."

"You said it wrong," Simão noted sourly.

"She knows what I mean." She faced Mama again. "*É triste*."

"*Sim*," said Mama, pulling a wrinkled handkerchief from the pocket of her apron and dabbing her eyes.

In the silence, Chelsea wished she hadn't come. She had thought she was becoming one of the family. Now she wasn't so sure.

Mama said something in Portuguese and left the room.

"Rosa must have had help from someone with a truck to take all her things," Chelsea said.

Simão nodded. "Mama was visiting Avó with a friend, and I was at the fish shop. When I came home to shower, I found Rosa was gone. She was not at my office. Nobody was answering my phone."

Chelsea bit her lip. Hire someone, she was thinking, pay her a decent wage. Or work out of your home. You don't have to be so damned important. Let Rosa run her own life. For God's sake, her boyfriend seems like a nice guy.

Of all the things she could think to say, she didn't dare give voice to any of them.

Without Rosa's pictures and knickknacks, the bedroom was cold and empty. How sad that she had to sneak out like this.

Beyond the lace curtains, the sun edged behind a cloud. Chelsea thought about where she might find Rosa. Her boyfriend's home was her first guess, probably the most likely. Mel might know her whereabouts, too, or at least he could tell her when Rosa was expected to bring in her next assignment.

Simão was staring at his stained shoes, his dark eyes shadowed in pain. Chelsea wanted to go to him, to hold him and be held. She was tempted to offer to find Rosa for him. But part of her was rooting for Rosa to escape. Like a slave, she thought.

"Is there anything I can do?"

"No," he said, not looking up.

Her ankle ached more than usual. She supposed she had spent too much time on it that morning. Or maybe it was stress. "I thought you might need my company tonight, but I guess I'll go home."

262

He just shrugged.

On her way down the hall, she looked into Simão's room. It was decorated in dark blue and green. A knitted afghan much like the one Chelsea had on her couch was spread across the foot, with Simão's open briefcase on top. A large wooden crucifix hung over the head of the bed. Simão's clean clothes were neatly folded on top of the mahogany dresser. Rolled-up blueprints leaned against the joining of the walls in the far corner. It was a man's room, dark, warm, smelling slightly of cigarettes and shoe polish. A framed photograph of Simão's late wife perched atop the dresser. Next to the photo, Chelsea saw a stack of Weekly Times newspapers. It was strange she had never really seen this room before, yet Simão had seen everything in her apartment.

Where did she fit in, she wondered.

Mama was in the kitchen, peeling potatoes into a brown paper garbage bag.

"*Adeus*," Chelsea called from the doorway.

No response. She walked back down the brick path. For the first time, she noticed weeds growing between the bricks. Some of the roses were dying.

Twilight. Her kitchen was gray. Everything was dim, blurry around the edges. Chelsea closed the curtains and sat down at the computer.

"Rosa Freitas ran away from home at the age of 26 to escape a brother and mother who refused to let her grow up and do the work she loved or date the man she had chosen for herself."

She sat back, reread the sentence and started a new paragraph. "Rosa is Portuguese, an immigrant from the Azores. Her brother, Simão, is head of the family, and he feels responsible for his grandmother, mother and sister. He supports them all on the meager income he earns working part-time at a Portuguese fish market and running a property business he calls Simão Freitas Enterprises. He has earned a position of pride in the community as head of a growing business and president of the Portuguese Chamber of Commerce. To the world, he presents the strong, confident face of a leader. But at home, the deep pain of loss shows.

"Simão lost his wife and unborn child. The wife, seeking a chance at a music career, went to an East Side bar, flirted with the wrong guy and was stabbed to death. Now, whenever one of the women in Simão's life shows signs of becoming worldly and independent, he panics for fear of losing them."

She stopped typing and sighed. Now was not the time to bat her head against Simão's macho beliefs. He needed her support. But so did Rosa. How awful she must be feeling right now, separated from her family, feeling as if she can never come home.

She wrote: "Such is the dilemma of the Portuguese family. The man is driven by such a strong need to protect and control the women in his life that he smothers them. In time, they rebel, and the family falls apart--or grows stronger."

The family unit. Devotion to family. Every Portuguese person she had interviewed had mentioned it. But where did devotion end and self-preservation begin? She suddenly pictured her mother serving her and her father pieces of leftover pie, having none herself because there wasn't enough. It was only pie, but wasn't it the same thing? Rosa wanted her own slice of pie.

She sighed. If she could think of Rosa's boyfriend's name, she could call and see if she was with him. But would Rosa want to talk to her? And if she did, would she then feel obligated to tell Simão where his sister was?

The amber letters on the computer screen glowed more brightly against the increasing darkness in the kitchen. Chelsea's eyes were fixed on the computer, but her mind was elsewhere. She remembered how she had always wanted to be a writer, how her father had been delighted with her first short stories, scrawled in pencil on newsprint with wide spaces between the lines.

When she worked on the high school paper, her parents let her stay late, walking home at sunset, so she could write her stories and work on the pasteup until it was ready for the printer. They cheered when she won a scholarship to Berkeley, letting her move into a dorm. Even when she moved to Sacramento with Jeffrey, they didn't try to stop her. What if she had been Rosa? Would she be writing her thoughts in spiral notebooks and hiding them under the bed? Would she be restricted to dating only men whom her brother approved of?

The telephone startled her. She looked around as if waking up from a long dream.

"Hello?"

"Chelsea Faust? This is Clark Egan from the Riverside Press-Enterprise. I got your name from the CNPA bulletin, and I'd like to talk to you about a job."

Four hundred miles away, she thought. "Yes, Mr. Egan, thanks for calling." Please make it a job I don't want.

Chapter Twenty

"Riverside!" Her mother's eyes were black marbles. "You can't be serious."

"It's closer than Washington, D.C." Chelsea felt herself shrinking back to eight years old as she sat in the oversized armchair opposite her mother on Saturday morning.

Her father was silent, staring at the photography magazines she had brought him. She had been surprised to find him in a new darkroom, happily organizing his negatives. But his mood turned somber after she dropped her bombshell.

"I haven't been offered a job yet, Mom. He just asked me to send a resume and clips."

"But why even consider it?"

"Mom, I have to consider every possibility. I can't live on unemployment for long."

"We can give you money," Dad said quietly.

"No, you can't. You--" She stopped herself. Why remind her father that he had lost his job and was barely getting by financially himself? "I couldn't let you do that."

His lips worked, but he said nothing. His hair looked thinner, the pouches under his eyes bigger.

"What does your boyfriend say?" Mom prodded. "Surely he doesn't like this."

"I haven't told him yet." She stood. "I've got to go. I've got work to do."

Dad tossed his magazine on the floor. "Wait. You just got here. Maybe, before you move away, you could give your old dad a little advice."

"On what?"

"Marketing photos. I know you've done some freelance pieces. Well, I need the extra income, so I thought I'd give it a shot."

"Really? That's great!" She sat down beside him. "You won't get rich, but I'm happy to help you. The daughter teaching the father. It feels strange."

"Just tell me what to do."

"Okay, first you have to figure out what kinds of photos you want

266

to sell and what types of magazines are most appropriate. Then you have to study the magazines . . ."

Her father listened closely as Chelsea shared her experiences. Her mother quietly set a cup of hot coffee on a coaster on the end table next to her.

"Thanks, Mom." They smiled at each other.

On the way home two hours later, she passed Fifth Street and went on to Little Portugal. Simão's car was parked outside his office. She might be rebuffed again, but Chelsea parked behind his Buick and walked up the stairs. As always, she smelled garbage and exhaust.

As soon as she knocked, the door was yanked open.

"Chelsea. Come in."

She stared. Simão hadn't shaved, his eyes were red, and he had a cigarette hanging from his mouth.

"I've never seen you smoke before."

He shook his head. "I quit. But I am so worried I had to do something. It is better than shooting myself."

Chelsea clasped his arm. "Shooting yourself? Why?"

He slumped onto the sofa, pulling her down beside him. She couldn't help remembering that first night they had made love here. But now gray daylight poured in, and everything looked dull.

"I have failed my duty to my sister. First my wife, then Rosa."

"No, Simão."

"Yes. Oh, I need her to help me here, but I can use the machine. What is important is that she is my sister. I am supposed to take care of her."

"She is not a child, sweetheart. She's a grown woman. She can take care of herself."

"Like you?" he said, pointing his cigarette at the cast on her ankle.

"Don't men ever make mistakes?"

"Yes, but they are stronger."

"They have bigger muscles, yes, but that doesn't always mean anything. We're just as smart, Simão, just as resourceful. And Rosa is not in trouble. She's simply in love with a man you don't approve of. I met him. He seemed nice to me."

"He is not Portuguese."

267

"So what? Neither is my father, but he's a wonderful man."

Simão stubbed out the cigarette in a small tin ashtray. "I know."

"You think my mother's parents didn't freak out when she married a German who wasn't even Catholic? But it turned out fine. You have to let Rosa make her own choices. Love her for what she is, not what you think she ought to be. She's a terrific woman, smart, talented, loving. "You should be proud."

"I suppose."

She rubbed his stubbled chin with the back of her hand. "I don't want to be torn between the two of you. I love you both."

He kissed her. His breath tasted of cigarettes and wine. "You have a good heart."

"Let me take you home and make you dinner."

"I am not hungry."

"Come over anyway. Let me prove that I can cook. We could go get your mother."

He shook his head. "She won't leave. She is waiting for Rosa. We will eat there. Maybe she will come home."

"Oh, Simão."

Would they ever be free of his family?

That Sunday, Five Wounds Church was crowded. As Chelsea limped up the broad steps with Simão and his mother, she thought of her childhood trips to Mass, with Mom nudging her and her dad up the aisle. Now as she followed Simão's mother, Chelsea felt as if she had been dropped into the scene from another planet. This wasn't her real family! Everyone around her was speaking a language she didn't understand.

Mama was greeting her friends. Chelsea heard Rosa's name, saw heads shaking, tongues clucking. What a shame the daughter had run off. But who was this pretty girl?

Chelsea nodded and smiled her way past the huge brass doors. She dipped her fingers in the marble holy water font and made the Sign of the Cross.

Candles glittered and statues beckoned on all sides of the T-shaped church modeled after a cathedral in Portugal. At right front, two men strummed guitars and three women sang in shrill voices. Chelsea could hear people chattering outside, but inside, a prayerful hush prevailed. White-haired women, grizzled men, and young couples with their children knelt, their hands folded on the backs of the pews, their eyes on the blood-streaked figure on the cross.

Following Mama and Simão into a pew near the middle on the right, Chelsea bobbed in a modified genuflection, her cast stopping her from going all the way down, and took her place on the kneeler.

It was nice to see a man openly devoted to God, she thought, watching Simão's eyes closed in prayer. Except when that devotion made him close-minded and disapproving, she added to herself. She remembered Simão's reaction to her sexy photo and hoped they were beyond that now. But Simão's rejection of Rosa's boyfriend still worried her.

Mama made the Sign of the Cross and sat back. Chelsea and Simão did the same.

Does Simão feel guilty about having sex with me? She glanced at his pious face and slipped her hand into his. He squeezed it and let go just as the priest and his procession entered the back door and the assembly stood in unison.

Mass was familiar yet different. Chelsea knew the order and recognized the main prayers, the Gloria, the Apostles Creed, the Lord's Prayer. But she didn't know the Portuguese words and struggled to read along in the tattered missalette she found in the pew. The sermon was a loss. Too many words, too fast. Instead she let her mind wander.

It was as if two sides of her personality were pulling against each other. One side was the professional journalist looking for a good job, wherever it might take her. The other was the good little girl who wanted a home and a husband just like her mother.

She glanced down at her leg, still covered with a cast from below the knee to the floor. Dirty and frayed around the edges now, the cast was due to come off next Thursday, and she was anxious to start walking and running again. The doctor had assured her the ankle would soon be as sound as ever. What a joy it would be to drive normally and to wear stockings and real shoes. Her ribs were already healed, and the cuts on her face were reduced to faint pink lines. Someday, she hoped, the memory of that night would also fade.

Everything was fine except for not having a job. Despite Simão's persistent offers to support her, she needed satisfying work, not only to pay the bills but to shape her days. Her identity was wrapped around being Chelsea Faust, reporter. Maybe someday she could stay home and write books, but right now she yearned to be back at work on a newspaper.

However, this handsome man beside her was changing everything. Something deeply ingrained made her want to cling to him and please him in every way, from how she dressed to being nice to his mother. But she felt as if she could never relax.

Mass went on. Songs, prayers, sitting, standing, kneeling. At the sign of peace, Simão kissed her gently on the forehead, his eyes soft with love. Mama kissed her, too. People on all sides reached out their hands. Chelsea echoed their *paz de Deus* and prepared to join them in the line to receive Communion.

She wondered if she was committing a sin. She hadn't been to Confession in years, and one wasn't supposed to take Communion without confessing first. But it was easier to join Simão and his mother at the altar than to explain why she couldn't.

After Mass, the church emptied into the plaza out front. It was a bright, cool day, chilly in the shade, warm in the sun.

On the way to Simão's car, someone touched her shoulder. She looked into the swarthy moon face of Joaquim, the man who had rescued her the night of the attack. With him was a small dark woman, his wife she assumed.

Olá, Joaquim," Simão said and the men shook hands.

"*Como está?*" Joaquim said to Chelsea.

Chelsea smiled. In broad daylight, his wide friendly face was appealing. "*Muito bem,*" she replied.

"*A perna?*" He gestured toward her ankle.

Chelsea counted in her mind. "*Quinta-feira.* Thursday it comes off." She motioned to demonstrate.

Joaquim nodded.

In a minute, Joaquim and his wife had moved off toward another group, and Chelsea, Simão and his mother were in the Buick, heading east. Now what, thought Chelsea. Do I go home? Inwardly she shrugged. What else did she have to do? But she looked around. What a

270

great day to take pictures. Or drive to Riverside and see if it would be a good place to live. Or take Simão back to her apartment and make love.

But there was Mama in the back seat, talking to Simão about Rosa and Avó and who knew what else.

Chelsea was surprised when they drove past their house, left little Portugal and stopped at a big supermarket on White Road. "The grocery store?" she said softly. "I thought you would shop at--"

"Trade Rite?" finished Simão. "Mama discovered by looking at the ads that their prices are much higher than the American stores. Here they have more variety, too. We come here every Sunday, when I am not working and can help her carry the bags. Rosa reads the labels for Mama. Then she and Mama spend Sunday afternoon baking together."

"Oh," said Chelsea, beginning to realize what lay ahead.

Three hours later, she worked at the kitchen counter in a borrowed apron, flour on her arms, dough coating her hands as she rolled out a pie crust under Mama's watchful eye. Simão sat at the kitchen table, a cigarette burning in the ashtray beside him, coffee cooling in a big gray mug as he scribbled on a yellow pad.

"*Sempre a trabalhar*," said Mama, shaking her head.

Always working, Chelsea translated. "*Sim*," she replied. Hadn't her own mother complained of the same thing about her?

When the pie was in the oven, the two women sat in the patio, sipping iced tea. Chelsea looked into the kitchen at Simão from time to time and sometimes caught him smiling back at her. That she would stay for dinner was a given. Mama had bought ham, sweet potatoes and corn, plus some beer for Simão. Chelsea, too, she indicated.

It was comfortable here. From the back porch, Mama's yellow parakeet twittered. A pair of blue jays darted between branches of the cherry and apple trees. A sprinkler turned lazily on the grass, spray wafting toward them on the breeze. It was like her parents' back yard, only smaller. If she had a book to read or something to work on, the afternoon would be perfect. Just sitting here made her sleepy.

It was as if Mama read her mind. She went inside, returning with a plastic bag.

"For me?"

271

Mama, nodded. "*Para bordar.*"

Chelsea pulled out an embroidery kit: white cloth, thread, a needle, and a tiny pair of scissors. Included was a colored picture of a rose design, marked off in squares. She stared, puzzled. She didn't do cross-stitch. With a chill, Chelsea realized that Mama had bought the kit for Rosa. Now that Rosa was gone--"

"*Mama, não. Não posso aceitar.*"

Mama gestured impatiently. "*Sim, sim, para você.* For you."

From the cloth bag beside her own chair, Mama took a crochet hook and lavender yarn and set to work on a striped afghan that already hung down over her knees. Chelsea sighed and unfolded the embroidery chart. She had embroidered as child; she could figure this out.

After a few minutes, she set the embroidery on the table and went in, down the hall to the bathroom with its crocheted toilet paper and Kleenex covers. She paused outside Rosa's empty room. They want me to take her place, she thought.

Simão met her on the way back and folded her in his arms, kissing her passionately. "I am very glad you are here," he whispered in her ear.

"But I have to go home sometime."

"Maybe you should stay here. We have a vacant room."

"No, Simão, I can't."

"Why not? You have no job. You cannot afford to pay rent. I can take care of you, and we can be together."

"I can take care of myself." Too harsh, she knew, but it was too late to take the words back. A red flush rose up Simão's neck. She struggled to think of something to calm him before they quarreled.

She put her fingers over his lips. "I'm sorry. I've been on my own for 10 years, Simão. It's a habit. But look, I can't move in here. What would people say? They know we are dating. They'll think we--you know."

Simão sighed. "That we are having a sinful relationship. We are."

"In your eyes."

He let it pass. "But if we got married--"

He stopped as Mama came down the hall. "*Mais fio,*" she said, disappearing into her room. In a minute, she returned with another

272

skein of yarn. *"Vamos para fora,"* she said to Chelsea, urging her to come back outside. Then she ordered Simão to do something. Chelsea didn't understand any of what she had said, but he answered impatiently. *"Basta, Mãe, basta."*

Enough.

"I have to do an errand," he told Chelsea. As he hurried out of the house, she was left with no choice but to follow Mama back to the patio and start stitching little x's.

It was 10 o'clock before Chelsea made it home. Simão didn't stay, pleading an early shift at the fish market. She was relieved. She felt as if she had lost track of herself for a whole day and she needed to get it back.

She had some negatives she had never printed, photos of Alum Rock Park, downtown San Jose and her parents. She gathered them up, traded her Sunday dress for torn jeans and tee shirt and started for the darkroom, tired but feeling as if she could not rest yet.

She was halfway out the door when the phone rang. She hesitated, listening.

After the third ring, Simão's voice came on. As she caught the essence of his message, she felt her face grow hot and her anger rise. He was asking her to work in his office, to take Rosa's place filing and answering the phone. He knew she was unhappy without a job and he needed someone, he said.

Without listening to the rest, she slammed the door and stomped downstairs.

"I am not a secretary!" she muttered. "I am a reporter! And I am not Rosa or Fátima! Besides, I don't even speak Portuguese. If you can't accept me for what I am, leave me alone!"

She flipped on the red light, locked the door of the darkroom from the inside and turned the radio up loud on the rock and roll station.

After midnight, she climbed wearily up the stairs, carrying a stack of barely dry prints which she spread out on the kitchen table. She leaned close to inspect her favorite, a shot of an old woman pushing a shopping cart down Santa Clara Street. In the background was a young woman in a dark suit and high heels, swinging a brief case. She walked by the shopping cart woman as if she couldn't see her.

Without the Weekly Times, she wasn't sure where she could get it published. Maybe she could freelance it to the Mercury News. Maybe she could approach an art gallery.

The phone rang again. Chelsea squinted to see the number on the machine. Four calls had come in while she was gone. Probably all Simão. Why didn't he just give up and go to bed?

In the darkroom, she had thought about Simão's request and tried to make herself understand that he had good intentions. She needed a job; he had a job to offer. She couldn't afford rent; he had a room to give. But he didn't understand who she really was. She was different from the Portuguese girls he knew. Although she had Azorean blood, she was 100 percent American, which in her eyes meant freedom for everyone, male or female, to do what they wanted with their lives.

The phone rang on, relentless. As she hesitated, the machine picked it up again.

"Chelsea." Simão sounded worn out. "Please answer. I am worried about you."

She picked up the receiver. "Simão, I'm here."

"Oh, thank God. I thought somebody came into your apartment and killed you."

Like his wife. Poor Simão. Would he always be this paranoid? "No, no. I just decided to stay up and print some photos in the darkroom."

"Is it safe?"

"Sure. I lock myself in, close the drapes; nobody even knows I'm there. This is the best time to do it. No traffic noise, no kids bouncing balls in the driveway. I got some good shots."

"Okay. Chelsea, did you listen to my messages? About working with me?"

Here it comes, she thought, but she had worked out what she would say. "Sweetheart, I can't, not right now. I need to use this time to really work on my book. Pretty soon I'll get another job, and I'll be too busy. Besides, I don't speak Portuguese, so how can I help?"

"That is not a problem. I need someone who can speak to the American businessmen. And most of all, I want to keep you near me."

She sank into a chair, her eyes on the photo of a deer she had photographed at close range at Alum Rock Park. "Oh Simão, we can be together every night and on weekends. I will come visit you in your office. You can visit me in mine. We're moving so quickly. I--we care for each other, but I'm afraid--"

"You do not love me?"

"Yes, I do. But let me finish. I feel as if I'm the substitute for your sister. You want me to sew like her and cook like her and even sleep in her room. Honey, I'm Chelsea. I'm a reporter. I'm American. You have to want me for myself."

"I do. You do not understand me."

"No. You do not understand me." From outside, she heard the faint chiming of the clock in the Pavilion shopping center downtown. It was 12:30 a.m., and suddenly she felt exhausted. Her ankle ached from standing so long in the darkroom. And now she was afraid she was ruining her romance with Simão over semantics. "You should be in bed, darling."

"I could not sleep while I was so worried about you."

"That's sweet but unnecessary."

"It will always be necessary until you are my wife sleeping by my side, where I can reach out my hand and touch your soft skin and know you are there safe."

"Oh, Lord. Are you proposing to me again?"

"Yes. Again. Marry me."

Chelsea closed her eyes. The room spun and she opened them again, forcing herself to concentrate on a photo of her father. What would Dad say? What would he think? He liked Simão. He wanted her to be happy. She knew what her mother would say. "Finally. Now don't be so damned independent you scare him away."

"Chelsea?"

The man deserved an answer, but she couldn't give the one he wanted. Not tonight. "Simão, thank you, but this is not the type of decision that should be made on the telephone at one o'clock in the morning when we're both half asleep."

"Maybe you are right." His voice was hurt, dry. "I will call you tomorrow. Perhaps we could go out to dinner, if you are not too busy."

"Sure. I'm sorry, Simão."

275

"Me too. Good night."

"Yes. Goodnight." She had an idea. "Simão?"

He was gone, and the night ahead stretched long and lonely.

Chapter Twenty-One

Two white envelopes stuck out of her mailbox the next morning. One was from the Redding Record-Searchlight. The other was from the San Francisco Chronicle. "Oh, my God," she whispered, sitting on the step.

The Redding paper needed a sports writer. "No thanks," she said, setting the letter on top of the grocery store ads. But the Chronicle had an opening on its general assignment photo staff. Please call to set up an interview, the letter said.

She took a deep breath and let it out again. "Oh, my God," she repeated.

For a long time, she sat, staring blindly at the cars moving past, her mind racing ahead to what it would be like to be a Chronicle photographer. Several of her idols had started there. Chronicle pictures went over the wire to papers all over the world. It was the paper everybody read when she was going to Berkeley. Of course, it was a union shop. Photographers didn't write, and writers didn't take pictures. But she supposed she could find other outlets for her writing.

The Chronicle! She pictured living in one of those seashell-colored apartments along 19th Avenue, where the air smelled of sea salt and Golden Gate Park was a quick jog away. Downtown, with its shimmering skyline, had Northern California's biggest library, the biggest theater, the finest opera house. The coastline was stunning. She could run along the beach for miles. What a place to live and work.

The salary would be good. She could buy a new camera or anything else she wanted. And it was only an hour away.

Inside she heard the telephone ring and started up the steps. It was probably Simão. If he proposed again, what would she say? She thought she loved him. But she kept hearing something Anna at the bakery told her that she left out of her story: "You are a career woman like I was. Marry a Portuguese man and your career is over."

Well, she couldn't get married. Not now. Not until she found a job and got her life back on track. If Simão really loved her, he would wait. If not, maybe it was best for both of them to find out.

Hampered by her cast, she moved so slowly the answering machine clicked on before she got to the phone. Still holding the mail, she stood and listened.

It was not Simão. "This is Reid Callan from the Riverside Press-Enterprise. Give me a call. I'd like to set up an interview."

As the machine beeped, she sank into her chair. Riverside?

At noon, she heated instant soup for lunch, but she was too excited to eat. Instead she gulped a large glass of ice water and dialed the Chronicle. A secretary arranged the interview for Thursday, Oct. 19 at 10 a.m. The photo editor was sorry it couldn't be sooner, but he would be in Europe for the next two weeks. Chelsea put her soup in the refrigerator and turned on the computer. Better write her book quickly. Soon there wouldn't be time.

She decided to put off calling the Riverside editor. Why go hundreds of miles away if she could work in San Francisco?

"San Francisco? That is how far? An hour?"

"Yes, Simão. About 50 miles north. It would take longer than an hour during commute times. I hear the traffic is horrendous. But I'd move up there if I got the job."

Simão shook his head. "What about you and me? I ask you to marry me, and you talk about moving away. Do you not love me at all?"

Chelsea stroked the soft dark hair on his chest. She was always amazed at Simão's body, so strong, so perfectly proportioned. The only flaw was a scar on his hip from an accident on a boat back in Faial. Do I love him? The attraction was pure animal. No logic to it at all. They had different plans for their lives, different ideas about men's and women's roles, and yet deep down they had the same values and the same roots, and their bodies and souls insisted on twining together even if their minds didn't.

"Yes," she whispered. "I love you very much. Try to understand. My work is everything to me. Maybe--" She scrunched down under the covers and pulled the spread over their shoulders. "Maybe we could find a place together somewhere in the middle. Redwood City, San Mateo, Palo Alto . . . ."

"My home is here."

278

"Yes. But--" She stopped herself. It was easy to understand why Simão would not want to give up his sweet little house with the flowers all around and Portuguese tiles on the wall. It was a home, not a temporary lodging like her apartments had always been. And what about Mama? Like Avó, would she be trapped living with her husband's family? But Mama was kind to her, and having her take care of the cooking and cleaning would free her to work. . . .

She tried to dash away her dream of an apartment in The City. "Maybe I could take the train. There's a station right off The Alameda, only a couple miles from here."

Simão rolled over and pulled her close, squashing her breasts against his warm chest. "I do not want to talk about this anymore. It makes me sad. I just want to hold you. Soon I will have to go home. Mama will not sleep until I return, and I have to get up at 5."

"I know." She burrowed her head against his shoulder. "You work so hard."

He shrugged. "It is what a man does."

And a woman, Chelsea thought. But her thoughts blurred as Simão rose up on his elbow and slowly began licking her, starting with her lips, then her neck, then her breasts. He eased the covers off and continued down her ribs and stomach, across her hips and between her legs. Chelsea gasped, her head falling back, her back arching as his tongue touched her. Where did such a conservative Portuguese man learn how to do this, she wondered. Then she gave herself up to the red heat that enveloped her.

After he left, she sat in her bathrobe, sipping tea and looking out at the dark, quiet street. She had never felt so deeply, physically content as Simão made her feel. When they made love, she was like a cat being stroked, pushing herself against the hand that pet her, begging for more. At those moments, Simão was all she needed. She would happily let her work become a hobby and devote everything to him. But when they were apart, doubts crept in. She chafed at the restraints he seemed to be putting on her. At the same time, she wondered if her mother was right. Maybe it was time to marry and settle down, perhaps even have children. If she let this chance go by, she might always regret missing the domestic part of life.

The door closed downstairs and she watched as Angie walked John to his car. John wore his uniform, Angie was in her robe. Their little girl was probably asleep inside. The couple walked slowly, arms around each other, reluctant to part. At the car, they hugged for a long time before John kissed her and got in the car.

Chelsea sighed. Sometimes her computer and camera were cold companions.

Finally, she thought, leafing through a People magazine in the orthopedics waiting room Thursday at San Jose Medical Center. Today she would get her cast off. She could wear real shoes and stockings and learn to walk normally again. Best of all, she would not have to look at a constant reminder of her stupidity that night she went out to photograph the errant councilman. The scars on her cheek had faded, and her ribs were fine. Her ankle was the last remnant. That and the loss of her job. But she had grown philosophical about that. It had to happen sooner or later. She and George P. Dunning were like gasoline and a lighted match.

She wondered what the Chronicle publisher was like. At a paper that big, she might never meet him. But at least when she went for her interview, she wouldn't have to explain why there was a cast on her leg or promise it wouldn't hamper her work.

"Chelsea Faust," called a harried Hispanic woman, reading the name off the front of a folder. Chelsea grabbed her purse and followed her into the back.

After a few questions, the nurse sent her to the cast room to have the plaster removed. Chelsea stared at the white wrinkled skin underneath and flexed her ankle. It was stiff, but it didn't hurt. Walking gingerly on bare feet, she went to the X-ray department for one last picture, then returned to the waiting room. It was a half hour before the doctor called her in. She wished she'd remembered to bring another shoe. She took off the shoe she had and shoved it into her purse.

"Looks fine," said the doctor, gesturing toward the film.

"It feels weird."

"I'm sure it does. After six weeks with no activity, it's bound to feel strange. But the bone has healed and you shouldn't have any problem."

Chelsea looked at her bare ankle dubiously. "How soon can I run again?"

The doctor smiled. "I don't see any reason why you shouldn't be back on track in a month or so. Take it easy at first, work your way up, you know, walk a block today, then two blocks tomorrow, and so on. You'll know when you're ready to run. By Christmas you won't even remember this."

"Wanna bet?" Chelsea stood, enjoying the feeling of standing on two equal feet. "Thanks." They shook hands, and she followed the doctor out to the exit. She felt sorry for the two people in the waiting room with casts on their legs. I am so lucky, she thought.

Outside the building, she wanted to dance in pleasure at finally getting the cast off, but it was too soon; her lower leg was like a piece of wood.

Never mind. Wait until Simão saw her with two good legs. And oh, what a pleasure it would be to shower without a plastic bag around her ankle. She could even go swimming at the gym again.

She knew she had a stupid grin on her face all the way to the truck. Inside, she nudged the accelerator with her bare toes and giggled. "Hallelujah," she said, shifting the truck into first gear and gliding out of the parking lot.

She had to pass Simão's office on the way home. His car was there, and she felt him pulling her like a magnet. But no, she was going to get a shoe on that foot first. Maybe take a long bubble bath. Then she would put on something sexy and lure her entrepreneur lover away from his work.

But he wasn't interested in romance.

When she walked up the stairs and let herself in without knocking, she found him scowling at the papers on his desk. Feeling beautiful and sexy in a soft white dress, glossy stockings and delicate white sandals on both feet, she bent to kiss his tanned forehead.

"Ah, *meu amor*, why does your government have so many stupid rules?"

"*Our* government. You live here now, too. America, land of the free, right?"

281

"No. Look at this. I buy this building, I make my plans, then they tell me I need a different kind of zoning to make offices here. Why did they not tell me this before? And what does it hurt to rent space for offices? People in offices do not make noise, they do not use dangerous chemicals, they do not cause big parking problems. I do not understand. C-1, C-2, C-3, what is the difference?"

Chelsea sighed and pulled up a chair next to him. She had covered enough planning commission and city council meetings to know zoning could be a sticky situation. Half the agendas seemed to be debates over people wanting to do things with their property that the zoning ordinances didn't allow.

She read for a few minutes. "You need a variance," she said.

"What is a variance?"

"A ruling that lets you do what you want as long as you can prove it won't hurt anybody."

"More paperwork, yes?"

"Yes. I'll help."

And suddenly, without thinking about it, Chelsea was drawn into Simão's business. Within minutes, she was on the telephone, plowing through the system as a representative for Freitas Enterprises.

There were papers to file, meetings to attend. Chelsea made lists of things they needed to do, then grabbed her purse. "I'm going to get the forms," she said.

It was only when she was down the stairs and on the way to her truck that Simão called to her. "Your cast is gone. You have two beautiful legs again."

Chelsea grinned back up at him and kept going. "I've got to get there before the office closes. Then I'll show you my legs up close."

It felt strange walking into the San Jose City Council chambers as an advocate rather than a reporter. Chelsea and Simão went together, arriving early, sitting near the front. Murmuring voices came from the back of the room and out in the hallway, where a crowd was gathering to protest plans to build a new 10-screen theater complex in south San Jose. She was grateful Simão's office building was earlier on the agenda. They could leave before the long public hearing started. She had sat through many such hearings, taking notes for hours as one

282

person after another walked to the microphone to speak for or against an issue.

She had her notebook tonight, but she wouldn't be taking notes for a story, only for herself and Simão.

The council members began to arrive. The mayor, a tall, athletic woman in a severe gray suit, poured herself a glass of water and talked to the Hispanic councilwoman from east San Jose. Another councilwoman, the only black person on the council, took a seat at the end of the table and looked through her agenda.

"So many women," Simão whispered. "In my country, you don't see women in government."

Chelsea nodded. "Maybe things have changed there, too."

"Perhaps, but women in the Azores are too busy at home. The men who run our villages talk all day sometimes. Who would feed the children or wash the clothes if the women spent all day talking?"

Chelsea sighed. "Maybe their husbands could do it." She grinned at Simão's disbelieving look. "Why not? It isn't that difficult. Men--" She stopped as Councilman James Slater sauntered in and stared down at her from the podium. As their eyes met, she wanted to look away, but she didn't want to admit defeat. Instead, she kept her gaze on him and conspicuously crossed her legs. The councilman was still watching her when a short Japanese man tapped him on the back and forced him to turn his attention away.

"Who is that big man?" Simão asked.

"That is the thug I photographed that night, the guy who had his goon beat me up."

Simão's face flushed. "I will tell him what I think. God help me, I may kill him."

Chelsea held him back with a hand on his shoulder. "No, sweetheart. He's a monster, I'd be the first to admit, but you need his vote. The rest of the council tends to follow his example on these matters. He used to be a city planner, and he's supposed to be some kind of expert. If you tick him off, you will never be able to have offices in your building. Hopefully, my arguments will be so logical that Slater would look foolish disagreeing. Don't forget, I know things about him that would destroy him."

283

The hallway crowd was filling the chairs around them. Next to Chelsea, a petite redhead handed out posters for her group to hold up during the hearing.

Simão picked at his nails and stared at the heavy black print on the agenda full of legal language he had trouble understanding.

She squeezed his hand. "It'll be fine. We're small fish tonight."

Still, she was nervous. She had never spoken to the council before, only sat taking notes. Some of the council members would recall her as a reporter and wonder what she was doing here. They might not know yet that she was no longer with the Weekly Times. After all, it had only been a few weeks since her byline last appeared.

The agenda item came quickly, after the council ran through a list of routine matters that left Simão obviously confused. But Chelsea had memorized their agenda number. When the mayor called 38, she hurried to the podium.

"I'd like to speak on this item."

"All right. Ms. Faust, is it?" the mayor said.

"Yes, that's correct."

"You're a reporter, aren't you?"

She swallowed. "Not at the moment, Madame Mayor. I no longer work for the Weekly Times."

"Oh. I hadn't realized. Well, what is your connection in this matter?"

Chelsea took a deep breath and started her speech. "Simão Freitas, the owner of this property, is a friend of mine. He bought this building in good faith, certain that he could turn it into offices and receive a reasonable return. Being somewhat new to this country, he did not understand the different commercial zonings and found himself with an unusable building. However, after careful study, he has determined that turning these apartments into offices would not disturb the neighborhood at all, but would in fact enhance it and bring more business to an area that needs it. He has also found that other similar buildings in the area have already been granted variances for this very purpose."

"I see," said the mayor, making notes. "Is Mr. Freitas going to speak for himself on this matter?"

"He feels his English is lacking when it comes to governmental

284

matters, but I can assure you he is a top-notch businessman. In fact, he is the current president of the Portuguese Chamber of Commerce. He has tenants ready to move in. All he needs is your approval. Thank you."

She started toward her seat, but Slater called her back. "Ms. Faust. How good a friend are you with Mr. Frietas?"

"Excuse me?" But she understood perfectly the leering look in his eyes.

"He's your boyfriend, isn't he?"

She could feel her face turning hot and was conscious of Simão about to leap out of his seat. "I don't see what my relationship with Mr. Freitas has to do with this. I'm a concerned citizen trying to help."

"Of course."

Behind her, she heard muttering.

"Ms. Faust, am I to understand that you no longer are employed at the Weekly Times?"

"Yes, I already mentioned that, but I don't see what--"

"How did that come about?"

"It's really not--"

The mayor stepped in. "Councilman Slater, we have a very full agenda. Ms. Faust's employment situation and her personal life are irrelevant to this issue. We're talking about a variance. If there's no further public comment, I'd like to call the question. Do I hear a motion?"

Chelsea retreated to her seat, wishing she could leave the building and hide. Simão squeezed her hand. "*Obrigado*," he whispered.

She shook her head, fanning her flaming face. "*De nada*."

"You are a brave woman."

"Shh. They're about to vote."

"I move we grant the variance," said the east San Jose councilwoman.

"Second," said the African-American councilwoman.

Slater's face wrinkled up and his eyes narrowed, but he voted with the majority.

Simão kissed her on the forehead and stood. "We are finished, no?"

285

"Yes. Let's get out of here."

As the phone shrilled, Chelsea turned from the Royal typewriter. "Freitas Enterprises." She listened, frowning. "*Um momento. Não falo Português.*" She punched the hold button. "Simão, you've got to take this one. He talks too fast for me."

"Okay." He winked at her as he picked up the receiver on his own desk.

Chelsea listened to the purr of his voice as he spoke Portuguese to the caller. It had only been 10 days, but already it seemed natural for her to be here. After she had won him the variance, Simão had insisted she come work with him, at least until she found another job. Having nothing else to do, except her book, she agreed. It would put her in a better position to meet women she could write about, she reasoned. It was also pleasant being with Simão all day.

She sat at the scarred wooden thrift shop desk and phone he had purchased for Rosa. Many mornings when they met at the office, they had only been apart a few hours. After Simão left the fish market, they shared morning coffee, worked a bit, went to lunch, and worked some more.

Chelsea handled the telephone, typing, English correspondence, and legal papers.

It was odd. After so many years in newspapers, she had thought she would feel out of place doing office work, but it was as if she had turned into another person working in another country. Despite her previous articles, most people in the Portuguese community seemed to think it perfectly natural for her to give up her job and help her fiancé.

Fiancé. She sat back, staring out at Santa Clara Street through the dusty window. She had not officially accepted Simão's repeated proposals, yet they both seemed to acknowledge their future marriage as a given. So did everyone around them. Watching and listening to him now, she thought, why not? She had never felt the same warmth and passion about anyone else. With Jeffrey, they were more like buddies who had sex. This was different.

The telephone startled her. Simão was on the other line. She grabbed the phone before it could ring again.

"Chelsea?"

286

"Angie?" Why would her downstairs neighbor be calling?

"Oh, thank God. I had a terrible time finding you, but I got this letter here for you from the Chronicle. They put it in the wrong mailbox, I guess. I was about to throw it away, figuring it was a sales pitch, but then I realized they sent it first class and it's addressed it to you."

Chelsea felt her stomach tighten. "The Chronicle? What does it say?"

"You want me to open it?"

"Yes."

Simão had finished his call and she could feel him watching her.

"Okay." Paper rattled over the line. Angie cleared her throat. "It is a reminder that you are scheduled for an interview on Thursday, Oct. 19."

She sighed, relieved. She was afraid the letter might tell her that it was canceled.

"This is for a job?"

"Oh, Angie. Full-time, with benefits, major exposure, the works."

"Well, good luck."

Simão was staring at her as she hung up. "This is about the job in San Francisco?"

"Yes. I've got an interview next week."

"I see." He picked up a stack of lined yellow pages. "Can you type this for me? I want to mail it today."

Chelsea's heart suddenly felt like a hunk of lead hanging in her chest. Everything was fine as long as she gave herself up completely. As soon as she remembered who she was, she felt like Dorothy in the Wizard of Oz, desperately out of place and longing to go home because nothing in Oz was real.

Chapter Twenty-Two

Chelsea clutched her black leather portfolio so tightly her fingers ached. Her black pumps beat a brisk rhythm on the polished sidewalk as she walked from the parking garage to the San Francisco Chronicle building. She wore her best suit, a black and white tweed, with a red silk blouse, and her long hair was corralled in a French braid.

She breathed in the cool salt- and exhaust-tinged air. San Francisco! She loved it all, the skyline as she drove up Highway 101, the ocean glinting in the distance, the saltwater-taffy-colored houses stacked up tight next to each other, the old ladies in babushkas waiting at the bus stops next to scrawny young men in black leather jackets and chartreuse hair. She read the famous names on the buildings she passed and felt the excitement of the city: Davies Hall with its glass walls, Max's Opera Cafe, Union Square, Macy's.

Up ahead, a young man with waist-length blond hair sat on the sidewalk playing bongos. Beside him, a black man squeezed haunting music out of a battered fiddle. As people passed, they threw coins into the open fiddle case. Chelsea reached into her pocket. "Great music," she said, adding 50 cents to the coins in the velvet-lined case.

The black man nodded and smiled, showing a gold front tooth. When she worked here, she would seek out sights like this to photograph.

Simão came to mind. If he could just see San Francisco, he would fall in love with it, too. Maybe it would remind him in some way of Portugal, with its ships and sea breezes.

Still, he was tied to his house and his business and his mama in San Jose. A man his age shouldn't have so many strings, she thought. But if her own mother were standing beside her, she would have complained that Chelsea herself was the one in the wrong. A person her age should have a family by now. A career would not keep you warm at night or support you in your old age.

"Shush," she whispered, then looked up to see Josh Bernal, one of the Chronicle's columnists, coming her way. "Good morning."

He nodded, preoccupied. Up close, he needed a shave, and there was dandruff on the shoulders of his navy blue jacket.

Well, we're all human, she told herself. I wonder what he's writing about today.

A block later, she stood before the big glass door. A burly guard with a nasty red bump on his nose greeted her. "Do you have some identification?"

She fumbled in her purse. "I have a driver's license and a press card. I'm here to see Mr. Smith for a job interview. I have his letter."

He studied the license and the letter. "Okay. Sign in here. It's on the sixth floor."

Her heart was beating like the bongos she had heard earlier. This was it. The Chronicle. Big time. In the elevator, she pictured herself riding up every day. She would get an apartment near the ocean. She'd have a space in the Chronicle parking lot, of course. No walking four blocks and paying $1.75 an hour. She would always carry her camera with her; the whole city would be her beat.

The doors opened, and she walked up to the first desk. Around her, reporters sat in cubicles, editors in glass offices. Computer keys tapped like rain. Phones burbled, faxes rang, conversations hummed.

"I have an appointment with Mr. Smith," she said. The young clerk, whose short black hair was moussed into a tall crew cut, frowned.

"He's not in."

"Excuse me?"

"He went out. I'm not sure when he's coming back."

The roaring in her ears drowned out all the other noises. "But we had an appointment for 10:00." She glanced at her watch, although she already knew that it was exactly 9:59.

"I don't know what to tell you. I guess you could wait over there."

"Thanks." She took a seat in one of the hard brown plastic chairs near the door.

The clerk offered her coffee, which she refused, and a newspaper, which she accepted. She stared at it but couldn't digest the words. She was down to the sports pages by the time a bulky man in a gold corduroy jacket and thick black glasses burst through the door muttering to himself.

He stopped at the desk to pick his messages out of a slot marked

Smith.

"Matt," said the clerk, "this woman has been waiting for you. She has an appointment."

Chelsea rose, barely keeping a grip on her portfolio as she stretched out her right hand and forced a smile. "Hi, I'm Chelsea Faust."

He stared, confused. Then his eyes suddenly gleamed with recognition. "Oh, Chelsea Faust. Didn't you get my message?"

"What message?"

"Oh dear. We'll be in my office," he told the clerk.

Chelsea followed him, barely able to keep up with his galumphing gait, past reporters, through double doors into the photo area and into a small glassed-in office. "That's why I don't trust these high-tech message systems. Have a seat."

She moved a pile of newspapers to the floor and sat on the edge of a chair identical to the one on which she had been waiting.

Smith sighed. "I'm afraid I have bad news for you. The job I originally wrote to you about isn't open any more. The guy decided not to leave. I'm really sorry you had to drive all this way."

Chelsea's face was a tight mask. She refused to let it show her disappointment. "I didn't mind. It's a beautiful drive. Won't you at least look at my work? In case you have another opening?"

He glanced at the clock. "I've only got about two minutes, but sure, why not?"

Forty-five minutes after she had walked in the front door full of hopes and dreams, Chelsea passed the guard again and emerged on Market Street. Smith had liked her work, but he had warned her that openings at the Chronicle were rare. Somebody practically had to die for a job to open up.

The sun, so bright before, was now hidden behind a wall of fog. The air was cold, and a biting wind tore at her face. "Damn!" she hissed, walking quickly, hating her stiff shoes and scratchy suit. She wanted her tennis shoes so she could run all the way to the ocean and throw herself in.

The Chronicle had not rejected her, she had to keep reminding herself. Smith had liked her work, even encouraged her to try freelancing something for him. But there just wasn't an opening on the staff.

To console herself, she had lunch at the Cliff House, then went walking on the trails around the old Sutro Baths nearby, ignoring her aching ankle.

She struggled over the sand and rocks in her good shoes and stood against a stone wall watching the waves crash against the rocks, exploding in white spray that turned to foam and slipped back over the stones into the ocean. Far in the distance, a freighter headed out of San Francisco Bay. Behind her, teenagers scrambled over the rocks, laughing and calling to each other as they crawled through the caves.

As she watched one wave after another, she felt she had come to a point where every choice she had would bring her pain. Either she could go alone to Riverside or wherever else she could get a good job, or she could stay here, marry Simão and become someone she was not.

How had things changed so quickly?

The tide was going out. Each wave was a little less spectacular. The wind was cold against her face, and she was tired.

"Let's go see the seals," she heard a young mother say to her little girl behind her; soon they passed her on their way down the steps toward the ruins of the Sutro Baths. It was time for her to move on, too. She should go home before the traffic got bad. After that, she didn't know. Back to answering Simão's telephone, she supposed.

Somehow, nothing was turning out as she had planned.

She had loitered too long, and now she was stuck in the afternoon commute. It was only 4 o'clock, but cars were already backed up on 19th Avenue, all trying to get out of San Francisco.

This is what it would be like every day if I worked here, she told herself. The commute from hell.

But I would live here, she countered. I wouldn't have to commute.

A horn startled her. She was boxed in on all four sides. "What do you expect me to do!" she hollered, although of course the sunglassed jerk behind her couldn't hear.

When she turned in to the driveway at 5:56, Simão was waiting on her front steps.

Chelsea frowned. Right now she wanted to be alone. She got out, feeling tired and rumpled after her upsetting day and the long drive. "Hi."

"*Boa tarde.*" He kissed her forehead. "Well, what happened?"

Might as well give him the good news. "The person who had the job decided not to leave. I'm back where I started."

Simão's eyes brightened and his lips twitched as he fought back a grin. "Oh, I am sorry you are disappointed." The smile won. "But I am very glad you are not moving to San Francisco."

"I knew you would be."

He pulled her close. "Do not sound so sad. It is not what God meant to be. You can work here. With me."

"It's not the same."

"I know. You can maybe, what do you call it, freelance or write books. Or write for a Portuguese newspaper?"

"I suppose." She could still see San Francisco disappearing in her rear-view mirror.

The mail arrived as Chelsea reconciled her checkbook. She was staring at the numbers on her calculator and the minus sign that preceded them.

"How could I be overdrawn?" Quickly she added the debits again and subtracted the total from the bank balance. Same result: $32.37 in the hole and a week before her next unemployment check arrived.

"But I haven't spent any money!" She looked back at the most recent entries: rent, telephone bill, gas and electric, groceries, fuel for the truck. All necessities. Except for her lunch at the Cliff House. But that was a special occasion.

Her savings account was down to $300. At this rate, she would be broke in less than a month.

She went out the front door and grabbed the mail. Mostly advertisements. And two more bills--her VISA card and truck payment.

"Damn." She sank to the step, staring at the windowed envelopes. A postcard dropped out of the supermarket newsletter. On the front was a photo of a cat hanging from a narrow branch, a worried look on its face. "Hang in there, baby," was printed below.

"I'm trying," Chelsea said. She flipped the card over. "I miss you.

The wife's still gone. She has the kids now. Dunning is still an asshole. I bought two of these, one for me and one for you. Forgive me for being a rat. Please call. Let's go out for a drink. Mel."

The familiar scrawl slanted across the card at a 45-degree angle.

"Oh, Mel," Chelsea sighed. How do you save a person who's destroying himself? She was surprised how much she missed him.

She looked down at the bills on the cement beside her. If only she could turn the clock back to before she lost her job.

Simão didn't know her financial situation. She had told him she got plenty of unemployment and had ample savings if she needed it.

Ample for what, she asked herself. She could pay her truck payment and VISA bill or her rent, not both.

Simão constantly badgered her to move in with him. Her parents had offered her old room. She had to do something. Working for free for Simão didn't pay the rent. Neither did betting on a book for which she had no contract. She could stall another month before the landlord evicted her. Maybe two if she begged. But what would she be left with then? Bad credit and the same lousy choices.

If a job offer came from far away, should she take it? Yes. She had always taken care of herself. She wasn't about to stop now.

"Ugh, too much thinking." The sun was warm, but an autumn breeze sweetened the air. She went in, laced on her running shoes, and set off on a gentle jog. Her ankle still wasn't up to full strength. One mile was all she dared. She wished she could go 20.

As she passed Discount Photo Supply on Fourth Street, she saw a familiar car in the narrow parking lot and stopped. "Dad?"

She went up the steps into the little store that always smelled of developer and fixer and found her father, chuckling over something with the bearded man behind the counter. He held a large bag bulging with supplies.

"Hi," she said. "You must be getting serious about this business."

"Gotta do something." He turned back to the clerk. "Denny, this is my daughter, Chelsea. You've probably seen her pictures in the Weekly Times."

"Oh, yeah," the guy said, extending a large hand. "You do good work."

"Thanks. Dad, what are you up to?"

"Just restocking the darkroom. I was out of everything." In his eyes shone a light that had been missing for over a year. "How about you?"

"Jogging. Have to work the ankle and blow the cobwebs out of my mind."

He nodded, gazing at her thoughtfully. "I'm glad you're here. I have a proposition to discuss with you. Let me drive you home."

This had better not involve me moving back in with him and Mom, she thought as she got into his car, feeling 12 years old again, going out with the first man in her life, the man who had taken care of her for all those years before she had to worry about jobs and money and other confusing grownup things.

Her father bounded up the stairs with the energy of a young man. He carried a large unmarked envelope.

"Iced tea?" she asked.

"Good idea. Thanks."

She put ice in two tall glasses, poured in tea from the pitcher she kept in the refrigerator and added a spoonful of sugar to her father's glass before joining him at the table. "So, what's going on? You look like you won the lottery or something."

Dad shook his head. "No, no, nothing like that. But I've done something you might find just as surprising."

"What already?"

He pulled a proof sheet out of the envelope. "What do you think?"

Chelsea grabbed the magnifying glass off her desk, bent over the first frame and gasped. "Slater?"

"That's right."

The whole sheet was the councilman and his friends under the Guadalupe Bridge. Some of the shots were blurry or faint, but several were clear and damning. She looked up into her father's eager face. "How did you do this?"

"By being crafty. I dressed up in old clothes, put a ratty old hat on my head, limped a little bit, and pretended to be drinking a lot. I hung out there, shared a bottle of wine and made up a hard luck story they fell for."

"But how did you explain the camera?"

"Oh, I said I used to be a professional photographer, but I fell on tough times and now I just carried it around and pretended to shoot. I said I couldn't afford any film."

"Wasn't Slater suspicious?"

"Well, the first night, sure he was. But I really didn't have any film. I opened up the back and showed him. So he decided I was just some kind of nut. It became a joke. Photo Joe and his empty camera."

"How many nights did you go out there?"

"Four altogether. I'd wait until they were mostly asleep, then walk back to the car and drive home. On the fifth night, Slater wasn't there any more."

"Oh my God. Mom must have had a fit."

"I told her I was at your place, playing security guard to make sure you were safe. You have to back me up on that."

"But I haven't been home much. I've been out with Simão."

"What a tangled web we weave, eh? Anyway, now I need to figure out what to do with these pictures. And I need a story to go with it. That's where you come in."

"I don't know much, but I guess I can do some research. I heard that Slater moved in with his girlfriend. It's almost time to file for the next election. I can find out if he has taken out papers. We can't sell our story to the Weekly Times, with Slater being a friend of the publisher, but the Mercury might take it."

"Worth a try."

"Okay. Dad, you make the prints, and I'll find out who to talk to at the Merc. My original informant said they weren't interested, but maybe he never actually contacted them. Anyway, they couldn't possibly have photos this good."

Her father squeezed her hand. "Well, I'd better get going before your mother gets worried."

She walked him to the door. "Thanks, Dad. I still can't believe you did this."

"After what he did to my little girl? Besides, I had nothing better to do." They hugged and she watched him walk to the car, the old bounce back in his step.

295

She couldn't avoid the question of what to do much longer. Simão was still pressuring her to move in with him. Her mother was harassing her to come home for a while. Dad kept talking about how they could work together in the new darkroom if she moved back.

"There's nothing to worry about," she insisted at lunch one afternoon at Denny's with Simão and her mother. Her father had gone to a meeting of the camera club he had just joined.

Money had come up indirectly. "They're having a baby shower for your cousin a week from Saturday," Mom said. "I almost forgot to tell you."

"God, another afternoon of giggling girls cooing over booties and Pampers."

When you have your own babies, you'll appreciate things more."

Chelsea sighed. "So, what does she need? What are you going to get her?"

"Well, her mother says she really needs a car seat. She's getting her a crib, and Louise is buying a high chair. I thought maybe we could go together on the car seat."

Chelsea closed her eyes, remembering her negative bank balance. "I don't know if I can do it right now, Mom. I, uh, I'm a little short till my next check."

"Oh, well, she'll understand, you without a job and all. I can buy it and put your name on the card."

"So you're rich all of a sudden?" Chelsea remembered guiltily that her father had been out of work longer than she had.

"Oh, we have a little stashed away." Mom was silent for a minute. Then, "I've been knitting a blanket for the baby. Maybe I'll just give her that. It was going to be for the birth, but I guess I could whip up something else."

Chelsea shivered in the chilly restaurant.

Simão quickly shed his jacket. "Here, put this on." As he wrapped it around her shoulders, Chelsea leaned against him. "Thanks." The jacket was heavy and warm, the silky lining smooth against her skin.

When the waitress arrived, Simão ordered a steak, and Chelsea asked for the fettucine. Mom had the chef's salad. "I don't know what got your father so hepped up on photography all of a sudden, but I'm sure glad he's interested in something. It's too bad it's such an expensive hobby."

"You can make a lot of money off it if you do it right," Chelsea said, wondering why she wasn't doing it if it was so easy.

"If you moved in and worked together, you'd both benefit."

"I don't have to live there to do that."

"How much money is in your checking account? Be honest."

"Oh, here comes the soup," Chelsea said.

Mom stirred Sweet 'n' Low into her coffee. "The other day your father was doing numbers in his head, how much you pay for rent and your truck and other things and how much you get for unemployment, and he figured you'd be broke by Christmas."

Chelsea colored and pulled Simão's jacket tighter around her. She was conscious of him listening very carefully. "Mom, Dad doesn't know everything about my finances."

"He knows enough, doesn't he?"

"I don't want to talk about this now."

"Chelsea Ann Faust, you are as stubborn as your German father. Worse with the Portuguese thrown in. Your life isn't that mysterious, and you aren't that high and mighty that you couldn't use a little help from your parents."

"What are you talking about, a loan?"

"No, no, no. You know we don't have money to spare. But we do have a house that's almost paid for. I'm saying you should get off your high horse and move in with us. We could both use your company and moral support, and if the three of us shared expenses, we'd all be better off."

Simão intervened. "I have asked her to live at my house. My sister's room is empty, but she always says no."

They were ganging up on her. "I like my apartment."

"Yes, at $600 a month."

"I'll get another job, Mom, one that pays more than the last one."

"When?"

They were both staring at her now, challenging her.

"Any day now. Have a little faith in me." She spied the waitress coming their way with more iced tea. "Let's talk about something else.

297

Simão, tell Mom about your new office building."

All she wanted at this moment was to escape. As soon as she got free of Mom and Simão, she would call the Riverside editor and arrange an interview. She would show them she could take care of herself.

Chapter Twenty-Three

The following Friday, she was packing. The Riverside job had been filled. More bills and another interview that didn't deliver a job had helped prove she couldn't go on this way. Then the landlord told her the rent was going up to $650. It was give notice or wait to be evicted.

"All right, Mom, you win," she had said on the phone. "I'm moving back in. But just for a couple months. I'll be out right after the holidays."

"Hallelujah. I'll get your room ready," her mother said. "I'll be over after lunch to help you pack."

"No, I'll do it. I've got plenty of time. Simão can help me with the heavy stuff."

"Well, holler if you need anything."

She hated giving notice. The landlord, a sharky property owner with buildings all over town, scowled when she told him. "I should know better than to rent to young single women. They never stay very long. I should stick with old people. Couples."

"I told you. Circumstances have changed. Besides, I was here almost a year."

"A year is nothin', sweetheart. Anyway, be out by the end of the month, and I'll inspect the place and send you what's left of your deposit. Leave me a forwarding address."

Chelsea sat back on the floor now, pulling her bathrobe around her, staring out the window at the gray October sky and talking to the air. "I feel like I never grew up. I'll be like a high school kid on summer vacation, reading, writing, helping my mom, going out with my boyfriend." She sighed. "We'll never be able to sleep together."

The door slammed below. John coming home from work. She checked the clock. It was almost 8 a.m. She forced one more paperback between the books in the box, folded the top together and shoved the box into the row along the wall. Time to get dressed.

She was just finishing her makeup but still in her robe when someone pounded on the door, a hard fist against the wood.

"Who could that be?" Simão's knock was gentle, and most other people rang the bell. But nobody came this early.

She put the cap on her mascara and went to look through the peephole in the door.

"Mel!"

She smelled alcohol the minute she opened the door.

Mel almost fell in. "Chel-sea," he said, his mouth twisted in a wry grin. "Hiii." His suit was rumpled, and his hair was uncombed.

"What is going on? Get in here, Mel."

"Gladly." Her former editor lurched inside, and before she knew what was happening he had thrown his body against hers. "I just came to say I love you."

"What!"

He drew his face back and looked at her through red, unfocused eyes. "I said, 'I love you.'"

Chelsea pushed him away. "It's 8 o'clock in the morning. I'm practically engaged, and you're here drunk, telling me you love me?"

Mel squinted. "Is that why you're packing? You're getting married?"

"No. I'm moving back home. Thanks to you and your friend George P. Dunning, I'm broke."

"Not moving in with your boyfriend?"

"No." She moved toward the kitchen. "Let me get you some coffee." The coffee was left over from the day before, but Mel probably wouldn't be able to tell the difference at this point.

He followed her and collapsed onto one of her kitchen chairs. "Chelsea. You're more beautiful than I remembered. Especially in that bathrobe."

"Mel, stop it." As the coffee heated, she sat next to him. She wanted to smooth his thin brown hair and straighten his shirt. "You're talking crazy."

"No, I'm not." He took the coffee, cupping his fingers around the flowered mug. "I'm a little drunk, but I've always had these feelings for you. I just thought, well, I was married and I was your boss and we've always been buddies. . . ."

"Right. Up until I got fired."

He sniffed. "You don't know how hard I tried to keep it from happening."

"I was just trying to do my job."

"I know. Best reporter in the West."

Wait until he saw the Slater photos in the Mercury News--if the editor ever called back.

She glanced at her watch. "Used to be the best reporter in the West. Now I answer phones in my boyfriend's office."

"For pay?"

"Not exactly."

The telephone rang. They both stared at it, but Chelsea didn't move. "I'm not going to answer it. How would I explain having another man in my apartment at this hour?"

"The plumber?" He chuckled and drained his cup as the phone stopped its sharp jangling and the machine clicked on.

Simão's voice: "I will be late a few minutes this morning. Please open up for me and call Mr. Almeida about those forms. *Obrigado.*"

"He ought to pay you."

"He doesn't even pay himself. He works at a fish market in the early mornings."

"Hard-working Portugees."

"Yeah, they are. Mel, I'm worried about you."

He shrugged and pushed back his chair. "No big deal. Well, I have to go. Thanks for the coffee."

As they walked to the door, she looked outside for his car. "Are you driving?"

"No. I got busted. DUI. I'm walkin'. It's good for me."

They both hesitated at the door. Mel reached for her hands and leaned close. They were the same height, eye to eye.

Suddenly he kissed her. Chelsea felt herself drawn to him, conscious of only her thin robe between her skin and his hands. Breathless, she pulled away. "Oh my God."

Mel nodded. "Wow. Are you sure you want to marry that guy?

"No," she breathed. "Go to work. Please."

Mel grinned, his eyes twinkling. "Okay. But don't hurry to get married. My divorce is final in four months and three days."

"Oh, Mel. Sober up on the way, okay."

He ran down the stairs and swaggered south on Fifth Street as Chelsea stood on the landing, still feeling his lips on hers and her blood racing.

Mel was drunk. But what was her excuse?

The telephone rang again. "Oh, Simão," she moaned, picking it up on the third ring. But it wasn't Simão.

"Jason Sparks from the Mercury News returning your call."

Now? She pushed everything else aside and took a deep breath. "Thank you for calling back. Until recently, I was a reporter at the South Bay Weekly Times, and I was investigating a rumor about Councilman Jim Slater. Well, I couldn't get enough evidence then, but I have photos now that prove he was up to some serious misuse of taxpayers' money."

"I see." Sparks sounded doubtful, but she ended up with a 3:00 appointment for herself and her father. Meanwhile, she had work to do.

She dialed Simao's number quickly and counted the rings until the recorder came on, then spoke in a rush before she lost her courage. "Good morning, Simão, I'm afraid I can't come in today. I have a meeting about a story with the Mercury News, and I have to spend the morning preparing my research. I'll stop by the office afterwards, if it's not too late. I'm sorry about Mr. Almeida's forms. *Bom dia.*"

Her face was hot as she hung up. He would be displeased, but she was a volunteer, not his secretary. Besides, with Mel's kiss still warm on her lips, she couldn't face Simão this morning.

As the Mercury News city editor looked over the pictures of Councilman Slater among the homeless, Dad picked at his cuticles and Chelsea clutched her hands together so tightly they hurt.

"Slater doesn't know you took these pictures?"

Dad shook his head. "No, he thinks there wasn't any film in the camera, that I was a crazy bloke who liked to click his shutter for the fun of it."

"You're sure he was living there?"

"Yes," Chelsea spoke up. "As I told you on the phone, I was working for the Weekly Times when I went out and tried to take

302

pictures. Slater's friend assaulted me and broke my camera. But he was definitely living there."

"Unbeknown to my daughter, I went out to track him down and found him living exactly where she said she had seen him. But I pretended to be one of the homeless. I figured it was safer, after what happened to her. Besides, it galled me that her own paper would try to cover this up."

"I hear you. But you see," said Sparks, leaning back in his chair, rubbing his eyes. "In journalism, we think it's important to be up front about what we're doing, not to trick people. Although, sometimes I have to admit it's the only way to get a story."

"Exactly," said Chelsea.

"I'm uncomfortable because neither one of you is on staff. As well as the fact that you were out there, Mr. Faust, on false pretenses."

Dad nodded, disappointment in his eyes.

"And I'm angry that we missed this story. Our own reporters should have caught it." Sparks shifted quickly through the pages of Chelsea's article. "Your pictures are pretty strong evidence, and your daughter has really done some legwork to back them up. Chelsea, you called everybody I would have asked you to call--cops, council members, sociologists, social services. I have to check on this one with my boss, but I think we can run it, and give it big play. There will be more stories dealing with the fallout after this hits the fan, but we'll do those in-house. My freelance budget is busted, and I want my city hall reporter to follow this up."

Chelsea nodded, her mouth dry.

"We'll pay you a total of $150, that's the best I can do, and credit you as freelancers. Unless, Chelsea, you want me to list you as a former Weekly Times reporter."

She shook her head vigorously. "No thanks."

They left their opus on Spark's desk, and he walked them back to the front entrance.

Chelsea waited until the big glass door closed behind them. "Whew!" she said, hugging her father. "We did it."

"Now we just have to wait for it to come out--and hope Slater doesn't come after both of us. You're still moving home, right?"

303

"Yes, don't remind me."

That night, she couldn't sleep. She was pleased about the Slater story being exposed but worried about the fallout afterward. What if he did come after her or her father or Simão? In his mind, they were a couple.

Well, she supposed they were. That's why she felt so guilty about kissing Mel. Her old friend fit right into her doubts about Simão, but she had stopped him before it went any farther. Did she really want Mel in that way? She enjoyed talking shop over Margaritas, but . . . No. That spark she felt with Simão just wasn't there.

She sighed and pushed off the sheets, too warm. Simão would be angry with her for not going to the office today. She and her father had gone out for espresso to celebrate, and it was after 5 when she got home. Simão hadn't called, so she spent a quiet evening alone, packing and thinking.

By 8:00, she missed Simão. When she called his home, his mother said, "Não está aqui. He is not home."

As she hung up, Chelsea remembered that he had a Chamber of Commerce meeting. Perhaps he would call afterward.

She stayed up late, just in case, and her imagination played a romantic scene. What if he called and said, "Chelsea, please will you marry me?" "Yes," she would reply. It would slip out so easily. "Yes."

Getting up stiffly, she looked at herself in the bathroom mirror. "Yes? Is it really yes?"

"Yes," she replied. "But that crazy Portugee has to get a few things straight."

Candlelight glowed from the center of the table, sparkling off borrowed silverware, china and wine glasses. On the stove, two big pots, also on loan from Angie, bubbled, one with raviolis, the other with fresh crab. Deli salads waited in the refrigerator next to two bottles of champagne.

Chelsea hurried back and forth, perfecting the last touches. She had French-braided her hair and put on a snug, low-cut black dress that had been buried in the back of the closet since she lived in Washington. She had spent her checking account dry for this evening's food,

304

flowers, and wine, but it was worth it.

Finally everything was ready. She switched off the overhead lights and waited at the window, trying to calm herself. She had told Simão she was going to a baby shower and could not see him until that evening but that she wanted him to come over for a special dinner.

"You are always too busy," he grumbled, but he said he had some chores to do anyway and agreed to be there at 6:00.

Tonight was the night. No point in putting Simão off a day longer. How many times can you turn down a man's proposal before he stops asking? She knew she was sounding like her mother, but it didn't matter. If it looked as if she was seeking someone to support her, it was just a coincidence. Simão wasn't exactly rich, and she still planned to get a job. Once he accepted that necessity, they would be happier. She was working for a newspaper when they met and fell in love; she would do it again as soon as a job opened up.

Her parents would be pleased. She looked forward to seeing the happy looks on their faces. She pictured her dad walking her down the aisle.

Lord, would the service be in Portuguese or in English? Bilingual. Had to be. Her parents didn't speak Portuguese, and Simão's mother didn't understand English.

As she watched out the window, Simão's car glided to a stop in front of her apartment and backed smoothly into a narrow space just opposite her door.

Chelsea rushed to the stove, giving the frozen raviolis another stir. They were starting to float to the top, ready. In the other pot, two scarlet crabs did an eery dance, intertwining, spinning together, apart, together, their claws catching and releasing.

The doorbell. She took a deep breath, patted her hair to make sure none of the ends had escaped and walked forward, feeling odd wearing high heels in her apartment.

Simão looked exhausted. Circles under his eyes showed the strain of working two jobs. She felt guilty for stranding him at the office the day before. But tonight would make up for it.

When he saw her, he raised his eyebrows in surprise. "Are you having a party?"

305

"A party just for two, you and me," she purred, kissing him gently on the lips. "Would you like some wine?"

He nodded. "Yes, please. Today has been a terrible day. Nothing went right."

"Oh?" She led the way to the kitchen, pulled a bottle out of the ice and started to open it. "I hope you don't mind that we have champagne instead. What happened?"

Simão wrinkled his brow, puzzled, but said nothing about the wine. "I stopped at the office and found a message from Mr. Almeida. He got mad at something and said he would not sign the lease. Then Pedro Sousa said we have bugs in 4B, then my telephone went out of order, and I could not get anybody to fix it because it was Saturday. I just--sometimes I wish I was a farmer like my father."

Chelsea held out the sparkling glass of Brut. "I'm sorry it went so badly for you. At least now you can relax. Put it all out of your mind."

He took the glass in his big hand. But he didn't drink. "Then, worst thing, my girlfriend is too busy to see me for two days in a row. She tries to get a job in a faraway city so I will not see her no more. Now she probably got it and she wants to celebrate. But I do not feel like a party. I am sorry."

She stared into his eyes until he looked straight back at her. "Simão." Her heart was beating so hard she was sure he could hear it. "There is no faraway job. I was thinking about what I would say to you tonight."

"What do you mean?" His eyes were hurt. "In American movies, when one of the couple has to 'think,' it always means they're going to say goodbye."

"Oh, no. Not always." She set her glass on the counter and took Simão's and set it down, too. "Not this time. Simão, this is going to sound forward, but you know me by now, I'm a pushy American woman. I want to marry you. I want to say yes to your many proposals. I want to be your wife."

Simão's mustache curved slowly upward and his eyes filled with tears as her words sank in. "You will be my wife?"

"Yes."

"Oh, thank God." He pulled her close then. She closed her eyes, breathing in his faint cologne, and hoped the moment would last forever.

"Simão," she said, savoring the feel of his scratchy cheek against hers. "I really do love you. *Amo-te muito*."

"*Te amo também*."

Finally they pulled apart. "Let's toast now, before the bubbles go away," she said.

"*Um momento*." To her surprise, Simão bolted from the kitchen and out the front door and ran down the steps.

She watched him from the window, leaning into his car, pulling something out of the glove compartment. "Oh my God," she breathed, knowing what it must be.

Simão beamed as he returned to the kitchen and held out a blue velvet box. Biting her lips, she opened it carefully. Now tears came to her eyes as a large diamond surrounded by five tiny ones sparkled in the candlelight.

"It's beautiful."

"*Sim*, like you. May I put it on?"

The ring fit perfectly. "Oh, Simão." She dashed away the tears that insisted on slipping down her face. He offered his handkerchief.

"I'll get makeup on it."

"*Não faz mal*." No big deal.

She started to laugh, and they were both chuckling as the stove timer went off.

"Dinner is ready."

It was a joyous, romantic evening. They fed each other raviolis and crab, toasted until they were tipsy, then took the candles into the bedroom and made love until 2 a.m.

"Simão," she whispered afterward, "I'm still going to get a job. But something close."

He sighed. "I know. I give up."

He stayed that night, rising at 5 to hurry home before his mother woke up. Chelsea was going to meet them later for church, and they would tell Mama the news. That evening, they would tell her parents.

She woke with the sun in her eyes, a big shaft of light beaming from an unusually bright October day. Lifting her left hand, she held it up and let the sun sparkle off her ring, creating tiny rainbows across the cream-colored bedspread. It was so cliché. Like every other engaged young woman she had ever known, she couldn't wait to show her ring to every woman she knew. Maybe she had never thought much about marriage before because it was beginning to seem as if it would never happen.

Stretching and yawning, she shoved the covers back and eased out of bed, reaching for her robe. They had fallen asleep naked. The bed still held the scent of their lovemaking, and her clothes were piled on the floor.

She imagined being together like this every night. It sounded wonderful.

Of course it wasn't the first time she'd lived with a man. There were those years with Jeffrey and a three-month fling with Peter the revolutionary at Berkeley, but those were different. There was no commitment. Nobody had ever bought her a diamond ring and pledged to spend the rest of his life with her and their children.

Children. Talk about your career-stoppers. But other women had combined both, and she would find a way to do it, too. Like Avó, she would have children and grandchildren. Maybe even great-grandchildren. They would be tall like her and Simão, with dark hair and eyes, and they would be bilingual. She had to get back into the Portuguese class. She had dropped out this semester to save money, but she needed to learn the language. If Simão could learn English, she could become fluent in Portuguese.

The kitchen was a mess. Leftover raviolis had turned to glue in the big white pot. Fishy water and bits of orange shell remained in the other pot. Dishes and glasses littered the table and counter. Next to her plate was the blue velvet box in which her ring had come. Simão told her he had been carrying it around for over a month and had almost given up on ever being able to present it to her.

The ring was much different from the one he had given his first wife, he said. Fátima preferred emeralds, but to him Chelsea was the fire of diamonds and the coolness of white gold.

308

She slipped the box into the pocket of her robe, started the coffee and let it brew while she cleaned up the dishes. Then she would have breakfast and meet Simão at church.

She was just sitting down with her coffee and a bowl of cereal when the telephone rang. She was tempted to let it go. But maybe it was Simão.

"Good morning, sleepyhead," her mother said. "You sound like you just woke up."

"I've been up a while." What did she want so early?

"Well, I wondered if you needed some help with your packing."

Packing! Chelsea had somehow forgotten for a moment about moving in with her parents. Maybe the plans should change now? "No thanks, Mom. I'm okay. In fact, I was just getting ready to go to Mass with Simão."

"Oh, so you won't be home?" Her mother sounded disappointed.

"Not for most of the day. But we wanted to come over tonight and show you something Simão bought for me."

"What's that?"

"Oh, I can't tell you; I have to show you. I'll see you sometime after dinner."

She hung up and returned to her breakfast. Knowing her mother, she was probably already broadcasting the news to all the neighbors and cousins that her bachelor daughter was finally getting married.

309

Chapter Twenty-Four

A few days later, Chelsea was in the bedroom before work, piling her summer shorts and tee-shirts into a cardboard box, when the telephone rang. Humming "Love Me Tender" with Elvis on the radio, she grabbed the phone.

"Good morning, Chelsea," said a very sober-sounding Mel. She remembered the last time she had seen him and swallowed guiltily.

"Mel. Hi, how are you?"

"I'm okay. Great story in the Merc. And your dad's pictures. How about that."

"Jealous?"

"You bet. I could kill Dunning for that whole situation."

Silence followed.

"Mel?"

"Yeah, I'm sorry. Sarge just slipped me a note. It says, 'Say hi to Faust.' So, hi."

"Hi back to Sarge. Mel, what can I do for you?" She knew it sounded cold, but this was so uncomfortable.

He sighed. "I've been calling for days, but I guess you were busy. First, I'm sorry for my behavior the other morning at your apartment. I meant what I said, but I had never intended to say it because I knew it wasn't mutual."

"That's okay. But about the drinking. I know it's none of my business. . . ."

His voice sounded muffled, as if he were trying not to be heard by the other nosy souls in the newsroom. "I know. I have to stop. I haven't had a drop since then. Six days and counting."

"Are you going to AA?"

"No, I just quit. I can handle it."

"You sure?"

"Oh, yeah. It was just a phase." She heard a commotion in the background, then Mel's voice got louder again. "The other reason I called is that I heard there's an opening at the Mercury. Somebody quit without notice, and this friend of mine over there called. It hasn't even been announced yet, but if you get your stuff in there, with a hearty recommendation from me and my friend. . . ."

Chelsea caught her breath. The San Jose Mercury News. That was even better than the Chronicle because she wouldn't have to move. With her story on the front page of today's local section, surely she would have a better chance than before. "Who do I call?"

She took down the name and number, thanked Mel profusely, and sank onto the bed, her head spinning.

She hadn't told Mel she was engaged. The biggest news of her life. But this was almost as big. Suddenly she had no interest in sorting clothes.

She dialed the number Mel had given her, asked for Jim Green and waited. The photo editor's voicemail answered. Chelsea frowned and left a message, giving both her home number and the number at Simão's office. Photo. The pictures in today's paper were shot by her father. The photo editor probably wouldn't care about her writing. But she had her clips from before, too.

At the office, Simão kissed her warmly, his hand lingering on her cheek. "Good morning. You look beautiful. Like a famous writer with a story on the front page."

Chelsea nodded, distracted. "Thanks." She wasn't ready to explain that she was dressed for a job interview. If the editor called, she was prepared to jump in the truck and go. Her portfolio lay on the seat, filled with photos ranging from her college days to her Weekly Times story of the Portuguese hall burning down.

"I have these letters that need to be typed," Simão said. "They must be mailed today." He handed her five sheets of yellow paper with his heavy all-caps print.

Thinking *I won't have to do this garbage much longer*, she tossed her purse in a desk drawer and sat at the typewriter, rolling in a sheet of clean paper. We ought to have computers, she thought.

Simão kissed her hair, then sat at his own desk and picked up the phone.

As she typed, cursing the mistakes she made every line, she wished he would leave for a while so she could speak freely with Jim Green when he called.

But why was she keeping this a secret? She should have shouted it the second she walked in. It was a great job, close to home. Yet she knew that even if Simão had agreed to the idea of her working, he would not be happy when a real job came along.

She sighed. Simão, waiting on hold, turned and winked at her, then began to speak into the phone in Portuguese.

The hours passed. She was putting stamps on the envelopes as the postal carrier approached the box in front of the office. She dashed down the steps.

"Just made it," said the wiry, red-haired postman.

When she returned, Simão was in the bathroom. Hastily she dialed the number to retrieve messages from her answering machine. No calls had come in. She hung up as Simão emerged.

"Did someone call?"

She colored. "No. Not a soul. I was just checking my messages."

"Ah. This afternoon, I thought we would visit Avó. Mama says she is not feeling well, and I think she would like to meet my future wife."

Chelsea swallowed. "Sweetheart, we have already met. Rosa took me there, and I interviewed her. Her life is fascinating."

Simão frowned, confused. "When did Rosa take you to see Avó?"

"Before she--um, before she left. Back when you thought I was corrupting her."

He clenched his jaw. "We must not talk about Rosa. We will go today at 4."

"Okay." But Chelsea glanced anxiously at the telephone. Come on, ring, she thought.

Avó was not in the hall in her wheelchair this time. Simão led the way to her room. Amid all the petite Asian women working there and the frail old people in wheelchairs, he looked especially tall, and his suit stood out gray and sharp. He could be a doctor, Chelsea thought, silently wishing for a moment that he was. Or some other professional, a lawyer or a professor, not a fish market worker and self-styled entrepreneur. But that was silly. He was Simão, and she loved him. He had done well for an immigrant from a little farming village. Soon his property would earn enough income to support the family and he could quit the fish business.

312

The sight of Avó drove her wandering thoughts away. The old woman lay in bed, looking deathly ill. Her white hair hung in loose wisps around her tiny grayish face, and her arms dangled out of the hospital gown, the skin sagging and bruised from shots and IVs.

A TV show was playing, apparently turned on by one of the workers, but Avó was unaware of it.

Simão bent to kiss his grandmother's withered forehead. "*Avó, estóu aqui. Simão.*"

The ancient eyes flickered open, and Avó tried to speak, but her words came out garbled. Then she noticed Chelsea and spoke swiftly and loudly as she grabbed for Chelsea's hand.

Holding the gnarled fingers, Chelsea looked to Simão for translation. But he shook his head. "I do not know what she is saying. She is much worse."

"What happened?"

"She had what they call a stroke."

"Why didn't you tell me?"

"I--I don't know." He slid a chair toward her. "Sit."

His eyes were on the old woman's. "*Ah, minha Avó.* I hope you are not in pain."

Avó squeezed Chelsea's hand.

"Avó," she said. "I am so sorry I haven't been to see you lately."

The grandmother answered with another stream of words she didn't understand. Neither did Simão. As she repeated them, he leaned closer, but didn't comprehend. Suddenly as she said the same thing a third time, Chelsea got the words.

"Oh my God, Simão. I know what she's saying."

"What?"

"Write my story."

"I don't understand."

"She told me the whole story of her life. I've got it on tape. Rosa translated for me. I wanted to put her in my book." Which I have not worked on for days, she thought. "She remembered."

Chelsea leaned closer, squeezing Avó's hand. "*Vou escrever a sua história.*" She looked at Simão. "Is that right?"

He nodded. "It is good."

313

Avó's eyes closed wearily.

Down the hall, dinner carts rattled. A cheery young aide in white bustled in. "Mrs. Freitas," she called. "Time for dinner."

"She is sleeping," Simão said.

"No, she is pretending to sleep. She does that all day. Whenever she doesn't want to do something. Mrs. Freitas, wake up. We have applesauce and stroganoff. Good stuff."

Avó didn't move.

Simão stood. "I will feed her. Thank you."

"Okay. I'll come back later." The aide hurried out.

Chelsea released Avó's hand and switched places with Simão. She watched as he tenderly rubbed the old woman's hand and kissed her cheek. "You must eat for me, for your Simão, if you still love me."

When the aide returned with Avó's tray, the old woman opened her eyes and waved toward the foot of the bed.

"I think she wants to sit up," Chelsea said. She found the control and raised the bed, then watched Simão feed his grandmother, one spoonful at a time, using the paper napkin to mop up the food that dribbled out the left side of her mouth. At that moment, her heart was so full of love for him she thought it would burst.

He was quiet as they walked toward the exit a little while later. The halls were silent now, all the residents at dinner in the dining hall or in their own rooms. Through the open doors, Chelsea saw other patients. A toothless Chinese woman sat swinging a spoon, splattering herself and her sheets with pureed broccoli. In another room, an old man lay facing away from them. The covers had slipped off, and she could see his bare backside. From another room, a woman hollered "Help, help, help!" yet no one seemed to be coming to her aid.

"We should tell someone," Chelsea said.

Simão shook his head. "No. She screams all day long. Nothing is wrong; she is just crazy. Avó says she can't hardly stand it sometimes. That is why until lately she spent all her time away from her room. So she can't hear. She can look out the front door and pray that somebody comes to visit her." He sighed.

Chelsea put her arm around his broad back and pulled him close. "I know it's hard."

"*Muito difícil.*"

314

In the driveway at Simão's house, he hesitated, not getting out. "Wait," he said, putting a hand on her arm.

"What?" Chelsea glanced toward the front of the house and wondered if Mama was watching them from the kitchen window.

His expression was serious. "You must write your book."

She stared at him, surprised. "I will."

"I mean, right away. You can bring your computer to my office and work there. I will not disturb you. Just if you can answer the telephone sometimes."

"I don't have a publisher."

"I know. You told me. I will pay for printing your book."

She kissed his cheek. "Simão, thank you, but do you have any idea how much it costs to publish a book?"

"No. I do not care."

"Thousands, sweetheart."

"Maybe our cultural society or the chamber of commerce will help. I have friends in the community."

"I know, but--"

"Shh. It is important to Avó that you tell her story. It may be her last wish. The doctor says she is very sick. And there are other women. You have talked to many of them already. We are losing a whole way of life. The young women, like Rosa, like--" he swallowed--"like my first wife, they are different. America changes them. They are--"

"They're like me?" Chelsea stared at his shadowed face.

"A little. Anyway, we must save our memories of the older ways. Women like Avó, they never learned to read or write. If nobody keeps track of what they said, we will lose it. You are a good writer, and you have a Portuguese heart."

"Oh, Simão." She hugged him. "How I love you."

They held each other a long time, then Chelsea opened her eyes and caught a movement at the kitchen window. "Your mother is watching."

"*Ai, Deus.* I will maybe have to build her a separate house for when we are married. But now I am grateful she is a good cook and takes care of me."

"My mother is teaching me how to cook."

315

Simão kissed her gently on the lips. "I know. You will be a very good wife. And someday, a good mother."

Chelsea rolled her eyes. "Me a mother. A few months ago, I was just a carefree reporter looking for a Pulitzer Prize."

"Well, when I am at work and the children are at school, you can go for that prize."

Chelsea tried to see his eyes, to see if he was kidding. It was too dark to tell. "You're not serious, are you? What if I wanted to work full-time?"

Simão sighed, his hand on the door latch. "We'll see. Right now, I am starving. Let us go inside before Mama comes out to get us and catches us kissing."

From the kitchen phone, Chelsea checked messages at home and at Simão's office. Green had not called and probably wouldn't tonight, so she might as well relax.

It was a cozy evening at Simão's house. During dinner, a cold wind came up and rattled the window screens. The trees in the back yard waved eerily in the full moon light. Mama's thick spaghetti sauce reminded Chelsea of her grandmother's. The secret was cumin, Mama said.

After dinner, they moved to the living room. Simão had built a fire while Chelsea and Mama did the dishes. Now she sat in front of it, staring at the flames. Her mind wandered as she watched the tongues of fire lick at the gnarled branches Simão had trimmed from the back yard trees months before. The crackling flames were blue at the top, orange-red at the base.

So much was changing at once. She replayed the scene with Avó at the hospital and thought of the manuscript she had left untouched for over a week. She hadn't packed it yet, but soon the month would be over, and it would be time to move.

Her stomach clutched at the thought. Back to Mom and Dad's. It was like failing, even if it was the practical thing to do. The other option was moving in here. It was a nice house, warm and cozy, but it was where Simão lived with his mother and his sister. Besides, in this straight-laced community, people would talk if she slept there before the wedding.

She thought of Jeffrey suddenly and how he would have laughed at the possibility of living with his mother. In his mind, the only guys who did that were gays or Mama's boys who never grew up. He wouldn't understand Simão and his culture.

Life in D.C. was so different. Chelsea found it hard to believe now how comfortable she had been in the midst of it, dreaming of the stories she would write and the honors she would earn.

She sighed so loudly Simão came to sit beside her.

"Are you sad, *meu amor*?"

She shook her head. "No, just thoughtful."

"What are you thinking about?"

"Nothing."

In truth, she was thinking about the job at the San Jose Mercury News, wondering how Simão would react if she got it.

He knelt at the hearth, poking at the dying embers, putting on another log with a hiss and flare of sparks.

Chelsea stared as the flames from the old log gradually reached up and encircled the new one like hungry monsters finding a new bone to gnaw on.

Mama sat contentedly in the corner, knitting and watching a Spanish movie on TV. Simão leaned against the sofa, watching Chelsea stare.

"You are so beautiful in this light."

"Thank you." She yawned. "I think I need to go home. I'm beat."

"I wish we were already married. Then you would never have to go home."

"You'd never make it to work on time."

"I do not care. The fish, they come whether I am there or not. Let Luís sort them."

Chelsea realized she had never heard this name before. There was a big chunk of Simão's life she knew nothing about. But now all she wanted was to be alone in her bed, sleeping. She got up stiffly and went to Rosa's old room for her coat. The room's emptiness chilled her. She returned quickly to the fire, standing in front of it until the backs of her knees felt as if they were burning.

"You are ready?" Simão said.

Chelsea kissed Mama. "*Boa noite.*"

Mama smiled benignly and said, *"Boa noite, filha,"* without missing a stitch.

In 30 years, would that be her knitting and saying good night to her children? Chelsea followed Simão out the door and gulped in the cold wind that mussed her hair and chilled her lungs.

Their good night was quick. It was too cold outside to linger, and Chelsea was half asleep.

As Simão drove away, she turned toward the piles of boxes in her living room. "What happened to me?"

Rain, so hard it sounded as if someone was flinging marbles at the windows, woke her before dawn. She groaned and rolled over, but sleep had stolen away.

She reached across the bed, feeling Simão's empty pillow.

Soon she would be back home, sleeping in the room where she had grown up, while Simão slept at his house in his musty male room, with his own mother down the hall. It was crazy. If she couldn't be here, they ought to be together.

She pulled the covers over her head, but it was no use. Her eyes wouldn't close, and her mind wouldn't turn off. She slipped out of bed and put on her robe. In a few minutes, she was sitting in front of her computer staring at the blank gray screen.

The rain had eased into a steady tapping, like pins dancing on the roof. From downstairs, she heard voices and a door closing. John was home from work.

She began to type. "A year ago, I was a reporter on my way to the newspaper big time. I didn't know what a *festa* was, I didn't speak a word of Portuguese, and I had never met Simão Freitas. Now we're engaged, and I'm working in Little Portugal.

"It started with an assignment. . . ."

Her fingers flew across the keys, their tapping blending into the rain on the roof. She had eight pages written by the time she instructed the computer to save and got up to start a pot of coffee.

Outside, the sky was gray, and the wet streets were black. Cars swished by as people drove to work. Simão would be at the fish market now. In two hours, he would hurry home to shower and change before going to the office. He would expect Chelsea to be there then.

318

Not this morning. She would call and tell him she was writing. He would understand.

The coffee gurgled and began to drain into the pot. Its aroma filled the kitchen and made the apartment feel warmer and cozier. Chelsea's stomach growled. She shushed it; she could eat later.

Now she had to continue the story of how she had become part of Little Portugal. It could be the opening to her book. She would share her own story, making the link between Americans like herself and the Portuguese immigrants past and present, tying them into one long chain of Portuguese-American women.

The rain slowed to a drizzle. She poured her coffee, sprinkled cereal into a bowl and kept working, oblivious to the increasing traffic outside or the passing time.

"This is good," she whispered as she paused and hit save again. What was missing was an ending. Would she really marry Simão and become a domestic stay-at-home writer, or would the restless rebel in her burst loose from the silk bonds her Portuguese husband-to-be wanted to tie around her? Simão wanted to get married in May. It gave them six months to plan, and they would be back from their honeymoon in time for the Dia de Portugal and the San Jose *festa*. It would also give her time to finish this book.

She sat back, drained, and looked at the clock. It was almost 9:30. She had been so engrossed she had forgotten to call Simão. It was odd that he hadn't called her when she didn't show up.

Not only had Simão failed to call, but she still hadn't heard from the photo editor at the Mercury News.

Was that job real or just a figment of Mel's imagination? She kicked at a box of books next to the desk. It was almost the end of the month. If she spent all her time at Simão's office, when would she finish packing? But if she got the job, she wouldn't need to move.

She picked up the phone and dialed. The machine answered, with Simão's voice in Portuguese. She had urged him to make a recording in both languages, in case an English-speaking client called, but he hadn't done it yet. She listened impatiently to the familiar voice speaking words she was pleased to realize she understood as clearly as if they

319

were English. Her class had helped, but mostly she was learning the language by osmosis.

The beep sounded.

"Simão, I started writing and got carried away. I'm going to take the morning off, maybe do a little packing. Let me know if that's a problem. See you soon. Bye."

The rain had stopped. Water dripped from the eaves, and the sky seemed a shade brighter. Chelsea stretched and headed for the bedroom. She needed to go for a run to clear her head before plunging into the book again.

Her shoes slapped on the wet sidewalk as she jogged south. As she approached the newspaper office, she saw Mel's Volvo out front.

I should never have gone this way, she thought. What if I run into Dunning? Besides, I can't stay out long.

She slowed and looked in the window. Sarge had his back turned, typing. A young woman she didn't recognize sat at her old desk. Mel was so close she could almost touch him if the glass weren't in the way. He was on the phone, taking notes, nodding and gesturing with his other hand.

Chelsea chewed on her lower lip. At this time of day, she would have been inside, where that girl was, writing, talking, or working in the darkroom beyond the door to the right of Sarge.

She hadn't seen a copy of the Weekly Times in a couple of weeks; she was losing track of what issues they were covering. They had probably abandoned the Portuguese community again, just as the men had predicted at the cultural group meeting. Just take their money for advertising, then forget they exist.

Copies of the latest issue were stacked in a newsstand out front. She bent to read the headlines: How to redo your kitchen, holiday makeovers, best restaurants.

"Fluff," she muttered, shaking her head. "Where's the real news?"

Something banged on the window and she looked up to see Mel tapping his Berkeley ring against the glass. He waved her inside.

She shoved open the heavy door and walked into the warm dusty office.

"Hey, Chelsea," Berta called from behind the counter. She had blue fingernails and a diamond stud in her nose now. "Coming back to us?"

She shook her head. "I don't think so." She went on to the newsroom, where Mel grabbed her in a big bear hug. He seemed sober. Instead of alcohol, he smelled like English Leather cologne.

Chelsea fought the blush that rose from her neck across her face as she pulled away from her former boss. "Hi. I was just passing by and couldn't help but look in the windows. The paper looks kind of soft. What happened to the news? I--"

"Hey, what's that big rock on your left hand?" Sarge bellowed.

She looked at her engagement ring as if she had never seen it before. "I don't know. I woke up, and it was there." She tried to smile. But Mel's face had sagged as if gravity had suddenly weighted it down.

"There goes another good one," Sarge said. "Get married, make babies, be happy. Me, I'm stuck here for the rest of my life." He grabbed his chipped and stained coffee mug and went out the back door.

Mel stood frozen in place.

"Say something, Mel." She wished the girl reporter wasn't listening, but the new intern was just as curious as Chelsea had always been. Anything happening in the newsroom was fair game.

He stared out the window. "I never thought you'd really do it."

"I--I don't know what to say, Mel. You knew I liked Simão."

Mel studied the big calendar on his desk. "I don't have anything scheduled this morning. You want to go someplace for coffee?"

God forbid she send him back to the bottle. Maybe that kiss in her apartment, though drunken, was real. She could work on the book later. "Sure. Matisse?"

The espresso bar was empty this time of day. They sat in wing chairs across a tiny dot of a table sipping lattés as Pavarotti bellowed "Pagliacci" over the speakers.

Mel kept staring at her, and she wished she had jogged north instead of south. "So, where's the hard news?" she asked. "The teasers on the cover were all fluff."

"New management decision. Coddle the advertisers, attract readers who don't care about news. The real stories are still there, just buried on pages 4 and 5."

"You agreed to that?"

"Yeah, I was drunk at the time. I'd have agreed to put naked couples copulating on the cover to save my job."

"Or pictures of kittens, puppies and babies."

"Yeah."

They were quiet. Pavarotti stretched for a high note. An old man wearing a beret came in, poured himself a cup of coffee and sat at a far table with the San Francisco Chronicle.

Chelsea scanned the prints on the wall, all impressionist artists, like Matisse.

"I stopped drinking," Mel said in a voice so low she strained to hear.

Their eyes met and held. "You told me that before."

Mel's eyes flicked away and focused on a painting over her head. "Then I got drunk again. This time I mean it. I'd like to say I did it all alone, just quit cold turkey, like I said I was going to, but I didn't. Sarge picked my face off the desk blotter one day, dried me out and dragged me to AA. 'Hi, I'm Mel, and I'm an alcoholic.' "

"Hi, Mel." Her lips twisted into a semblance of a smile.

"Sarge has been doing this meeting gig for 20 years. I had no idea he was a drunk. I've never seen him take a drink. He'd smoke, curse like a longshoreman, abuse man, woman, and beast to get a story, but he'd never take any booze, just 20 cups of coffee a day. Now I know why. It's like I've been let into the secret fraternity. It's so cliché, too, the drunk newspaperman." He sipped at his latté.

"Mel, I'm sorry."

He shrugged. "So, that's the big excitement in my life. Kathy's still gone, and I get the girls on alternate weekends. I'm trying to support two households on one lousy paycheck, and now the girl of my dreams is getting married to some Portuguese guy."

In the bright light coming from the front window, the lines radiating from the outside of his eyes and the dark circles underneath stood out. He had aged over the past few months. Mel's was a face she had loved for years, but had never thought of romantically, probably

322

because he had always been attached to Kathy, first as her boyfriend and then as her husband. He and Chelsea had been buddies long before they were co-workers. "Mel," she said quietly. "Are you teasing me, or were you really interested in me that way?"

"Jesus. Well, might as well 'fess up. I've been spilling my guts at the meetings so much, I'm getting used to it. Chelsea, I've had a crush on you that goes back to when you were a gangly freshman in a mini-skirt and peasant blouse. Since I've become unattached--good word, isn't it, like unhinged--anyway, I started thinking maybe. . . See, before, I always figured your career would take you away from me. You were so talented, so much more than I was, and so ambitious, you wouldn't stay here. When you went to Washington, that confirmed it. Then you came back, and my wife left, and I thought, well maybe, but I guess I moved too slowly. Somebody else got there first. And I'm the one who sent you out to meet him."

Chelsea closed her eyes. If only Pavarotti would shut up. He was singing so loudly she was getting a headache. "I didn't know," she whispered.

Her mind was buzzing. Did she ever like Mel enough to want to date him, fall in love, and marry him? Perhaps. She had always felt comfortable with him. But she had never had the kind of feelings for Mel she had for Simão.

Mel had given her no hint before that kiss in her apartment. He had watched her with Jeffrey and other boyfriends for years and then with Simão. But if he loved her, why did he let her be fired from her job? Jealousy? Weakness?

"Did you hear from Jim at the Mercury?" he asked suddenly.

She shook her head. "No."

"Shit. I'll call him again, nudge him. If you're still interested."

"Oh, yes. Absolutely. Of course, Simão would rather I stay home and bake bread and raise little Simãos and Chelseas."

Mel winced. "Please, don't paint any domestic pictures."

"Sorry. So when are you going to leave this miserable job?"

"I'm thinking about just shooting Dunning and taking over."

"Seriously. You could move to another city."

"I know. I'm starting to look. I can't get used to the idea that I

323

could move anywhere I want, as long as I could still see the kids every two weeks. In fact, I should move. I can't afford to keep the house." A large group in business suits came in, and Mel looked at his watch. "It's almost noon. We'd better go back. If I don't get ahead today, deadline tomorrow will be a real bitch."

"Ah, deadline."

They squeezed past the businessmen and headed south on First Street. The sky had partially cleared, and sun glinted off the puddles in the street. As they walked, Chelsea slid her arm around Mel's slim waist. He did the same around hers.

She sighed. "This is nice."

"Until your boyfriend comes after me with a machete."

"He wouldn't do that." But after a minute, she quietly took her hand away and walked a little faster.

Chapter Twenty-Five

The phone machine light was on when she slipped into the apartment just before noon. She knelt in front of the machine, rewound the tape and pushed play, expecting to hear Simão's voice asking when she was coming to work.

"Ms. Faust," said a deep disk jockey voice. "It's Jim Green from the San Jose Mercury News. Mel Cohen suggested I contact you regarding an opening we have in our photo department. Please call me at 920-2000 as soon as possible."

"Oh, thank God," Chelsea said, sinking into her chair. Finally. She dialed the number right away and was soon on the line with the photo editor.

"Mr. Green, this is Chelsea Faust. You called about a job?" she began, trying to sound casual.

"Yes. It would be on our metro desk. Your former editor spoke very highly of you. He thought you might be just what we're looking for. Jason Sharp on the city desk also put in a good word. So, if you're interested, I'd like to set up an appointment to meet you, look at your work, and talk about the position."

"Sure. I could come today." Don't sound so desperate, she scolded herself.

Green chuckled. "How about tomorrow? Today's half over, and I'm pretty booked this afternoon. Things slow down for us in the mornings. So how about tomorrow at 10?"

The pace of a daily. Even that excited her. She supposed she'd be working nights and weekends. Simão would hate that. "Sure. Great. I'll be there." Could she speak in anything but one-syllable words?

She raced to the bedroom to trade her running clothes for a dress. In a minute, she was out the door again. To celebrate, she would stop at Togo's for lunch. And then, time to report for work and give Simão the good news.

Mel had given her a copy of the latest Weekly Times. Now at Togo's, as she ate her turkey and avocado sandwich, she turned the pages slowly, stopping to stare at a drawing. It was Rosa's work.

Why was she surprised? Rosa would not give up her first paying

325

art job easily. But that meant she was still in the area. Mel must know how to reach her.

She would take this to the office and show Simão. But then, no, maybe she should find Rosa herself and talk to her alone first. After all, she knew Simão still partly blamed her for his sister running away.

The thick sandwich oozed avocado and mayonnaise all over her fingers. What happened to the healthy diet she used to eat? She sighed. She didn't run as often either. Everything was different now.

At the next table, a couple of teenagers giggled as they shared a bowl of nacho chips and sipped extra large Cokes. Beyond the rail, customers wearing everything from suits to torn jeans lined up all the way to the door to buy submarine sandwiches.

Halfway through her lunch, Chelsea couldn't eat anymore. Too many butterflies in her stomach. There was so much to think about. Mel. The job possibility. Rosa. Her upcoming marriage. Moving in with Mom and Dad. The book. Besides, she was late. She wrapped up the second half of the sandwich in a couple of napkins, grabbed her iced tea and went out.

Simão's car was not parked in front of the office. The red door at the top of the stairs was locked, and the lights inside were off. Chelsea reached under the eaves for the spare key and let herself in.

His briefcase sat open on a chair. The desk was in disarray, although Simão never left without straightening his papers first. A cigarette smoldered in the ash tray. On Simão's omni-present yellow pad, 6:43 was scrawled across the middle in dark letters written so hard they left an impression all the way to the bottom of the pad.

Chelsea stubbed out the cigarette, opened the curtains, and pushed the button on the answering machine.

Three messages, all in Portuguese, all related to business. Nothing from Simão.

She felt a chill and turned the thermostat on the wall up to 70. The old heater roared into action, sending warm dusty air through the vent overhead.

Simão was probably just out on business, she told herself. Or maybe one of his *companheiros* had dropped in and invited him for coffee. Or perhaps he ran out to get some lunch. But what was that 6:43?

She pulled out a letter to type. All she had to do was keep busy. He'd be back any minute. She stared at the neat block letters without seeing them.

An hour passed. When the phone rang, she jumped on it. "Hello? *Bom dia?*"

But the caller spoke Portuguese with an accent so thick she couldn't make out more than a couple words.

Please speak more slowly, she asked him in Portuguese. But she still didn't understand, and when she asked him to repeat his message a third time, he hung up in disgust, muttering something about *a mulher estúpida*, the stupid woman.

"Oh, nuts," Chelsea sighed. Would she ever understand this language? Would she always be an outsider? And where was Simão?

At 3:30, she couldn't stand it any longer. She put on her coat, went back down the stairs and climbed into the truck.

For a minute, she sat behind the steering wheel, thinking, as cars passed by on Santa Clara Street. He could be anywhere. But all she could think was to try his home. Maybe he had gone there for some reason. Perhaps he was ill. Or Mama needed him. Or guests had come from out of town. Perhaps that was it. 6:43 could be the arrival time for their flight. She would have a chance to meet some more of his family. But why wouldn't he have told her?

Or maybe Rosa had returned. Simão's sister was fresh on her mind from perusing the newspaper at lunch. She missed Rosa's friendship, and she knew Simão and his mother still grieved over her departure.

As Chelsea turned the corner, she expected to see Simão's car and perhaps one or two more. The lights would be on. Happy voices would ring out into the winter air. She would knock and be welcomed into the love of her new family.

But there were no cars. The windows were dark, and the only sound was a lone mockingbird singing from the peak of the roof as it dried its feathers in the lukewarm sun.

Chelsea walked up the path. The blooms were sparse and wan this time of year. The grass wasn't as green as it had been a couple months ago either.

She knocked gently. Perhaps Mama was asleep. Simão had said she often napped this time of day.

When there was no response, she tried the knob, not expecting it to turn. But the door opened easily and Chelsea found herself alone in the darkened hallway. She sensed immediately that no one was home.

Her first thought was burglars. But everything seemed to be in place, the TV sitting in the living room, Mama's radio on the kitchen counter, Simão's Wall Street Journals neatly stacked on the table.

It was strange to be here alone. She walked slowly down the hallway, peeking into Rosa's empty room on the right, Mama's room, with its pink afghan and the scent of roses and face powder, at the end, Simão's room on the left. She went in, smelling tobacco, fingering the tweed jacket that lay neatly on the bed in a dry cleaning bag, running her fingers over the rough black cover of the Bible that lay on the nightstand beside the bed.

A car swished down the street and stopped out front. Chelsea's heart pounded. What if they caught her sneaking around in the house?

But she would be living here in six months, right?

She hurried to the kitchen and peered out the window, leaning over the stove. The car was a green Pontiac, and the driver, a young Hispanic man, was walking toward a house across the street.

She sighed.

Now what? There was no note, no sign to indicate where Simão and his mother might be. She could wander around town all day and not locate them. She supposed the best place for her was at the office, where Simão expected her to be. But the glow of dealing with callers whose language was gobbledygook to her and typing business letters when she should be writing her book was quickly fading. Simão needed to hire someone else--for pay. Someone Portuguese.

Besides, after tomorrow, she might have to give her future husband notice, because she would be working for the Mercury News. Please, God, she added.

She was about to go out the front door when something thumped against the sliding glass doors in back. Her heart pounding, she turned and burst out laughing. The neighbor's huge orange tabby cat was pacing outside, its mouth opening and closing in meows she couldn't hear.

The cat lived two doors down, but it often spent its days in the Freitas backyard, away from the dog and children at its own house. She knew Mama kept a bag of dry cat food in the cupboard next to the potatoes. She set her purse on the hall table and got the bag, barely able to keep the cat outside as she filled its bowl.

Soon it was purring, its head deep in the dish, crunching at the food.

Chelsea locked the back door, went through the house, and left, locking the front door behind her, too.

He'll be at the office, she thought on the short drive back. He just stepped out for a minute. Mama is probably with her friends. Simple explanation for everything.

But at the office, nothing had changed, and no one had called. She stayed until 5:00 and went home, still wondering.

Sleep was impossible. Between worrying about Simão and thinking about tomorrow's job interview, there was no way she could relax. She turned on the clock radio. Soft music poured into the darkened room. Closing her eyes, she let herself float with the notes. Gradually she dozed.

She woke to an annoying commercial for a local car dealer.

The moon had disappeared, and the sky was beginning to lighten. At 5:30 a.m., she slapped off the radio and sat up, a plan forming.

She dressed quickly, dashing cold water across her face, combing her hair with long hasty strokes, grabbed her purse and went out, shutting the door softly behind her so as not to wake the sleeping neighbors.

The pre-dawn streets were quiet, and most houses she passed were dark. On Santa Clara Street, the stores wore their closed signs, and the parking lots were empty. She slowed as she passed Simão's office, but there were no cars around, and the curtains were still open, as she had left them yesterday.

She had never been to the fish market just up the street, but now she drove straight there. Sure enough, Simão's car was parked out front. She parked hers beside it and got out, feeling butterflies in her stomach as she heard men shouting in Portuguese.

329

The fish smell hit her first as she came around the back and found the big warehouse door open. Crates of iced salmon, cod, and crab were lined up in rows leading from an immense sink where a wiry old man wrapped in a stained gray slicker stood, pulling the guts out of a salmon. Behind him, two men threw fish from the bed of a pickup truck into a bin behind the old man. They worked quickly, bending, lifting, tossing, the fish landing splat atop the others, spraying the air with salt water and scales. One of the two men was Simão, dressed like the old man in a worn-out slicker. The other man looked familiar, but Chelsea didn't know who he was. Probably she had seen him at church or on the street.

Everything was wet, slimy and smelled of the sea. As Chelsea stared, teeth chattering from the cold, Simão looked up.

His eyes were swollen, his face somber. "What are you doing here?" His voice was hoarse, subdued.

"I-I have been looking for you since yesterday." She gazed at the other men, wondering if they understood English. "I went to the office after lunch, and you weren't there. You weren't at your house. Last night--"

"I was at the hospital. Avó had another stroke; she is near death. You did not come to work, you were not at home. I could not take time to look for you wandering around the city." There was no mistaking the scolding tone in his voice.

"Oh my God." Avó. She should have guessed. "I'm sorry, Simão. I was writing. And then, I went out for a walk, but you could have called."

"I did call about 10:30. You were not there."

"I didn't get a message." She realized with a pang of guilt that she had been with Mel at that time.

"I had no number to leave you."

The other man said something to him, and Simão nodded. "I have much work to do. I want to finish quickly and return to the hospital. "

"I'll go with you." But she remembered her job interview that morning. Simão still didn't know about it.

He stared at her. His eyes were so sad she wanted to rush up and hold him. She moved a step closer, but the older man erupted in a stream of protest.

330

"This is no place for a woman," Simão said. "Go home. I will call you later."

She nodded and turned away.

Her tennis shoes slapped on the wet floor. Behind her, the men spoke words she didn't understand.

As she slipped past the big door, she realized the sun had come up. It was another overcast morning, cool and windy. She could still smell fish. Her stomach growled. It would be nice to take herself out for breakfast. But she didn't have much money left, and she needed to shower and dress for her interview.

"I should have asked what hospital," she berated herself. "I could have gone there."

She could try all the local hospitals later, but she would have to wait until after her interview, by which time everything in her life might have changed.

Chelsea parked in the visitors' lot and walked down the sidewalk along the vast windowless Mercury News building. As she neared the entrance, she looked into the empty fountain. It had been shut off for the winter, and leaves had collected at the bottom.

Two women, one in a blue suit much like her own, and the other in a red polka-dot dress, passed her, nodding a greeting. Chelsea smiled back. Might they soon be her co-workers?

Up the steps and past the big double doors, she noted the old printing press in the lobby. Couches surrounded a table on which stacks of the latest Mercury News were piled. A heavyset security guard stood watch behind a wide counter.

"Can I help you?" he asked.

She took a deep breath. "Yes, good morning. I have an appointment with Jim Green."

"Ah." The guard ran his finger down a list, then picked up the telephone receiver in front of him and dialed three digits. "A miss-- what is your name?" She told him. "Chelsea Faust is here to see you." He listened and nodded. "He'll be out in a minute. Have a seat."

Chelsea perched on the edge of one of the couches and picked up a newspaper, but her mind was buzzing too fast to read. Across the room behind another counter, three women sat with headphones over their ears, answering incoming calls. Every minute or so, she heard, "Good morning, San Jose Mercury News, how may I help you?"

Behind the guard's counter, signs pointed to advertising on the right, editorial on the left. She strained to see what lay beyond.

"Chelsea?"

He came up behind her, and Chelsea gawked. Jim Green was short and balding; he wore what hair remained in a long black ponytail. He was dressed in jeans, a green silk shirt and gold suede vest. A holdover from the '60s, Chelsea thought, feeling self-conscious in her "dress for success" suit with the frilly white blouse. This isn't how I usually look, she wanted to tell him.

"Good morning," she said, rising on legs suddenly gone wobbly.

His handshake was firm and friendly. "Come on back."

She followed him through a maze of cubicles not unlike those at the Chronicle. She and her father had come through here the day they met with the city editor about the Slater story.

Jim Green led her to a conference room. "Coffee?"

"Okay. Thanks."

He went to get it himself and was back in a minute with two Styrofoam cups, taking the seat next to her. "I'm not supposed to drink this shit, but I've decided life's too short, and I need a jolt to get going in the morning. Especially today. We were out shooting a fire at 10 o'clock last night. Don't you know that screwed up the schedule. So, show me your stuff."

Chelsea opened her portfolio, then sipped her coffee as he paged through her work, occasionally nodding, grunting approval. "Hmm," he said when he got to the fire at the Portuguese Hall. "Not bad."

She smiled nervously. "Thanks."

"When can you start?"

"What?"

He grinned, showing stained brown teeth. "Mel told me all about you. I've read your resume, and I've seen your work. I don't see any reason to mess around. You want to work here, right?"

"Definitely."

"Mel said you're a pit bull with a story, a hard worker, usually get along with people except for publishers who are pricks, you're single and unattached, and a hell of a photographer."

Chelsea's mind was spinning. "Actually, I'm engaged," she ventured, wondering why she even mentioned it.

"Aw, hell. But I guess we have to allow it. Legally I'm not supposed to ask, but does that affect your availability for work?"

"Oh no, not at all." She felt as if she were lying.

"Good. Can you start Friday?"

"Sure."

"Great. 10 o'clock. Be here. You'll work 40 hours, the pay is $2,040 a month, plus paid benefits, seven sick days, two weeks vacation, the usual stuff. You'll have the option to join the union, which most people do, but as management I can't offer an opinion on that."

Chelsea glanced at the clock over Jim Green's head. "You mean that's it? I've only been here for about 10 minutes."

"Well, I'll have you fill out some papers on Friday. Then we'll get started. You've got all your own gear, right?"

She nodded. Maybe with this job, she could buy a new camera. Dad's was a workhorse, but it was old-fashioned.

Green leaned back, hands behind his head. "So, how tight are you with the Portuguese community?"

She shrugged. "So so. My fiancé is from the Azores." She hoped he was still her fiancé. "He's the president of the Portuguese Chamber of Commerce."

"Cool. We need an in to that part of San Jose. You'll be a real asset. Helps our company's diversity drive, too."

Chelsea suddenly focused on what he was saying. "Excuse me? I don't understand."

"You're a woman and you're Portuguese. Two notches on the old affirmative action meter." Chelsea's face must have registered her shock because he hurried to add, "It's no big deal. Everybody's something. Me, I'm half Jewish and half Puerto Rican. They love it. Roberta, whom you'll meet Friday, gets the older woman segment. Mike's Irish-African American, if you can picture it. We've got it all.

We work in this diverse community, and the more pieces of the puzzle we can put together, the more complete a picture we'll get. Do you speak the language?"

"Portuguese?"

"Yeah."

"A little. I'm not exactly fluent."

He shrugged. "Well, you probably know enough to pose people for pictures." He looked past her at somebody waving from the hallway. "I'm being paged for a meeting. Come Friday at 10 a.m. Park in the visitor lot until you get a pass for the employee lot, which I'll arrange if you remind me. Tell the guy at the guard desk you're the one I said to send on back. Bring your camera and your social security number and we're in business." They shook hands, and that was it.

As she passed the silent fountain, Chelsea realized her underarms were wet. She breathed in a big gulp of cold air and moved toward her truck on shaky legs.

I got the job, she told herself. I got it, I got it, I got it. Suddenly her life was coming back into focus. She would be working full-time on a newspaper again. She wouldn't have to move out of her apartment.

There was just one problem. Simão.

Simão's car was not in front of the office, and the lights were off, so she drove on to her apartment, thinking she could start calling all the hospitals in the telephone directory until she found one with a Mrs. Freitas as a patient.

But there was no need. Simão was sitting on her porch in a black suit, staring blankly at the street. As Chelsea came closer, she could see he had been crying. His eyelids were swollen, his lashes still wet. He clutched a soggy handkerchief in his hand.

Her brief exultation over her new job was replaced by cold fear.

"She died," Simão whispered.

Chelsea closed her eyes, feeling the wave of sadness come up from her heart. "I'm so sorry." She hurried up the steps, setting down her portfolio and purse, and sat beside Simão. As she grasped his hands, her engagement ring flashed in the weak sunlight. "Was it the stroke?"

"Her heart went at the end. Everything just sort of stopped at

334

once, I guess. At least, we had an opportunity to say goodbye." His voice was hoarse, and he kept his eyes focused on the street, away from Chelsea. "Except for Rosa. Avó kept for asking for her *neta*, her granddaughter, and I kept saying, 'She is coming,' even though I knew it was not the truth."

"Oh, Simão." Chelsea pulled him close. She felt guilty. If she wanted to, she could have found Rosa through Mel. She knew her drawings were still appearing in the newspaper. Rosa would have wanted to see Avó at the end.

He drew back and loosened his necktie, unbuttoning the top of his white shirt. "Where did you go? You are all dressed up."

"Now is not the time."

"I want to know. If you are to be my wife, you cannot keep going to places without telling me."

As Chelsea felt her face turning red, he added softly, "I would worry too much. You can go wherever you want to, but I just want to know you are safe."

Clearly, he was thinking about Fátima. One death often brings back others, Chelsea thought. Avó's death reminded her of her own grandmother's passing. "I'm sorry, Simão. There's something I didn't tell you. I had an interview at the San Jose Mercury News for a job. And I got it. I start Friday."

"Oh no, you cannot." He looked as if he had been struck.

"What do you mean no? It's a wonderful job. I may have to work some nights and weekends, but oh, Simão, it's a great job. And it's right here in San Jose. Besides, we need the money."

"We do not need as much now. With Avó gone."

Chelsea closed her eyes. He was right. Simão would now be free of the nursing home payments. Still, he had the house and his business. Besides, she wanted to work. "I know, but--"

"You cannot work Friday. We leave tomorrow morning for Faial."

"What?"

"Avó's wish was to be buried at home with her ancestors. Mama and you and I, we are going to take her body there. The next plane is not until Sunday. We cannot wait that long. I have already reserved tickets."

"Without asking me?"

"There was no time, and I did not know where you were. You must come with us. You are part of the family now. Besides, I want you to see my home."

"Oh my God." She realized she had been gripping the bottom of her jacket so tightly it was damp and wrinkled. She opened her hand and stood slowly. "Let's go inside. I think we both need a drink."

Simão rose, too. "No. I have to pick up Mama at the church. She wanted to pray an extra rosary for Avó to make sure her soul goes straight to Jesus."

Chelsea pictured Simão's grandmother in the nursing home and remembered how eagerly she had poured out her story. Was she in heaven now telling that story to Jesus? It was a simplistic view. Chelsea wasn't sure what happened to people when they died. But if anyone went to heaven, surely Avó did. And her own grandmother. They might be talking together now. In Portuguese.

Simão had already gone down the first step. Chelsea reached for his arm.

"Wait. What about--when will I see you again? Do you and Mama want to come for dinner? She won't feel like cooking. I'll go to the store." Simão was shaking his head. "Simão, I'm not sure what I should do."

"Pray for Avó. Begin to pack for two weeks in the Azores. It is cold there this time of year. We will leave at 7 a.m. If I don't hear from you tonight, that's it. We go without you."

"But, Simão, I can't."

"You cannot go? If you want to be my wife, you will be on the plane with me tomorrow morning. Tell the newspaper they must wait, and if they cannot. . . ." He shrugged and moved on down the stairs toward the sidewalk.

And he was gone.

What had started as a wonderful event had turned into a nightmare. She went in and poured herself a glass of burgundy, left over from a dinner with Simão, and sank into the chair before her blank computer screen.

"Damn," she whispered as the wine warmed her throat and stomach. Avó was dead. She empathized with Simão's pain and wanted to help him through it. But Simão's demand that she go with him to the Azores, or else, wasn't fair. Would he never consider her career important? If he really loved her, he would try to understand. She would love to go to the Azores with him, but not now.

But that was the way of the Portuguese man. He had to be in charge.

Could she get time off for a death in the family, even before she started? If Jim Green was so high on her talents, maybe he'd be willing to wait a couple weeks.

She reached for the phone and dialed the Mercury News, but as Green's extension started to ring, she hung up. He had said he needed somebody right away. She didn't dare beg off. By the time she got back, he might have hired someone else.

Swallowing the rest of her wine quickly, she changed into her sweats, grabbed a sheet of negatives off her desk and headed for the darkroom.

337

Chapter Twenty-Six

Avó's wrinkled face stared at her through the liquid in the developer tray. She had the same eyes as Chelsea's great-grandmother, dark and perpetually suspicious. No wonder, considering the hurt she had suffered in her life. Those eyes seemed to accuse her now. She should have been there with Simão at the end. And she should be working on Avó's story.

And her own Grandma Silveira's story. It hadn't been so bad for her back in the Azores, although certainly it must have been painful to leave her family behind when she was only a teenager. But the real difficulties came later, trying to support a family of eight without a husband, working days at the cannery, nights cleaning the church, doing whatever she had to do so her children wouldn't go hungry.

Chelsea sighed. Great-Grandma Silveira had died when she was a toddler. Her oldest daughter, Chelsea's grandmother, had died a few years ago, worn down by diabetes and heart trouble. Chelsea had been working in Washington and never got to talk to her before her death. If only she could have captured their stories in person instead of hearing them in bits and pieces from their descendants.

Tears were coming as she lifted the print out of the developer tray, dipped it into the stopbath for 30 seconds and dropped it upside down in the fixer. She started toward the enlarger to make another print, but suddenly she was crying so hard she couldn't see. She sank onto the old wooden stool, weeping alone in the red light that filled the converted laundry room.

The sobs gradually eased, leaving her feeling washed out and weary. She made a few more prints, trying to concentrate on her work without thinking about the past or future, but she couldn't keep Simão out of her mind.

How was he paying for the plane tickets to Portugal? Weren't they terribly expensive? She could hear her mother telling her, "Go. He's your fiancé, and what an opportunity. I wish I could go to Portugal. There'll be other jobs. If they can't wait for you, too bad. What if you had another job? You'd have had to give two weeks notice. This is just like that."

"But the guy at the Merc knows I'm unemployed," Chelsea

338

whispered. "He knows I'm available. I said I'd be there Friday. I said being engaged was no problem."

She inserted a new negative into the enlarger and tried to focus the reversed image on the tray below. But her eyes were tired, and the picture was blurry. She clicked off the light and put the negative back into its plastic sleeve.

She emptied the trays and waited impatiently for her finished prints to be washed so she could hang them up and get out of here. She felt trapped in this room and trapped in her life. Escape was all she wanted, but where and how she didn't know.

At last she emerged into gray twilight. A chill wind tugged at her blouse and fingered her hair. The weather matched her mood. She locked the door and headed south on Fifth Street.

When she walked in, Mel was on deadline, frowning at the computer screen. It was 5:00. He had one hour to finish laying out all the pages, writing the headlines, and marking the photos for the printer.

The writers were finished with their stories. Sarge leaned back in his chair, toying with an unlit cigarette, talking to one of his police buddies on the telephone. The new intern was gone. Berta was helping a customer at the counter.

It was terrible timing, but she didn't know who else to turn to.

"Mel?"

I should go, she thought when he turned around. The skin on his face sagged, and his eyes were bloodshot. "I'm gonna kill that bastard," he said without a greeting.

"Dunning?"

"That's the one. He waits till 5:00 to decide he wants to write a weekly column and put it on the lead news page. It doesn't matter to him that it kicks out 20 inches of solid newswriting, or that it takes me two hours to turn his gibberish into English. Oh, no, he doesn't give a damn. It's his paper; he can do what he wants."

"True." For the first time, Chelsea was glad she didn't work there anymore. Things would be much different at the Mercury News.

"So what's up with you? How'd the interview go? Jim said you were coming." Mel punched a couple keys on the computer and the story disappeared from the screen.

"I got the job."

"Of course. I gave you such a glowing recommendation Life Magazine couldn't turn you down. So why do you look like he told you that you should turn your camera into a piece of modern sculpture where it would do more good?"

"Oh, Mel." She sank into the chair beside his desk. "I know you're on deadline, but I have to talk to somebody. Simão's grandmother just died, and now Simão and his mother are going to take her body back to the Azores. It was her wish. He insists I go, too, or the marriage is off."

"So what's the problem? Don't you want to go to the Azores? That's Europe, Chelsea."

"I know, but I'm supposed to start at the Mercury on Friday."

"Oh. Call Jim and tell him somebody died. He's got to wait."

"Didn't sound like he would. She's not immediate family."

"I think he has to."

"Yeah?"

"Sure." Mel patted her knee, then shook his head. He spoke in a low voice so Sarge couldn't hear. "Sorry. Engaged woman. Former employee. I'm not supposed to touch you like that. If only you weren't so damned gorgeous." He cleared his throat and raised his voice again. "Does Rosa know about her grandmother?"

"I don't think so. We haven't been able to find her."

"She calls me once a week. On Thursdays. I give her assignments. She drops them off on Mondays. I don't know where she's living, but she gets the job done."

"You don't have an address or phone number?"

"Nope. It's in the area, that's all I know."

"Mel, I've got to find her."

"Sorry. I can't help you with that."

She stood. "I'd better let you work. You really think Jim Green will let me take two weeks off before I even start?"

"Sure. Just call him."

"Thanks. I feel much better." She leaned closer and kissed his forehead. "You can touch my knee any time."

Mel smiled, showing his slightly separated front teeth. "I'll remember that."

She hurried back down Fifth Street to her apartment. She would call Jim Green and get time off. Then somehow she would find Rosa. Everything would be fine.

She was going to Europe.

Jim Green sounded stressed. It was noisy in the background, a radio going, people talking. He was probably on deadline, too, but she had to let him know as soon as possible. Then she could tell Simão the good news.

"What? Say it again. It's hard to hear in here." He sounded like he had a cigarette in his mouth despite the no smoking signs Chelsea had seen around the office.

Chelsea raised her voice. "I'm sorry to bother you on deadline. This is Chelsea Faust. We met this morning. I'm afraid I've had a death in the family, and I can't start work Friday. We have to go to Portugal for two weeks. But then, I'll be back and ready to work."

"You can't start Friday? Shit. Hold on." Soft music filled her ear. Green came back in a minute. "Let me get this straight. This morning, you were available to work any day, any time. Now you can't come in for two weeks?"

"Yes. You see, my fiancé's grandmother died--"

"Your fiancé's grandmother."

"Right. And she wanted to be buried in the Azores, so my fiancé is going to take her there, and he insists that I go, too, as part of the family, and since I've never seen where he came from--" She could tell by Green's silence that she was in trouble. A desperate try. "I could take some great photos for the travel section while I'm there. Write a whole feature. Then I'd still be working."

"Yeah." She could hear him flipping through a pile of papers. "We don't do travel in this department. Most of that's freelance anyway. Look, I need somebody like yesterday. I've got other applicants who could start tonight if I had time to do the paperwork. I should have known when you said you were engaged to a Portuguese guy that work would not be the priority. Maybe you can try for the next opening. Probably in a year or so."

"But--." She couldn't believe this was happening. She wished

341

with all her heart that she hadn't called, but then she would lose Simão. If only she could make him understand. She remembered her mother's argument. "Well," she said, "If I had had another job, I would have had to give two weeks notice."

"That's one of the parts I liked about you. No delays, no strings. Maybe you should just marry this guy and make little brown Portugee babies."

Chelsea's mouth flew open. She swallowed hard, not sure whether to sob or strangle him. "I can't believe you said that," she choked out.

"It's so true. Look, babe, I'm sorry for your fiancé's grandmother's death, but all old people die, and if you're gonna need time off every time an old Portugee kicks, you can't work for me. I need somebody nights, weekends, whenever. Even if it's your day off, I call your pager and you're there. Maybe you don't understand daily newspaper work."

"I do! I worked at--"

She heard a buzz on Green's line. "I've gotta go," he said. "I'm sorry this didn't work out. Your photos are really good. Try freelancing something for travel. Thanks for calling."

And he was gone.

The sun had set. She sat in her dark kitchen staring at the gloomy sky. A few hours ago, everything had been wonderful. She finally had the job of her dreams. She could keep her apartment. She was going to marry Simão. Now it was all shattered. As things stood at this moment, she had lost both Simão and her job.

But a man who would make her choose between him and her work? What kind of husband was that? Yes, but what kind of boss would say such hurtful things to her, even if he was on deadline and understaffed?

Her face was burning. How could she let any man cow her that way? Did she even want to go to the Azores?

The telephone rang. She hesitated. Why answer? It could only bring her more grief. She sat frozen in place as it rang once, twice, three times and the machine clicked on. "This is Chelsea, leave a message at the tone."

"This is your mother, Chelsea. I'm sorry you're not home. I have great news. Call me right away."

Chelsea's face crumbled at the sound of her mother's voice. The machine went silent as she dashed the tears away with her fist. She walked stiffly across the kitchen for another glass of wine, and tried to think clearly. Jim Green was obviously a jerk. Like her former publisher. Like too many men. She was better off not working for him. But this was the Mercury News, the biggest daily in the Bay Area. It won all the awards every year. It had sister papers all over the country and bureaus all over the world. It might be worth putting up with another creepy boss. She shuddered, remembering her showdown with Dunning at the Weekly Times.

Things weren't so bad, she told herself. She could move to her parents' house and then marry Simão in six months. And she could go to the Azores, where not only Simão came from, but her own great-grandmother and grandfather. It would be terrific for her book, and she could do a story for the travel section, too. Several stories.

She took a long drag of wine and felt it slide warm down her throat and into her empty stomach. Taking deep breaths, still sniffling, she went to the phone and dialed Simão's number, ready to tell him she would be on the 7 a.m. flight with him and Mama.

No one answered.

It was hard to know what to pack. She put mostly skirts and dresses in her suitcase, suspecting Simão's homeland was as conservative as he was. His family would never approve of her running around in jeans and men's shirts as she did here.

She grabbed the pages she had written for her book and a thick spiral notebook and set them beside her suitcase, along with her camera.

Her excitement grew as the suitcase filled up. She was going to the land she had seen in Simão's mother's photo albums, the place where her great-grandmother grew up, where Simão had played as a little boy. She could almost smell the salty ocean air and picture the green fields dotted with white houses.

It was almost 10, and she still hadn't reached Simão. She dialed both his numbers again. No answer at home or the office. She left a

343

message on the office machine, telling him she would be joining him after all.

She was too keyed up to sleep. Where could they be? Church? No service went on this late. A social event? Not likely when Avó had just died. Perhaps they were with Simão's uncle. But Chelsea didn't even know his last name.

Over and over, she dialed Simão's numbers to no avail. Finally she dialed another number, one she knew would bring a human response.

"Hello?" Mom's voice was cautious.

"Hi, Mom, it's me. I'm sorry to call so late."

"What's wrong?"

"Nothing." Well, except losing the job and Avó dying and her quarrel with Simão. "I'm going to Portugal tomorrow morning."

"What do you mean?" Her mother didn't bother covering the mouthpiece as she bellowed, "Carl, pick up the other phone!"

"What's going on?" Chelsea heard him say.

"She's going to Portugal. I can't believe she waits until now to tell us."

"Mom, will you stop yelling for a minute?"

"Hi, sweetheart," her father said.

"Hi, Dad. Now, both of you, calm down. Simão's grandma died this morning. She wanted to be buried in Faial. Simão and his mother and I are taking her body back. We have to go tomorrow because the next plane isn't until Sunday, and we didn't want to wait that long."

"My, my. How long will you be gone?" Mom asked.

"Two weeks."

"And when are you moving home?"

"Oh God." In her excitement, Chelsea had forgotten the landlord's deadline. "Dec. 1." She stared at the calendar. "Three days after I get back."

"That's not much time."

"I'll manage." Maybe she and Simão should get married sooner, so she would only have to move once. Where was he? They had so much to talk about.

"My grandmother came from Faial, too. You might have family still there for all we know. Try to look them up while you're there."

344

"And take lots of pictures."

"Oh, I will, Dad."

"Do you need a ride to the airport?"

"No thanks. Simão will pick me up." But so far he didn't even know she was going. He might be calling right now. "Look, I've got to go. I need to get some sleep." A lie. She would never sleep. "I'll send you a postcard."

"Well, good luck," Mom said.

"Have fun."

"I will, Dad."

She had barely hung up when the phone rang again. She snatched it up. "Simão?"

"No, Chelsea, it's your mother. I forgot our big news. Your father got a photo spread accepted by *Modern Maturity*."

Big time. "Oh Mom, that's great. Maybe getting laid off was the best thing that ever happened to him."

"Maybe. Well, you'd better go to bed if you're leaving the country tomorrow morning. I wish we could go with you."

"Me too. Maybe next time. Bye, Mom."

She dialed Simão's house again. No answer.

Her bags packed and waiting by the door, she dressed for the trip and sat in the dark living room, clutching the portable telephone in her hand. She had been calling Simão's house for hours with no response.

At 4:30 a.m., so tired her eyes felt red and raw and it seemed as if everything must be a bad dream, she made a final pass through the apartment, checking windows, making sure all the stove burners were off, looking for anything vital she might have forgotten. Then she went out into the dark, cold night.

It took two trips to lug her things down the stairs. She climbed into the truck, rubbed her face, trying to wake up, and drove quietly down Fifth to Santa Clara Street.

The city was asleep. No one seemed to be stirring, except at San Jose Medical Center, where the emergency room was brightly lit and a knot of people lingered in the doorway.

She turned down Simão's street, holding her breath. The house was dark, and his car was gone. Parking in the driveway, she hurried to the door and peered in the windows. It was all as deserted as that afternoon she had gone there alone.

Her heart was beating too quickly. She forced herself to take a couple deep breaths. Suddenly she heard a noise behind her and gasped. Then she shook her head at her own foolishness. It was a little black terrier, the chain around his neck jingling as he ambled up to sniff her feet, probably curious about this other creature stirring in the night.

Reaching into her purse, she pulled out her notebook and wrote: "Simão, I am going with you. I'll meet you at the airport. Chelsea."

Her heart sank. Which airline? Which terminal? As the drivers behind her grew impatient, she studied the signs, trying to remember which airlines went overseas.

She parked in the long-term lot and hurried into terminal C.

"TWA?" The woman behind the information counter shook her head. "That's in the new terminal." She pointed. "Out that door. You'll have to drive there."

She nodded and went back out. Already, her bags were starting to pull the muscles in her back and shoulders.

Seventy-five cents poorer for her stay in the wrong parking lot, she exited the airport and reentered, heading for Terminal A, which looked more like a modern office building than an airport. She drove into the underground garage, parked, and followed the signs into the building.

Just when she felt she couldn't carry her suitcase another step, she saw the red, white and blue TWA sign up ahead and felt a new spurt of energy. If she could just determine which gate the plane was leaving from, she could find Simão and Mama, get her ticket and relax.

None of the destinations on the video screen sounded Portuguese. The woman behind the counter was doing paperwork. Like most of the terminal, it was quiet around the TWA counter.

"Excuse me. Can you tell me what gate we leave from for the Azores?"

"Azores?" The clerk pursed her bright red lips. "We don't have a flight to the Azores."

"What?" Chelsea swallowed. "You know where it is, right?

Islands off the coast of Portugal."

"Yes, ma'am, but we don't go there from here."

"You have to. My boyfriend is leaving from here around 7 a.m." She glanced at her watch. It was only 5:45. Maybe she was too early. "Can you check?"

The woman sighed and punched keys on her computer, finally tapping her frosted nails against the screen. "There are no direct Portugal flights from San Jose. You have to either go to LAX and hook onto TAP, the Portuguese airline, or fly to Boston and go from there."

Chelsea relaxed. "Oh. Then they're probably heading for LA or Boston." She stared at the screen again. No Boston flights were listed. Los Angeles departure was at 7:30, Gate 6. "Okay, thanks," she said. "Let me make sure my friends are there, then I'll be back."

The woman shrugged. "Whatever."

As she started away, her camera case making her neck ache, the suitcase dragging at her shoulder, Chelsea hesitated and turned back. "Can I leave my suitcase here for a few minutes?"

The ticket agent shrugged again. "All right."

"Thanks."

She jogged toward Gate 6, impatient as her purse and camera crawled through the X-ray machine and she crossed through the metal detector.

She approached Gate 6, eager for her first sight of Simão and Mama. They would be happy to see her. She would be relieved. Everything would be all right.

She rounded the bend. At Gate 6, she saw rows of empty plastic chairs. One bald man sat sipping coffee and reading a paperback book.

Beyond the windows, the sky was growing light. Red streaks threaded the gray as a beam of bright yellow sunshine broke through, lighting up the gray seats.

Chelsea sat down to wait, fighting off the feeling that her quest was hopeless.

The waiting area filled with passengers, the 7:30 plane came, they walked through the carpeted tunnel and boarded the plane. The doors closed, and the plane taxied down the runway, soared into the air and took off for Los Angeles.

Chelsea walked wearily back to the counter.

A different clerk was working there now, an older woman.

"I left my suitcase here," Chelsea said. "I need it back."

"What suitcase?"

Oh no, Chelsea thought. But the woman was already reaching behind her. "Is this it? I would have checked it aboard if it had had a tag."

"I don't have a ticket," she said, her voice leaden.

The woman shoved the bag back over the scale and Chelsea took it. "Thank you."

Outside, it was a bright sunny day, as if in mockery of her mood. She didn't know what to do now. Her stomach felt as if it were gnawing itself. Was she growing an ulcer? Why not, she thought.

She hated to leave the airport. But she knew in her heart it was already too late. Somehow they were already on their way to Portugal, and she was still here in San Jose. Simão would think she chose her job over him.

He must have changed his flight. But why didn't he call?

He probably thought I didn't care.

She tossed her bags into the truck, paid $3 at the exit and drove home.

Maybe he would be there.

But the space in front of her apartment was empty.

She trudged up the stairs, dragging her suitcase. The neighborhood was awake now. From downstairs, she could hear the baby crying and a radio playing. Traffic had increased with the beginning of the morning commute. Everyone seemed to be going somewhere except her.

She sighed. It was over. She would have to pick up the pieces and start her life alone again. As she went in, she saw she had a telephone message. Simão?

But when she pushed the button, all she heard was a phone being hung up.

"No, don't hang up!"

She considered going back to bed, but she was fully awake. She started the coffee, then leaned into the refrigerator, looking for breakfast. She pulled out the milk, closed the door and grabbed the granola from the cupboard. She was just about to take her first bite when the phone rang, startling her so badly she dropped wet cereal all over the table.

She jumped up, banging her knee in her hurry. "Hello?"

"Chels, it's your old friend Jeff."

"What? Jeff?" The last person she wanted to hear this morning.

"Yeah, remember me? I know you've got somebody else, but hey, that's no way to greet a former love of your life."

"I'm sorry. I was expecting somebody else." Get off the line, she thought. "I'm expecting a very important call."

"Okay, I'll be quick. I'm coming out there next week. Can we get together?"

"Are you bringing your girlfriend?"

"What girlfriend? Oh. No, that's history. This trip is for business. But I want to see you."

She covered her face with her hand. How could she deal with next week when she didn't know how she was going to get through today?

"Chels? You still there?"

She took a deep breath. "Yes. Look, Jeff, I can't think right now. I was supposed to be on a plane to the Azores this morning, but, well, I missed the plane or something, I couldn't find them, and I was supposed to start a new job tomorrow, but Simão's grandmother died and I couldn't start for two weeks and the guy said well, forget it--"

Jeffrey chuckled. "Stop. You're talking Valley Girl gibberish." His voice softened. "What happened, sweetheart?"

The tears were coming. Jeffrey, that sleaze, could always get to her. "I had the best job of my life, and I blew it because Simão insisted I go with him to the Azores to bury his grandmother in her homeland."

"His grandmother? For that you gave up the best job of your life?"

Chelsea nodded, brushing away the tears that coursed down her cheeks. "Yes."

"Baby, I always knew you were crazy, but now you've proven it. Call the employer back and tell him you were temporarily insane and you still want the job."

"I can't. I'm sure he's already given it to someone else."

"It's worth a try. And what about this jerk of a fiancé who orders you around?"

Like you never did? "He didn't order me to do anything." But she remembered his words, "If you are not on that plane. . ."

"Sounds like a jerk to me."

"He's not a jerk." Chelsea pictured Simão, his eyes full of tears, begging her to come with him. She was the jerk to value her job over him.

"Does he even speak English? He didn't go to college, did he?"

"He's been working hard all his life. And yes, he speaks beautiful English." She remembered the fish market, the smells, the splat of fish landing in the tray. Jeffrey would find the whole scene beneath him.

And that's what's wrong with today's politicians, she added to herself.

"Ah, methinks thou dost protest too much."

"Shut up, Jeff."

"Well, all I really wanted was to get together next week when I come. In fact, if you wouldn't mind, I need a ride from San Francisco airport Wednesday at 10:45."

Chelsea's tears stopped, and her eyes widened. What nerve this guy had. He insults her and her fiancé, then asks for a ride from the airport.

She stared out the window at the gabled roof next door, a decision forming in her mind.

"Chelsea?"

She nodded to herself. "I'm sorry. I'm leaving for the Azores on Sunday." Before she could hear his jeering response, she hung up the phone.

Chapter Twenty-Seven

Chelsea stood alone in her kitchen talking to herself. "Jeffrey McNeil doesn't know the meaning of real work, and he certainly doesn't understand about family. He'd cheat his own mother to get ahead in his career. I was right to leave him.

"And Jim Green, that photo editor at the Mercury. He has no heart. He's a sexist, racist jerk. I don't want to work for him anyway."

Simão is sexist, too, a small voice told her.

"Yes, but he loves me. Besides, he's just afraid I'll get killed like Fátima." She sighed. If only she'd had these revelations before he left, she could have been more supportive instead of thinking only about her precious career.

Maybe it was the lack of sleep, but everything looked different now. She should write Jeffrey a thank you note for helping to put things in perspective, she thought as she ate her cereal.

Yes, it seemed crazy to mess up a good job opportunity for the death of her fiancé's grandmother. But when her husband-to-be begged her to go with him to her funeral, how could she say no? Wasn't he ultimately more important than any job? Shouldn't he be?

Chelsea nodded. Yes. In the few romance novels she had read, men and women did incredible things for love, suffering imprisonment, scandal, bankruptcy, all for the one they loved. Of course, these were fiction, but this time maybe she should be a little more like the romantic heroines she had read about.

Look at all the Portuguese women she had met who had left everyone and everything behind to come to a new continent with their husbands. They worked in factories, canneries, and dairies, scraping by with 13 kids and no money, living in a land where they didn't know the language or the culture, all for love of their husbands and children. Young people gave up their dreams of education and careers to take care of the older people. She had heard it over and over. Family was the most important thing.

All Simão was asking her to do was to marry him and write books and freelance articles for a while instead of working round the clock for a sexist jerk who made fun of her Portuguese heritage and hired her just to pump up the paper's "diversity."

351

Staring into the puddle of milk at the bottom of her cereal bowl, she sighed and reached for the telephone book.

She flipped through the yellow pages. What was the name of that travel agency she and Jeffrey had used? Worldwide. She flipped to the W's.

"Worldwide, this is Sherry, how may I help you?"

"Hi, this is Chelsea Faust. I need to fly to the Azores."

Simão was right. The next flight was Sunday, and it was only Thursday now. But that gave her time to find the last missing piece to the puzzle. She dialed another number, one she knew by heart.

"Weekly Times," chirped Berta's familiar voice.

"Hey, Berta, it's Chelsea."

"Hi, how's it goin'?"

"I don't know. Is Mel in?"

"Yeah, he's on the other line. Want to hold?"

"Sure."

Suddenly Tony Bennett's voice swelled in her ear. Since when did they have telephone Muzak, she wondered, gazing around her apartment at the stacks of boxes. Maybe later today, she could take some of them to her parents' house. The more she got done before Sunday, the better. She wouldn't have much time when she got back.

At least she was already packed for her trip. Except that she had forgotten to get a passport, which was first on her list today. Maybe she should get more film, and another lead-lined bag to carry it through the X-ray machines at the airport. Of course, money was getting short. She would have to charge her plane ticket. And once she got there--well, she'd figure that out when she arrived.

"Hello?" Mel sounded rushed.

"You're not on deadline, are you?"

She could hear his shallow breathing over the phone line. "Chelsea?"

"Yes, it's me."

"I'm sort of on deadline. I've got a meeting with Dunning and the stockholders from our parent company in forty-five minutes. They want reports on everything I've ever dealt with, it seems, plus they've moved the deadlines up on us, and Sarge is out sick. It's nuts around here."

"What's wrong with Sarge?"

"I don't know. He woke up with chest pains. He wanted to come in, and I said no way, get yourself to the hospital and don't come back until you're certified okay. I don't want him dropping dead at his desk. The way he lives on coffee and cigarettes, I don't know. So, what's up? Time is money, kid."

Chelsea smiled. She missed Mel. "Listen, I need to find Rosa. You've got to give me her phone number. I know you have it."

"Ah, Chels, I can't do it. She made me swear, said she'd quit if I breathed a word to anyone, especially her family, which I guess includes you. Her work has caught on with the advertisers. I can't afford to let her slip away now."

"Damn it, Mel, her grandmother died. They were very close. She needs to know, preferably before the funeral."

Mel was quiet. Chelsea could hear him tapping his fingers on the desk. "I can't give you her number, but I can tell her to call you when she comes in this afternoon."

"When's that?"

"Two o'clock. That's the best I can do."

"I thought you were my friend."

His voice softened. "You know I am. But I can't give you Rosa's number." He cleared his throat. "Did you start the new job yet?"

Sigh. "Nope. I'm not going to. That's a long story."

"I thought you'd be perfect for it."

"Yeah, me too. Anyway, tell Rosa to call me. It's really important."

"Okay, okay. But I can't guarantee she will." Suddenly he was silent. Then, "Oh God, those guys in suits must be the stockholders. They're early. I'll talk to you soon, Sweetheart."

"Bye Mel. Good luck."

Her errands finished by noon, she had the rest of the day to kill. Everything for her trip was already packed. She knew she ought to box up some more of the things in her apartment and take them to her parents' house. But she didn't want to have to explain why she wasn't already on her way to Portugal.

Slowly, as if in a trance, she went to the bedroom and got her running shoes, tying the laces so methodically it reminded her of when she was a little girl and her father taught her to tie her shoes by having her copy him tying his. Things were so simple then.

Shoes on, she braided her hair and stuffed it into a blue baseball cap, grabbed her keys off the hook by the door and went out.

She ran quickly to Santa Clara Street and turned east, so full of restless energy she thought she might run all the way to Alum Rock Park.

Clouds had covered the sun, but rain was still hours away. She breathed in the cool air and watched the stages of her life pass by.

There was the Weekly Times office and then the Mexican restaurant where she and Mel used to eat. She wondered how the meeting with the newspaper brass was going. She hoped Mel was standing up for himself and for the paper. Don't let them turn it into an advertiser, she silently urged her former editor.

She passed San Jose State University, where a Portuguese woman who worked there had told her not to marry a Portuguese man because they were too macho. The students loitering on the lawn outside the speech and drama building looked so young.

The college gave way to stores and churches and then the sprawling San Jose Medical Center where Joaquim took her the night the councilman's thug broke her ankle.

She ran on, starting to feel tired but unwilling to stop.

Simão's office was ahead on the right. They had made love the first time there, then worked together side by side until the morning when her job and Avó's death separated them.

She sighed and ran farther into Little Portugal. Five Wounds Church loomed on the left, its tall spires reaching high into the gray sky. The new Portuguese Hall was going up next door. As she passed, she could hear the workmen shouting to each other in Portuguese.

The bookstore, the bakery, and the dress shop were filled with memories. From the cafe across the street, old men in porkpie hats stared at her in her shorts and tee shirt. She could feel the women gazing from their shops, but she was no longer paranoid. This was America. If they couldn't accept her as she was, too bad.

Gradually the Portuguese names on the shops yielded to Spanish and Vietnamese ones. She passed the piñata shop and the Vietnamese clothing store.

Her legs were tiring, and she began to wonder if she could run all the way back. Still she went on, setting the intersection with King Road as her goal.

Breathless and sweating, she reached King Road and the entrance to the old Calvary Cemetery. Stone benches lured her in. She slowed to a walk and passed under the arch, walking between the graves.

Above, the clouds had turned dark and threatening. She was likely to get drenched on the way home. But she had to rest a minute.

The bench was cold under her thighs. She shivered, fighting to slow her breathing and clear her head. Gradually she became aware of the names on the gravestones. She read them in wonder. "Sousa. Machado. Gomes." All Portuguese.

She walked slowly down the row. Suddenly she gasped and knelt to look more closely.

Fátima M. Freitas, 1965-1991, native of Portugal, beloved wife.

"Fátima," she whispered, touching the letters. This was where Simão had buried his first wife. She would have been a year younger than Chelsea.

In front of the stone was a clear vase with three fresh roses. Simão had been here recently, probably just before he left.

Chelsea sank onto the grass and stared at the slight rise in the lawn, the barely noticeable discoloration between the new and the old grass.

She rested her chin on her knees. "Fátima. He still misses you a lot," she said aloud. "Look, he brought you flowers. He's so afraid I'll get hurt that he doesn't want me out of his sight. Well, except for now."

She looked up at the glowering sky. She couldn't stay much longer. "I guess you know Avó died. You knew her better than I did. I wonder, did she tell you her story? Simão went back to the old country to bury her. I should have gone, too, but all I could think of was my job.

"I might have lost him. I can hardly stand to think it. You know, I thought he was so overbearing sometimes, and so sexist, you know

355

how he is, and so different from anyone I've ever known. I'm American, you see. I didn't know anything about being Portuguese until I stumbled into it a few months ago. But my great grandma came from the same island you did."

She heard a car roll through the gates and park nearby. She hushed, suddenly feeling foolish sitting here talking to the air. But she needed someone to talk to, and she and Fátima had a lot in common. Tears filled her eyes, and she kept her face turned away so the newcomer wouldn't see.

Go on, she silently told the driver, her eyes fixed on Fátima's grave. But footsteps crunched on the gravel, coming toward her. Wiping her face with the back of her hand, she turned slowly and stared in amazement.

"Rosa!"

"*Bom dia, minha irmã*. My sister."

In a flash, they were in each other's arms, weeping and laughing at the same time.

Finally Chelsea gasped for breath and pulled back, looking at her friend. Rosa seemed stylish in black slacks and white sweater. "Rosa, where have you been? I missed you so much."

"I missed you, too."

"And Simão--it's killing him."

"It is only his pride."

"No. He was really hurt." She still struggled to breathe. "I wish I had a Kleenex."

Rosa dug into her purse. "I got one."

"Thanks." She wiped her eyes and pulled in a long breath. "I sure didn't expect to see you here."

"I come two times a month. There are others in our family here, too. See, my uncle and aunt and their little baby." She pointed down the row to gravestones Chelsea hadn't noticed before. "That's another cousin."

These might soon be her own family. It gave her an eery feeling, part warmth, part pain. "I didn't know there were so many Freitases in San Jose."

Rosa nodded. "Many. Some are not our family. The name is very common among the Portuguese."

"I know. Not like Faust."

"No." Rosa grinned.

Chelsea wrapped an arm around her friend's waist. Rosa had lost weight. "Can we sit down for a minute?"

"Sure."

The bench didn't seem as cold now.

"Rosa, do you know about Avó?"

"She has died. I know. I went to visit, and they told me."

"Oh. But--"

"I had not been there for two weeks, and I felt bad. I should not be kept away from my Avó because I did not want to see my brother or my mother, I decided. So I went yesterday. They said she passed away. I was too late."

"I'm sorry, Rosa."

New tears filmed Rosa's large brown eyes. "I wanted her to know I still love her. Now I can never tell her."

"Oh, Rosa. She knew." Chelsea stared at her hands, not knowing what to say. "I didn't see her at the end either."

Rosa didn't answer for several minutes, but sat staring at the graves marked Freitas. "When is the funeral?"

"You don't know about that?"

"What?"

"Simão and Mama have taken Avó to Faial to bury her there."

"Faial? *A sério?*"

Chelsea shrugged. "He said it was her wish." Suddenly the words came out in a rush. "I was supposed to go, but then I got this job, and I said I couldn't go. I changed my mind and asked for time off, and the guy decided he didn't want me to work for him after all, but Simão had already left. Now I'm afraid he hates me. I got a ticket for Sunday morning. I don't know how I'm going to find him. . ."

She stopped as inspiration hit. "Rosa! We could go together! Look, I have a charge card with an outrageous limit. Let's go call my travel agent right now. It will be so great. You can be my interpreter.

357

You'll know where to go when we get there. And Simão and Mama will be so surprised."

"I don't know if I will be welcome."

"They love you."

Rosa played with a new ring on her left hand, a smooth gold band with a small round diamond. "How is Mama?"

"Sad. She misses you very much. That house is not the same. It's got this giant hole in it where you used to be."

"I am not going back there. I am getting married."

Chelsea had noticed the ring. "That's terrific."

"When you and Simão marry, you can fill my room with your things or even someday a baby."

"Wait a minute, slow down," Chelsea laughed. "I'm not ready for that yet. Maybe we could make it part office and part darkroom."

"Good idea. I saw your article in the Mercury the other day. They said on the radio Mr. Slater is going to resign."

"I didn't hear that. For once in my life, I didn't even think about the news. All I could think about was Simão. Well, good."

A cold wind tore at their clothes. Chelsea shivered.

"You must be freezing," Rosa said. "You are almost naked."

"Yes." Her teeth were chattering. "I didn't expect to be gone this long."

"Let me drive you home."

Chelsea stared at the dark green Nissan beyond the fence. "You didn't have a car before. Where did that come from?"

"It is Mark's." She tugged Chelsea to her feet. "He has two."

"Really?" So she was marrying a guy with money.

They paused in front of Fátima's grave.

"Simão brought flowers," Chelsea said.

"I know. He comes every week, always with roses, even in winter. Part of his heart will always be here."

As Chelsea considered what it would be like to marry a man who still loved his dead wife, a raindrop splashed off her nose, then another on her hair.

"It's raining," she said.

"We must go. Hurry." The raindrops suddenly came hard and fast, turning the granite stones from light to dark gray as the two women ran across the grass to Rosa's boyfriend's car.

They had two days before their trip. Rosa and Chelsea had lunch together, then Rosa left to tell her fiancé the news. Chelsea went home.

She was paging through the Mercury News, looking for the international weather listings, when she came across the obituaries and suddenly wondered if anyone had arranged to put something in the newspapers about Avó's death. Seeing nothing, she decided to write up a notice.

She sat at the computer and typed quickly. As she concluded with "funeral services will be held in her native Faial, Azores," she felt an ache in the pit of her stomach. She felt bad about Avó, but even more she missed newspaper work. It had been a part of her for so long. She stared at the Mercury News section on her desk with her story and her father's photos and knew she wasn't ready to let it go. Writing books was fine, but she loved the adrenaline of cranking out stories on deadline, being where things were happening, the ego boost from seeing her name in the paper. Simão would never understand.

Perhaps she could still find a job that fit into their lives. But today she had to deliver Avo's obituary.

First stop was the Mercury News.

She had been nervous and cocky last time she came here, waiting to be let into the brightly lit area hidden beyond the guard station. She remembered how impressed Jim Green had seemed to be with her photos. She remembered, too, how he had emphasized her Portuguese ancestry. Well, here she was, submitting an obituary for her Portuguese grandmother-in-law.

The guard nodded absentmindedly as she handed him the sheet of paper. "Okay, thanks. I'll see that it gets back to the local editor."

And that was it. She was on her way out the door, past the antique press, the fountain and the parking spot for the employee of the month, and back on the freeway.

The Portuguese Tribune occupied an old storefront in the middle of Little Portugal. Chelsea approached nervously. The paper was

359

published in Portuguese, and she didn't know whether she should try to speak Portuguese or just admit straight out that she was a *gringa*. After all, she had written her obit in English.

To her surprise, the heavyset woman who came from the back room when she rang the bell said, "May I help you?" in English.

How did she know, Chelsea wondered, blushing. "Yes, I-I have an obituary for the grandmother of my fiancé." Her face was burning up.

"Your fiancé?"

"Simão Freitas."

The woman nodded. "Ah, Simão. I heard his grandma died."

Everyone knew everything around here. "Yes. And I was, um, I am a newspaper reporter myself, so I . . ."

The woman scanned the sheet of paper Chelsea handed her. "Okay." She took the paper to the back, leaving Chelsea in the lobby filled with photographs from the Azores. Soon she would be seeing those places in person.

Her last stop was the Weekly Times. She pulled up at the curb, parked in a one-hour spot, and slid out. It was strange here, too. For so long, she had been part of the staff, carried a key to the front door on her chain, and knew everyone who worked at the paper, from Berta at the front desk to Joe who oversaw the carriers who delivered the finished product.

Someone new sat behind the front desk, a middle-aged woman with dyed blonde bubble hair and half glasses perched on her nose. She was dialing a phone number with the eraser end of a yellow pencil when Chelsea walked in.

"Can I help you?" she asked, looking over her glasses.

Chelsea swallowed. "I need to talk to Mel."

"Mr. Cohen is in a meeting right now. Would you care to wait?"

She walked to the door of the newsroom and peered in. Sarge was there, his back to her, and the new intern sat at her old desk. "I'll just go talk to Sarge."

The woman raised her eyebrows. "I believe he is on deadline."

"No. His stories aren't due for a couple more days." Chelsea started through the door.

"Now really." The receptionist was out of her seat and starting toward Chelsea. "You can't just go in there."

Chelsea summoned as much diplomacy as she could muster. "I used to work here. Check out a few back issues. I'm Chelsea Faust. My byline is all over the place."

"Well, I don't know."

She was about to give up and hand the woman Avo's obituary when the publisher's door opened and a small man in a gray suit came toward her. As he got closer, she gasped. "Mel?"

"Chelsea?"

His face was chalky, his eyes glazed with shock. He suddenly looked much older than he was.

"Are you all right?"

"What are you doing here?"

"I brought an obituary."

"Oh. Simão's grandmother?"

"Yes. She was local, so I figured, why not?"

"You can leave it on the desk."

He passed her and kept walking toward the door.

"What are you doing?"

"Leaving. I suggest you do the same before the stockholders come out of Dunning's office."

"Why? What's going on?" The look on his face frightened her.

"Come on. Outside," he whispered, glancing at the new receptionist.

Once they were in the cool air, Mel took a left and walked south on Fourth Street. He said nothing until they paused near the shop where Chelsea bought her photo supplies. "I need a drink."

Chelsea saw that his hands were shaking. "No, you don't. Please, tell me what's going on."

He sighed and collapsed onto a bus stop bench. "That bastard sold the paper. It's going to be a shopper, all ads. No hard news at all. I'm supposed to fire Sarge, get the intern writing advertorial and tap into news services that cater to advertisers to fill the rest of the space. It won't be city council and police, but how to refinish your floors and oh by the way use brand X wax. I told them I quit."

361

Chelsea took the seat beside him, watching an old woman in rags pushing a shopping cart under the freeway overpass. "I didn't think even Dunning was that sleazy."

"Money talks," Mel muttered, looking at his hands. "I've still got ink on my fingers. I didn't even finish this week's paper."

She grabbed his hands and held them tight. "What are you going to do?"

"I don't know. If you hadn't stopped me, I was going to bury myself in a bottle of tequila until I died, the world ended or we had another big earthquake. With luck, a building would fall on me."

His hands were icy. "There are other jobs, Mel. You're a good editor. Or you could write. I bet you'd love to get back into writing stories or even a book. Think of this as a new opportunity."

"Is that what you're telling yourself?"

That silenced her. She too was unemployed because of the same publisher, and she had just lost herself a great job opportunity at the Mercury. But there were other consolations. She studied the weave of Mel's jacket, one she suspected he had had for at least a decade. "I'm going to Portugal. With Rosa."

He turned, his eyes starting to focus. "You found her?"

"She found me. In the cemetery. When I told her what was going on, it just made sense for us to go together."

"That's good. And then what?"

"I guess I'm getting married."

"You guess?"

"If he's still talking to me."

"Oh." Disappointment showed in his eyes. "What about work?"

She shrugged. "I'll freelance and write my book, I suppose, until I find another newspaper job in this area."

A bus approached and slowed. Chelsea released Mel's hands and waved the driver on by.

The late-afternoon light was dimming. Somewhere beyond the thick cloud cover, the sun was setting. Chelsea wondered what time it was in the Azores.

Mel startled her by running his hand gently along the side of her cheek. She turned, looking into his eyes.

"Mel," she whispered.

Suddenly, he pulled her close and sealed his lips against hers. She closed her eyes as he kissed her cheeks, her eyes, her forehead, her neck. She was vaguely aware that they were sitting out in the open on a busy downtown street where anyone could see them. Anyone but Simão, a small voice said. As Mel's hand brushed against her breast, she moaned. "Stop. Please."

Mel drew back. "Oh my God. I'm sorry, I couldn't help it."

Chelsea couldn't breathe. "It's my fault, too," she said.

"You're engaged."

"You're still married."

"We're both unemployed and upset."

She nodded. "Exactly."

"Let's go to your apartment."

She swallowed. "Mel, no."

He stood and pulled her up. "It's our last chance. If you say no, I'm going to the liquor store."

"That's blackmail," she whispered, but they were already walking toward her apartment.

Chapter Twenty-Eight

The plane seemed to be flying into endless night as they chased the darkness through one time zone after another.

Rosa was excited, chattering about the aunts and cousins they would see, the church, her old school, the farm where Avó grew up and the one where she and Simão had lived until their father died.

She talked too about her fiancé and the wedding they were planning. He had a big all-American family that had taken her in and made her feel as if she could do anything she wanted. He loved her art and wanted her to go to college, she said. She would study and paint and sell her work at the galleries.

Aside from grieving over Avó, all that was missing in her life was Simão and her mother. This trip would surely reunite them, and then everything would be perfect.

Chelsea only half listened. Everything felt so odd. Being on this airplane in the middle of the night somewhere over the Atlantic. Listening to Portuguese flight attendants ask if she wanted *"Café o chá."* Hearing other passengers conversing in Portuguese. The menus were printed in Portuguese, and the pilot and flight attendants made all of their announcements in Portuguese first, then English.

As they had welcomed the passengers aboard, she had found herself tongue-tied, unable to remember any kind of response. She just nodded and smiled.

And now, listening to Rosa babble on, she felt as if she had already landed in another country.

She turned her engagement ring slowly around on her finger and tried to remember Friday night with Mel.

When they reached her apartment door, she had gently pushed him away. "I'm sorry, Mel. We can't do this. I love Simão. Besides, what would keep you sober tomorrow? Please, go home. Maybe you could visit your parents or your brother in Oregon for a while. Just forget all this. And me, too."

Mel nodded, still clutching her hand, rubbing it slowly. "A day late and a dollar short, huh?"

She kissed him on the forehead and nudged him toward the street. "Quitting the Weekly Times was a bold move. Now you're free to race me to the Pulitzer Prize. Don't you dare start drinking again. I'll call to check on you, and if you get drunk, I'll never speak to you again."

She watched him walk away, looking small and old.

Back in the dark apartment, a copy of Avó's obituary sat next to the computer. She shook her head. Avó would not have approved of her bringing Mel here. Then she remembered Martin, the handsome man who had helped Avó on her farm. Maybe she would have.

Her suitcase and camera bag sat in the corner, waiting for the trip to Portugal. She wished she could leave for the airport right now. What would she say to Rosa about Mel? He was her boss, too. Nothing, she decided.

Now on the plane, as Rosa paused in her monologue, Chelsea sighed.

"What is wrong?"

"Nothing. I guess I'm just nervous."

"About Simão?"

"Yes. I hope I'm doing the right thing."

"Do not worry. Simão will be happy. You will see."

"Um hm." She stared again at her ring. She could never tell anyone what had almost happened with Mel. Not Simão or Rosa, her own parents, or any of her friends. She was marrying Simão, end of story.

She opened the in-flight magazine and pretended to read. Mel was terrible husband material, not that she was thinking of him that way. But he drank, he didn't have a job, and he was generally unstable. Not like Simão. Tears filled her eyes, and she stared hard out the window, trying to see something in the blackness below.

She was relieved when the attendants started shuttering the windows for the movie. She would have two hours to bury herself in a film and compose herself. If only she could sleep, as many of the other passengers were doing.

The movie was in Portuguese, with English subtitles, and the plot was confusing. Soon, despite her anxieties, her eyes grew heavy and she dozed.

When she woke, it was morning, and the plane hummed with excitement as people prepared for the landing. Rosa, clutching her purse in her lap, gazed out the window, eyes shining. "I cannot believe we are almost home."

"How much longer?"

"The pilot announced it will be one half hour. But soon we will see the first island and then come down at Terceira."

"And transfer to Faial."

"Yes. On a smaller airplane."

Chelsea smoothed her hair with her hands. It seemed like days since she had showered. "This is still home to you?"

"Oh yes. I was a little girl here. My father was alive here. Yes. It is home. Here I do not have to struggle to remember the words. They just come to me easy like I was born knowing how to say anything I want."

Chelsea nodded. "That's the way English feels to me. I guess we start learning in the womb." But her mind strayed from the conversation as she strained to get her first glimpse of the Azores.

"Your great-grandma never went back or nobody in your family?" Rosa asked.

"I guess none of them could afford it. Or it was so far that they never considered it. No, when they left, they left forever."

"And now you, their granddaughter, return in their place."

Chelsea nodded. It gave her an odd sense of being part of history. "Hey, is that land down there?"

Rosa beamed. "Yes. Oh, it is beautiful."

The seatbelt light flashed, and they felt the plane lowering in the sky. Below them, the island of Terceira took shape. It was a patchwork of emerald fields marked by black rock walls. As they got closer, Chelsea could see cows in the fields, the ocean lapping against the rocky shores, white houses, a church steeple, boats.

"I'm coming home, Grandma," Chelsea whispered amid the roar of Portuguese conversation all around her.

A blast of Portuguese came over the loudspeaker, then in heavily accented English, "Ladies and gentlemen, welcome to Terceira. The temperature is 65 degrees and clear. For those transferring on to Faial, the plane will leave in one hour."

They sank closer and closer to the ground until the wheels gently touched the runway. The passengers whooped and applauded.

As the plane stopped, they grabbed their bags and joined the throng in the aisle. "*Vamos, minha irmã,*" Rosa said.

Outside the windows, Chelsea could see small cars, men in shirtsleeves, and odd-looking pickup trucks with wooden beds.

The airport was small and spare. They stood in line to pass through customs. The attendant merely glanced at their passports and nodded them on without checking their bags. Then Rosa grabbed a cart and headed toward the gate for Faial.

Chelsea stood in the middle of the confusion, feeling very tall and very American. And warm. Although the temperature was mild, the air was so humid it was hard to breathe. Her stomach churned with nerves and too much rich food. She also needed a restroom, but feared what she would find. All her life she had heard horror stories about European bathrooms.

"*O quarto de banho?*" Rosa said. "*Ali.*"

Suddenly her friend was refusing to speak English. Chelsea sighed. As long as Rosa kept it simple, she would be all right. She headed toward the door marked "*Mulheres*" and found restrooms that were immaculate and very private, the toilets hidden in little rooms with floor-to-ceiling doors.

Afterward, she dried her hands under a blow dryer.

An old woman looked up at her and smiled. "*Estados Unidos?*"

"*Sim.* California." Suddenly home seemed very far away.

"*Vás casar aqui?*"

She was asking if she was going to get married here. Was her ring that obvious? Did she look like a mail-order bride reversing the age-old custom of going to America to marry? "*Não. Ali.*" There. She nodded to the woman and hurried out to where Rosa waited with their luggage.

"*Vamos?*

Chelsea nodded, following her to the gate. She was warm in her slacks and long-sleeved shirt. The other women she saw wore blouses and skirts, sans hose. The men wore hats and sweaters over their open-necked shirts.

Outside on the blacktop, a small blue and white plane waited to take them to Faial. Soon the passengers filed out and up the steps. The plane was no bigger than a bus, Chelsea thought as her long legs bumped against the seat in front of her.

As they took off, she picked up the magazine in the rack. The stories were printed in both Portuguese and English, but the English was such a literal translation she couldn't help laughing.

"It is funny?" Rosa asked.

"They need an editor."

She looked at her puzzled, then forgot their conversation, exclaiming, "Oh, I can see Faial!"

This island looked much like the last except that as they drew closer Chelsea realized the fences were not made of rocks but flowers. She remembered Simão telling her about them. "Hydrangeas. *Hortênsias*, we call them. They grow wild all over the island."

They crossed over a larger port than Terceira's, more white houses and a church, and descended toward the runway.

So this was the land of her great-grandparents. And of Simão.

"Rosa, I am so nervous," she said, walking across the blacktop toward the terminal. She half expected to see Simão inside, even though they had not told him they were coming.

"So am I," Rosa said. "Remember, I ran away in anger. I am dating a man who is not Portuguese, and I am going to marry him. In fact, I am living with him. My brother and my mother may take one look and spit on me."

"No, they wouldn't do that."

"I do not know. They were so angry."

"Oh Rosa, if they do, I will spit back for you."

Rosa grinned. "You are a crazy American, like my Mark. Let us get our bags, and then we will find a taxi."

"To where?"

"To my village. My aunt still lives there, and I think that's where Mama would go. Her house is near the church and the cemetery."

"Oh." Despite the heat, Chelsea's teeth were chattering.

The Portuguese taxies were black and green. The driver, a young man in jeans, tee shirt and an American baseball cap, looked them up and down, shrugged and tossed their bags into the trunk. He didn't talk to them, his attention occupied by the loud rock music coming over his radio.

But the boy was a good driver. Chelsea stared at the village around them as they squeezed down narrow streets barely wide enough for the little taxi. They drove between whitewashed, tile-roofed houses, occasionally passing a small cafe where men in hats lounged just as they did in front of the Tamar Cafe in San Jose.

They passed several churches, a school, and a milk processing plant. "What's that?" Chelsea asked as they approached a tiny building painted red, green and blue.

"It is an *Império*. A chapel to the Holy Ghost. We have them all over the islands for our *festas*."

They came out onto a broad boulevard along the edge of the marina. Boats of all sizes bobbed in their moorings, many of them tied up to a huge wall on which letters were scribbled.

"What's all that?"

"The wall? Sailors used to believe, and some still do, that if you leave a message on the wall before you go out to sea, you will have good luck."

"It reminds me of our graffiti."

"But it is good graffiti." Rosa was watching the cross streets. As they approached a broad green park dotted with red benches, she leaned forward and spoke to the driver.

He nodded and veered left.

Gradually the tall buildings gave way to scattered houses, and then to a narrow road bounded on both sides by a wall of blue hydrangeas.

"I've never seen so many hydrangeas in my life."

"Yes, they are all over the island. But we are getting close now." Rosa's fingers were gripped together nervously. Chelsea felt butterflies in her stomach.

A half hour from the airport, they passed a series of farms and a tall brown and white brick church. There in the road sat a boy on a donkey.

Rosa gasped. "He looks like my cousin Alberto, but he would be older. Could this be his son, Neno? He was just a little boy, but my aunt said he was all grown up now." She leaned forward again. "*Senhor, pára aqui, faz favor.*"

The driver scowled, but eased to a halt. Rosa leaped out of the car while it was still rolling. "Neno?"

When the boy nodded, looking puzzled, Rosa blurted a stream of Portuguese. Chelsea heard Rosa's name and her own, and Simão's. As the connection became clear, the boy grinned and gestured up the road.

Rosa ran back to the car, out of breath. "He is my cousin. He was just a baby, Chelsea. Now look. He is 15. I cannot believe it. Anyway, he says Mama and Simão are at his grandmother's house, my aunt's, and the funeral is later today. He must wait for the milk wagon, but he told me how to get there. This is a good sign that God is with us."

Chelsea nodded, so jittery she couldn't speak.

As Rosa rebuckled her seat belt, the car jerked forward, and they were thrown back against the seat.

"We are almost there," Rosa said, glaring at the driver.

Chelsea nodded, her throat dry, as they moved swiftly into another village.

Rosa leaned over the back of the forward seat, directing the driver. They turned left, then right, then right again, passing another *Império*, a little park with a large statue of the Virgin Mary, a field of black and white cows. They pulled into a dirt driveway in front of a tiny white house roofed with black slate.

"*Vinte-nove mil escudos*," the driver said.

As Rosa dug into her purse, Chelsea noticed a little boy in black pants and a baggy shirt come around the corner. As he saw them, the boy shrieked and ran into the house next door.

"We've been spotted," Chelsea said, pulling in a deep breath as the driver opened their door.

"A neighbor, I think. You cannot sneak around here. Everybody knows everything." Rosa clasped Chelsea's hand. "It will be all right."

"I hope so."

Rosa slipped out, giving a handful of American money to the driver, who looked at it, nodded and stuffed the bills into his shirt pocket before going to the trunk to get their bags.

Chelsea followed, watching the front door.

It was Simão she noticed first, so tall he seemed in danger of hitting the frame above the door. He stood staring, shading his eyes with his hand. Chelsea could see he had adopted the Azorean dress, dark slacks and an open shirt.

"*Obrigado*," the taxi driver said and spun away in a cloud of dust, leaving Chelsea and Rosa standing in the dirt with their bags.

"*Mãe de Jesus*," they heard Simão mutter. Then he was stumbling down the steps toward them. "Mama!" he hollered back into the house as he hurried forward.

Chelsea bit her lip. Would he accept her and his sister, or would he send them both back on the next plane to America?

But as he neared, she saw tears in his eyes. Suddenly she and Rosa were both enveloped in his big arms. To her shock, Simão was weeping, then sobbing.

Slowly he let her go and embraced his sister. "Rosa, Rosa, *minha irmã, onde estavas*? Where have you been?" His accent was thicker than Chelsea remembered.

He pulled back and looked at his sister. "You look very American."

Rosa smiled through her own tears and nodded. "*Sim*. Chelsea, she was so afraid you would send us away."

His tears started anew. "*Não. Nunca.*" He turned to Chelsea, and they fell together like two halves of a puzzle.

Chelsea was crying now, too. "I'm so sorry."

He stroked her hair. "*Não.* It is my fault. I am too stubborn. Thank God you are here."

As she leaned on him, smelling his salty skin, he asked, "What about your job?"

"I had to give it up to come here. The boss wouldn't wait."

"Oh, *meu amor*. I am sorry." He pressed her tight against him. "We took an earlier flight to L.A. I really did not think you would come."

Beside her, she heard Rosa yell, "Mama!" as she embraced her mother.

Simão raised his head. "Come, meet my family." His arm around her shoulders, he walked her to the house, where she kissed his mother, then looked in surprise at another woman who came out behind her. She looked just like Simão's mother, only shorter.

"*A minha Tia Cristina.* My aunt," Simão said.

"I'm not surprised. They look so much alike. Um, *muito prazer em conhecer à senhora*," she said, using her textbook Portuguese.

The woman laughed, showing missing teeth in the sides of her mouth.

"Too formal," Simão said, grinning. "We will teach you. Tia speaks English anyway, so do not worry."

"Come inside," Tia Cristina said. "Let us give you something to eat and to drink."

"Oh no, thank you. We ate so much on the plane."

But Simão's aunt wasn't listening. "You must eat. Look how thin you are. And Rosa, you are skinny, too. Beautiful, but skinny." Then she spotted the ring on Rosa's finger. "Both of you are getting married! Ai, Maria. You must tell me all about it."

And they were hurried into a house that reminded Chelsea of Simão's little place in San Jose, except that the TV and the stove looked about 30 years behind the times.

Tia Cristina led them into the dining room. She poured wine all round and brought out a plate of fresh bread and goat cheese.

Chelsea sat next to Simão. He buttered a bite of bread and raised it to her lips.

"You will taste no bread like this in the United States."

She opened her mouth as he gently set the bread on her tongue. A sweet heavy taste flooded her senses as she savored it, chewing slowly. "This is fantastic," she said, smiling at Tia Cristina.

"I will teach you how to make it while you are here."

Mama shook her head. "*Não poderá obter os ingredientes,*" she said.

Chelsea understood. "Even at the Portuguese grocery store?"

"Bah," Mama said. "*Não. Os homems. . .*"

Simão chuckled. "Trade Rite is run by men. Mama thinks they do not know how to cook, so they do not buy all the right things, and being Portuguese men, they do not listen to their wives. Ah, Mama, *todas as mulheres são feministas.* Everybody's a feminist."

"It's the men's fault," Chelsea said with a smile. "But I do want to learn how to make this bread. It reminds me of something my grandmother used to bake."

"Her great-grandmother was from Faial," Rosa said.

"Ah," Tia Cristina said. "So you are Portuguese."

"Half. My mom says I'm a half-breed."

"You have a Portuguese heart. I can tell."

Just then the door slammed open, and a little girl about 3 years old came in. When she saw the company at the table, she stopped and stared.

Chelsea stared back. The toddler looked so much like her own photos at that age that she could have been her child. She had the same dark hair, chocolate brown eyes and pouty lips. There was also a hint of mischief that struck Chelsea as very familiar.

Tia Cristina laughed. "That is my granddaughter. Her name is Anna Maria, but we call her *'a terremota'* for she is like an earthquake, always shaking things up. *Venha aca. Estas são as tuas primas Rosa e Chelsea dos Estados Unidos."*

The girl stood, digesting that information, then came up to Chelsea and pulled at her shirt sleeve.

Tia Cristina chuckled. "Look at that, she wants to sit in your lap."

Chelsea scooted her chair back and reached out her hands. "Come on."

The girl was heavy as she pulled her up onto her lap and stared into the mirror image of herself. "If we had a daughter, she would look like this," she whispered to Simão." For the first time, she seriously considered what it might be like to be pregnant, to care for a baby, to be a mother.

"We must get married soon and start a baby. We are getting old."

"Who is getting old?" said a booming voice from the doorway. Simão's cousin Alberto stomped into the room, his steps heavy in his work boots. Neno followed, grinning as he grabbed a slice of bread and collapsed into a chair in front of the fireplace.

"We all are," said Simão, rising. "Come meet Chelsea, and here is my little sister Rosa."

"Oh my God," said Alberto, shaking his head. "I think we are getting old. Rosa was just a teenager." He hugged them both, then pulled up a battered chair from the corner and cut off a slice of bread. He chased it with a long swallow of wine.

"How come everybody here speaks such good English?" Chelsea asked Simão.

"Well, my cousin and his family lived in America for a little while. They decided to move back here. But they keep their English because Alberto's wife, Tilde, has a shop by the Hotel Fayal, where she sells her sewing and other things. Many of the customers speak English. So she must, too. Sometimes the whole family works there, when they are not busy with the cows. You milk them in the morning and evening. In between, if they have food, you don't do much anyway."

"That true?" Chelsea said, looking at Alberto.

"*Não.* Cows keep you working all day. Besides, we have to grow their food and our food. It is a lot of work."

As they sat talking, Chelsea could feel herself growing drowsy, partly from the wine and partly from the hour. She was about to excuse herself to take a nap when Tia Cristina suddenly jolted her awake.

"*Ai, Deus, que horas são?* What time is it?"

When Alberto said it was 2:00, she jumped up from her seat. "It is time to get ready. We must go. Simão's avó is waiting."

Chapter Twenty-Nine

It was a small group standing around the grave. This cemetery behind the little brown and white brick church was not like San Jose's vast Calvary Cemetery with its neatly mowed lawns and straight rows of marble stones. The wildflowers grew up around their legs, and the graves were placed willy nilly with a variety of wooden crosses and handhewn stones. Nearly every one had a photograph of the deceased encased in a glass frame. Simão assured Chelsea he had already given a photo to be placed at Avó's grave. He had taken it from the wall of his house.

The only mourners were the family, the two mothers with their grown children, and Tia Cristina's granddaughter. Alberto's wife Tilde had closed her shop for the funeral, and now she was sneaking shy glances at Chelsea and Rosa.

There were no tears. The tears had already been shed at home. As the others prayed aloud in Portuguese, Chelsea's mind wandered back to the last funeral she had attended, Aunt Julia's. How long ago that seemed. And how different with her cousins cracking jokes and her mother and aunt gossiping about what people were wearing.

She was impressed by the faith of this family living in this simple house, working with cows and embroidery, not newspapers or politics. As they listened to the words of the priest, Chelsea felt they really believed that Avó was now in heaven with Jesus, that all of her suffering was over, and that they would see her again when they died.

How much easier it would be to believe totally, to not be so damned educated.

Simão squeezed her hand. "Are you all right?" he whispered.

She nodded. "I'm fine. Are you okay?"

"Yes. I miss Avó, but she is with God, and that is where she should be. She earned a place right next to Jesus and the Virgin Mary."

It was over quickly, and they adjourned to Tia Cristina's house for more food. Alberto brought out his accordion and played. They refrained from dancing out of respect for Avó, but they sang, and Chelsea hummed along, wishing she knew the words. The feeling was familiar, as so many things felt here. Perhaps it was all those Portuguese women inside her.

375

Lulled by the music and wine, she fell asleep leaning against Simão's shoulder, feeling his deep voice vibrate against her cheek.

He kissed her gently. "You must go to bed. In America, it is late. Come on."

He led her to the little room where her things were laid out next to Rosa's. No sleeping together with her boyfriend here, she thought drowsily.

She took a quick trip to the bathroom, marveling again at the pull-chain toilet, rustled through her overnight bag for her nightgown, and was soon in bed, thinking she might sleep forever.

Cows don't care if the farmer had a party the night before. They still need to be milked. As Chelsea slept, Alberto rose at dawn, groaning over his coffee, and left for the fields. Simão went with him. It had been nearly three years since he had seen his cousin, and he missed talking to him. Neno soon followed.

Rosa was up early, too. When Chelsea finally stirred around 9 o'clock, she heard the other women talking quietly in the living room. Looking through the open door, she saw they were all sewing. Of course, she thought, they have to keep adding to the merchandise in Tilde's shop.

She felt movement on the other side of the bed and turned to find little Anna Maria tugging on the covers. "Chel-see?"

"Oh, my goodness. Hi there." Chelsea had never been around children much, except for her American cousins' kids. She never really knew what to do with them. But this one was doing it all for her. "Want to come up here?"

The child knew little English, but she understood Chelsea's patting-the-covers gesture, and scrambled up, reminding Chelsea of a cat she had as a child. Chelsea pulled her close, rocking her slowly back and forth. "You are so cute. You look just like my own little girl would if I had one."

She just giggled, apparently not understanding a word. Chelsea shrugged and kissed her soft cheek. Then they heard Neno's donkey outside, and Anna Maria jumped off the bed and raced out, letting the door slam behind her.

Chelsea remained in bed, listening. Mama was humming. How

she must have missed sitting and sewing with her sister and her daughter. Chelsea would never be a real substitute. While they sewed, she would want to be off writing or taking pictures.

As she grew fully awake, her stomach growled, and she longed for a cup of coffee. With a sigh, she left the soft, comfortable bed, put on the robe someone had left on the chair for her, and went to wash up.

"So, where are you getting married?" Tia Cristina asked as Chelsea entered the living room. "We have been talking about weddings. It is so exciting. You and Rosa both! We may have to fly back to America to see it."

"They could get married here," Tilde suggested.

Chelsea shook her head. "No. That would be beautiful, but I want my parents to be there."

"Make them come here."

"Tilde, why should they?" Tia Cristina scolded. "Her father is not Portuguese."

They all went silent, then Tia set down her sewing decisively. "You must have breakfast, Chelsea. I will get you something."

"No, I--"

"Don't argue with my mother-in-law," Tilde said. "She loves to serve people. We have not had company for maybe two years. And now, this is wonderful. But it makes me homesick for America."

Mama said something. Chelsea, not understanding, looked at Tia Cristina.

Tia sighed. "My sister says it is safer here. She is still thinking about--oh, I don't know if I should talk about that."

"Simão's first wife," Chelsea said softly as Tia nodded. "Mama is right. Sometimes it isn't safe there. You have to be careful. I know Simão worries a lot."

"He should," Tia Cristina said. "Now, you want coffee, yes, all Americans want coffee first thing in the morning. And I have fruit and bread. You eat. Then I give you something to sew."

When Simão returned with Alberto, Chelsea was carefully stitching a simple red flower on a large linen tablecloth. She looked up at the two men. They were dressed alike and so handsome she could hardly stand it. Simão's face was already more tanned than she

377

remembered, and he wore a felt hat like his cousin's. The lines around his eyes only made him more attractive to her.

"Look at you, still in your bathrobe, sewing with the women. What has happened to my liberated Chelsea?"

She smiled up at him. "I've been domesticated."

He kissed her on the cheek. "Well, come on, get dressed. Tilde doesn't want you messing up her tablecloth anyway."

"Hey, I did okay."

He inspected her work and nodded. "You are very talented. Now, I want to show you my island. Hurry, before it gets too hot and we have to come back for our *sesta*."

Chelsea was glad she had brought lots of film. She could have spent all day just photographing the hydrangeas. Up close, their scent filled the air, and their blue color was so intense they didn't seem real. Walls of flowers marched up and down the green hills, and she shot frame after frame until Simão handed her a big round bloom and insisted they move on.

They rode Tilde's Volvo past the fields of cows to a parking lot where tourist buses were lined up and dozens of camera-toting visitors struggled down a narrow path. They parked the car and joined them.

"Where are we going?" Chelsea asked.

"You will see."

Suddenly they turned a corner and Chelsea gasped. In front of them lay a vast crater, miles deep and miles across. "My God, it's huge."

"*Sim*, we are lucky. Most days you cannot see it because of the fog."

Even now, fog hung along the edges and seemed to be creeping toward the crater. Chelsea raised her camera and began snapping pictures. They had barely started back before the crater was hidden in fog.

Next they drove toward a corner of the island that Simão told her had been devastated by a volcano. Although nearly 20 years had passed, many of the homes remained just as they had been, their roofs caved in with lava rock on top, weeds growing through the floors.

Maybe she should have brought even more film, she thought,

shooting one frame after another, thinking of Avó's story.

"Come on," Simão said, hugging her against him. "There are nicer things to see."

It was a long day. They saw windmills, statues and craft fairs. They walked along the marina and peered inside the windows of an *Império* to see the gilded altar inside. They lunched on fish stew and fresh bread at a seaside cafe, and watched the ferry from Pico unload. Finally they stopped at the park Chelsea had seen on their way from the airport and sat on one of the red benches.

Simão kissed her lightly on the lips. "How do you like my island?"

"I love it. It's--you can't imagine how it feels to be where my great-grandparents lived as children. It's like going home, even though I've never been here before. I wish my mother could see it."

"You will write about it and take many pictures to show her."

"Yes." She leaned against him, so comfortable she could fall asleep. "Simão?"

"*Sim?*"

"I love you so. I'm sorry I--"

"Shh, *meu amor*," he said. "I know. Your work is very important to you. Just as mine is to me."

She opened her eyes wide. Was this the same man she had argued with back in San Jose?

He stared out at the boats. "When I came here, I was surprised to find my cousin's wife running a business. She does all the work. Alberto just helps count the money." He smiled. "Alberto, he told me, he had a hard time with this, she is not home to take care of Anna Maria or cook or anything, but it is okay. Tilde is happy. If she had to stay home like those women you see behind the curtains all day, she would not be happy. Like you."

"Simão Freitas, you have changed."

"Not completely. You will not go out at night to get hurt, and you will let me buy your beer when we go to a party."

She rolled her eyes. "*Ai, os homems*. Men." It was time to change the subject. "Anna Maria is so cute. She looks just like the pictures of me when I was her age."

379

Simão nodded. "*Sim.* And I will tell you a secret. Tilde is going to have another baby in about six months. Alberto said not to say anything to Tia yet. She would not let Tilde keep working if she knew. But a woman can sew and sell things with a big belly."

She looked into his glowing brown eyes. "Simão, suddenly I want to have children, too."

"Good. How about 8?"

"Kids?! No way. I meant maybe two or three. And maybe we could wait a couple of years. Until your business makes us rich." She jumped up, pulling him by the hand. "Can we go to the hall of records and see if we can find my ancestors?"

They passed tall buildings, a park, narrow passageways. Suddenly they came out into a vast open area occupied by a modern white building.

Simão paid the driver, and they hurried up the steps. Inside, people were lined up, applying for permits, recording deeds. One couple was buying a marriage license.

It was nearly an hour before they reached the front of the line. Simão spoke for her, telling the girl she was looking for records of her great-grandparents from around 1907.

From a stack against the back wall, the girl took three five-inch-thick volumes and opened the first one.

Chelsea stared. "It's all written by hand."

"*Sim.* No typewriters."

In the ornate flowing characters of the turn of the century, names were listed in columns for births, marriages and deaths.

The records were organized by first names. Chelsea remembered reading that surnames weren't used much in the Azorean villages, but now she despaired. "How will I ever find the right ones?"

"How old was your great-grandfather when he left?"

"16."

"Go back 16 years from 1907." He gently turned the pages.

Suddenly in the listings for 1892, a name caught her eye. Maria Anna Silveira, born Dec. 2, to Alfonso and Maria.

"I think that's her, that's my great-grandmother." Her heart pounded as she continued backward and found her great-grandfather's birth as well. Then, hurrying forward 15 years from Maria's birth, she

380

found a marriage record. The next year, another birth was recorded. "Uncle Henry," she whispered. "They brought him with them as a baby."

June 1907 was the final entry for Maria and Francisco. Emigrated to *Os Estados Unidos* on an American ship.

An odd sense of déjà vu engulfed her. She was standing here on the island her great-grandparents left almost 90 years ago. Their names were in the record book. Now she was here. It was almost as if she should write her own name on those thick yellow pages to complete the story.

Chelsea copied each of the entries into her notebook. Then she took out her camera and carefully focused on the writing, hoping enough natural light was coming through the windows.

At last, she reluctantly closed the ancient book of records. "I guess that's it. Thank you very much," she told the girl.

"You are welcome."

Simão kissed her forehead. "Unless you want to look up my name in the book, we will go home and rest now. *Sesta* time."

As they walked out into the sunny afternoon, she breathed deeply of the humid salt air scented with hydrangeas. "Why would anybody leave here?"

Simão hugged her against him. "They want to be liberated like Chelsea Faust and rich like Simão Freitas." He kissed her, lightly at first, then with increasing passion that made Chelsea tremble.

"I wish we could be alone together," he whispered.

"Maybe that's the real reason they went to America."

"*Sim.*" They were laughing as they got into the car and started home.

Their trip was a whirl of sightseeing, meals at Tia Cristina's and with other families in the village, and mornings spent sewing with the other women while Simão went to the fields with Alberto.

On their last night in Faial, the whole village gathered at the church hall for a party.

Chelsea put on an embroidered blouse and long blue skirt she had bought from Tilde's shop. Rosa helped her wind ribbons into her long hair and pin it up in a thick braid. As she stood in front of the discolored mirror brushing blush on her cheeks, Chelsea thought her eyes looked darker, her skin more tanned than ever before. Looking back at her was a woman who looked every bit as Portuguese as the others who had lived here all their lives.

She wondered how her great-grandmother had looked as a girl. In the few years that Chelsea knew her, Grandma Silveira was short and overweight with a gray bun and feet that were perpetually swollen. She always dressed in black or dark blue. She had lived a hard life, and it showed. But what was she like when she was Chelsea's age?

With a start, Chelsea realized she was already almost twice as old as her great-grandmother had been when she got married. By now, she had had all but one of her eight children. Yet Chelsea still felt like a young girl.

She finished with the blush and began applying mascara, then glossed her lips with pink lipstick. The final touch was a pair of earrings Simão had purchased for her, small silver rings engraved with entwined roses.

"*Que linda*," she heard from behind her and turned to face Simão, who was gazing at her with a warm light in his eyes.

"How long have you been watching me?"

"A few minutes. I could watch you all night."

She kissed him lightly, mindful of her fresh lipstick. "Soon."

"When?" His eyes were suddenly very serious.

She pulled him back into the room and patted the bed. He sat down next to her. "We talked about May before, but let's pin it down," she said. "It's December now. We don't want to do it at Christmas, do we?"

"No, but not too long. January, February, is winter."

"March?"

"Lent."

"Right after Easter then?"

Simão reached into his pocket and pulled out a little calendar. To Chelsea's surprise, the dates went down the card instead of across. "*Sim*, May, before the festas start. May 15. It is a Saturday."

382

Chelsea nodded. "Okay. May 15." Putting a date on it made the wedding suddenly very real. But she would have done it today if she could.

"Too long," said Simão, and then to her surprise, he crushed her lips with a kiss and eased her backward on the bed.

Her heart pounded as she returned the kiss and wished they could close the door and be alone for a while. But already footsteps were coming across the wooden floor and Tia Cristina was clucking her tongue. "Young people in love. You cannot control them."

They sat up, Chelsea blushing and Simão busily straightening his shirt.

"We have set a date," Simão said. "We are getting married May 15."

"*Ah, optimo!* We will celebrate tonight. Now, let us go to the party."

Music poured out of the brightly lit hall as they parked Alberto's car and walked toward the open door. Chelsea was nervous. She felt as if she was being presented to the whole village for approval. But Simão laughed at her qualms. "They will love you. How could they not? You are beautiful and smart, and you have a good heart."

"Oh, Simão." She was about to kiss him when Tia Cristina gave her a warning look. Instead she squeezed his hand and he squeezed back. "This is silly," she whispered in his ear. "I am 28 years old, and you're older than I am."

"I know. But to the old women, we will always be children."

"Ah, Simão!" said a gray-haired man at the door, pulling him down to kiss both cheeks. He bussed Chelsea likewise, along with Rosa and the others. Simão introduced him as the mayor of the village.

At the door, a woman handed Chelsea and Simão each a glass of red wine and led them to one of the long tables set up along the sides of the hall.

In front, a band of village men played, mostly in tune, on an odd collection of well-worn stringed instruments. Three women, dressed alike in scarves, white blouses and full red skirts, sang, their voices shallow and piercing to Chelsea's American ears.

They had barely sat down when the band struck a chord that sent everyone into the center of the room. "Come, it is the *chamarrita*," said Simão, pulling her to her feet.

She remembered her mother and her aunts talking about this dance. "But, I don't know how--"

"I will teach you. It is easy."

Around her, the villagers bobbed and spun to the music, responding to calls from the bandleader. It reminded Chelsea of the American folk dances she learned in school. With Simão as a partner, she barely had to think. He moved her easily. As the red wine went to her head, she let herself get lost in the music and the dance. It was as if Chelsea Faust, all-American journalist, had completely disappeared, and she had become an Azorean teenager, from her braided hair to her dancing feet.

The air smelled of sweat and hot sausage by the time the music stopped.

The women brought huge platters of food to the table. Suddenly famished, Chelsea sampled linguiça, morçela, and other sausages. There were also potatoes, fresh bread and cheese, green salad and endless quantities of wine.

She ate and drank and tried to follow the threads of Portuguese conversation around her. That was the only thing that separated her from the others, her lack of the Portuguese language. She promised herself she would continue her classes, practicing with Simão's family to become at ease in the language by the time they were married.

There was one other difference. She had an English-speaking family at home, including a German father who wasn't Portuguese at all. Reaching into her purse on the bench beside her, she pulled out her camera and turned on the flash. She had to capture this evening as much as she could for them. She eased out of her seat.

Simão looked up, a question in his eyes, then nodded when he saw the camera. "It is good. This is a night to remember."

She photographed the musicians, the dancers, the people eating, the women in the back drizzling sauce over the flan and ice cream for dessert. They looked up and smiled for the camera. Photography was a language they all understood.

Chelsea memorized the faces, the smells, the sounds of the music until they were engraved in her heart. She didn't know when she would return, but she knew that with Simão as her husband, she would be back sometime.

Had her great-grandmother felt this way the night before she left? Had there been a party? Surely it had not been as happy a time. Grandma Silveira had been so young, and in those days, once you left, there was little chance of coming back.

She was grateful for airplanes, telephones and a reliable post office which kept them in touch.

The last frame of film shot, she was putting her camera back into her purse when Tilde touched her arm. "Would you walk outside with me?"

Simão was deep in conversation with the gray-haired man across the table. "Sure," Chelsea said.

The air had turned foggy, and Chelsea could hear a horn blowing at the marina.

"Are you having a good time?" Tilde began.

"Oh yes. This is wonderful. I almost feel like I belong here."

Tilde clasped her arm. "You do. You are one of the family. Your great-grandmother was born here, right?"

"Yes, but it was a long time ago, and things are very different in America than they are here."

"I know. That's what I want to talk about." They came to a bench. "Shall we sit down? I get tired quickly these days."

"Oh, yes, the baby, I almost forgot. Sure." The bench was damp, and a cold breeze chilled her face. "Now, what do you need to talk about?"

"Fátima, Simão's first wife, was my best friend when we were young girls. We play together, we become women together, we marry the two cousins. Simão is like my brother. When Fátima died, it was very bad. We were in America then. Alberto had thought he could make a better living there. But when this happened, he said it is not safe, it is not worth it, better to be here with family. So we come home."

"I didn't know that."

385

"No. We almost become American like you. Anyway, the thing is, Simão, he never got over it. Sometimes he seems too, what do the Americans say, macho, but it is only because he is afraid."

Chelsea nodded. "I know. I haven't helped matters any. I've gone out and gotten myself in trouble, probably driven him nearly crazy. But you can't live always in fear."

"No. But you must take care of Simão and help him to be less afraid. It is good that you brought Rosa back to him. I know it was very hard for them to be apart."

"It sounds like you knew everything that was going on."

"Simão's Mama writes letters all the time. She tells everything. I knew all about you before you arrived."

"I wonder what she said."

Tilde squeezed her hand. "She said you were beautiful, smart, and strong-willed enough to handle Simão, and she hoped you would get married soon."

"Really?"

"Yes. She also said you were lonely and needed a husband."

Chelsea laughed. "That's what my mother always says, too. Well, we're making them both happy."

Another breeze seemed to blow right through her.

Tilde felt it too. "It is cold. Let us go in." They stood and Tilde hugged her. "We will try to come to California for the wedding. I have many friends there I would like to see. But with the baby, I don't know. Maybe later."

"I understand."

As they approached the door, Alberto looked out. "What are you crazy women doing? It is cold. Come on, Simão wants to introduce his future wife to everybody."

Simão held out his arms, and she slipped into them.

In the midst of the celebration, she wondered where she could publish her pictures, but that would have to wait until she got home. It was time for another *chamarrita*.

Chapter Thirty

Simão was so nervous his hands shook as he knotted his necktie.

"Relax, it will be wonderful," Chelsea told him. She was on the other side of their bedroom, packing film into her camera case.

"I wasn't this nervous on our wedding day," he said. "But of course, the mayor and two congressmen and the Portuguese consul did not come to our wedding."

"Maybe they should have." She zipped the case shut and set it next to her purse. Slipping into her white high heels, she went to Simão and kissed his cheek. "It was a perfect wedding, was it not?"

Simão nodded. "Yes. Oh, damn." He tore off his tie and threw it on the floor. "I cannot do this today."

"Here, let me." Chelsea put the tie around her own neck, deftly knotted it and slipped it over Simão's head. "My father taught me when I was a girl, so I could help him. He almost never wore a tie, but when he did, it was my job. I thought I was so clever."

"You are clever." He glanced at his watch. "*Ai, Jesus.* We must go."

As they drove toward the San Jose Historical Museum for the dedication of the Portuguese museum site, Simão stared straight ahead, his jaw tight, his eyes dark with nerves. This project was their dream. When António from the bookstore had found an old postcard depicting the *Império* that stood next to Five Wounds Church near the turn of the century, it became the catalyst for the museum project the cultural group had talked about for years.

The museum would be built in the shape of the *Império*, with space upstairs for exhibits and events and downstairs for storage of photographs and memorabilia of all sorts documenting the Portuguese experience in Santa Clara Valley.

At first, it sounded like a pipe dream, but now they had the blessing of the city, an architect's rendering of the *Império*, and a space set aside for the Portuguese Museum.

Simão wore a black pin-striped suit and red tie. His thick black hair was freshly cut. Chelsea stared at his handsome, serious face and felt her heart swell with love.

It was a month after their wedding, the memories of which she

387

would treasure forever. All of the friends and relatives from both sides had come, except Alberto and Tilde, whose baby was due within the week. But they would be here today.

Like today's event, the wedding ceremony was bilingual. Father Noia, Five Wounds' pastor, recited each section first in Portuguese, then in English. At the reception afterward at the rebuilt Portuguese hall, they danced the *chamarrita* and all the modern American dances, too.

Chelsea and Simão honeymooned in Monterey for a glorious week of romance, sightseeing, fishing, and dinners overlooking the bay. Chelsea found hints of California's Portuguese heritage everywhere, in the names of the streets, in the Portuguese-run Captain's Cove restaurant where they ate one night, and in the history of the canneries that used to dominate Cannery Row.

It was time someone honored that history and put it together in one place, she thought.

Today it was happening.

Cars streamed into the museum parking lot. Simão parked next to the fence. He got out slowly, stiff with stage fright, as Chelsea looped her camera case over her shoulder.

"Come on, sweetheart, you're going to be great."

"It is a long speech to give in two languages."

"No, not too long. Besides, you get it over with first, and then all you have to do is introduce people."

"*Ai, Jesus,*" he sighed again.

Chelsea hugged him. "Come on. Let's go get 'em."

San Jose Historical Museum was a re-creation of turn-of-the-century San Jose. Old houses had been moved there from various locations in the city, and replicas of the old hotel, stables and firehouse had been built. In the center of the complex was a big plaza circled by folding chairs. At the southern end of the plaza, next to the Ng Shin Gung Chinese temple, an area had been marked with white ribbon and a sign: Future Home of the Portuguese Museum.

As they approached, they were thronged by people. Members of the cultural group, one of the congressmen, and the Portuguese consul from San Francisco all came to shake Simão's hand. Over their shoulders, Chelsea spied Rosa and Mama walking up. With them were

Tia Cristina, Neno, Alberto, Anna Maria, and Tilde carrying a baby wrapped in thick blankets. Chelsea's mother and father were already seated near the podium. She waved, they waved back. She was trapped in the crowd, being introduced to Simão's friends and the dignitaries who had come.

When she could break free, she went to hug her parents. "Hi. I'm glad you made it."

"This is pretty impressive," said her father, taking a quick photograph of her.

"Get a picture of the sign, dear," Mom said.

"I will, when it's not so crowded."

"We'll have to compare photos later. Enjoy the program. I have to sit next to Simão with the big shots."

As she walked over, her heels sinking in the soft grass, someone pulled on her skirt and she turned to find Anna Maria beside her in a white dress and big red hat.

"*O que é isto?*" asked the child, pointing at the sign.

"*Isto é o nosso museu.* It is our museum," Chelsea said, stroking the little girl's hair. "It will be an *Império*, just like you have at home, with lots of pictures and Holy Ghost crowns and tablecloths like your mother and grandmother make, and we will have parties there . . ."

But Anna Maria had stopped listening. "I want something to eat," she said in plain English.

Chelsea burst out laughing. "You little stinker, you speak English. Give me your hand, so you don't get lost. Let's see what they have."

They were filling Anna Maria's plate with slices of fried linguiça, fresh California strawberries, Azorean cheese, and sweet rolls from Anna Silva's bakery when Chelsea heard a familiar voice behind her.

"Hey, Faust, do they let the press eat at this shindig?"

She turned. "Mel!" Her former editor stood grinning at her in a tweed jacket, white shirt and blue jeans, a fisherman's cap over his thinning hair.

"Jeez, you look great," he said as they pulled out of line. "Who's your friend?"

"This is our niece Anna Maria from Faial."

Mel shook his head. "She could be yours."

389

"I know. Wait until my parents see her. So, what are you doing here? You're Jewish."

"I'm the press."

"What are you talking about? You didn't go back to the Weekly Times, did you?"

"Hell, no." He reached into his back pocket and pulled out a multi-folded newspaper. "I started my own rag."

"How?"

"Got a grant. I don't know if you remember, but I was good at that academic stuff. I convinced this foundation that San Jose needed an alternative to that hunk of advertorial we used to work at."

"Let me see."

On the front page was an article about the museum dedication, as well as a report on financial problems at the county jail. Chelsea stared at the second byline. "Sarge works for you?"

"Yep. He couldn't stay at that paper after they destroyed it. Besides, he needs to take things a little easier since his heart attack. And look at this."

The headline read: "Giles a shoo-in for vacant Slater council seat."

"Fred Giles? The guy who ran against him four years ago?"

"That's the one. Southern accent, buck teeth. Remember?"

"My God. He was the guy?"

"That's your Deep Throat. He admitted it to me, said he never intended to get you in trouble."

"Oh well. Water under the bridge." Chelsea shook her head. Anna Maria had plunked herself on the grass and was busy eating. "I'm so happy for you, Mel. The paper looks great."

"There's just one thing missing."

He was staring at her, a smug smile on his lips. His eyes were clear, his expression happy and relaxed. He obviously was sober and had at least temporarily beaten the demons that were killing him before she went to Portugal.

"Me?"

"*Sim, senhora.* You. Will you do some stories for me?"

"As staff?"

"Well. . . ." He shrugged. "I don't have the budget yet. Even

Sarge is sort of freelancing. He was old enough to retire on Social Security anyway. Hell, I'm doing nights at the local Safeway to pay the bills, but if you could find time. . . ."

"Are you kidding? Now that my book is at the printer, I'm dying to get back to work. Want me to start with something about the museum?"

"I hoped you would. My pictures are worse than horrible."

"You're on." Chelsea saw Simão looking anxiously toward the food tables. "I'd better go. Simão's having a heart attack over this. I'll get something to you ASAP." She kissed Mel on the cheek and took her niece by the hand. "Come on, Anna Maria."

It was time. The crowd was taking their seats, and Simão had an empty place for her between him and António. He introduced to her to a state assemblyman and the mayor of San Jose, then reached into his coat pocket for his notes.

"It's good news. Just tell them," Chelsea whispered.

Then Simão was at the microphone, tall, handsome and confident. "*Boa tarde*. Good afternoon, ladies and gentlemen. This is a wonderful occasion for which we are gathered, the dedication of a museum to the Portuguese of Santa Clara Valley."

Chelsea turned on her tape recorder, slipped out of her seat and focused her camera on her husband. She remembered the first time she saw him, back at the Portuguese parade a year ago. She hadn't understood anything about her heritage then, but she knew this man was the most fascinating person she had ever met. He still was.

It was a good thing she had brought lots of film, she thought, turning her lens on the dignitaries, then her family--her mother and father, Simão's mother, Rosa and her new husband, Tia Cristina, Neno, António and Tilde, their baby, and Anna Maria. With role models like her mother, her Aunt Rosa and her Aunt Chelsea, Anna Maria was bound to be a strong woman who would not be afraid to do anything she wanted, not like the old-fashioned Portuguese women who let men rule their lives. But then, thinking about it, Portuguese women had always been strong in their own way.

Simão was near the end of his speech. She had heard it many times as he practiced. But now, with the sunset at his back and the

391

Portuguese museum site in front of him, and so many important people listening, it sounded different.

"The Azorean dream was to come to America and make a new life. We have done that for generations. We have become part of the fabric of America. Our family values, our hard work, our love of God and the land, we bring this to California to help make it the great state that it is.

"And now, we have a new Azorean dream. To preserve the stories of those generations who came before us so that our children and their children and all the generations to come will be able to see and hear about all that people like my grandparents and my wife's great-grandparents and all the mothers and fathers have done for us.

"This museum is a dream come true, and I thank you all for coming to share it."

"Amen," Chelsea whispered, clicking one more shot for the family album. And page one.

About the Author

Sue Fagalde Lick's maternal great-grandparents emigrated from the Azores Islands in the late 1800s, settling in the San Jose area. A longtime newspaper reporter and editor, she is the author of *The Iberian Americans, Stories Grandma Never Told: Portuguese Women in California, Shoes Full of Sand*, and *Childless by Marriage*. She and her dog Annie live on the Oregon Coast.